LIBERTIE

ALSO BY KAITLYN GREENIDGE

We Love You, Charlie Freeman

LIBERTIE

a novel by

KAITLYN GREENIDGE

ALGONQUIN BOOKS
OF CHAPEL HILL   2021

Published by
ALGONQUIN BOOKS OF CHAPEL HILL
Post Office Box 2225
Chapel Hill, North Carolina 27515-2225

a division of
WORKMAN PUBLISHING
225 Varick Street
New York, New York 10014

This is a work of fiction. While, as in all fiction, the literary perceptions and insights are based on experience, all names, characters, places, and incidents either are products of the author's imagination or are used fictitiously.

LIBRARY OF CONGRESS CATALOGING-IN-PUBLICATION DATA

Names: Greenidge, Kaitlyn, author.
Title: Libertie : a novel / by Kaitlyn Greenidge.
Description: First Edition. | Chapel Hill, North Carolina : Algonquin Books
of Chapel Hill, 2021. | Summary: "Coming of age as a free-born Black girl in
Reconstruction-era Brooklyn, Libertie Sampson is all too aware that her mother, a
physician, has a vision for their future together: Libertie will go to medical school and
practice alongside her. But Libertie feels stifled by her mother's choices and is constantly
reminded that, unlike her mother, Libertie has skin that is too dark. When a young man
from Haiti proposes to Libertie and promises she will be his equal on the island, she
accepts, only to discover that she is still subordinate to him and all men. As she tries to
parse what freedom actually means for a Black woman, Libertie struggles with where
she might find it—for herself and for generations to come"— Provided by publisher.
Identifiers: LCCN 2020040086 | ISBN 9781616207014 (hardcover) |
ISBN 9781643751764 (ebook)
Classification: LCC PS3607.R455 L53 2021 | DDC 813/.6—dc23
LC record available at https://lccn.loc.gov/2020040086

10 9 8 7 6 5 4 3 2 1
First Edition

For Ariel and Ariel and M. Ariel

LIBERTIE

Se pa tout blesi ki geri

Not all wounds heal

1860

I saw my mother raise a man from the dead. "It still didn't help him much, my love," she told me. But I saw her do it all the same. That's how I knew she was magic.

The time I saw Mama raise a man from the dead, it was close to dusk. Mama and her nurse, Lenore, were in her office—Mama with her little greasy glasses on the tip of her nose, balancing the books, and Lenore banking the fire. That was the rule in Mama's office—the fire was kept burning from dawn till after dinner, and we never let it go out completely. Even on the hottest days, when my linen collar stuck to the back of my neck and the belly of Lenore's apron was stained with sweat, a mess of logs and twigs was lit up down there, waiting.

When the dead man came, it was spring. I was playing on the stoop. I'd broken a stick off the mulberry bush, so young it had resisted the pull of my fist. I'd had to work for it. Once I'd wrenched it off, I stripped the bark and rubbed the wet wood underneath on the flag-stone, pressing the green into rock.

I heard a rumbling come close and looked up, and I could see, down the road, a mule plodding slow and steady with a covered wagon, a ribbon of dust trailing behind it.

In those days, the road to our house was narrow and only just cut through the brush. Our house was set back—Grandfather, my mother's father, had made his money raising pigs and kept the house and pens away from everyone else to protect his neighbors, and his reputation, from the undermining smell of swine. No one respects a man, no matter how rich and distinguished-looking, who stinks of pig scat. The house was set up on a rise, so we could always see who was coming. Usually, it was Mama's patients, walking or limping or running to her office. Wagons were rare.

When it first turned onto our road, the cart was moving slowly. But once it passed the bowed-over walnut tree, the woman at the seat snapped her whip, and the mule began to move a little faster, until it was upon us.

"Where's your mother?"

I opened my mouth, but before I could call for her, my mother rushed to the door, Lenore behind her.

"Quick," was all Mama said, and the woman came down off the seat. A boy, about twelve or thirteen, followed. They were both dressed in mourning clothes. The woman's skirt was full. Embroidered on the bodice of her dress were a dozen black lilies, done in cord. The boy's mourning suit was dusty but perfectly fit to his form. At his neck was a velvet bow tie, come undone on the journey. The woman carried an enormous beaded handbag—it, too, was dusty but looked rich. It was covered in a thousand little eyes of jet that winked at me in the last bit of sun.

"Go, Lenore," my mother said, and Lenore and the woman and the boy all went to the back of the wagon, the boy hopping up in the bed and pushing something that lay there, Lenore and the woman standing, arms ready to catch it. Finally, after much scraping, a coffin heaved out of the wagon bed. It was crudely made, a white, bright wood, heavy enough that Lenore and the woman stumbled as they carried it. When the coffin passed me, I could smell the sawdust still on it.

My mother stepped down off the stoop then, and the four of them lifted it up and managed it into the office. As soon as they got it inside, they set it on the ground and pushed it home. I could hear the rough pine shuffling across the floor.

"You're early." Mama struggled with the box.

"Don't start with me, Cathy," the woman said, and Lenore looked up, and so did I. No one, except Grandfather before he died, dared call Mama "Cathy." To everyone except for me, she was always "Doctor." But Mama did not bristle and did not correct, as she would have with anyone else.

"Word was you'd be here at midnight."

"We couldn't leave," the woman said. "He wasn't ready."

The woman knelt down in her dusty skirts and drew a long, skinny claw hammer from the handbag. She turned it on its head and began to pull at the nails on the coffin's face. She grunted. "Here, Lucien." She signaled to the boy. "Put some grease into it." He fell down beside her, took the hammer from her hands, and began to pull at the nails she'd left behind.

Mama watched, eagerly. We all did. I crossed the room to stand beside her, slipped my hand into hers.

Mama started at my touch. "If you'd only come later."

The woman's head jerked up, her expression sharp, and then she looked at my hand in Mama's, and her frown softened.

"I know we've done it differently. This time we really tried," she said. "Besides, my Lucien sees all this and more. If you do this work, Cathy, your children will know sooner or later."

Mama did not take advice from anyone, certainly not advice on me, but she said nothing at this softest of rebukes, only watched the woman and her son.

The boy, Lucien, pulled hard, and when the final nail was out, he and Lenore pulled at the splintering plank until it gave a terrible yawn. And then I saw:

a man curled in on himself like a dried mulberry leaf,

his skin gray, his eyes open and staring,

his pants damp. He smelled sharp,

like the spirits Lenore used to cut Mama's medicines.

The woman gasped and reached for the boy and held him close. Lenore gasped, too. Mama let go of my hand and knelt down at the side of the coffin. She held her ear over the man's open mouth, and her eyes went blank, that look she always got when she left this world and entered the one of her mind.

She stood up suddenly. "The arnica, please," she said to Lenore, who hurried to the shelf over Mama's worktable.

Lenore held the big glass jar close to her chest, then set it down beside the coffin. Without looking at her, never taking her eyes off the dead man, Mama held out her right hand.

"Thirty grains," she said. "Exactly. Don't skimp me, girl."

Lenore counted them out.

One . . . two . . . three . . .

I watched the yellow pellets move from the jar to Mama's open palm. Mama wet the fingers of her free hand with her spit, the better to gain purchase, and then pinched each grain, one by one, from her right palm and fed them into the dead man's mouth.

fifteen sixteen seventeen

"He wasn't like that when we put him in, Cathy," the woman said.

Lucien turned his face into her side, and I felt a flash of pride, that a boy bigger than me couldn't watch what I could.

twenty-one twenty-two twenty-three

Thirty seeds passed between his lips.

The last five left them yellow.

Mama stood up. The man lay still in his coffin. Mama put her hands on her hips, frowned. Then she knelt down suddenly and whacked his back. The man sputtered and coughed and made the lowest moaning sound. His eyes blinked, and he rolled them up to look at all of us, from his resting place.

"There," Mama said.

The woman sighed. "Cathy, I don't know what we would have done—"

"Well, we don't have to wonder." Mama wiped her hands on her skirt. The man in the coffin was still groaning.

"He was so eager to keep going," the woman said. "He and his sister came to us three days ago. He said he should leave before his sister. That he was strong enough to make it first. But when he saw how he had to come, he got scared. He was shaking something fierce."

"I told him, 'Me and Manman took a girl not but ten years old this way, and she was brave and didn't cry the whole time,'" Lucien said. He was much recovered now and had stepped away from his mother's side. "I said, 'Be brave, Mr. Ben.'"

"Last night, he disappeared," the woman said. "That's why we left at the wrong time. He went missing and almost killed us all. He was down in Market Square, begging for whiskey to help him through. I said, 'You fool,' but he was already drunk by the time he got back. Pierre told me to wait till he sobered up, but if we'd done that, he would have kept yelling, drawing even more attention to us. It took Pierre and

Lucien both to get him in the box, and the whole time he was hollering that we were trying to kill him. He kept saying 'Damn, nigger, what'd I ever do to you?'"

Mama started to laugh but caught herself. Instead, she said, "How did you get him to be quiet?"

"I soaked that rag in some laudanum and stuffed it in his mouth, and then he fell right still. When we nailed the top on, I swear he was still breathing."

Mama shook her head. "You always overdo it, Elizabeth," she said, and then we all heard a great whoosh as Mr. Ben sat up in his coffin and began to cry.

"That black bitch right there promised to get me out. They all said she can get you out. No one ever said it was like this. In a goddamn coffin." Mr. Ben was upright, and I could see him clearly. The color came back to him—his skin was a dark brown. I liked his face. It was soft and, I thought, handsome, made more so by his cheeks and chin. They rounded in to the pout of a spoiled and much-loved baby. I could not tell how old he was—his skin was smooth, but his hair, what was left of it, was turning gray and clipped close to his skull. He wore a graying shirt and britches and no hat. His hands were enormous and calloused. He was crying, loud, racking sobs that I did not think a grown person could make. He made no move to leave his coffin, and my mother and the woman made no move to comfort him.

The woman said, "Behave yourself, Mr. Ben."

Mama pursed her lips. "Is this his final destination?"

"We take his sister to Manhattan next month."

"Then perhaps Mr. Ben can wait for her there. Mr. Ben," Mama said, "you will have to stay the night here, but I trust we can count on you to be quiet?"

Mr. Ben did not look at her; instead, he gazed up at the ceiling. "As long as I don't ever have to sleep in any coffin."

Mama laughed. "Only the good Lord can promise that."

MAMA HAD LENORE set up a bed for Mr. Ben by the fire, and she and the woman—Madame Elizabeth, she'd said to call her—took Mr. Ben by both elbows and helped him stand for the first time in twelve hours and walk around the room before settling down.

Mr. Ben went easily enough to sleep, and Mama and Madame Elizabeth fell to talking.

I was too cowed to say anything to our visitors. With the other people who came to see Mama at the house—her patients, and the runners from the pharmacy closer to town, and all the women in the committees and societies and church groups Mama headed—I had been trained to make polite conversation and ask, "How do you do?" But Madame Elizabeth was different. She spoke to Mama as if we had not all just seen her raise a man from the dead. As if Mama was the same as she.

"Cathy," she said when Mama stood over Lenore as she made up Mr. Ben's cot, "you work this poor woman to death."

As they talked, I did not dare to interrupt them. I did not want to be sent away to bed. Mama brewed strong sassafras tea for both of them—they had seemed to agree, without ever speaking it aloud, that they would both stay up the night to make sure Mr. Ben made it. I sat very still and close to Mama, and the only way I was sure she had not forgotten me was when, after she finished her mug, she silently handed it to me, because she knew that I believed that the sweetest drink in the world came from the dregs of a cup she had drunk from.

From their talking, I learned that Madame Elizabeth was a childhood friend of Mama's. She had a husband, whom she called Monsieur Pierre. "A Haitian Negro, so you know he's unruly," Madame Elizabeth said, and Mama laughed.

"Oh hush," she said.

He and Madame Elizabeth owned a storefront down in Philadelphia—Madame Elizabeth ran a dressmaker's shop on one side of the house, and Monsieur Pierre ran an undertaker's on the other.

"You are doing well?" Mama asked, and Madame Elizabeth stood up, stamping her feet so her skirt hung down straight.

"Well? Well? Look at this dress, Madame Doctor." She turned. It was, indeed, a very fine dress. The lilies embroidered on the bodice stretched tendrils down to the skirt—a queer embellishment on a mourning dress that she had clearly worn over many travels.

"You play too much," Mama said. "A dress like that draws attention, and that's the last thing any of us need."

"We're doing the Lord's work in a cruel world, but that doesn't mean we can't do it with style," Madame Elizabeth said.

Mama looked at the fire. "If we are found out because you insist on introducing yourself with an ostrich feather, I don't know that I, or the Lord, can forgive you."

"Well, ostrich feathers are déclassé." Madame Elizabeth took the hem of her dress in her hand and artfully shook it. "Pierre always hated them, and lo and behold, the ladies say they're no longer in fashion. So nothing to worry about on that account."

They fell into a practiced quarrel, one that must have been older than me, centered on Mama's bad dress sense. Mama did not care for beauty; this was true. Like all the women in our town, she dressed for work—in heavy dark-colored gowns that could bear the mark of other people's sweat and tears and spit and vomit, and never show the stain.

But where others took care to tie a scarf at an angle or thread sweetgrass through a shirt cuff, Mama did not care. She was not scraggly. She was always neat, and on Sundays she allowed for the vanity of a hat with a big sweeping brim, which was decorated with the same set of silk flowers she'd won in a church raffle before I was born. But when one of the ladies' groups she belonged to would occasionally fall into giddy talk about the newest bolt of fabric or a new way of tying a head scarf, she would always quickly steer the conversation back to what was at hand. She would have been mortified to know it, but I had heard some of the women point to those same silk flowers on her hat that had not changed position for many seasons and call them "more reliable than springtime."

Madame Elizabeth teased Mama about the cramped practicalities of their youth until finally she turned to me, the first she had acknowledged me since she came in.

"Do you think she was always this way?" She glanced sideways at my mother.

"You turn my own daughter against me?" Mama said, but she was laughing, really laughing, in a way I had not heard before.

"When we were girls at the Colored School"—Madame Elizabeth leaned in, her voice low, as if I was as old as she and Mama—"I used to be so terrible at arithmetic. But not her. She was the best at it. Oh, so quick! You'd think the devil was giving her notes."

"Elizabeth!"

"But he wasn't of course. She was just so smart, your mother. Smarter than the devil, but good. But not all the way good. Can I tell you? Can I tell you a secret, my dear?"

"Don't listen to her." Mama went to cover my ears, but Madame Elizabeth drew me to her and held me close to her lap, and mock whispered, loud enough for Mama to hear: "Do you know what your clever mama would do? She'd ask me to dye her ribbons purple for her. Yes, even your good and smart mama wanted a bit of purple ribbon. And me, being her bestest friend, being her kind Elizabeth, mashed up all the blackberries I could find and dyed those ribbons the prettiest purple anyone in Kings County had ever seen."

"And extorted me and forced me to agree to do your arithmetic for you in exchange," Mama said.

"But can you blame me?" Madame Elizabeth's breath was so soft on my ear I shivered. "Your mama has always been the brightest."

Madame Elizabeth stroked the plaits in my hair and ran her fingers over my brow. "Lord," she said, "your girl may be dark, Cathy, but isn't she pretty."

"Libertie is beautiful," Mama said, gazing happily at me, and I flushed warm, because Mama did not often comment on anyone's appearance, unless it was to note that their skin had gone jaundiced or developed a rash.

"It's a shame she got her father's color," Madame Elizabeth said absently, and Mama stopped smiling.

"It's a blessing," she said, very distinctly, and Madame Elizabeth's hand paused.

"You aren't scared?" she said. She was stroking my face again. I did not want her to stop, but I could see from Mama's face that she wished that she would. "This work grows more dangerous, you know. You are all right. You're bright enough they hassle you less, maybe. But she's too dark."

Mama stood up abruptly. "It's less dangerous work if your help-meets come to you at midnight, as promised, not dusk," she said. She bent over Mr. Ben's cot.

Madame Elizabeth let go of my face.

"I told you why we missed our time."

But Mama didn't answer. She held her palm over Mr. Ben's open mouth.

"How is he?" Madame Elizabeth called.

"If he makes it through the next hour without any upset, he should be recovered."

Madame Elizabeth looked over at her son, who had fallen asleep in Mama's leather examination chair. Lucien, like Madame Elizabeth, had brassy velvet skin, and it was blushing now, in the last heat of the fire.

"Lucien's good-looking as well." Madame Elizabeth glanced sideways at Mama. "Perhaps one day, he and Libertie will make us proud and marry."

Mama was still watching Mr. Ben, but she smiled. "And move my Libertie all the way to Philadelphia, away from me? I couldn't bear that," she said. But she was pleased, I could see, that Madame Elizabeth, even in jest, considered me worthy of her son.

"What did Mama do with the purple ribbons?" I asked before I could stop. I cursed myself. Surely, now they would send me to bed. But Madame Elizabeth pulled me onto her lap.

"She wore them every day, because she knew they looked so fine. She was wearing them the day she met your good and kind father. She only let me borrow them once, when I asked her because I was going to a lecture at the lyceum. And, wouldn't you know, it was there where I met my own good man, Monsieur Pierre. He was fresh from Haiti, and I do believe meeting him is because of those lucky purple ribbons. Maybe she'll let you wear them one day, too, and you will tell us of finding your love with them."

"Tall tales," Mama said.

The rope on the cot whinnied as Mr. Ben turned over in his sleep. He began to cry. He was saying something, a word gargled by the bend of his neck. Mama gently lifted his head, and he sighed. Then he shouted, "Daisy."

"He certainly is giving us work," Madame Elizabeth said.

"We grow too bold. You should not have taken him."

"He insisted. In his state, it's safer to keep him moving. Once his sister comes, she can take him on to Troy or Syracuse. Or Canada."

"He won't be safe till he's out of this country. Even then, he will probably still be in danger," Mama said.

"Daisy," Mr. Ben cried again.

"His sister said that was his girl," Madame Elizabeth said. "He took up with her, and then she ran. They got word last spring she died. That's what finally made him despair enough to leave, his sister said. She'd been trying to get him to work up the courage for forever. Their mother gone, brother gone, and then the girl he'd started to love, for just a little bit of comfort, gone, too. That's why he's here."

"He's running away, not running towards. They're the most dangerous kind," Mama said. "They have nothing to lose, and so they grow reckless."

"He won't harm us, though."

"Let us hope," Mama said. She did not sound convinced.

MY MOTHER NAMED me Libertie for a dead man's dream, the dream of my father—the only other dead man I knew before Mama resurrected Mr. Ben.

My father died when I was still in Mama's womb. He was a traveling preacher, and on one of his trips west, he fell ill. By the time he made it back to her, it was too late. Even Mama, who I believed could heal everyone, could not heal him. In his final moments, as he lay sweating his life away in her arms, he told her to name me Libertie, in honor of the bright, shining future he was sure was coming.

Father was one of those who'd stolen themselves away and come up north. Did he come in one of Madame Elizabeth's coffins? I do not know. Mama did not like to talk about him. His name was Robert. I know it only from tracing it on his gravestone with my finger. He is buried in my mother's family's plot—he, of course, did not have his people up here. His gravestone reads ROBERT SAMPSON, and then, underneath it, instead of his time on this Earth, only one word: FREEDOM.

Although Mama did not like to talk about my father, she did like me to take care of his grave. Every other Sunday, after church, we stopped in the burial place and washed down his stone and pulled up the weeds. One of the first presents she made me, when I was four or five, was a small pair of scissors to wear at my waist, so that I could trim the grass that grew over him. "It's his home now," was how she'd explained it to me. "We have to make it comfortable for him."

While Father was the one dead man I knew, I knew of a dead little girl, too: my mama's sister. She was also buried in the family plot, but her stone had no name, and Mama wouldn't tell it to me. Mama did not like to speak of her, either. She was not a name, not a memory—just a white stone that only Mama was allowed to tend and a glass jar on the parlor's mantelpiece, where Mama kept three braids clipped from her sister's head right after she passed. The dead girl's braids sat gathering dust in the bottom of the jar, curled in on one another like the newborn milk snakes we'd sometimes find asleep in the barn. I only learned how the little girl passed from Lenore, who told me one day, plain, while Mama was on a house call and had left me to help wash the sheets.

As she beat the linen clean, Lenore said, "Pneumonia." The dry cough racking the small, sweaty body, the muffled air: it was a painful way for a child to go. "Back then, there was no colored doctor, man or woman, in the county. If you wanted to go to see a doctor, you had to find a white person willing to accompany you—white doctors did not treat colored people if we came alone. Your grandfather was light enough. He could get by. But the little girl who passed, she couldn't. She was too dark. They would have known her to be colored. They would not have taken her for white, as they would have if it was your grandfather or your mama who fell ill."

"Your grandfather had a white friend," she continued. "A Mr. Hobson, who he sometimes chewed tobacco with. So he ran to him to see if he would accompany his daughter to the hospital. But when he reached Mr. Hobson, the man was playing cards and did not want to get up from the table—not yet. Mr. Hobson waited a hand, and then another, just to make sure he was losing, and by the time he had gotten up and gotten back to the house, your mother's sister was gone."

Lenore ended the story matter-of-factly. "Your mama became a doctor because she watched her sister die."

I think it is also why, even though Mama could have gotten by, she always made it clear she was a colored woman. They let her into the medical school alongside two white women before they realized their mistake, though she was quick to point out she'd never deceived anyone, never claimed she wasn't a Negro, always signed her real name and address. And then, of course, she married my father, who must have been dark, because I could never get by the way she could. But Mama saw that as a mark of honor, a point of pride for her Libertie. Almost as if she'd planned it.

I know that they met at a lecture. Maybe one where Madame Elizabeth met her Haitian? I never had the courage to ask. Mama only told me that the lecture was about the country being founded for us in

Africa. It was a lecture about whether or not American Negroes should go. Should free men leave? Mama did not want to—I know that. And I know that my father always did. So I am named for his longing. As a girl, I did not realize what a great burden this was to bear. I was only grateful.

Where did Father go? Where was he now, since he was not here on Earth with me and Mama? Every other Sunday, I lay on my father's grave and imagined that new place he'd journeyed to in death: Freedom. In the muggy summertime, in the hot July sun, I imagined Freedom was a cool, dark cave with water dripping down the walls—like the one where Jesus slept for three days. And in November, when the wind bit the tips of my fingers and turned them red, I imagined Freedom was a wide, grassy field on a warm and cloudy day.

What did Father do, now that he was dead? He went to more lectures. Since it was the only thing I knew about him, about how they met, I imagined that was Freedom to him. In Freedom, he sat in the cool cave or in the wide field in a pew like we had at church, but comfortable, and he closed his eyes and listened to learned men and women make the world anew with words. And at his side were two seats: one for Mama at his left and one for me at his right. I imagined that when I died and made it to Freedom, whenever that would be, I would have to spend eternity very politely pretending to like these lectures as much as Mama and Father did. It would be hard to do that forever, but Mama would be happy, at least, and I would have my father's hand in mine, while I sat, slightly bored but loved, in Freedom.

WE ALL SLEPT in the examination room that night—me curled on Mama's lap, and Madame Elizabeth and Lucien collapsed on each other, and Mr. Ben still in his cot.

I woke up first, a little before dawn. It was strange to be awake without Mama, but it gave me time to very carefully crawl down off her lap and creep across the floor and sit, hugging my knees, right by Mr. Ben's pillow, so I could get a better look at him. Mr. Ben was the first person I'd ever met who had been brought back from death, and I watched him avidly for signs of what Freedom had been like.

I saw where his lips were damp with spittle, and I smelled, on his breath, the dried flowers that my mother had made him eat. And then I had the shock of watching him open his eyes, very slowly, to stare back at me.

"I been awake for hours," he said.

I nodded.

"You her girl?"

"She's my mama."

He whistled. "She must've liked her niggers black to get a girl like you."

I had heard worse. It was the refrain of so many when Mama and I walked in the street.

"Mama says I'm like a mulberry."

"Yeah, you a pretty little girl—no denying it. Just dark. Where your daddy at?"

"He's dead."

"So who else live here?"

"It's just me and Mama—and her nurse, Lenore, who comes every morning to help with the patients."

He propped himself up on his elbow and winced. "Lord, I'm dizzy." He contemplated the ceiling for what felt like a long time. Then he looked to the window that was just beginning to turn white with the rising sun. "She own all of this? From doctoring? Just from doctoring?"

"Mama grew up in this house. Her daddy owned it. He was a pig farmer. We still have some of his hogs, but we don't raise 'em to sell anymore. You don't know about his hogs?" I warmed to the telling. What a change, what a delight to have a stranger in the house, someone who did not already know everything about me, as was usually the way with Mama's visitors. "His hogs used to be famous. Grandfather was very religious, and he taught every hog born under his care to bow its head in prayer before it ate at the trough. He'd say the Lord's Prayer with 'em, Mama says. A few of the pigs here are old enough to still do it. Sometimes . . ." I leaned forward to share this secret with my new friend. "Sometimes, I say the Lord's Prayer really loud when I'm feeding 'em to see which ones will bow. But they don't listen to me like that."

This confidence was lost on Mr. Ben, though, because he wasn't paying attention. He was looking up, over my shoulder, and I turned to see that he was looking at Mama, who had stirred in her chair, and who was watching Mr. Ben back.

"That's enough, Libertie."

She stood up and stood over Mr. Ben. On her face now was a familiar expression, one I had seen often enough in the examination room, and when I accompanied her on her house calls.

When Mama was diagnosing someone, when she was calculating how best to heal them, she got this look. Her eyes emptied out and turned dark, and her brow went completely smooth, and she stared for a good three or four minutes. She did not respond to anything—not a patient's babbling, not the sound of the wind at the door, not the distraught mother saying, "Please, please, please," not the cries of the baby who was too young to understand the failings of its own small body. Certainly not to me, the girl at her side holding her bag, watching her disappear from me and go deep into her mind, where the right answer nearly always was. She'd leave me behind, leave us all behind, to commune with the perfection of her intellect. And when she returned, it was with a resolve that was almost frightening to see.

It was sad and cold to be outside her caring. It had scared me as a smaller child, made me cry.

As consolation, Mama had explained that one day I would join her when she left for her mind like that, that one day I would be a doctor, too, standing beside her, both our minds flying free while our bodies did the work. And we'd have a horse and carriage, and a sign with gold letters on it that said DR. SAMPSON AND DAUGHTER. "Wouldn't that be nice, Libertie?" she'd said.

And that had been a kind of hollow comfort when she left me behind for her calculations.

Mr. Ben was watching her now. "It feels like I'm dying. Am I gonna die?"

Mama's eyes filled up again, and she was back. "Not yet," she said.

He propped himself up on his elbows. "This the worst pain I ever felt. I was whupped till my back was ribbons when I was a younger man, and I thought that was dying, but this is different. It feels like there's a hole in me, in the very center of me, and the wind's running through it."

Mama sat back. "That's a problem of the spirit."

"So medicine women are supposed to fix that."

"I'm a trained doctor," Mama said, straightening up. "I fix the body. The spirit can tell me what's wrong with the body sometimes. But what you are describing—you can talk to Reverend Harland at the church about the spirit."

"Seems you should be able to do it all."

I did not think, then, that Mama was even listening. If she had heard it, I was sure she had discounted it, because all she said was, "You will stay here to rest."

The next morning, it took Mama and Madame Elizabeth and Lucien, struggling, to lift the empty coffin back onto the wagon bed it was so unwieldly. Finally, they slid it home.

Madame Elizabeth was just taking up the whip to prod the mule when Mama seized her friend's hand and kissed the knuckles where they wrapped around the switch.

Madame Elizabeth looked startled. Lucien smirked—oh, how I hated him for that.

For Mama looked genuinely pained. "If you should run into any trouble—"

"We won't," Madame Elizabeth said.

"But if you should . . ." She held her friend's hand for a beat more, then flung it away from her. "Be safe."

Mr. Ben had come outside for this last bit. He bent his head slightly in the wagon's direction. "Thanks, mamselle," he said with slight mockery, to which Madame Elizabeth rolled her eyes.

Then she called to the mule, and they were on their way.

Mama stayed to watch them go. Mr. Ben stood beside her.

"Y'all ain't afraid of getting caught?" he said.

"She's very good at what she does."

Mr. Ben sniffed. "When she's not trying to murder a man."

Mama glanced at me, then looked back to the road, where the wagon moved slowly away from us. "You made it here well enough."

"Back in Maryland," Mr. Ben said, "where I was before . . ." He looked down at his hands. "Before I was sold the first time, there was a group of niggers like you gals. They did what you doing. They got fifteen out. And then they was caught. You don't want to hear what happened."

Mama glanced again at me, then back at Mr. Ben. "We most certainly do not," she said.

"What happened?" I asked.

"Blood—"

"That's enough," Mama said. "Mr. Ben, if you're well enough to stand and well enough to talk, do you think you're well enough to help us today?"

He sniffed again. "I suppose so."

"Good," Mama said. "The best way to help is to stay quiet and stay out of the way, then. Don't let anybody who comes to the house see you yet."

"Your neighbors don't know you in this business? Mamselle Elizabeth told me she was bringing me to an all-colored town."

"We are," Mama said. "You'll settle well here. But it's best if we allow people to truthfully say they thought you came here on your own. Generally, we take care of each other here. But I don't want to put anyone into a position of lying for us. It's too dangerous. Besides, you know as well as I do, Mr. Ben. Even with our own, you can't trust everybody."

He looked out over the yard again, to the barn and the squat crab-apple tree, to the hog pen with the two pigs just now rising from the mud to wander, to Mama's medicine garden and the small field that lay just beyond it, where we grew the vegetables for the kitchen, to all the things that I'd just told him she owned.

"I suppose that's right," he said. "Just because a person's a nigger doesn't mean they know the life you do." Then he looked at Mama and stalked back into the house.

I slipped my hand into hers.

"What does he mean, Mama?"

"He has just suffered a great shock to his system and won't make much sense for a while."

"Because you and Madame Elizabeth got him free?"

She took her hand out of mine and knelt so that we could look each other in the eye. I did not like this at all. I preferred looking up at her, tilting my head back till all I saw was her chin. Eye to eye was more frightening.

People said Mama was a beautiful woman, but I think what they really meant was she was light enough to pass. She had large eyes, true, set deep in her skull, but they were more owl-like than anything else. She had a heavy brow, hooded, that made it look as though she was about to scowl, even when she was laughing. Her skin, of course, was pale but it was sallow. It was her one vanity, the only one she allowed me to witness anyways—she dried lily petals in the spring and ate them year-round, to make the tone of her cheeks even. It was, up until this moment, my favorite secret we shared between us. I was the only one who saw her do it. Her nose was straight—I think this is what people meant when they called her beautiful—but it was severe. Her lips were the only pretty thing about her, the same as mine, full and always resolving themselves into the shape of a rose. When I looked at her, I never saw my own face, and maybe that is why I found it so disturbing, these times when she'd kneel down to look me in the eye.

I preferred, at that age, to think of us as the same person. I was still young enough for that.

She looked me in the eye and said, "What did you say?"

"You got him free. You and Madame Elizabeth. You got him here to be free."

She looked me steadily in the eye. Finally. "This is true."

I expected her to stand again, but she did not. "You cannot repeat to anyone what you just said to me—"

"But why?"

"This is not a game, Libertie. What we did, what we are doing, is very dangerous. If you tell somebody, it would not end well for us. We would go to jail, Mr. Ben would go back to bondage, and you and I would never see each other again. Do you understand?"

I did not, entirely. But to admit this would not please her, so I nodded.

She stood up and put her hand on her hip. The sun was finally out, and we could see, in the new light, Lenore coming up the road. Lenore was not a big woman, but she still managed to roll her hips when she walked, and she liked to ball her skirts in her two fists and switch them this way and that, to keep the dust off her. Mama was insistent that no dust be brought into the examination room, except by her patients themselves, and made Lenore wipe herself down with damp cloth and beat her skirt with a straw brush before she could join her each day, so Lenore had devised this method to make it a bit easier.

She made her way to us, where we stood, glanced at me.

"The girl up?"

"I woke up before anyone," I said proudly.

Lenore gave Mama a look.

"I told her," Mama said. "She says she can keep a secret."

"She a child," Lenore said.

"I can do it," I said again.

Lenore looked steadily at my mother, and my mother looked back for a bit, then lowered her eyes.

"It's not safe for the baby to be up," Lenore said.

"I'm not a baby," I insisted.

Lenore sighed. "Grown folks know when to keep quiet. Babies run they mouths every which way. Y'all can't help it." Her voice was drained of malice. She was merely stating a fact. This wounded my pride even more. Worse, she was not even looking at me when she said it; she was looking at Mama.

"Dr. Sampson, I won't get sold to a slavecatcher because a child can't stop talking."

"Nobody's saying that's going to happen," Mama said.

"Still"—Lenore moved past her, to the house, to start the fire burning for the day—"you can't trust babies with the ways of the world."

We were alone together again.

"I am not a baby, Mama."

She looked at me skeptically.

"I can help. I can do what you do. Let me help."

"You cannot, Libertie."

"Mama," I said, "you always say that when I am big, you and I will have a horse and carriage together, with 'Dr. Sampson and Daughter' written in gold on the side. You promised me, when I am big. You said that. You did. So let me help you now."

She sighed.

"I am eleven, nearly twelve in July. Let me do it, too, Mama."

She was not looking at me anymore, but at the dusty road that Madame Elizabeth had left on and Lenore had returned to us on. "I suppose it was inevitable," she said.

"What does 'inevitable' mean?"

"If you're to join us in this work, Libertie, the first lesson is the one Lenore said. Don't ask so many questions. Only listen and learn."

THIS LESSON DID not appear to apply to Mr. Ben.

The whole day, all he did was question.

"What's that you've got going there, Miss Doctor?"

"Lord, why does the house smell like greens gone bad?"

"Y'all don't stop at noon to eat?"

"But I still don't understand who pays you for all this work, because you know niggers ain't got no money."

Mama tried, politely, to answer his questions at first while Lenore flat-out ignored him from the start. It was not so bad in the morning, before patients, and before John Culver, the pharmacist's son, came running for more supplies. Usually, in those hours, Mama and Lenore worked in a silent dance, the only sound being the fire crackling and the glass tops of the medicine jars shifting as they reached for this or that to make or measure.

But the silence of their work seemed to unnerve Mr. Ben, and any time the house began to quiet down, to start the rhythms of women working, he was compelled to speak and break it.

"Does every woman in New York make a biscuit as dry as this?" he said as he reached for his third one that morning.

Mama was only half listening.

"If my woman, Daisy, was still here," Mr. Ben said, "she'd learn you. Even you, Miss Doctor. Whoever heard of a woman knowing how to make a pill but not a biscuit? It's not natural. Daisy would learn you, though, if she was still with us. She was sweet like that. She was the type to learn you if you asked."

Lenore looked up sharply. "Mr. Ben, you're bothering the doctor."

And Mr. Ben said, "She can nurse and listen at the same time, can't she?"

A few moments' silence. Then.

"Miss Doctor, this tea is weak," he said.

No answer this time from Mama or Lenore, who had pointedly decided to ignore him.

"Miss Doctor," he tried again, "why don't you ever put on new ribbons? My Daisy always tried to make herself pretty, and she wasn't half as rich or important as you. But she knew how to make herself look nice. If you thought of looking nice, then maybe you'd find a man to come here and live with you. You're not too old for all that, Miss Doctor."

At that point, Lenore moved as if she would show him the door, but Mama held up her hand to stay her. She took a deep breath, and then she turned, a tight smile on her face.

"Mr. Ben, I do believe you have not seen the rest of our town. Libertie, take Mr. Ben for a walk."

"Mama . . ."

"You said you wanted to be of service in our work. Well, be of service," Mama said.

So I took Mr. Ben's hand in my own and led him out into the afternoon sun. When I went back for my cloak, I overheard Mama and Lenore.

"Honestly, it's a wonder how that Daisy woman got with him in the first place," Lenore said, and Mama laughed outright. "When will he leave?"

"His sister will be here soon."

"It's too much, Doctor."

"We can bear it," Mama said.

I took my coat and left.

WE WERE THE sole house on the way to town—Grandfather had cleared the brush himself and tried to sell the lots along it to other colored men, but most men, if they were buying, wanted to live closer to the school and the church. Because we were the only family on that road, and had the privilege of naming it after ourselves.

"Sampson Lane," I told Mr. Ben proudly.

He nodded. He looked above us, where the tree canopy stretched, through which we could see the white sky of spring.

"It's colder up here in New York," he said. "I didn't think a place could be colder than Philadelphia, but Kings County has it beat."

I did not feel right talking badly about our town, but I also felt my cheeks stinging in the bitter air. I nodded politely, not committing to my guest's belief but trying to be neighborly, which is what we learned in Sunday school.

Our house, and the road that led to it, were all on higher ground than the rest of our settlement, and as the path sloped down, as our feet began to angle to the earth, the ground became wetter. My boots were spotted in mud, and Mr. Ben's began to squelch.

"I'm sorry," I said. "We will tell Mama, and she will find better shoes for you."

"She will, will she?" he said.

"You don't like Mama," I said. It had not occurred to me, up until then, that anybody, anyone colored anyways, could dislike my mother. I always saw people speak to her with respect, and even the sick children, who knew to be afraid when they saw a doctor, did not have dislike in their fear, only a kind of awe. So it was a revelation to meet someone who disliked her, and it was so strange that I did not understand it as a threat.

Mr. Ben did not deny it. He only kept walking until finally he said, "You always been free?"

"Yeah," I said.

"You ain't never been a slave? Your mama neither?"

"No," I said.

He sighed. "They tell us over and over again what's not possible. White folks say this ain't possible, this place ain't possible. But it's real.

It's a glory, but it's . . . it's . . . I wish my Daisy was still here to see it with me. She told me there was places like this. She said if she was ever free, she'd spend all day in silk and she'd paint her face pretty. I wish she was still alive to see it. She knew what she would do with freedom. It wasn't man's work she'd do with freedom. Not like your mama. She knew better than that."

Then he stopped, and was silent, and seemed to have gone away to another world, too. Not the one where Mama went to figure out how to make a body work right, but somewhere else, probably with his Daisy in her silks. But in the moment, I decided to apply Mama's new lesson for me and not ask questions.

"This it?" Mr. Ben said.

Sampson Lane had reached the crossroads, where the main road stretched to downtown and the waterfront—the journey most people who lived here made every dawn and dusk for their livelihood. In the other direction, the road stretched deeper into Kings County, to the farms some of us worked. The final fork spread south. Around us was some of the land cleared for fields, the cabins and houses built close together so that neighbors could share gardens and animals and conversation.

There was the schoolhouse, which was empty now, because it was spring and most children were working. It would start up classes again in a few weeks, when they returned, and I would sit there, too, away from Mama.

There was the low, rambling building that was Mr. Culver's pharmacy. His son, John, was regularly running from Mama's to here, passing messages between the two of them. Out front sat six glass vials, filled to the brim with blue and green and red liquid remedies—the sign to all, even those of us who did not know our letters, that Culver's was a place for medicine. I knew the front room well. Culver's also was our general store, where we could buy seed and burlap and thread from a welcoming face, not the begrudging white ones downtown who sold the same, at two times the price for colored people.

And finally, there was the church, the building everyone was proudest of. It had been the first one built, after our grandfathers bought land here, and it stood back, next to a little glen of trees we took turns pruning to keep pretty, and the graveyard shaded lower on the hill, protected from any passerby.

Mr. Ben looked around. "This it, then?" he repeated.

"We play over there," I said, pointing to the other side of the churchyard, where in the summertime a meadow always sprang up, which I and the other children liked to run through. In this new spring, it was bare, but I tried to explain it to him, what the future glory would look like. "We run so hard there you feel like you're bursting."

His face was unmoved.

"But I guess it's all just mud now," I said, trailing off.

A crow called above us, wheeled in the sky, and settled on the branch of the nearest tree, shaking a too-new blossom loose.

Mr. Ben said, "I couldn't see what this place looked like on the way in. I could only hear what this town was like, when I was in that box."

"What was it like?" I said. "In there."

"Awful, gal. What kind of a question is that? What you think it like, to be shut up in the dark with nothing but yourself all around you?"

He made another turn, looked up at the sky again, which seemed too white and was closing in around us.

I was seized with the wild desire for him to love our home as much as I did. He had said he was lonely for his Daisy, but maybe he was lonely because of being in the box, of having been so close to her in death but then being snatched away to rise up. I knew part of making a guest feel comfortable was to introduce them to those they might have something in common with. That is what they taught us girls in deportment at the Sunday school, anyways. And he seemed to enjoy talking about the dead. I pointed to the churchyard again.

"That's where my daddy is," I said. "Mama's sister, too. They're dead like your Daisy. Like you were. 'Cept Mama couldn't bring them back. She did that for you, though."

He looked at me from the corner of his eye and smiled slightly. "They all in there, then?" he said.

"Yeah." I thought about it for a minute. "Not all of 'em, though. Mama's sister's hair, it lives in the glass jar in the parlor. But all of my daddy's in there."

Mr. Ben nodded. He was quiet for a moment, and then he spit in disgust on the ground. "I don't even know Daisy's resting place."

He limped to the middle of the crossroads, turning first in one direction, then the other. He looked up above him again, at the sky. Then he said, "Let's go back to your mother's." And so we did.

He allowed me, though, the kindness of slipping my hand in his as we walked back home.

Dinner was eaten in near silence. Mr. Ben seemed to be thinking still of our trip to town, and Mama, she ate not for pleasure but for utility. She often said that if it was not for Lenore, I would not know good cookery at all. She seemed to notice that there was a sadness around Mr. Ben, because she said, at the end of a meal where the sole talk was between our tin spoons scraping our plates, "Is everything all right, then?"

He looked up at her, hard, for a minute. So hard Mama startled.

Then he looked back down at his plate and said, "Yes, ma'am."

It was my job to clear the table, to take everything to the basin of water Lenore always left, her last duty before the end of the day. So I did not hear how it started between them, only how it ended.

I had taken our plates and come back for the pitcher when I saw Mr. Ben by the parlor mantelpiece, running his hand along it. Mama was still at the table. She had taken out her accounting ledger for the day. She was back in the world of her mind.

Mr. Ben ran his fingers along the family Bible that sat there, then over the little mirror in a gold frame that Mama displayed and the bowl where Lenore put cut blossoms from the tulip tree outside. He skipped over the jar with the braids in it. His fingers next ran over a pile of newsprint.

"What's this?" he said.

Mama glanced up over the greasy spectacles on her nose, narrowed her eyes. "Ah, that? That is our newspaper. They print it once a month. It has lots for sale, and news of the church. And here . . ." Mama got up to stand beside Mr. Ben.

"I can't cipher," he said.

"Of course," Mama said. "But, you see, there's a primer in the back."

She rustled the pages to the very end. She held her hand over the paper and read aloud the print there. "See? This part are words to learn. 'Free.' 'Life.' 'Live.' 'Took.' 'Love.' 'Loves.' 'Man.' 'Now.' 'Will.' 'Thank.' 'God.' 'Work.' 'Hard.' 'House.' 'Land.' 'Made.' 'Slaves.'"

With each word she spoke, I saw him wince, as if the words had pricked his finger.

"And these," Mama said, "are the sentences to learn. 'I am free and well.' 'I will love God and thank Him for it.' 'And I must work hard and be good and get me a house and lot.'"

"'Work hard,'" he said.

"Yes."

It was quiet between them for a bit, only the fire crackling.

Then Mr. Ben panted out, as if it was taking him great effort to do so, "There was a nigger back in Maryland who learned how to cipher. You wanna know how he learned, Miss Doctor?"

"How?"

"He took pot liquor fat and dipped pages of the Bible in 'em. Dipped 'em in till the pages was clear through. Greased the Word and hid it underneath his hat, and that clever, pretty nigger walked around with the Bible fat on his head, and if any white man saw it, he wouldn't know it as the word of God. He'd only see some greasy, dirty papers on a nigger's head and leave 'im be."

"Well, that's marvelous," Mama said gravely. "That's quite beautiful."

"You think?" Mr. Ben sucked in a gulp of air, cleared his throat loudly. "I always thought it was a whole lot of work. But"—he pointed at the newspaper held between them—"we must work hard and be good even in freedom. That's what you telling me. With rules like that, don't it make you wonder what freedom's for?"

He let his fingers run along the mantel again, from the Bible, to the mirror, to the flowers and back again, skipping over the newsprint.

"You got so many pretty things, Miss Doctor," he said. "Such pretty things. My Daisy was the same way. She kept three stones she'd found: pink ones, and a white one, too. And a shell she'd found down by the wharf. She even had a mirror like this," he held up the mirror and set it down again. "She wanted one something fierce. 'Course, she didn't need one. My eyes were enough of a mirror for her, I told her. But she said no, she needed a mirror. To see herself. First thing she bought with the money from her market garden, even before she tried to save for freedom. She loved looking at herself in that thing. Sometimes, I'd have to beg her to put it down so my Daisy would talk to me."

He picked up the mirror at last, cradled it in his palm. "Do you think someone like that belongs in freedom?" Mr. Ben said. "I mean, if she'd lived to make it here. Do you think she would have been able to work hard and have her lot of land to earn her freedom, like that paper says?"

"We all work hard," Mama said. "I do not follow what you mean, Mr. Ben."

"I told you about my Daisy, didn't I?" He still would not look at her. He carefully set down the mirror. "She was almost as fair as you. No, fairer. And big brown eyes. And hair down her back in curls, when she let it out. Almost like . . ." He let his fingers run again along the mantelpiece once more, until they lit on the last thing he hadn't touched. The jar with the braids coiled at the bottom.

His back was still toward Mama. When he picked up the jar, he didn't see her flinch. But I did.

I moved to remind him. "Oh, you know what that is, Mr. Ben," I began, but Mama shot me a look so pained I stopped my explanation.

"Her hair was almost like this then," he said. He held the jar up to better catch the dusty braids in the light.

"Nah," he said, turning the jar around in his hands. "Daisy's hair was finer."

He set the jar back down and turned around. He was watching Mama's face carefully, as if tracking which way it might turn. "Who'd all that belong to, then?" he said.

Mama took her glasses off her nose so that she could see him more clearly. "My youngest sister," she said. She cleared her throat. "It is a keepsake."

"And what happened to her?" Mr. Ben said. "You lose her to the body or the spirit?"

Mama took in a sharp breath. She made a low, guttural sound, as if something was wrenched from her throat. And then she looked quickly down at the newsprint in her hand. I could see her eyes moving back and forth, making some kind of calculation. I could see, in the fever of it, one eye wet and watery. She looked up.

"I think," Mama said, her voice entirely steady but her eyes wet, "that we have come to an end with our time together, Mr. Ben. I think perhaps this is your last night here and you should wait for your sister in town. The back room at Culver's will have you. He takes in many of our new arrivals, and—"

"So that's it, then," he said.

"Yes," Mama said. "I believe it is."

She turned to me, still crying, her voice deadly level. "Libertie, please make up Mr. Ben's cot for him. Make sure it's comfortable for his last night here with us. I will be working in the examination room. Be quick, girl. We have a long day tomorrow."

And then she gathered up her ledger in her arms and walked out of the room. Mr. Ben watched her go.

He would not look at me, only at the fire, as I made his bed for him.

"Why did you go and do that?" I said as I pulled the cot closer to the fire for him.

"Leave it alone, girl."

When the bed was done, I stood beside it. I did not know exactly what I was waiting for, what I hoped I or he would say. I knew I should say something in defense of Mama. If Lenore was here, she would have loudly cursed Mr. Ben the whole time. But he looked at me with a sadness so deep it startled me. I could not say anything to reprimand him. Instead, I stepped forward and hugged him fiercely.

He smelled of fresh-cut grass, up close. I had not expected that. He was still in my arms for a moment, and then he put his own arms around me once, a quick, tight squeeze, the tightest I'd ever known, the air squeezed out of my lungs. And then he let me go.

"I'll be all right, girl," he said. "You go on now."

I WAS OF an age then when I had just left Mama's bed for one of my own, and even though I wished to comfort her, I did not wish to give up my hard-won independence of a cot to myself, under the eaves.

I stood by her examination room door while she sat with her back toward me, bent over her books.

"Mama," I began.

"Go to bed, Libertie."

So I did.

I did not see Mr. Ben to Culver's back room. Mama decided to take him there herself after Lenore came. She said, "You stay here, Libertie. You asked for your education to begin, and so it begins today."

As Mama walked down the road with Mr. Ben, neither of them speaking or looking at each other, I imagined what secrets I was about to be initiated into. What big-woman ways I was about to learn. What I would be able to chart about hearts and spleens and tongues. But Lenore only turned to me and said, "You can start with the cats in the barn."

We had a band of stray cats that had lived in the hay there since Mama was a girl. Big nature-raised hooligans with gnarled and matted fur, and sometimes sores on their sides. Whole generations that Mama and Lenore took care of, nursing their battle scars and birthing their litters. They terrified me. Even from far away, I knew them as too rough to be pets.

"Not them," I said.

Lenore smirked. "Your mama said it's how you'll learn to care."

So I took the bucket that Lenore usually did, and filled it with what she fed the cats—guts and bits from the kitchen, ground up for them. In the dim light of the barn, I could hear them all around me, and soon a few came closer and rubbed up against me. I felt panicked. Not because of their sharp teeth or their hissing, but because of their need. They wanted so much from me. The smell of their food made me ill, not because it was putrefying but because of how much it made them want me, made them mimic the action of love to get it, swirling around me, their softness hiding a deep, yawning hunger inside of them, just below their skin. I could feel it humming when they got too close. Their need was monstrous.

I fed them quick and ran from the barn, and when Mama came back, I wanted to tell her all of that, that their need was too much of a burden to carry. How could she do it? How could she see them so naked and yearning, and not want to turn away?

But Mama looked so tired, her face was so worn, that all I could say when I saw it was, "I don't like the cats, Mama."

Lenore sucked her teeth. "You bother her with that?"

But Mama was too tired, even, to hold my silliness against me. She did look disappointed, though.

But now that the idea of my taking on her work had gripped her, had become something she favored, Mama would not let me give up.

"You have to learn," she told me. "Care does not come natural to me, either."

What a lie, I thought. I could still see her, in my mind's eye, walking slow and steady beside Mr. Ben, who had picked up her dead sister's braids and tossed them aside, but who, I could tell, she understood had not meant it.

"But care, it is our lot now," Mama was saying. "It is our service to others that defines us. We are doers of the Word."

She sighed. "If you cannot keep the cats, you'll learn how to keep the garden."

The garden is no small thing to a homeopath. Mama kept a huge one to grow the most common things she needed: elderflower, ginger, mint, aloe. She was so orderly in everything, and the garden was no exception. The herbs were close by the door, and everything else was in neat rows, labeled clearly on posts made from scraps of wood. Up until now, the garden had been mostly Lenore's domain. But Lenore was so busy with everything else she'd been paying it less attention, and the garden had begun to be unruly. When they needed something from it, Mama would question Lenore, and Lenore would think for a minute, and they would argue back and forth about where it should be.

"You will keep it in the correct order, Libertie," Mama said. By which she meant the order of her imagination.

How was I to learn her mind? Before I could take over the garden, I would have to make a more diligent study of homeopathy, Mama's discipline of medicine. "The guiding principle," Mama had told me, many times as I grew, "is that like cures like." But it was, as all things Mama insisted were straightforward, more complicated than that.

I was allowed a rest from my regular chores, and Mama had me sit in her examination room with her materia medica, the big black leather-bound book that listed every remedy and the diseases they belonged to.

Yarrow	*is for*	*Anemia and Colic and Bed-Wetting and Hysteria and Nosebleeds and Hemorrhages and Varicose Veins and When Women's Wombs Lose Children*
Bitterwood	*is for*	*Indigestion and Fever and Heartburn*
Datura	*is for*	*Drunkards and Stammering and Ecstasy*
Belladonna	*is for*	*Nymphomania and Gout and Hemorrhoids and Delirium and Depression*
Calendula	*is for*	*Burns and Knife Cuts and Flesh Wounds*
Daisies	*are for*	*Acne and Boils and Giddiness and Railway Spine*

Milkweed	*is for*	*Syphilis and Leprosy and Swelling of the Hands and Feet*
Chamomile	*is for*	*Restlessness and Waspishness and Bleeding Wombs*

I had to transcribe what I read into notes, to remember which substance was for which symptom. And then, the next morning, I took my scrap of paper and searched for each plant in its proper place, and recorded if it lived and flourished, or if it had become overgrown or invaded the space of another.

I did not have an eye for recognizing plants on sight, and I spent many frantic minutes comparing the description of a leaf pattern or a petal to what was flowering before me. The only things I could recognize with any ease were pansies. Not very impressive, as pansies grow everywhere and are known even to fools. But when I saw a thatch of them in my mama's lanes, they cheered me—panting yellows and purples and blues.

Pansies	*are for*	*Obstinate Skin*

In my new life of study, I thought often of Mr. Ben. He lived in the back room of Culver's now, a place I had never seen, only heard about. Culver himself had found him so waspish that he'd offered to pay Mr. Ben's way across the river to Manhattan.

"To Mr. Ruggles's place in Manhattan, on Golden Hill. Ruggles and his friends would help him." This was Lenore, gossiping with Mama in the mornings while she banked the fire and I sat, head propped in my hands, reading the materia medica.

"And Mr. Ben refused?" Mama said.

Lenore nodded. "He said he'd die if he crossed the water. He said he'll drown. Said he's seen it in a dream. Says the water's full of dead niggers calling his name, and he'd rather stay here, on land."

"His sister can't come soon enough," Mama said.

But she did not come for another month, perhaps two. When I went into town sometimes, to bring a note to Culver or his son, I would see Mr. Ben wandering the crossroads, turning one way or another. He always had a smile for me. Weak, but he gave it. He never called me Libertie, though. Instead, he called me Black Gal.

"Hey there, Black Gal, and good morning to you."

"What you doing for your mama, Black Gal?"

And it was with a sense of pity, which we both could feel between us, that I would return his greeting, show him what was in my bag, raise my hand back to him.

What I wanted to say each time was, *How could you do that to Mama?*

What I wanted to say each time was, *Mama can be your friend.*

What I wanted to say each time was, *I wish I could be your friend, but this is too sad a start for friendship.*

I was that age when I was not young enough to speak that frankly, yet I was not so old that I could pretend the sadness did not exist. So I raised my hand and smiled at him and then went home, to read the remedies and wonder what it meant to care. I had been so cavalier in my request to Mama, to be inducted into her world of secrets. It was overwhelming enough to care for bodies that had turned against themselves, that had sickened and soured on miasmas and disease, that had collapsed under the burden of fevers and chills.

It was still another thing to care for someone like Mr. Ben, who was of whole body, I knew, but of broken spirit.

But Mama said when the spirit broke like his had, it was not our realm.

I was not so sure.

Sometimes, I tried to talk to her about it. I would venture to her, as we sat side by side in her examination room, "What do you do with someone like a Mr. Ben?"

To which she would say quickly, "I do not know what you mean, Libertie."

And we would be left in silence again.

Once, bored by the rows of flower names stretched out before me on a long night of study, I went out at night into the garden, to walk along the rows.

I absently rubbed my fingers along a yarrow bush's leaves. After a few minutes, they began to swell and my tongue thickened. I looked down at my fattened fingertips in the moonlight and looked up and saw Mama through the window, sitting at her desk behind the muslin curtain, working through her ledger. As I watched her, I reached for the yarrow leaves and ripped five of them off the branch, stuffed them into my mouth, and chewed them. It did not take long before my cheeks and mouth began to itch. I ate three more leaves. Two more. And then I ran into the office, and finally Mama looked up from her ledger.

I had the satisfaction of seeing her startled, but she was not scared. She treated me as she would any other of her patients. I could not speak at that point, could barely breathe. I only held up the last few yarrow leaves that I clutched in my hand, and then she nodded and went to work.

She laid me down away from the fire. She went over to her shelves of medicine and reached for one glass jar—she didn't even have to look at the label. She called for Lenore, her voice clear and strong, and when Lenore came in and saw my swollen face, she gasped.

"Keep her mouth open," Mama said. "The danger here is losing air."

Mama made my remedy and then came over and placed it under my tongue herself.

It was a kind of heaven, made dreamier because of my sick state—the room all hazy and warm, my mother's face steady above me. I watched it as closely as I could, and saw her disappear again into her mind. But it was all right, because I knew, this time, when she went there she was thinking only of me. Of how to keep me alive. Of where my lungs and tongue connected, and how deeply I was taking in air, and what to do next to bring my body back. To be at the center of my mother's work was a wonderful place to be. Mr. Ben had had that experience, and as I lay there, sick, I allowed myself to feel the full envy of it. I craved her care, even though I knew I should not.

I fell into a restless sleep. One of the times, when I surfaced from oblivion, I heard Mama whisper to Lenore as she gazed at my face, looking for signs of progress, "She looks just like . . ." And then there was nothing. She was gone again, into her mind.

I realize, now, where she was going. And I know, now, how cruel this all was. I should have known then. I'd seen her face stricken when Mr. Ben held up her dead sister's hair. With the same unconscious cunning all young children possess around their mothers, I had devised the best way to get her attention—make her relive one of her most painful memories—the sick little-girl body, limp in bed, the small gasps for breath, the throat closing, the skin flushing from brown to a deep velvet and then emptying out into gray. What kind of daughter who loves her mother does something like that?

She worked on me all evening, and I would have been brought close to death all over again, from the sheer joy of that attention, if Lenore had not leaned over me while Mama was distracted and shook her head.

"Your mama is a saint," she said, and the way she said it, I knew she knew what I had done. Lenore, who knew and saw all, saw all that Mama, with her big heart and big brain, could not see. I had acted so small. Lenore, God bless her, could see petty a mile away.

I could not meet her eye.

Saints have big enough hearts that they can care for the whole world. Their hearts are so large they dwarf normal people's—and their hearts aren't dumb like human hearts. It is stupid and selfish to ask a saint to use such an extraordinary organ solely on you, even if you are the saint's daughter.

I did not get away with anything like the yarrow trick again for a long time. Even though, in shame at my audacity, it still occurred to me, many times, to try.

ANOTHER WEEK PASSED. It was a too-warm spring that year. So hot we wished for the cold and gray of March. Our settlement was in a valley, not the fine, cooler tracts of land that the white people had reserved for themselves, and so it was always warmer in our town, we imagined, than elsewhere. Culver's shop was even busier, with its pump out back, where we children liked to play at catching the final dribbles of cool, rusty water to rub on our tongues and splash behind our necks.

Mr. Ben liked the pump, too. He liked to sit out there, as the sun went down, before heading into Culver's back room. By the pump, he was always mumbling that name, Daisy, turning it over and over in his mouth, a kind of lullaby he said to soothe himself, to encourage him to keep lifting one foot in front of another, without his woman by his side.

The boldest children used her name to rechristen him. I took this as a sign of hope—you knew a newcomer belonged to the town when they got a nickname. The children called the new name after him at dawn, as he made his way to the wharves downtown, as he left all of us at Culver's. They called it to him as he stood on Front Street, palming a penny before passing it to the woman with a rush basket full of eels and taking the slinking black coil down beneath the wharves, to cook over an open fire, because, as he loudly cried to anyone who would listen, he had no Daisy to cook it for him. They called it to him as he emerged from under the docks in the dusk, to venture out along the board, and look out across the angry gray river to Manhattan and softly whisper to his love across the stinking, cold, and unforgiving waves.

So by the time his sister Hannah came at the end of May, no one bothered to call him Mr. Ben anymore. Everyone called him Ben Daisy.

Miss Hannah came to us in the same coffin Ben Daisy did. The first time I saw her was when Lucien and Madame Elizabeth performed the same sleight of hand they had with him—set down the coffin, pried off the lid. But instead of a lifeless body, there was Miss Hannah, eyes shining bright, looking avidly up at us, her hands clutching a small, irregular yarn handkerchief to her chest. She sat up in the light immediately, put her free hand to her back and winced, and stretched out her other hand to Madame Elizabeth, handing her the piece of cloth.

"How I passed the time on the journey," she said. "Took a line of yarn with me and weaved it the whole way."

Mama looked very pleased at that, and Madame Elizabeth beamed. Miss Hannah was a steadier hand than Ben Daisy could ever hope to be.

Miss Hannah was impatient to see her brother, but Mama asked her to stay for a moment, to drink a cup of tea. "You'll see him soon enough," she said.

"But my brother," she kept saying, even as she clung to Lucien's arm, her legs still soft from lying down for so long. "He made it all right? He doin' fine?"

Mama would only say, "I'll take you to him." Her voice was even, but she would not look Miss Hannah in the eye. I had never seen my mama ashamed of anything before, so I did not know to recognize it. I stayed close, eager to hear what Mama would say to Miss Hannah.

"Ben Daisy is—"

"Ben what?" Miss Hannah said.

Mama reddened. "It is what the children sometimes call him here."

"Why would they say that?"

"He, well—"

"He has a good Christian name." Miss Hannah kept talking. "We was gonna choose ours together, when we got free. We was gonna be the Smiths, on account of our mama saying our daddy always wanted a smithy someday. Why you call him by that woman's name?"

"Then you know her?"

Miss Hannah sniffed, in distaste. "Before we agreed to run, he fell hard in love with that woman. I thought it would be good for him. He was just beat something awful for trying to run, and after that I thought he was lost to us. He only stared at the wall. But then he found Daisy, and she liked him enough. I hoped it was a good thing. Have a little fun, remember what sweetness this world can hold, so he'd want to stay here in it. He was talkin' 'bout drowning before he met Daisy. But he met her and he was happy. For a while. He turned sick with love. That Daisy, he'd do anything for her. She didn't deserve him. You know, he'd save up what little money he could and buy her butter to lick.

"And you know how that little girl repaid him? Three springs ago she ran away without him, even though she knew me and him was fix-ing to run, too. That little girl didn't even warn him or nothing, just up and disappeared. They found her body a few miles away, with the man she run with, both of 'em torn apart by the paddyroller's dogs.

"And every spring like this, he pines for her worse and worse. I thought he'd do better when we made our escape. That's why I had him go first, even though it was risky. He didn't even want freedom anymore. He says she's his love. Says she's all he's ever had. Easier to love a haint than this broken world. For him, anyways. And if I have to hear that Daisy's name one more time, I'll scream."

Miss Hannah set down her mug and glared, back and forth, at Mama and Madame Elizabeth, her chest heaving.

"We'll take you to him, then," Mama said, her voice low.

And the five of us—me, Lucien, Madame Elizabeth, Mama, and Miss Hannah—put our cloaks on to walk through the dusk to Culver's back room.

I did not understand then. Can a child, who has so few memories, no history of her own, know what it is to be haunted? To understand a ghost is to have an understanding of time that is not possible for a child. Children can feel spirits, but they do not discriminate between the living and the dead the way adults do. For them, it is all the living. And so I did not understand the look of anguish on Mama's face as we got closer to the reunion, and I did not understand why Miss Hannah was so angry at a dead woman, and I still did not understand why I felt so sad around Mr. Ben.

But I was about to learn.

THE ONLY PEOPLE allowed in Culver's back room were new-comers. More and more often, new people were appearing—not just the ones brought by Madame Elizabeth, but those who found us on their own. If you saw an unrecognizable face in town, someone new walking down the roads, who tried to stay close to the underbrush so that they could run, we all knew to send that person first to Culver's. In those days, you did not ask about the past of the newly arrived.

They'd stay for a few nights, and then they would find a room or take a lot from one of the deacons of our church and put together a home of their own.

It was not families who arrived like this. It was mostly men. We welcomed them, of course, and most of them eventually settled in. But a few of them, maybe four or five, never fully joined us. Even after they'd found places to live and women to love, they still returned to the back of Culver's pharmacy to meet up with those most like themselves.

The back-room visitors would sit and watch Culver work. It was where Culver mixed up the different-colored remedies of his shop. He poured each one into the saltmouth and tincture glass bottles, as tall as a child.

Culver sold the back-room people beer and rum, even though we were a dry town. But the deacons and Reverend Harland pretended not to know Culver's back room, only obliquely mentioning it in their sermons, and Culver was careful that only colored people drank there. The few times white men tried to come and sit, they just saw Culver painstakingly measuring out the granules and liquids that turned the remedies their necessary hue.

Like every child in our village, I knew the people of the back room well. All had been christened with their own nicknames, which we sang to them. The people of Culver's back room had all lost themselves. They had returned in their minds back to the places they'd run from, the places they didn't name, even to their fellow travelers. So maybe when the boys yelled at them and the girls braided their names into song, we were trying to call them back to us. At least, that's what I tell myself now. The alternative hurts too much to bear.

There was Otto Green Leaf. Otto lived only four houses down from Culver's. It was a straight line home for him. But one night, he didn't return home, and when his wife called for him the next day, the three or four men in Culver's back room searched for him for hours. They found him in a field, two miles away. He said he'd gotten lost. His wife brought him home, but he kept wandering out, to sleep among the cabbages. He could only sleep in dirt, it seemed, from then on. After he'd found his way out of Culver's room, you'd see him every morning rising from the fields, his shirt covered in mud and dew, blinking at the dawn.

There was Birdie Delilah, the only woman who regularly went to Culver's. She became certain that her daughter, whom she'd lost in some way she never told any of us, had returned to her in the form of the woodpecker who lived under Culver's eaves. All night, she sat in Culver's back room, drinking corn whiskey until her eyes shone, waiting for the woodpecker to start her pestering when the moon was high. At the sound of the first knock, Birdie Delilah's whole face, which before had been dour and cold and slick with sweat from the burn of her drink, would light up, and she would begin to suck her teeth in response to the bird, steady in her conversation.

And there was Pete Back Back, who came to us still covered in sores from the whipping that drove him to run. No matter what Mama did, what compresses or dilutions she tried, his back wouldn't heal and his wounds remained as fresh as the day he first got them.

They were all there when we arrived with Mr. Ben's sister. The room was warm and small and dark, lit only by a few lamps up high. It smelled sharp and too sweet. When my eyes adjusted and I saw all the regulars, I was not so afraid. Mama and I had seen the people of Culver's back room out and about in town so often they no longer scared us.

But when Madame Elizabeth stepped in behind us, she drew her shawl over her mouth, and Miss Hannah, coming in right behind her, poor Miss Hannah began to cry.

Ben Daisy was sitting up, talking to Pete Back Back, who was steadfastly ignoring every word out of his mouth, in favor of the drink in his hand.

"She smelled like the ocean," Ben Daisy was saying. "I only smelled the ocean once, back when I was in Maryland, but that's what she smelled like. Good, clean salt. I told you 'bout her hair, didn't I? And her eyes? I'd tell you about the rest, but a lady's present . . ." Here, he looked sideways at Birdie Delilah, and then he looked up and saw his sister and he stopped talking.

Miss Hannah stepped a little more forward. "Ben?"

"So they got you here, too, did they?" He peered past Miss Hannah and caught Madame Elizabeth's eye. "So you managed not to kill my sister this time, like y'all did me?"

Madame Elizabeth did not respond. On her face was a look of the utmost pity, which seemed to annoy Mr. Ben even further.

"She got you good, Hannah."

"Ben, you look a mess."

"You would, too, if you'd been through what I have," Mr. Ben said. "Drug here in a coffin all by myself."

Miss Hannah knelt down beside him and touched his arm. "I came that way, too."

He wouldn't look at her. Looked down at the floor instead. Took another sip of his drink.

"They tell you the food here is horrible?" he said.

Miss Hannah gasped, laughed, then finally allowed herself to fully sob.

She turned to Mama. "You let my brother live like this?" she said, her voice breaking. "You let 'em all live like this? These people are not well."

Mama put her hand up to her mouth and only nodded.

"You said you was a doctor. She said . . ." Miss Hannah turned and looked at Madame Elizabeth. "She said you knew how to help people and make 'em safe."

"I tried," Mama said, but then stopped herself. Her words sounded so lost, in this small, hot room.

"He can't stay here," Miss Hannah said. "None of 'em can stay here."

Culver looked up from his bench. "No one's forcing anyone to stay. We stay together because we like it."

Miss Hannah ignored him, pulled at her brother's arm. "Come on," she said. "Come with me."

He did not move at first. He did not move for a long time. We all stood, and watched, while she pulled at his arm and said, "Come with me," until it became almost unbearable—her ask, his refusal.

But finally, he stood up and put his arm through hers, and Miss Hannah guided him from the room.

I think it was that—more than Miss Hannah's shaming, more than Ben Daisy's glassy eyes and his lips muttering nonsense, it was the fact that he would follow his sister out of the room, because of Miss Hannah's patience, that convinced Mama of how badly she had failed. And I saw her, standing right there beside me, disappear again, into the world of her ambition.

She was going to make him right.

I DO NOT know when, exactly, she started it. The letter she sent to begin it all, she wrote alone—she took the rare step of not dictating it to me. She must have written it that same night, when she realized she had lost Ben Daisy, because it was only a week or so later that I stood beside her in Culver's shop as she looked at the mail that had come for her and she turned to me, the envelope still in her hand, and bent down, and she hugged me, hard—she never hugged hard—and told me excitedly, "We can begin."

That afternoon, she gathered me and Lenore in her examination room and told us that she had decided to run a proving.

A proving is when you bring together a small group of volunteers to take a new dose, a new remedy. It is a way to test what can be a cure. Everyone tracks their reactions to the substance, minutely, and then you compare notes. With enough provings, you begin to understand the cures that are available to you, what will produce those reactions in the body, that push and pull that homeopathy rests on.

Since Mama was a colored woman, other homeopaths did not invite her to partake in their provings. She had to read the medical journals carefully, comparing articles and footnotes, making her own notations. She was looking for their mistakes. She had been doing this for years— it was what she often did late at night, when the books were done and committee work put away.

For this, her first proving, she told us that she wrote away to a man out west, a scientist like her. A colored naturalist who had recently come back from West Africa, where he had taken an all-black group of explorers. A wondrous thing. I remembered reading aloud an article to her about it a few months earlier. It had appeared in the *Mystery*—a newspaper Madame Elizabeth sometimes brought us with one of her emptied coffins. There, on the front page, was an account of his tour. I noticed the article because it had the place I had been named for, my father's dream, in the title: "Martin Delany's Exploration of Liberia."

At first, when I'd read it aloud, Mama, as always, was skeptical of any talk of homelands and empires—"It is futile to imagine, Libertie," she said. But she made me stop and read one line, three times, to make sure she understood:

*The Emigration Board of Commissioners has asked Mr. Delany
to make a scientific inquiry into the topographical, geological and
geographic qualities of the Niger Valley to determine whether it
can host a colony of American Negroes.*

So Mama had remembered him, and had sent him her secret letter,
and now, in the palm of her hand, she had the results.

Delany had sent a small package, passed hand to hand, through
every African Methodist Episcopal preacher in the North. All the way
from Ohio, to us, in Kings County. Reverend Harland himself had
delivered it to Culver's counter, though he'd felt a need to write, underneath Delany's hand, the admonishment *For good, Doctor.*

Mama bristled at that. "As if it would be for anything else."

Now, in her examination room, Mama had me unwrap the package
for her. I pulled at the twine and the paper—"Gentle now, Libertie,
gentle with your hands"— until it fell open. Wrapped in the brown
paper were ten dried seahorses, curled over one another. Their skin was
a low, dusky yellow, the same color as the oranges we studded with
cloves every Christmas and left to desiccate in our linen trunk to keep
our good cloth smelling sweet. I looked up at Mama. "Just as Delany
promised," she said. "He's a good man."

The very first task was to grind the dried seahorses into a gray powder, which smelled like the bottom of a privy and clung to the palms of
your hands in a fine, damp silt.

"'The male seahorse can be found in the estuary of the Niger River,'"
Mama read from Delany's letter, as Lenore ground and I was instructed
to transcribe into a notebook, what was to be the experiment's log. "'He
is a solitary creature. He does not swim in packs. He only interacts
with his female counterpart to mate. He floats through the dark, temperate in-between world of brackish water alone, with only his secret

for creation.'" Here, Mama broke off. "Delany believes he is some sort of poet, I suppose," she said, and frowned. She did not like flights of fancy. She especially resented them when people tried to mix them up with science.

When Lenore had finished grinding, we moved on to dilution. Mama had told us she would begin this trial with a 2C dilution, which meant we added one hundred grams of water to one gram of seahorse, and then another hundred grams, until we had our solution.

Finally, Lenore passed the vial over to me for the succussion. I took the vial and slapped it against the special board of leather and horsehair Mama had in her office for the purpose.

As I pumped my arms up and down, shaking the cure, Mama read some more. "'The male seahorse is a virtuous beast, romantic and loyal, steadfast in his heart and in his affections, the moral light of the animal kingdom. The male seahorse is not a profligate; he is frugal with his affections. When he mates, he mates for life. Every morning, he wakes and performs a dance with his partner—it is not a mating dance, but a dance that reaffirms their commitment to each other and the deep affection and love between the two. If he loses his mate, he will remain alone for the rest of his short life, unable to replace her with another.'"

Here, Mama stopped. "That's it," she said. "Make sure to get that part when you write the notes, Libertie."

When the solution was done, Mama told me to put it on her highest shelf. And then she sat down and wrote a letter of apology to Ben Daisy.

It did not seem to be a great burden for her to apologize, and I remember thinking this strange. I had never seen my mother do it before, but she wrote this letter with ease, as if she was sending off a note to Madame Elizabeth. When she was done, she handed it to me, to bring to Mr. Culver and ask him to read it to Ben Daisy or Miss Hannah the next time they came in.

On the way to town, I carefully ripped the edges of the letter open to see what she had written there, but it was only pleasantries, a single sentence with "profound apologies," and an invitation to Ben Daisy, and Ben Daisy alone, for tea in a few days' time.

He came. I was surprised he came, but he did. It was the end of the workday, and he had clearly had a good one downtown—he smelled of clean sweat, and he was smiling when he walked in. "What's this?" he said, laughing. "You sure you happy to see me?"

Mama smiled and nodded. She had asked Lenore to make a cake. She placed the cake in the middle of her examination room table and led him there. She took her place on the small wooden seat.

"Now," Mama said as she spread her skirts out about her, "how are you, Mr. Ben?"

He looked taken aback, but he answered. "Fine, Miss Doctor, just fine," he replied. "Figure I may as well pass the time with you ladies, and now that I've got such a warm welcome, you'll be hard pressed to get me to leave." He laughed again.

Mama laughed, too. They talked for a bit more. Mama reached over to cut Ben Daisy a slice of cake, and when he caught that, he smiled, a little meaner. She placed the slice in a square of cloth, put it in the palm of his hand. He hunched over to eat it, looking at her sideways.

I sat on a stool in the corner. Mama had told me beforehand to only begin when she gave me the signal. At last, Mama lifted one finger, and I picked up my pen.

"I wish to talk to you a bit about Daisy."

I watched his shoulders slump forward, ever so slightly, and then back upright, as if he had remembered something. "So that's what you want," he said.

"You miss her," Mama said.

It was quiet for a bit. But then Ben Daisy trusted himself enough to say "She was a fine gal. I miss her something terrible."

"What if I could give you something," Mama said. "Something to help with the pain."

"I've already got that down at Culver's." Ben Daisy laughed sadly.

"But Culver's whiskey doesn't help you," Mama said.

"It'll do what it'll do."

"But it makes you listless and miss your work. It makes you quarrel with your sister."

Ben Daisy was quiet. Then he said, "What does Hannah want from me?"

"Nothing," Mama said.

"That's right. It's all nothing." Ben Daisy lifted his head off the back of the chair and put his hands on the arms, ready to push himself off the big leather seat and out our door.

That's when Mama said, "You wouldn't want Daisy, if she were here, to know you like this, though, would you? If she were able to see you. Are you the man she'd wish you to be in freedom?"

Ben Daisy lowered himself back into the chair. "So, what are you proposing?"

Mama stood up and told me to fetch the solution. She measured some out, very carefully, into a smaller vial and handed it to him.

"You take this," she said. "One swallow, and one swallow only each night. It's night, isn't it, that the pain's the worst?"

Ben Daisy sighed. "Night is when it all catches up with me," he said.

Mama instructed him to return the following afternoon, and for every afternoon after that for five days. "You see how you feel," she told him. "And if it seems to help, tell your friends down at Culver's. It may help them, too."

When he'd left, she sat and began to dictate to me again.

"We have in our midst," she said, "a group of men, and a few women, who, upon discovering our community and life here in freedom, find their souls still oppressed. Their bodies are here with us in emancipation, but their minds are not free. Their spirits have not recovered from the degradation of enslavement, despite the many hardships and privations they have suffered to come here.

"Indeed, I argue that it is precisely because of these hardships and privations that when they arrive here, with us, some part of them does not return. When they arrive, I can treat the physical effects of their enslavement—the yaws in their limbs, and the scars on their backs and heads, and the bones that broke and were never set. But I have, up until now, not been able to treat what would be called the mental effects, the spiritual effects, which do not respond to prayer or clean living or even the embrace of friends.

"I believe the root cause for this is an intense solitude and loneliness, even in their freedom. At least, that is how some of them have described it to me. We have seen this illness before," she said. "In the cases of those we love, like Mr. Ruggles and Miss Sojourner Truth. They were afflicted by this deep and abiding loneliness even in freedom and took to drink, and then the water cure, lying in bathtubs and wrapped in cold, wet sheets to try and soak it out. And it has not done much for them. If all these good and kind warriors are felled by this disease of feeling, what hope is there for any of us?

"And what is at the root cause of loneliness? It is a lack of love. I believe if we can treat this deficit of affection, we can begin to see an improvement in those new to freedom. We can make them whole in both body and in spirit and see a real change in their condition. They will ingest this substance, which is made of the solitude and longing for love of the ocean, and it will rebalance what has been made unsteady inside them. Take Mr. Ben, who is lost in amorousness, who is able to do nothing but pine. We will realign his affections, so that he no longer loves what is dead but loves us here, the living. He will be filled with agape. He will love his fellow man. It is what I attempt to test, in my proving. He will be my first patient."

Then she raised her hand again, her sign that we were done for the day. She gathered the pages I had written, so that she could read what I'd taken from her own voice and correct it.

Ben Daisy took the solution faithfully. During that time, he did not appear any different—he still walked with one shoulder up high, and the other men still walked a little bit ahead so that they did not have to be in conversation with him. No one else from Culver's came to Mama's door. Either Ben Daisy didn't tell them to come or they were unimpressed with his progress.

The only time we saw his sister was at church on Sundays. Miss Hannah sat in the back pews, near the door, and her brother never came with her. We sat in the pews in the front, because Mama's father had been one of the men to build that church. When Mama was a girl, she and her brothers and sisters took up two whole pews. But now, of the old family, it was just me and her left sitting up front—the rest of the seats given away to friends. When we passed Miss Hannah on the way to our pew every Sunday, she would stiffly nod in Mama's direction, but she didn't smile. If Culver had read the apology aloud to her, it had not impressed her at all.

When Ben Daisy came back to our house two weeks later, it was in the last bit of light. His shirt was wet from work, and when we let him in, he sat sideways in his chair and we could smell the drink on him.

"I can't give it to you if you've been to Culver's already," Mama said. "Tell me the truth."

"No, ma'am," he said. "This is from one of the other men. They knocked a ladleful of cider on me, and that's why I smell like this. I'm as sober as a judge." Ben Daisy gave her a glassy smile.

Mama looked at him, and she came to some sort of decision.

"Libertie, my record book," she said, and I went and fetched it for her.

She took the book and looked at the columns of numbers. Then she licked her thumb, very carefully, and smudged out one. She dipped her pen in ink and wrote something else over it. Then she sprinkled some sand to let the ink dry.

As she rubbed the grains from her fingers, she said, very steadily, "A dose and a half today for Ben Daisy, I think."

Lenore sucked her teeth.

"Yes," Mama said.

Lenore took the little steel file she used, and measured a few more grains onto the slip of paper she'd set on the scale.

By the time the dose was prepared, Ben Daisy's head had begun to loll, and Mama had to hold his chin steady as she placed it in his mouth.

The other times he'd taken it, Ben Daisy had only grimaced at the taste—"Golly, Doctor, you can't cut this with nothing?" This time, he truly gagged. His knees rose up to his chest and he coughed, and Mama stepped back, surprised, then called for water.

She poured it in a slow trickle in his mouth until he was swallowing good and steady, and then she let him go. He slumped back in the chair, breathing heavily. Another cough. A third. He swallowed. And then he vomited something green and awful-smelling, all down the front of his shirt.

I jumped forward, Lenore cursed—"Oh damn"—and Mama stepped back again.

"Get it off," she said to Lenore. She grabbed one sleeve. "We've got to get it off."

Between the two of them, they managed to get the shirt over his head.

Ben Daisy lay in the chair bare-chested, his belly soft in his breeches, his eyes still closed, his breath in shuffles. Then his eyes flickered open, and he slowly sat up straight.

"You all right?" Lenore asked.

He put his hands on his knees, shook his head gently.

"Sit still, sit still," Lenore insisted. But Ben Daisy stood up, creaking, and made his way toward the door. By now it was dark; the sun was gone, and the fireflies of Kings County were out.

At the door, he looked out over the fields and watched the lights scatter across the long grass, as if everything was new to him. Then he gave a deep sigh, like the sound the water makes when the ocean turns over. And he lurched out into the night, still bare-chested.

"Well," Mama said. "Well," she half laughed. She was nervous.

"Should I run after him?" Lenore asked.

"No," Mama said. "I am sure he will be fine." But she did not look certain.

The next evening, just as Lenore was to leave for the day, the office door swung open and Ben Daisy stood in the frame.

"What did you give me?" he said.

"Why?" Mama asked. She snapped her fingers for my attention, and then pointed to the ledger book. I reached for a pen to transcribe their conversation.

"All day long," he said. "All day long, it's felt like this."

"Like what?"

"I hear it lapping at my ear, you know. I hear it crashing."

"Sit down," Mama said, guiding him to the leather chair. "Tell me what you mean."

"I hear it, in my ear. Lapping, lapping. It's been lapping all damn day, Doctor."

"Were you able to work?"

"I had to stop a turn and box my own ears, I did. Nothing came out."

"Lie back," Mama said. "Let me see."

She snapped her fingers again, and I put down the record book, took one of the slim white candles she used for close examination, and lit its wick in the fire. I placed it in the small glass lantern and came and stood at Mama's side.

"Steady, there, Libertie," she said as she lifted my arm herself, so I could get the angle of the light right.

She settled down into the little chair and leaned forward. She took his ear in her hand, as gently as a lover, and stretched the lobe very carefully, so that she could see inside.

"And it's so damn cold!" Ben Daisy said suddenly, rising up.

Mama sat back.

"So cold all the time. And my mouth, I tell you, it tastes like salt. Ever since yesterday. It just tastes like salt in my mouth. And Hannah, she says my breath stinks like the wharves. What do I care," he said. "That sister of mine finds every way to tell me I'm wrong. But the foreman said it, too, this morning."

He sat back down. As he spoke, indeed, a deeply salty smell filled the room. It was not necessarily unpleasant. Just very strong.

"I feel," he said. "I feel . . ." He slumped back down. "I feel like I'm falling underwater."

Mama lifted her chin. "Note that down, Libertie." She was trying, very hard, to conceal her excitement.

"Well," she said after a moment, "there is not much I can do for the smell of the breath. But chew these, twice a day." She handed him a bundle of mint leaves. "And come back again next week—"

"Like hell I will," Ben Daisy said.

"Just to talk," Mama said quickly, and Ben Daisy grumbled and then moved toward the door.

Mama watched him go and then turned to me.

"Is he cured?" I asked. I was excited.

"We shall see," she said. She was not going to play her hand.

All week long, I asked Mama if she thought Ben Daisy would come back to us, and she said, "It's not for me to decide, Libertie. It's up to him." But I could see by Saturday she was as nervous as I was, even though she would not say it.

Sunday morning, we headed to church and walked past the stony-faced Miss Hannah to our pew, as always.

Reverend Harland began the sermon—about Belshazzar's feast and the disembodied hand that had appeared to him and had begun to write on the wall the thoughts of God. Reverend Harland was talking about rulers dishonoring God and the calamity that would follow, but while he talked, I tried to think of that hand, floating in the air. Were its fingers long or stubby? Its palms jaundiced? What color was its skin—deep black or warm brown or the same pink as Mama's cheeks? Did that hand also float above a pyramid, or in a distant desert, shimmering in the heat? And did Belshazzar, who saw the wonder, ever think in the moment of astonishment to keep the marvel to himself, to keep a secret, to not reveal it, to revel in the mystery of words untranslatable?

The sermon ended, and so did my speculations. The singing was about to begin. The choir assembled, and then, as they were about to start, we heard a loud, off-tune voice, too straw-like to be called a tenor, rise from the back of the church.

> *Oh Lord,*
> > *Oh Lord,*
> *Oh Lord,*
> > *I'm saved again.*

We all turned to see who it could be, and it was Ben Daisy, his shirt now cleaned and pressed, his hat back on his head, singing as loud as he could while his sister stood beside him, crying tears of joy and sharp embarrassment.

After that, Mama was revered. Everyone could see Ben Daisy was cured. He was the first man down the road at dawn, heading to the fields. He helped out the reverend at church. He stopped drinking altogether. He only went to Culver's to pay the few cents he could, to settle his debt for all the corn whiskey he'd drunk in the past.

The others came out of Culver's back room and began to take the cure with Mama, too—Otto Green Leaf and Birdie Delilah, and even Pete Back Back, whose shirt was still wet from his never-closing wounds.

Ben Daisy was truly a new man, anyone could see, and Reverend Harland dedicated a special sermon to it that next week.

"The psalms tell us that the Lord heals the brokenhearted and binds up their wounds," Reverend Harland said. "He determines the number of the stars and calls them each by name. Great is our Lord, and mighty in power; his understanding has no limit. The psalms tell us to sing to the Lord, as Ben Daisy has done, with grateful praise and make music to our God. For the Lord delights in those who fear him and who put their hope in his unfailing love. And he sends his word to melt the snow; he stirs up the breezes, and the waters flow."

Afterward, when everyone had surrounded Mama to congratulate her, Ben Daisy pushed through the scrum of people, and hooked his little finger into Mama's and shook it—a queer offer of thanks, I remember thinking.

"You done it," he said with a wink. And then he sighed, "I can't wait to tell Daisy all about this."

Mama looked taken aback, but then she smiled and said, "I'm happy for you." She did not ask me to note that exchange in her little book, not yet.

Ben Daisy was cured right before Pinkster. Pinkster was what the old ones celebrated, the ones who had been alive for slave days here in Kings County—so ancient they seemed to me then, as old as the hills all around us. They all spoke in that strange singsong accent of old New York. They had celebrated Pinkster when they were young, and their hips still moved, and it was a queer kind of pleasure we all took, to make sure they could still celebrate it in their old age.

Every Pentecost, we young ones were instructed to make the old ones gingerbread and gather bunches of azaleas. In Sunday school, we worked to make the paper crowns that would sit on top of their graying heads. A few men Mama's age practiced the old songs on the drums, but they did not teach them to us children. They were the rhythms of the past, and only the old ones remembered them for sure, lifting their walking sticks to pound in time, sucking their teeth in disapproval when the beat was off.

At Pinkster, we crowned a King Charles, who was in charge of the festivities. We built him a grass hut, and he teased the children and paraded for the old. Usually, it was one of the church ushers, who would dance and twirl around town. But that year, because of his miraculous recovery, it was unanimously decided that Ben Daisy should lead the celebrations.

On Pinkster morning, I and the other girls in Sunday school woke up early, when the day was still cold. All week, we had been gathering rushes from the fields, setting them out to dry, and pounding them flat. We had been weaving the strands into thick walls, the green of the grass fading to a fragile brown. And now, we pieced them together, finishing the huts we were to celebrate in.

When we were done with the largest hut, the girls sent me to find Ben Daisy and lead him to it. He was standing in the crowd with the others, our neighbors and friends, waiting for the celebration to begin. I took his warm hand in mine and brought him into the enclosure.

The day was one of those sharply cold sunny ones, where you panted in the light but any bit of shade chilled you. It was even cooler in the largest hut, under all the grass. Ben Daisy stood peering out onto the churchyard. The old ones, already gathered in the hut, sat in a corner, skeptical of a newcomer having the place of honor.

The drums pounded, and everyone started dancing. I ran out of the hut as soon as I could, to spin in a circle with the other girls, their hands soft and slipping through mine as we tried to hold close, and to run up and down the yard. Pinkster was the only holiday when everyone tried a little cider—every other celebration we kept temperate. But on Pinkster, because the old ones celebrated it, a beer or two was allowed. Which is to say that someone may or may not have slipped Ben Daisy a sip of something that afternoon.

At the height of the day, when all our bodies were still humming from the dance, Ben Daisy stood in the doorway of the hut, paper crown pushed back on his head.

"A yup, a yup!" he called. He was getting into the spirit of it. Some others began to clap, a syncopated rhythm, to his name.

Ben

       Day

             Zee

Ben

       Day

Zee

"That's me," he called over the din. "That there's my name. And soon you will meet my Daisy, too."

One of the children laughed. "Truly?" the child said.

"Truly," he said. "Daisy came to me just the other day. I wish y'all could have seen her. She's here right now, in fact. But she's shy."

Some people laughed louder, thinking he was playing.

"I tell you, she looks marvelous now. She's got long curly hair all the way down her back, and she's got a pink silk gown."

"Oh really? Where'd she get that from?"

"She's got a silk gown," Ben Daisy continued. "It's pink and white, like nothing you've ever seen. And on her finger, one diamond ring so bright. Oh, I can't wait for y'all to see her."

"So where is she now?" someone else called, giggling.

"She's on her way. She came to visit me just last week, but she couldn't stay. But she's coming back, to live with me and mine. You hear that, Hannah?" Ben Daisy called. "You gonna have to make room for my Daisy."

I turned to look for Miss Hannah in the crowd. She was listening, her face stricken.

"To Daisy," he cried, holding up his hand in benediction, and the children chanted it back to him. I myself joined in, chanting and laughing till my voice was hoarse, even though I knew I should be scared.

So I made sure to whirl myself harder, dance faster, the rest of the night.

As night came, the old ones remembered Pinksters past: who was known for the freshest oysters and the sweetest bread, who could be counted on to stay awake the longest, who was the best dancer. They did not, of course, mention that they had celebrated all these feats while enslaved, that the whites had banished Pinkster and stopped observing it with them once they gained their freedom. The old ones spoke of it as its own day of release, as if it existed outside of time, and none of them mentioned how it used to end—with the men and women and children tearing down the grass huts and returning to their masters, saying goodbye to their loved ones owned by other men, with sometimes nothing but a blade of grass tucked away to remember them by, until they met again the following year, if they were lucky.

Miss Hannah came to Mama the next day, crying in her reception room. "You didn't fix him," she said. "He's as bad as ever. He really thinks that dead heifer is coming to live with us."

"He can't believe that," Mama said.

"He does. He really does," Miss Hannah sobbed. "You've only made it worse."

The next week, at church, Mama called to Ben Daisy, "How about you come and see me again."

"I haven't got time for that, Doctor," he said. "I need to buy some things for Daisy, to make her comfortable."

And he left Mama to go ask Miss Annie, who headed the church's auxiliary club, to bake him some cakes. "Little ones," he said. "Dainty ones, because Daisy eats like a bird, you know? But they've got to be pink and white. That's what she told me. Have to be pink and white." Miss Annie grumbled about it, but she agreed to make him three cakes, because he was willing to pay for them.

A few days later, he saw me again on the road to Culver's.

"Hey there, Black Gal."

"Hey, yourself," I said, wary. I could smell on him that he was unwell.

"I've heard," he said, "you grow pansies nice."

I paused. "I do."

"I'll give you a penny for five of them, for my Daisy."

I knew I should not agree to give him anything for her. "But how are they going to stay fresh?" I asked.

"Won't need to stay fresh long, because she's here," he said. But his voice was uncertain.

I felt a spasm of conscience. "I could," I said carefully, "press them for you. If you'd like."

"All right. But don't cheat me, girl," he said, smiling again.

"I can give them to you," I said finally. "Find me after church."

I did not tell my mother. By then, Miss Hannah had enlisted the reverend, and the three of them spent evenings talking about how best to fix his strange behavior. "Give it time," Mama kept assuring. "It takes a while for the dose to even out." She seemed to believe it, even though the reverend and Miss Hannah perhaps did not.

I do not know what I believed at that point. I thought my mother infallible. But I had also been up close to Ben Daisy, smelled the salt water of his breath and seen the dullness of his eyes. I trusted my mother, but I knew that Ben Daisy had no hope of becoming a steady man.

Still, I was a craven little thing. I wanted the penny he promised for myself. While I was tending the garden, I snipped off the heads of five pansies, big and wide. That was the least I could do for him—give him the hardiest ones. I dropped them into the pocket of my apron, and then, at night, when Mama was bent over her books, I bent over my own and placed each flower's head between the pages of my ledger, right in the corner, up close to the spine. Then I shut the book and did not open it again until later that week, when they had dried and turned crisp and thin, their color only dimming slightly.

The Sunday morning I was to give them over to Mr. Ben, I wrapped them up in a piece of fine paper pinched from Mama's writing desk.

Ben Daisy and I were to meet in the little copse by the graveyard. When I saw Mama and Lenore were caught up in the talk of the other women in the churchyard, I went closer to the trees, calling for him underneath my breath.

"Ben Daisy," I hissed. I stepped past the stones of my father and Mama's sister with no name, past where the land dipped and sank over their final resting place, into the cold shadow of the fir trees. "I have your pansies for you."

There he was. I could see his back was straight. He was the sweetest I had ever smelled him. But when he turned to me, his face was broken. "Forget them."

"But why?"

"She's already here. Saw her last night. On her finger was three wedding bands—one, two, three—all real gold, too. I said, 'What's the meaning of this Daisy?' And she only laughed."

He began to cry, great shaking sobs, while I stood beside him with the dried flowers on their sheet of paper, wishing he would stop.

"She betrayed me," he said. "She betrayed me all over again."

"At least take your flowers, Mr. Ben," I said. But he was sobbing so hard, his hands shaking, that he couldn't hold them.

"Here." I looked over at the crowd of parishioners. My mother stood in the middle, searching for me, I knew. "Kneel down."

He sat at my feet while I peeled each papery flower off the page and stuck them, carefully, into the band of his hat.

The church bell rang. The crowd began to move into the chapel. I had to take my place at my mother's side.

"Black Gal, your penny," he called.

"You can keep it," I said, and hurried toward the church.

I had expected him to follow me and join his sister in service, but he didn't. As I rushed to the doors, I looked back to the graveyard. Ben sat on the ground in the green and brown, his head still low. As the door swung shut, I swore I saw, through a flash in the trees, the figure of a woman rushing toward him, the long trail of her pink silk skirt fluttering in her haste. The church door closed, I walked to my pew, and when I craned my head to try and see him out the window, no one was there. I thought it must have been a shadow, that my pity for Ben Daisy had led me to yearn to see what he did, to bring the dead woman back for him and me—as if that would have healed anything at all.

During the service, I kept seeing that penny in Ben Daisy's hand, and I thought about the woman who he'd claimed had come to him at night, who wore the rings of other lovers on her fingers, who could not even manage to be faithful as a spirit. Was this what caring for another did? Resurrect them, even in death, to only become your worst fears? Did Ben Daisy suffer from too much care? Mama thought he did not have enough of it. But it seemed to me as though Ben Daisy had too much.

In the following weeks, he did not go to work with the other men anymore. He did not leave his bed in the room he shared with Miss Hannah. He even stopped saying that name. He became a ghost. When Mama tried to talk to Miss Hannah about it, she would only shake her head and say, "I don't know, Miss Doctor," before walking away.

One Saturday night, Pete Back Back came to Mama's door. He would not sit in her big leather chair, only stood in the middle of her examination room.

"Ben finally left his bed last night. Agreed to have a tipple with me," Pete said. "We drunk from Friday night into this morning. Culver threw us out at dawn. Said we was unruly. So we walked to the water-front downtown.

"We stood on the wharves. We looked at the ferries. I got paid Friday, so I still had a few coins in my pocket. The wind was blowing the stink of the river into our faces, but we was happy. We was the clos-est thing to free any nigger's ever been," Peter told us. He stopped for a minute, his eyes wet.

"We went to go sit down by the water, to rest awhile. We was going to sit on the bank, near the wharves, when suddenly Ben Daisy lifted his head. All around us, we could smell flowers. I swear to you, Doctor, the air changed. The wind coming off the river was so soft and warm. Ben, he caught a whiff of that water, and he looked up and out across the dark river. He smiled. And then he bolted.

"Before I could stop him, he ran to the end of the wharf, calling 'Daisy!' He leapt into the river, and the water closed around him. And he was gone."

"What do you mean, gone?" Mama said.

"I tried to call someone to help me get him out." Peter rubbed at his shoulder. "Some of the kids who live by the wharf, they dived into the water to try and find him. Dived in right after him, they did, but when one of the boys came back up, he only said Ben Daisy was gone, and then they all scrambled out of the water, as if they'd took a fright. That boy wouldn't tell me what he saw down there, but none of them would go back in, even when I begged them to."

Pete Back Back took something out from underneath his shirt. "Only this was still there, floating on top of the waves."

It was Ben Daisy's hat, the pink-and-white pansies I'd pressed for him still tucked into the band, the whole thing dry as bone.

"I can't bring myself to tell Miss Hannah. So I stopped here first," Pete Back Back said. He still would not meet Mama's eye.

That night, after Peter left, Mama said three prayers: one for Ben Daisy and one for his sister, and the final one for Daisy herself. "May her spirit finally rest." And then I watched as she took her ledger down, the one she'd been keeping her notes in about the experiment, and, with her pen, scratch something out, write something new on the page. Then she tore the whole page out of the book altogether and took it with her to her bedroom, and I never saw it again.

The proving was over. Mama wrote the conclusion for it herself, so I do not know how she explained it. She would not let me read it, and she never published anything about this study. In a few years' time, this failure would be overshadowed by the hospital for women and children that would make her name, and the consulting room downtown, and my eventual life of ladyhood. But that particular night, she bundled up the last little bit of seahorses in a brown envelope and carefully placed it on the highest shelf.

Nobody in our village would say that Ben Daisy had died. Miss Hannah, in her grief would not allow it. She stayed on with us, her eyes hollow. Ben Daisy's hat with the dried pansies she took to wearing on her own head. And when we spoke to her of him, if we ever spoke to her of him, we only said the river had him.

That first night when we'd learned of Ben Daisy, I asked Mama, "What happens to the dead?" We had cleaned the examination room, put everything in its rightful place, and we stood side by side, washing our faces and hands before bed.

"Why, they go to heaven with our Lord and Savior. You know this."

"But what happens to their thoughts and minds?"

"What do you mean?"

"Where does their will go?"

Mama looked as if she was about to cry. "It has been a long day. Hush, please, Libertie."

"But what happens? Where is Ben Daisy? Is he in the same place Father is and . . . and . . . everyone else?"

"Libertie, you ask too much of your mama sometimes."

And so I understood. Mama did not have an answer. Mama did not know. That great big brain of hers could not tell me where Ben Daisy was. And because Mama didn't know, the dead were not to be spoken of. They were all of them in another country.

Eventually, we learned, from whispers, what the boys said they saw when they jumped in the river to rescue him. That underneath the water, the boy swimmer had seen Ben, had tried to pull him up, but he was stopped. Ben was wrapped in the arms of a woman, her skin glowing golden in the waves, the pink of her dress flashing through the murk of the river, her hair long. She had looked at the boy as he swam close and reached for Ben Daisy's hand. He said she was the most beautiful woman he had ever seen, and she'd beckoned to him, as if to welcome him into her arms, too. He said he was overcome with the desire to swim into them until she smiled at him—with a mouth full of thousands of pointed teeth. Then Ben had tugged his hand out of the swimmer's, had waved softly and turned his whole body inward, like a baby's, to be cradled in the arms of the woman in the water. And the boy kicked away, up to the surface, before he could be tempted to join them.

Ben Daisy and his woman sleep in the river
Sleep in the river
Sleep in the river
Ben Daisy and his woman sleep in the river
Even past Judgment Day

That was the song, I am ashamed to say, that I made up after hearing this story, and the other children sang it, too. It became the anthem of our schoolyard for a year, and children still sing it today, I am told. I sang it because of all that I did not know and could not know about what happened. But even at that age, I knew curiosity could be heartless and I made sure not to sing it around Miss Hannah or my mother.

My heart hurt, and I was full of disgust, though for who or for what I did not know. I only knew I did not ever want to care for another if it made me act like Mr. Ben. If it made me wander the fields of Brooklyn, pressing flowers for someone who would never come. If it made me speak another's name until it became my own, even when I was guaranteed no answer. If it made me try to heal my people and fail so disastrously. If it made me put my brother in a coffin to get him free and still have him die anyways.

Care, I decided, was monstrous.

It was as clear as Ben Daisy's hat, floating on the waters. I would not be a doctor, no matter what Mama wished. I could not deceive others, and I could not deceive myself, as she did.

Sa ki bon avèk yon kè, sè ke li pa pote jijman

What's good about the heart is that it does not reason

W as freedom worth it if you still ached like that? If you were still bound on this Earth by desire?

It was a blasphemous thing to think, and I could not speak it to anyone, except to the plants in Mama's garden. I whispered it into the open blossoms' faces in the mornings, and then I carefully ran my thumb over each velvety petal. I knew my words were poison, and I was certain they could kill whatever good lived there.

Who was the woman Ben Daisy loved enough to die for? I looked for her where we'd all last seen her—in the water. I looked at the bottom of our well, in the muddy pools that collected in the ditches by the path to downtown. I looked for her in the pond, just past our settlement, where we took our laundry to wash. I looked for her in the wetlands, where the turtles and frogs and dragonflies swept through, where the men sometimes fished on Saturday afternoons. I stood, the tongues of my leather boots stiffening with mud, my feet sinking into the ground, and breathed in that murky smell of lake beds, and knew, in an instant, she wasn't there. Despite what Ben Daisy had said about her love of cakes and sugar, I did not think a woman who could drown a man in her arms lived in anything as sweet as fresh water. Her domain was brackish. She would live in salt.

The few times we went close to the waterfront, when Mama had to travel downtown and take the cart, I would lift my head to try and catch the smell of it over all the other scents—the rotted fruit in the gutters, the sweet blossoms of the trees planted in front of the nicer houses, the warm breath of horse manure, the sweat of all the bodies teeming around us. At the very top, maybe, when the wind was right, I could smell that other woman's home. Mostly, though, I listened.

If you listen closely, water, when it laps against the sides of a bucket, when it mouths a riverbed, sounds like hands clapping. It sounds like a congregation when prayers are done. But what is its message? It is not deliverance, I don't think. It is not salvation. It is something just underneath that, something that even Mama couldn't reach with her mind. So what hope was there for me of finding it?

A few times, riding beside her in our cart or walking beside her through our town, the rhymes I'd started myself about women and water ringing in our ears, I asked Mama, "Is the woman in the water real?" but she would only say, "I've taught you too well to fall for nonsense." It was a flash of her old assurance, which had gone somewhere underground, inside her, after Ben Daisy was gone.

After he left us, whenever new people came to us, whether by Madame Elizabeth's coffins or, when that route became too dangerous, by secret means of their own, Mama looked at them with sadness. She did not try to feed them ground seahorses. Instead, when they came, when she encountered them at church, she touched their shoulders and told them to come speak to her about what ailed them.

She still saw patients. She still gave aid. But she no longer imagined new cures, and when the people came with something strange, she looked at the remedies already written and did not offer her own.

People distrusted her. They did not always stop at our pew, first, after services to say hello. Reverend Harland was sympathetic, Mama was sure, but sometimes I caught him watching her, his eyes clouded over. Miss Hannah said, to anyone who would listen, "You can't trust a woman without a man to fix anything in a man's heart. How she know what wrong if she never even live with a man up close? You can't trust a woman without a man to ever understand what's needed," and though most people ignored Miss Hannah, you could feel the air shift around Mama when she entered a room, as if people were deciding something about her.

At night, she no longer disappeared into the trees of her mind but, instead, had me sit across from her while she drilled me on the habits of all the plants in the garden, of the uses of the parts of tongues and ears, of the mechanics of a stomach and a lung. It was as if she had become scared that all bodies would sink, as Ben's had, and that my voice, naming the parts of anatomy, singing of bile and blood, could somehow keep them on the surface. While I recited, her brow creased and worried, and she would mouth the words as I said them. When I was able to finish a list without error, she breathed so heavily it was as if she'd just run a race.

Mama and I were still haunted by Daisy and Ben, so when the war began, it was easy to ignore it, at first. And we did not know how long it would last, or who, exactly, was our enemy, when it started.

Some men in our town talked about joining right away, about convincing the white people to let us fight, convincing the white people that we were worthy enough to die. Or that's how Mama talked about it when no one else could hear, when it was just me and Lenore listening. "They think that will fix it," she said. "That white people will finally respect us when we're dead." And then she sighed and shot a glance to Lenore, who rolled her eyes and sighed, too.

I think, those first few months of war, I learned a whole new language from just their sighs.

BUT THEN IT was at our door. That spring, two years into the war, some of the men had left us to join the armies fighting two states over, maybe marching near.

The other ones, they came to us in July, by rowboat, deep in the dark. They found Mama's by midnight.

It was a family who came first. A mother and father, the mother's dress torn, her children balling the cloth of her skirts in their fists. They would not let go for anything—that's what I remember most—their tiny fists tight on muddied homespun, the mother holding the top of her dress to her chest, to keep herself decent. The father had a hat clamped to his head, the brim sticky with blood from his own brow. He wouldn't take it off while his children were in the room. Mama had to wait while the mother distracted them.

When Mama took off the hat, the father closed his eyes. He did not cry out, because he did not want to scare his children. Then he said, "They've gone crazy. The whites in Manhattan have gone crazy. They took Gold Street and Pearl Street, and then they made it all the way to Forty-Second. They're burning our churches. They are shouting that they won't fight for niggers, not ever. They surrounded our orphanage, so we were told.

"We were hiding in the house, till we heard that. That's when we picked up the babies and ran. One of 'em threw a bottle at my head, but we kept running.

"The white men were looking for anyone colored they could find. The white women were reaching out, trying to catch any colored child who ran by. When they caught one, they'd dash 'em against the stones in the street and cheer.

"On our way to the dock, we saw three men hanging from lamp-posts. The whites were hoisting up a fourth when we reached the wharf.

"We paid all we have in the world to an oysterman for his boat to take us across. We knew not to stay downtown, because there were too many whites there, and we were not sure who was friendly and who would attack. We slept under some pilings, or tried to, and when night fell, we walked to you. We knew it would be safe. Mr. Culver told us to come to you for our wounds. Said this one too deep for him."

Mama only nodded. She had learned, since Ben Daisy, you let them talk. She called me over after the man's head was bandaged.

"With luck, there should be more coming," Mama said. I looked at the man, blood drying on his closed eyelids. *So this is luck*, I thought. Mama said, "We have to be ready."

She told me to run to the houses of as many women as I could think of. To find as many of them as I could. I did. I ran down our dirt road and to the main drag, past the church. To Miss Annie, the schoolteacher, and to the choir director and her sister, Miss Nora and Miss Greene, and to Reverend Harland's daughter, Miss Dinah, to the women who lived on the other side of the churchyard, and even to Miss Hannah. To her door I ran, and said, "Come with me, sister, if you can."

I brought them all to the crossroads, where Mama and Lenore were waiting with the cart. Mama had her doctor's bag, and Lenore had lined the cart bed with blankets. Together, we made the long trip to the waterfront. Mama had Miss Hannah sit with her on the driver's bench. I walked steadily beside them, and I saw Mama, every so often, lean over and whisper in Miss Hannah's ear that it would be all right. We all knew Miss Hannah hadn't been downtown since Ben was lost, but she was determined now. Miss Hannah gripped Mama's arm, and Mama said, "There will be so many of them. You'll only have their want to think about." Mama had Miss Hannah hold a blanket over her other arm, to keep her hands from shaking.

But when we got to the waterfront, the whole stretch was empty. There were no boats. "Where are they all?" Miss Dinah said, and only the waves slapping the bottom of the wharf answered her. By then, it was just after dawn. The water before us was first a long line of silver and then a sudden wall of cloud and fog. The smoke from all the fires the whites had set was rolling over to us, across that wide expanse of river, and it mixed with the muggy July dawn until one swirling mass of white and gray sat on top of the water.

I had never seen smoke mix with fog like that before, how it hovered like a curtain between this world and maybe the next, from light to dark, from heaven to hell, from sleep to consciousness. That was where the woman in the water lived even now—I knew it. I knew it in my bones. And I felt how foolishly I had spent the last year, looking for her in common well water, when she was here all along. While I stood with the women on the dock as they tried to see what was coming to them through the veil, I prayed to her, that woman,

Let 'em through, let 'em through, LET 'EM THROUGH.

I heard the tiniest drop of a wave, the sound a fish makes when it turns over on the surface of the water and falls back to its home. Was that her? Was that her byword? I thought it was. I knew it was, because the next thing I saw, finally, was something nosing its way through the clouds.

It was a long boat, with four rowers—two at the bow, two at the stern—followed by two more. As they got closer, I could see that the rowers had kerchiefs wrapped around their mouths, to keep from breathing in the smoke as they worked, and their hats pulled down over their eyes, to keep them from stinging in the wind. Between the rowers, on the boats, were tens of children. What was most eerie about it all was that the only sound was the water slapping the oars. Even the babies were silent.

But then the first boat docked, and the women all around me took in a deep breath, and they began to sing.

Deep   *river,*
                                          my
          home
                     is
                              over
                                        Jordan
          Deep
                     river,
                              my
                                        home
                     is
                              over
                                        Jordan

By the time we got to the chorus, a baby in one of the boats began to cry, a big robust yell, as if he was trying to harmonize with us. And the women all around me broke out in whoops. "That's it," Miss Annie called out. "Keep it up." And then the other babies began to cry, as well, and I have never seen a group of women happier to hear a bunch of infants bawling at five in the morning.

We got the children out of the boats. A girl my age, her face streaked with soot, her arms covered in scratches, her skirts dark with something damp, held a fat baby in her arms. When she clambered off the boat and up onto the dock, she looked at me, looked in my eyes, came straight toward me, and handed the baby off before crouching down to sit, lowering her head to enter the peace of the fabric stretched between her knees. Mama saw her, saw the stain on her skirt, and went to her first, shielding her with her body so the others couldn't see or hear what she was asking.

I carried that baby all the way back to our house. She was not yet a year old, by the look of her. Still too young to walk. She lay against my chest. I could feel her spittle pool on the front of my dress. She was so heavy, and with every step, I could feel her chest rise and fall. It unnerved me. I tried to match her rhythm, to breathe along with her, but her heart was beating too fast. Still, despite all this, she would look around, keep her eyes wide open, staring at something in the tree branches above us—part of the past, or the present, or maybe the future, that I could not see. I kept praying to the woman in the water, even as every step took me farther from her. *Don't take this one with you. Keep her here with us. Let her spirit leave the water and come with me to land.*

The baby was still in my arms at noon, when we had gotten some of the survivors to our houses, some of them to the church.

"You can put the baby down," Mama told me.

I looked up at her. "I can't," I said. By which I meant if I gave up the weight of that baby, the whole weight of what had happened across the river—the fire and the hangings and the beatings and the white women dashing babies' brains and whatever had been done to that girl from the boat who had handed me the baby, that had made her hold her dress between her thighs—all of that weight would take the baby's place, and I knew I was not strong enough to hold it. Not yet.

Not then. Even if I made a million prayers to the woman in the water, I knew it wouldn't help.

And Mama, my mama, she looked at me and she understood. She said, "This is the hardest part of our work." She said, "Keep the baby close if you need to. But you can't carry her all the time." And she had me sit in the nicer armchair in the parlor while the women of our town crowded into the room.

They had gathered there, all sweating in the full heat of the day, their apron fronts and pinafores damp, their voices merging together into a new song, this one made up of just the question they asked one another in the room over and over again:

What to do?

"Look at that baby's skin," Miss Dinah said, gazing at the girl in my arms. "Covered in rashes, even worse than the singe from the burns."

"And that little boy who rode with me in the cart, his feet were too tore up to walk." Miss Hannah said this, in a hollow voice, looking straight ahead, back to being stuck in between this world and the one with her brother in the water.

"That one," Miss Clara said, pointing to the baby still slumped in my arms, "her father left her with the orphanage when he went to go and try to join the war. They told him she'd be well cared for. What's he going to come back to now?" Miss Clara was the youngest member of the women's club at church. There, she was given to making righteous statements that made the other women shuffle and shift, embarrassed by her blunt holiness.

"One of the girls said the white people went around and marked every colored person's home in Manhattan," Miss Annie said. "With red chalk, they marked it. They marked the homes of our white friends, too. So they knew who to burn." As she spoke, she fanned herself with her hand in quick, sharp strokes, trying to shift the weight of humidity with the palm of a hand.

"What terrors," Miss Dinah said. "Can you imagine? I mean, can you imagine, your very own neighbor marking your house to attack? Can you imagine all those people you pass in the street every day, planning for your demise?" Miss Dinah leaned forward and said, in a gruff, low voice that I suppose was meant to be that of a terror, "Mark 'em all and burn 'em down." I'd heard Miss Dinah try on this voice before, at church meetings when she was describing certain devils, and it had always raised a laugh. But not now. The accent only curdled in the hot air.

"Surely, the governor can stop it," Miss Clara said uncertainly. "He'll send troops to make it stop."

Mama looked at Miss Clara, with her high, smooth neck and clear brown skin. "You understand less than I thought you did if you think he'd lift a finger."

Miss Clara blinked, and her cheeks darkened.

"One of the men says"—Miss Annie leaned forward, eager to stop the sadness and share what she knew—"the mayor begged the governor for help, but the governor plans to come and cheer the rioters on."

"He'd do it," Mama murmured.

"How can you be so hopeless?" Miss Clara said.

Miss Annie sat back in her chair again. "It is not being hopeless. We have to plan for the worst of what white folks do. Because they always choose the worst. They do what they do, and—"

"We do what we can," Mama said. She took a sip of water from her tin cup.

"I hope the governor burns," I said, from my seat at the corner.

I had thought Mama would nod in agreement. Some of the other women did. I saw Miss Clara and Miss Annie smile when I said it. But Mama looked at me sharply. "It's a sin to wish such a thing on another person," she said. "Even on him."

I thought of the woman under the water, who I was sure had the vengeance in her to do something horrible like that, and I directed my thoughts to her. *Burn him up. Drowning's too good for him.*

Mama stood up. "To work," she said. Even then, our household had more than the households of the other women—more jars of preserves, more salt pork, more cloth, more firewood. And so we spent the afternoon taking stock of the pantry and of the root cellar, dividing what we had to feed everyone, which household should take from the extra barrel of salted cod and which needed more blankets.

We did not know it then, but this is how we would spend the rest of the war. All of us in that room there became a sisterhood. We called ourselves the Ladies' Intelligence Society—it had started as a kind of joke, when the few men in town asked the women where they were going, why they spent so much time at Dr. Sampson's house. I was a mascot of sorts—the doctor's girl, who was always in the room.

We were hell-bent on plotting. How could we get information from Kings County to Ohio, to Maryland, to Virginia, to the West, about the children left in the destroyed orphanage? How could we find their parents? It was from hours of those meetings that we found the father of the baby I'd carried off the boat, got word to him, were able to send her to relatives in Massachusetts. She was no longer in my arms, but I could still feel the weight of her there, pressing. Whenever I did, I'd fold my arms over my chest and pray again, to the woman in the water. *Keep her safe. Keep them safe. Keep us safe.*

"After the war" became everyone's refrain. We read of men dying every day, even as a few of those made their way off the battlefield, their eyes wide with horror. Whenever the war ended, if it ended, whoever won, we knew there would be colored people in need of aid. And what could we do, from the safety and comfort of our town that the whites had overlooked? What would help them best?

"A school," Miss Annie said. The women all nodded; that was a given. "Homes," Miss Dinah added. But it was Mama who cleared her throat and said, "A hospital." She looked around the room. "For colored people," she said. "We cannot live in freedom if we are not well."

There was a moment of silence as the women turned the idea around, and Mama, very carefully would not look at Miss Hannah, who was crying now. But Miss Annie, Miss Clara, and Miss Dinah nodded, and it was decided then that this was what their efforts would go toward. A hospital, for whoever made it out alive, to become whole again.

It was hard planning, oftentimes hours of talking with no clear answers. But when the women got going, the whole room began to vibrate. Sometimes, it seemed that the white walls themselves flushed when the women raised their voices. How strange it was to sit around them, at their feet or in the corner, and hear them shout, these same women who all week long told me and the other colored girls in town to speak softly, to keep our heads down and our backs straight, to train our eyes to overlook the insults the world outside of town heaped at our feet. Those women told girls like me to ignore the present-day horrors around us, to look only toward the future, toward another place that did not exist yet.

But here, in the room, I could imagine that I was already there. The women would begin the meeting sitting upright, but by the end, they would be sprawled. Leaning against seats, arms crossed over stools, sipping water, laughing, shouting back and forth.

You knew a meeting was getting work done when Miss Dinah

began her sharp, piercing giggle. It was uncontrollable, a little hyster-
ical, and did not necessarily prompt the other women to join in. It
was more like the whistle of a teakettle; it told you pressure was high,
waters were rolling to a boil, that something was happening, and that
whatever it was, it was as wondrous and yet as deceptively common as
water transforming into air.

I have never in my life felt anything as powerful as whatever force
was in that room while those women talked, and I began to believe that
it was the talking itself that did it, that perhaps women's voices in harmony were like some sort of flintstone sparking, or like the hot burst of
air that comes through a window, billowing the curtains, before rain.
Sometimes, I imagined the whole room lifting up from their talk—
lifting up and spinning out, out, into the future times to come, when
everyone would be truly free. The time I thought we were all planning
for.

To bring them back down, when a workday was done, they would
turn to some sort of amusement. It had to be something calming,
something sober. "We need to rest a little in order to keep going," was
what Miss Annie always said.

They decided on trading compliments. They'd write them down on
slips of paper, unsigned but addressed to the lady they wished to compliment, and then put them in an old flour tin Mama had. At the end
of the meeting, they'd draw the slips out one at a time and read the ode,
and then the fun began in guessing the author.

Everyone saved their praise by pasting the compliments into little books they stitched together and then passing them around to
be signed by every lady present—a record of attendance. They made
bindings out of the rags they had around, stuffed into the bottom of
their sewing baskets. 'Friendship albums,' they called them. Everyone's

album started neat and clean and pretty, of course, but it was every woman's goal to have a ruined one, a book with worn pages and extra leaves stuffed in, one bursting at the seams, because that showed how loved you were.

Mama was jealous of the other women. Sometimes, at the end of a meeting, I caught her fingering the pages of her own album, looking from hers to theirs. Hers were always a bit neater, a bit cleaner, and much thinner. Even after all she'd done for the orphans, even as the group conspired about how to make her a hospital, even after all that work, Mama would lift the other women's heavier books and sign them, smiling, while only a few of them signed hers. Ben Daisy still stood dripping over her, a rebuke.

I suppose I should have been angry at the other women on behalf of Mama. If I was a loyal daughter, I would have felt that. But at the end of every meeting, I looked at Mama's thin book and only felt sorry for her, not mad at them. *Is everything at least forgiven underwater?* is what I would have asked the woman in the water if I could have, but I did not really want to know the answer.

I did not know what to do with a vanquished Mama. I saw her hurt, but I still thought she could overcome it. She never spoke of it, so to me, it was another thing to add to the load she carried. "Everyone has their own burden, Libertie," she was fond of telling me whenever I complained about my inability to do arithmetic or when another girl was mean or petty. So I thought she could solve this setback, that it was temporary, that it was something Mama could fix with her cleverness.

Once, in her office, I found the discards of her attempts at praise for the other women, written on the backs of notes to the pharmacist and on the discarded labels of old medicine bottles.

You've done fine work, and I look forward to your work improving even more.

Although at first I was not sure, I see now you are a true Christian woman.

It was as if she could not, in spite of herself, break her reserve and warmly compliment any of these women, who'd discarded her from their care.

"You see, I am not very talented at this."

I started. Mama was standing beside me, watching me read her weak words. I think it was the first time she admitted a failing to me.

I felt a little flush of embarrassment for her.

"Libertie," she said, "write something for me. Kind, but not too kind. Nothing that would inspire envy."

"You cannot do it?"

"I do not have a way with words, like you do." She sighed. Then she said, very quietly, "The only good poem I've ever written is you. A daughter is a poem. A daughter is a kind of psalm. You, in the world, responding to me, is the song I made. I cannot make another."

My heart filled but quickly sank, because what freeborn thing can bear to be loved as much as that?

The least I could do was write a poem for her.

They were supposed to be anonymous. That was the whole point. It was my job at the meeting to take the unsigned works out of the box and read them to the room, with no bias. At the next meeting, when I took out the paper written in my own hand but elongated to look like Mama's, I stood up before them all and sang the love my mama had for the women there. The love she would have sung, if she'd had the voice for it.

True women friends are fine and rare
You search for them, here and there
The bonds between us bloom like a rose
For we are companions true affection has chose
Within our hearts lie trust and faith
Our true friendship, bonds will never break

Mama was not a good poet. Neither, at fourteen, was I.

But those women heard that awful poetry and smiled and clapped, and when I revealed it was my mama who wrote it, they said, "Very fine, Dr. Sampson. Very fine indeed." It was as if she had proven that she was one of them again, because she could praise them so warmly, even if the praise was clumsy. Maybe because of that. It was what they had been waiting for, and there was a kind of thawing in their relations.

Even rude love is better than no show of love at all. That must be why you took Ben Daisy, I thought to the woman in the water.

That is how I remember the rest of the war: my hands covered in the flour dust from long-baked biscuits at the bottom of the tin of love poems, the tips of my fingers stained with black ink, and Mama searching for every opportunity to be useful. I learned during the war how to scheme for the best way to set the world right, to change it. And I knew that this change was wrapped up in the love notes these women wrote to one another and dropped into a box, even as the world around us burnt.

Which world was burning, anyways? I wrote this question out to her, the woman in the water. After each meeting of the Ladies' Intelligence Society, I took what little bits were left of the poems and made a book of my own.

What did Ben Daisy say she liked? Pink and white and gold. Cakes and candy. Scent bottles and silk. I left pansies alone, but I collected everything else I could for her.

These things were hard to come by in our hamlet. We did not eat or buy sugar, because slaves made it—Mama was one of the few who were righteous enough to observe this boycott. But then, with the war, it wasn't to be had anyways. So I took to dripping honey in the pages of the book, underlining each question to the lady with a thick golden smear. Into the honey, I pressed flower petals, and then I let the page dry and started another one.

The songs I wrote in my book were made for the woman under the water, the one who offered something other than this world.

> *Is the water really better?*
> *Should we all just try to drown?*
> *Is your love better than this world?*
> *Which world is burning, anyways?*

I thought it was the world that drove Ben Daisy under the water, that kept Pete Back Back pocked with sores, that conspired to steal and beat and kill the children of the women around as soon as they left their wombs. So, what was there, really, to mourn? In annihilation, I saw a celebration. My book to the lady became a place to celebrate the destruction of all the devices of this world that had tried to snare my people and snap us in two, that had sworn to kill every last one of us one way or another.

And even as the wider world did not agree, did not even care what the women around me thought or believed, discounted colored women as entirely irrelevant—the thing to remember, I learned, was that these women, here, loved one another and cared for one another as no other.

Even for my shifty, jumpy, defeated Mama, they cared. And from that care grew a steady foundation.

WHEN THE WAR ended, I ran through the streets with everyone else, crying and saying my hosannas. Finally, the world I had dreamt of, had prayed for, was on its way.

A bunch of us colored girls and boys ran all the way down to the waterfront. We danced on the boards of the wharf, and I even leaned over the side to whisper into the waves of the water a "Thank you." I half believed, even though I knew I was fooling myself, that this was all her doing.

We left the riverbank at dawn, headed for home, and I walked backward the whole way, while the other girls laughed and the boys called me silly. I looked toward the river. I watched the sky for fires and probed the earth for blood.

Now, the newspapers were full of longing, not battles. White people longing for their sons' bodies, hoping they were whole. If their bodies did not come back intact, then what would happen to these good white Christian boys on Judgment Day? They would stand up in their graves and topple back down, as on some overgrown battlefield their errant leg or lost foot would rise without the rest of them. They made it sound like a horror. But I read each notice as the reports rolled in during that jostling year after the war, and prayed to the woman who had taken Ben Daisy under *Keep their arms scattered and their legs separated. Keep them without integrity when Judgment Day comes.*

It was a small price to pay, in my opinion. The war had broken bodies apart, and that seemed to be what caused so much terror among the whites, what made them shoot their own president. But I had stood in Culver's back room and seen the people broken from slavery, I had held that orphan girl in my arms, I had seen so many die from those same white people's hatred that I could not muster any sympathy for their terror, and I could definitely not feel it on my own.

They did not care for us. I would not care for them. I would only care for the women around me, the woman in the water, and Mama, of course.

It was the closest I'd come, at that point in my life, to a state of jubilee. Something that people had told us was impossible for two hundred years was here—colored people were free, the slaveholders were defeated, and everything around me led me to believe that it would be this way forever.

IT WAS FINALLY time for the Ladies' Intelligence Society to show their care for the world, which they did with a building they bought for Mama's hospital downtown. They decided that a location near the wharfs could serve more of the colored women in Kings County, and maybe some others adventurous or rich enough to take a boat from lower Manhattan. A COLORED WOMEN'S HOSPITAL was painted carefully on the sign there, and we all cheered when it was finally raised up and nailed above the door.

The women of the LIS painted the walls of Mama's hospital waiting room a deep red and raised money for the padded leather benches there. Walking into it was like walking into some expensive womb. It was dark and warm and designed to calm the patient, while she sat, scared, shocked by the betrayals of her own body.

When patients climbed the stairs to the examination rooms, they were called to a kind of rebirth. They passed through a hallway painted a deep, peaceful white and emerged onto a floor with wide windows and the white muslin curtains Mama put such stock in. They rose to a world of light. In the bright light, their bodies were not a shame, not a secret, and they were examined by the light of the sun "as the good Lord intended," as Mama would say. For some of the women, it was the first time they had ever exposed as much as their stomach to the sun, and sometimes they would break into tears, overwhelmed by the light. But even the most conservative of them, the ones who insisted there must be something indecent about all that brightness, came back to Mama and the hospital, to be tended.

As Mama and Lenore examined them, and I stood back, ready to assist, Mama named each part of a woman as she touched it. "This is your sternum. This is your rib. Here is your navel, but you knew that. Here, what I push on here, is your womb and your ovaries. This is your mons pubis. These are is your labia, minora and major. This is your prepuce. Pardon."

I stood in those examination rooms, and I heard her say this every day, to every woman, like a kind of benediction. And when I was not with her in the hospital, when she had me stay at the house to tend the garden or look after the land, sometimes in the middle of the day, I lay in the garden, felt the hot earth on my skin, and contemplated how my own limbs joined together. I traced for myself my sternum, my ribs, my navel, my womb, which I imagined as empty and small as a coin purse, my ovaries, which I could palpate with my own hand, my own mons pubis, my own labia, which I touched and thought the thrill I felt was merely the daring of touching something private in the light of the sun.

It was so quiet at the house without Mama and Lenore that I listened to my own pulse, could track my own breath, could maybe even hear my own body growing.

My mother was giving me the great gift that no other Negro girl my age, anywhere on Earth, I am sure, had experienced before. What other Negro girl had the freedom to lie in a garden on a workday afternoon?

Because of this, I was not scared or disgusted by my body changing, as I knew other girls were.

I'm sweating jewels, was how I explained it in my book to the woman in the water. Red rubies in my drawers, yellow pearls at the seams of my blouse, black diamonds across the bridge of my nose. I eagerly wrote to her about the wonderful rude shock that came when I woke up one day and realized that I now smelled like a woman. *I will be what Mama knows, what Miss Annie and the LIS know, what we study all day in her hospital, I wrote.*

One day at the house in a planning meeting, as the women talked about how to raise just a hundred more dollars, two hundred, to keep the hospital open, Miss Annie sniffed loudly while I walked by and said, "Womanhood is nothing but tears and sorrow." Then she looked at me. "I can smell it on you, Black Gal."

I was not offended, because I knew Mama saw honor in my changing body—how my measurements grew millimeter by millimeter, how the numbers that described me shifted. She told me she was proud. It was as if the change in my body was one she had willed herself, not the same cycle every other girl went through.

I think Mama thought if she gave me that space, I would reproduce her spirit and her will in exact measure. Like a cell dividing itself.

This new world of adult busyness and abundance that Mama was building at the hospital seemed as robust as my own body. I saw them as one and the same—that Mama's fortunes were changing right when my body was felt like a kind of omen, one I thanked the woman in the water for. I thought she had heard my cries for blood and revenge and was making them real for me, in the sweetest way possible: in Mama's prosperity.

I did not even realize that what I had grown into was a different person than my mother until she had COLORED painted off the hospital

sign. She sent for a boy to do it maybe a year and a half after the hospital was open, after the fourth or fifth charity bazaar the LIS had run
that came back with diminishing funds. All over the country, colored
people were building things that seemed bigger than Mama's hospital
for women, that the colored men and white people preferred to fund.

The possibilities for colored people seemed so many, so varied, each
more fantastic than the last, but which one was right and which one
should they choose? If I could have, I would have chosen all of them—
every idea, one after the other, seemed correct. A school for freedmen; a
letter service to reunite those separated by the auction block; a caravan
to Canada; another one to Kansas; Mama's hospital. *Why can't we have
all of it, all of it?* I wanted to say.

The Ladies' Intelligence Society told Mama they could not raise
the money solely for her hospital, in the way that they could during
the war. And certainly not solely for a hospital just for colored women,
when colored men were back and needed healing more. "We do not
like it," Miss Annie said, "but we think people will be more amenable
to your cause if we raise money for you and other things."

Mama did not even bat an eye. She only nodded, once, and said,
"Well, then."

And so Mama decided to change the hospital name. "It's a sign of
the reconciliation, of the harmony of the times we now live in," Mama
said to me and Lenore as we stood beside her, looking up at the boy
on his ladder in the street. "Here it is, only two years after the end of
the war, and white women will sit side by side colored women in our
hospital waiting room, willing to be treated because they know, deep
down, their organs are the same."

But I knew, and she knew, this was not true. Because after the boy
came down off his ladder, she had him put a rod up on the waiting
room ceiling, and then she instructed Lenore to hang a scrap of red

velvet on it, to make a little curtain, so that the new patients she admitted, the white women, could pull the curtain shut and avoid the sight of colored women beside them.

The white women came because Mama was colored but not too colored. In fact, her color worked in her favor. She would never be invited to a dinner party, or a lecture, or sit across from them in a private club. They would never run into her in their worlds and be reminded of their most embarrassing ailments: a stubborn and treacherous womb, smelly fluids, bodies insisting on being rude and offensive. Mama could restore these women's bodies back to what they wished them to be, make them well enough to join this world again—and they would never encounter her in their real lives, this woman who knew exactly what was beneath their skirts.

The first time I touched one of these new white-woman patients, she flinched. I remember, she was only a few years older than me, a young bride who'd come in with thrush between her legs, too embarrassed to see her own doctor and be found out. *Found out of what?* I wrote to my woman in the water.

I grasped the white woman's elbow to help her to the examination table, which she did not mind, and then I began to feel at her middle, as Mama had instructed at the start of the appointment, and she batted my hands away. "Off me," she said. And when Mama looked up, from where she was standing in the corner, preparing for the examination, the woman said, "Your girl is molesting me."

And Mama, my brave mama, did not come to my aid. She only narrowed her eyes slightly, and then she said, "Come take notes, Libertie," and she herself went to touch the woman's middle.

And so I understood. Mama was light enough that the white women did not feel awkward when her hands touched them. Mama, to them, was not all the way black. When the black women they knew outside the hospital touched the white women, they touched them with what they told themselves to be dumb hands. They did not have to imagine those hands as belonging to anyone, least of all someone thinking and feeling. But I'd touched that white woman with a knowing of what was deepest inside her, and she'd recoiled—it was beyond her imagination.

After that, I noticed how the white-woman patients watched me while I assisted Mama. They stared at where my dress tightened on my chest, at the roundness of my arms, at where my skirt darted at my hips—stared openly, because they knew I would not rebuke them—and then they would sigh, exasperated, and look away.

The older ones, I could understand their jealousy—the jealousy of age for youth, I thought it was. *Dried up corncobs*, I wrote of them in my never-ending letter to the woman in the water. But the patients about my age, I did not understand. I had grown up free, only around colored people, and I could not fathom their scrutiny.

And Mama chose them over me, every time.

When the women flinched, when they scowled at my body, Mama ignored them. Sometimes, she said, "Come stand here, Libertie," so that I was out of their eyesight. But Mama, dear Mama, my fierce Mama, never told them to stop.

Mama acted as though the white women's pain was the same as ours. As if when they cried, they grieved for the same things lost that we did. Mama did not seem to mind that a woman who came to our waiting room and sat on the other side of the velvet curtain could not be comfortable. Even when she came at her most vulnerable, when she had to be vigilant for some sort of abuse, she had to stare at that velvet curtain and wonder if on the other side of it was the very white woman who had caused her pain to begin with.

How, when the world was splitting wide open for colored women, could Mama choose to yoke herself to the very white ones who often were trying to sew it all up for us? "There's prudence and practicality, and then there is a complete failure of imagination," Miss Annie said shortly after Mama took COLORED off her sign, and that was all any self-respecting member of the LIS allowed themselves to say in front of me.

There was no drawn-out fight. The women in the group did not argue that way. Instead, one Sunday at church, our pew was empty, except for us. No one gathered around Mama's seat as soon as the sermon was over, as they had when we were plotting. We were back to the same loneliness we'd lived in after Ben Daisy. Mama had squandered every good feeling those women had ever mustered for her.

I saw Mama raise her hand to Miss Annie, and Miss Annie raise hers back limply and then turn to one of the other women she was talking to. I saw Mama register this, set back her shoulders, turn, and say, "Home, Libertie. I'm too tired for socializing today."

She gave up co-conspirators for customers, I wrote to my woman.

"What does it feel like?" I asked Mama one Sunday as we walked back home from church.

She looked at me, startled. "What do you mean?"

What does it feel like to lose your friends? is what I wanted to ask, but I knew it was an impossibly cruel question. So I only said, "What does it feel like to heal someone?"

But this, too, was a mistake, because my mother looked ahead and said, "I've never thought about it, Libertie. I don't know that I can answer."

How could she?

How could she?

It was the rhythm I walked to all the way to our house, up the steps of our porch to the front door.

I stood in the parlor and watched Mama unpin her bonnet until I could not take it anymore. "How can you treat those white women," I said, "after what you've seen them and their husbands do to the people who came to us? They marked our houses for destruction not three years ago, and you welcome them as if it was nothing. All the blood and sweat you mopped up for years, the bones we set right. All the people we lost—"

"You are so young, Libertie," she said. It infuriated me. "The world is bigger than you think." She was still watching her reflection in the parlor mirror.

I tried to meet her eyes, but I couldn't. I looked at the glass jar with her sister's braids in it, untouched since Ben Daisy—no one brave enough to touch it since he left us.

No, Mama, I wanted to say. *The world can live in the palm of my hand. The world is in the burning between the thighs of the colored women who seek you out for comfort. The world is in the wounds on the heads of the fathers, and in the eyes we treated, burnt by smoke from the fires the white mobs set.*

I can measure the world. Can you?

But I didn't have the courage to say that. I lowered my eyes. For a time.

"I've raised you wrong," Mama said to her reflection. "I've raised you all wrong if some white folks being cruel is a surprise to you."

I felt my face go hot with anger again. "I am not surprised by the cruelty, Mama," I said. "I am surprised we are expected to ignore it, to never mention it, to swim in it as if it's the oily, smelly harbor water the boys dive into by the wharves."

Mama finally took off her bonnet and set it down. She turned to me, her eyes exacting. "You want to write poetry?" she said. "Or do you want to get things done?"

"I want a clean pool to swim in."

She snorted. "Always with the flowery talk. You're spoiled."

"Call me spoiled," I said. "I won't rot if I swim in clean water, though."

She picked up her bonnet and folded it tighter in her hands, her only sign of distress.

She said with a sigh, "You are becoming too old for these scenes, Libertie. You can keep asking me your questions, your accusations full of God knows what. But the answer is never going to change. And I am tired." She set the bonnet down again, crossed the room as if to leave.

"But I am tired," I called after her, wanting to make her feel something, wanting to make her react, feel the same slippery sense of unease I'd felt when I saw that our pews were empty and that our friends had left us. "I am very, very tired, Mama. I am tired of bending over women's stomachs, and I am tired of feeling for babies' limbs under skin, and I am tired of smelling the sickroom breath of women who won't even look me in the eye."

Mama stopped at the door and turned. "If you are tired at sixteen years old, you understand how tired I am of having this argument with you. You can do as you please. But I won't have this discussion anymore."

And she left, calling over her shoulder, "Put the kettle on will you? A cup of tea would be nice."

I sat down in the parlor, in the seat in the corner where I'd watched my mother plan and plot and scheme and heal. Where I'd loved her and wanted only her understanding. I sat there for a long time, as the room darkened around me, as I heard her move about upstairs in her regular ambulations. I had my little book in my lap, full of notes to my woman in the water, but I could not write now. I saw my own handwriting, childish and looping large, and I thought of what she would think if she saw it, and I imagined she would feel only disgust with me, what I imagined was the same disgust my mother felt now, walking about her office, setting things right for the work-day tomorrow. Mama had fled into her mind, away from me—and I should be used to the cold by now, I should, but I still could not bear it.

It was a question of good. I had never doubted before that Mama was good. But here she was, discounting everything I asked in exchange for the money of these women, for the sake of the gold lettering on her building downtown. I could not, in all conscientiousness, call that righteous or good.

I am a fool, and maybe you are, too, I wrote in the book, and then I closed it, and sat back, and cried.

The next morning, we rode into downtown as if nothing had happened—Mama telling me the tasks ahead. Indeed, it felt worse to know that our reckoning had not even been a reckoning for her, it seemed, just a slight annoyance at the end of the day. Here was another break between us. She could not even see when we were at odds with each other.

I thought it had not affected her at all, until a few weeks later when she looked up from her books as I brought her a cup of tea one night and said, her voice cool but her face blushing slightly, "Cunningham College in Ohio has accepted you for further studies. I think it's for the best, don't you? I have taught you all I can here." She took off her glasses and smiled wanly at me. "I think I cannot teach you anymore."

I did not even protest. I said nothing and understood I was to leave her, had been banished, for wishing her to ask more of the world around us.

Se lè yon sous seche, moun konn valè dlo

It's when the spring goes dry that people appreciate the value of water

She sent me away, so I'd send her away, too, I resolved. I would banish her from the very recesses of my heart, from my consciousness, to forge a new self that had not ever been touched by my mother.

In the weeks leading up to my departure, she did not speak to me of it at all. It was Lenore who directed how to pack my trunk, told me what route I should travel, reminded me to never look a strange man in the eye. Mama went about her work as if I would be there with her forever.

So she wants silence, I wrote to the lady. *I'll give her the silence of the grave.*

On the morning I left, she told Lenore to take me to the ferry to Manhattan. "I should stay at the hospital," she said. But as I climbed into the cart, she stopped and held my hand and kissed it, in that same desperate way I'd seen her do to Madame Elizabeth.

"You write to me, you hear?" she said, her voice strangled. "You write to me everything that happens to you so I can know it."

I kept my hand in hers for as long as I could. *Let me stay with you, and I wouldn't have to write anything at all*, is what I wished to say. But I only said, "Yes, Mama."

And then she threw my hand away, and the silence rose up between us again, as inevitable and heavy as an ocean's wave.

Dear Mama,

The train was tolerable. The stagecoach was not. I had to sit on the top, at the back, because at first I was the only Negro traveling and there was a white family, moving to Ohio. The wife did not want me to sit beside her or her children. But after the first stop, a Negro man and his son joined me. The man was named Mr. Jonathan, and he taught me how to press my body forward into the wind. He said it was the best way to endure the ride. He told me I have a habit of looking back over my shoulder at the road behind us, and that is no good when you are traveling through open country.

The land here is strange. I find it all too flat. Not like the hills in Kings County. The air, though—that, I can concede, is better. The first few days out of New York, my nose dripped a thin black liquid that made the coachman laugh. He told me it was all the soot of the city, fleeing my nostrils. I must confess, I bunched my cloak into the balls of my hands and rubbed my nose at his rudeness.

The stagecoach left me in a town called Butterfield, and the college is five miles farther than that. There was one cart waiting to make a mill run, luckily, that agreed to take us—otherwise I would have walked the five miles, pulling the twenty pounds of clothing and quilts and books in my trunk behind me.

On the ride into school, I sat beside two other girls, one plump, one stout, both with skin the color of damp sand. The thin one leaned in to all three of us and said, "At night, you can't see nothing in these fields. You, for instance, out in those fields you'd be nothing but eyes and teeth."

I knew it was a joke, but when I heard it, it shot through me and I spent the rest of the ride turning suddenly, trying to catch, out of the corner of my eye, glimmers of teeth and eyes from the fields. Or maybe just another girl as dark as me who folded down into molars and corneas as soon as the sun set.

I will stop myself from speculating further. I know you do not like poetry. I will write another letter to you when I've gathered enough facts, not just impressions, for your liking.

Your

Libertie

I had resolved to wash her influence off me like dust from the road. But everything in that place she'd banished me to looked to me exactly like Mama. The gray sky that arched above me was the same color as her front tooth, and the fields smelled like the inside of her shawl, and the wind in the trees, I thought, sounded just like the whisper of her voice when she was being urgent.

The cart stopped a quarter of a mile before it reached campus, in front of a wide, low log cabin, set back a little, with a short, rough-hewn fence in the front.

As I headed up the path in the dusk, my trunk trailing behind me, the door opened. A woman stood there. When I reached her, I realized she was shorter than me—the top of her kerchief only came up to my shoulder. She was almost as dark as me, too. She looked up at me, laughed at my dirt-smeared face. "You look like you walked here from Brooklyn," she said.

She came out behind me and pushed me inside. "Leave the trunk," she said. "One of the boys will get it."

This was where I was to board—the home of an old friend of Mama's, Franklin Grady. He was from Kings County, too, and had moved out west to study law at Cunningham College, run for over twenty years by abolitionists, an experiment in Negro education. The woman who greeted me was Grady's wife, Madeline.

Grady had been there since before the war, since the days of spiriting away, and now that war was over and there were so many ways for a Negro to get ahead, he had chosen to stay at the college, to become its first Negro dean of law. Indeed, as Mama had told me, all the teachers were Negroes—drawn out to these fields to grow the teachers and doctors and farmers and lawyers our race would need in freedom.

I realized that Mama had sent me to a place that was the antithesis of her hospital. There would be no white students behind a velvet curtain in the classrooms of Cunningham College, claiming reconciliation. But Mama also knew, as did I, that I couldn't get away with the trick she'd pulled so many years ago—register at a white medical school and be taken for merely a white woman, not a colored one, until first semester marks came through.

The Grady household was not like mine. There were three rooms—the big front one, with the hearth, the back room, where Grady, Madeline, and the three children slept, and then a smaller room, where Mr. Grady's books were kept and where he went to work on the cases that came his way. The main room was hot. Hanging from the ceiling, draped over every beam and surface, were skirts and shirts and pants. Enough clothing for a regiment. "Keep looking," Madeline Grady said as I craned my neck up to stare at the ceiling beams through the leg hole of a pair of bloomers. "They'll be here till Wednesday."

Then she moved off, out the door to the yard, where more clothing hung out to dry.

She did not ask me to follow her, and I was at a loss as to what to do, so I sat down on my trunk and waited, while the two boys who were supposed to help me drag it in stood in front of me and stared. "Hello," I said, and they both ran off with a start to hold on to their mother.

Mrs. Grady came back in to the room and began to pull down some of the skirts and shirts and throw them over her arm. I moved to help, but she held up her hand. "There'll be time enough for that once you're properly settled in. Sit still. Play at being a lady," she said, and then laughed again.

I stayed on the trunk, awkwardly. When she came back in again, she pushed one of the boys forward, who held out a branch he'd broken off from the oak tree out front.

"Well, take it, then. Beat the dust out you, at least," Mrs. Grady said.

When Grady came home, that's what I was doing—hitting my knees and ankles until the dust from the road danced in the air. I was the only one to greet him, because Mrs. Grady and the boys were back outside, wringing the last of the gray water out of strangers' shirts.

Grady blinked at me once, twice. His cheeks flushed pink in the heat of the room—he was, perhaps, a little bit darker than Mama, and much, much lighter than his wife. But he was also clearly a Negro—he would not have been able to get by. He was short, too, with a round, pleasant face decorated with freckles and a broad, friendly nose, across the bridge of which perched the same small spectacles that Mama always wore.

When he saw me, though, he frowned as if I was a misplaced book.

"That's the girl, Libertie," Mrs. Grady called from the yard, and Grady grunted in response.

Later, at dinner, I told him, "Mama says thank you for your hospitality, and I do, as well," but he only managed to mumble a reply into his soup.

"She's asked me to give you this," I said, and I handed him the small pamphlet on prayer by Reverend Harland that our church had commissioned to be printed to celebrate the end of the war.

"Well, go on. Thank her," Mrs. Grady said. Let your own pickaninnies learn good grace." That made him smile, slightly.

He glanced at the title, then read it aloud. THE GLORY OF TOMORROW it said in proud, correct letters.

"Mama doesn't like that," I said. "She says it assumes too much."

"Huh," Grady said. "Well, Cathy never did put too much stock in forecasting."

"I, for one, agree with her on that," Mrs. Grady said to her bowl of soup.

"But you know Reverend Harland," I said. "He just refuses to respond to any of Mama's hints about unseemliness."

I blushed then, unsure if I had offended Grady with my irreverence.

He said nothing, only picked up the pamphlet carefully and carried it back to the room the rest of the family respected as his study.

It was to always be like that. He rarely stayed in a room when I entered. At first, I was sure the awkwardness would dissipate. Before I'd left home, the gossips at church had told me that Grady had been my mother's sweetheart before she met my father. So I was curious to meet him, to see if he could explain her to me, tell me what she had been like when she was young and gay, before she'd become this woman I could not understand. But it was perhaps this past connection that made Grady wary of me.

And so, to learn about him, I was forced to watch his wife.

I could not determine what about her made her the reason Grady had never come back to Kings County but instead had chosen a place with fields full of eyes and teeth. Madeline Grady was nothing like my mother. She liked to gossip and she liked to sing loudly, off-tune. She told me once, sighing, that if she had to spend another night at the college listening to lectures about the Negro condition, she would maybe yawn so wide she'd swallow her own nose.

That first night, she watched me as I put my Bible and my anatomy book—the two books I had managed to pack—under the pillow next to the mess of blankets she'd set up for me by the hearth. "Lord," she said, fanning the pages with her thumb, "imagine reading all of this. Sometimes I wonder."

"Oh," I said, understanding what she meant. And then I decided to be brave. "I could teach you," I told her shyly.

She shook her head. "I said 'sometimes,' girl. Not all the time." She laughed. "Grady reads enough for both of us."

I lay on the cooling hearthstones and wondered. Just that night, before we all retired to bed, Grady had read from their family Bible and Mrs. Grady had sat beside him, a child on her knee, patting in time to the cadence of the words. *But she does not wish to read them for herself?* I thought. It was even more strange to me because at the college, though I had yet to meet them, I knew there were women who had scrimped and saved and walked a thousand miles to be able to read a book. There were women Madeline Grady's age who stayed up late each night to learn the alphabet. And here she slept beside a man who not only read books but wrote them. And she'd never rolled over in bed and said, "Teach me."

I stopped myself from thinking further then—it was bad enough that I could hear, in the dark, the whole family shifting and sighing and passing gas in the next room. I did not have to imagine the Gradys' marital bed. But still, it was as if Grady and his wife lived in a kind of willed blindness.

I thought, *I have never seen a more incurious woman.* I thought, *My mother is better than Madeline Grady, at least.* I thought I was better, too.

Grady and his wife had married late, and their children were much younger than I was. They had a girl and two boys still in short pants. Grady, in contrast to his gruff indifference to my presence, doted on the boys and girl. He was always reaching for them—running his hand over the clipped scalps of the boys or suddenly squeezing the fat of the little girl's knees. I had never seen, up close, a family with a father, and whenever Grady made one of his sudden attacks of affection, I felt my cheeks burn and I had to turn my eyes away because they stung, as if a glare from the sun had suddenly caught them. I could not shake the feeling that I was seeing something I was not supposed to see.

Being in Grady and Madeline's house, I remembered the silence of my mother's. All those evenings spent where the only sound was her breath as she sighed over her reading, and sometimes the surprise of a log breaking into fire in the hearth, and here, at the Gradys', there was noise always around and within us. I realized that I had been raised up in something like a shroud, the muffling shroud of my mother's grief—for my father and maybe for life. To be at the Gradys' meant I was faced with life, and sometimes it felt like too much for my ears and my heart.

I would have written to my woman, if I could. But the Gradys' house did not have the long stretches of privacy that living with Mama did. There was no place to hide away and write verses. No ground to lie on and build myself anew. Those first few days, overwhelmed by the thunder of Madeline Grady pouring water into tin tubs, I found a corner of the front room and sat, facing the wall, the shroud of other people's laundry providing a cover. I had my book in my lap, my pen in my hand, when the youngest Grady toddled over and placed her chubby hands on my knees over and over again, until I put the paper aside to play with her.

The little girl tumbled away, satisfied. Through the piles of dirty petticoats, as I sat alone in the corner, I could hear Madeline Grady teaching her children her trade.

"Grady says a boy isn't ready for a proper education till he's seven," she'd told me that first day, "but it's never too early to learn to press."

"You've got to press the memory out of 'em," she told the children, who stood back in a circle, frightened of the heat, as she laid out each shirt and pulled the wrinkles out of the cloth. I heard the thud of the iron, the creak of the cotton, and I closed my eyes. When classes started, I told myself, I would be pressed clean at Cunningham—the wrinkles of my mother's passivity and stunted ideas smoothed out of me.

As Mrs. Grady worked, the room filled with the smell of other people's sweat, and she said, "Lord, it'd wake the dead."

She said this constantly about her work and did not wait to hear a laugh in response, but I provided one, because I wasn't sure what else to do. She teased Grady all the time, and he seemed to enjoy it. But for me . . . should I laugh at each one? Should I stay serious and ignore her? Should I add my own? She had a freedom I had never seen before. The freedom to laugh. Mama would have dismissed her for that. I felt myself doing the same, but then stopped.

The point of an education was to learn to do better, wasn't it?

Dear Libertie,

I trust you are finding the Gradys' home comfortable. I do not know what you mean when you say I do not approve of poetry. I am eager to hear of where you live now.

You did not ask about the hospital. It is doing very well. We are busier than ever, and Lenore has asked me to hire a girl to help her, now that you are gone. We have so many patients I fear we may have to turn some away. I have written to Madame Elizabeth for advice.

Reverend Harland has suggested that we stop serving unmarried women, and that we cannot do, as you know.

Miss Annie put on a wonderful concert last Sunday, all the children singing truly beautifully. I went downtown to hear the most interesting lecture on botany—I have included a clip, describing what was said, from the Eagle. I have also been twice to the theater the past few weeks—a very good Macbeth and then something very silly that a patient told me all the girls go to see. I enjoyed both— even the sillier show, I think. I suspect you would have, as well.

Please write as soon as classes begin.

Your

Mother

My anger had retreated in the face of my confusion at this new place, but now it came back, in such a rush that it made the letter tremble in my hand. I read it and read again—astonished. I read only for her cruelty then, not her longing. Her longing, I thought in a blaze of fury, was irrelevant and probably false.

There was no theater that admitted colored patrons downtown, so she had passed, as easily as that, to see her *Macbeth* and her silly play, in order to be able to talk more directly with her patients. A feat she would not have dared if I had been home and at her side. I crumpled the page up, tore it into smaller and smaller pieces, threw them into the wind as I walked to the Gradys' door.

I cannot not share myself with her, I told myself. My hand trembled again, slightly, at the memory of the strength of her hand holding mine. Write me so I know where you are.

But if she did not want my rage, which part of me did she wish to know the location of?

Dear Mama,

The college has remarkably progressed in the twenty years since its founding. I know you would be very proud of what the race has been able to accomplish here, what Negro men and women have been able to build when we take care of our own.

When the college began, classes were held in an abandoned barn on a stretch of land that the ten founders saved and schemed to buy. Over the years, they have saved to erect, one by one, additional buildings, so that today there is a lecture hall as fine as anything in Brooklyn, complete with old logs set up as columns. Beside each log is a chisel, and the male students, when they have an idle moment, drive the chisels into the wood, to flute the columns and make them truly Ionic. They are already half done.

There is a small chapel, used in shifts on Sundays, since it is the only colored church for many miles. People come from all over, not only the students, to worship there. There is a full brick building set up as the main hall, and another building where some of the students and teachers eat and sleep. It is all arranged around a bald square of dirt that will soon sprout grass and be the campus common. The agriculture students tend to it each day. Past the square and four buildings is the road into town, and then only the fields. At night, the lanterns in the windows of the college are the only light for many miles.

The college is run under the strict belief that silence is a sign of great intellect. Work begins at 5 a.m.—the boarders are expected to wake and wash, and then most of the students are assigned duties to keep the campus running. The young men clear brush, chop wood, construct outbuildings, and grow the small field of wheat and the market plots down near the river. The girls clean the campus, launder, and cook the food for all faculty and students. I am exempt, as a day student. But every day, as I walk from the Gradys' to class, I pass my classmates bent over in the fields.

The oddest thing is that we are expected to even do hard labor in silence. No one is allowed to sing any of the songs we all know to make work go faster. If anyone starts the melody to make work not so weary, he is dismissed from his post and sent to work alone in the woodshed.

It is a very queer custom, one that makes the campus dreary, in my opinion, though everyone else does not seem to think so. When chores are over, the campus erupts into chatter, and people laugh and talk again, as if nothing had happened.

Love

Dear

Libertie,

Silence is a virtue, and it is good that you learn this now. I am so glad to hear the college is thriving and that you are finding a home there.

You did not send back any notes on the botany lecture I sent. I suspect they have perhaps passed this letter in the mail, or maybe you are so deep in study you have forgotten to send. Make sure you do when you have a moment. I am curious of your opinion.

You must also make sure that you are avoiding any strong spices. Does Mrs. Grady cook with onions? It is not healthful for you. Be sure to continue your exercises twice daily—rotate the ankles, flex the wrists—to stay flexible.

You also must send me your list of classes, the names of your professors, and which books they have asked you to read. I am enclosing three articles from the latest Journal of Homeopathy, and I ask that

you write back your analysis of the arguments and your rebuttal, if
any, and send to me as soon as you are able.
    Your
    Mother

I would send her nothing. I had nothing to give her except petty
rebellions like this.

The other girl students were all assigned to the courses for teaching.
They were taking the ladies' course of study, which was concerned with
how to best direct a class. I was the only woman in the men's course,
the only girl taking biology and chemistry and rhetoric.

In lecture, I sat at the front, a bit to the side, at a separate desk. The
men all sat on rows of benches. I could not pay attention to lectures
and take my notes and see them at the same time, but I was aware of
them there, behind me. When I'd first walked into the lecture room,
I had wrinkled my nose—I had not smelled anything like that before.
Not a bad smell, just the heavy murk of young men that was caught
up in that hall. It was so overpowering I was not sure if I could even
differentiate one man from the other. They were just a cloud of scent,
pressing at my back as I tried to sketch the shape of a fibula. I smelled
it everywhere on campus, and it made me long for the company of
women even more.

The boys were polite enough—they waved to me at the end of class
sometimes. But that was not enough company for me, and I was lonely.
I would have tried to befriend the girls as we sat in the dining hall. In
that room, though, we spoke only in whispers.

I learned there was a kind of hierarchy. There were some girls who
had stolen themselves away before the war. They were a kind of aristoc-
racy, and they tended to stick together. At meals, they bent their heads

and spoke without even looking at one another—they had perfected a way to speak even below whispers, even beyond glances. Sometimes, in their silent language, one of them would communicate something to make another laugh, and it was in those moments that I felt it keenest that they were better than me. Not a single one of them would ever, I guessed, be as wasteful with their time here as I was, sitting at the front of a classroom of men and wondering what they thought of me. Those girls knew something about the world that I did not know, could never know.

Then there were the freeborn girls like me, from places like Philadelphia and Manhattan and Washington, DC. I should have naturally made friends with them. I heard them tell their histories to one another—their mothers were all, they claimed, "at home"; their fathers were clerks or tobacconists or preachers. No one would claim a mother or father who was a servant. It was strange since we all knew that each of us must have scrimped and saved to sit at that table. My own mother, in the weeks before I left, set the clinic's books in front of me and showed me the column she had added for her calculations: *Libertie's Education.* But not one girl would admit this fact. Something stopped me from telling them my mother was a doctor. I was not sure how they would respond—eagerness and solicitation seemed somehow worse than scorn. I did not want to still, hundreds of miles away, be relying on Mama for my position. So I chose to keep my distance from them until I could understand any of this better.

But the truth soon came out, and I began to catch them watching me. I only smiled at them and bowed my head and hurried on. My boldness had burnt away, and the strangeness of the place had engulfed me.

"You know, every last one of them up there at that college are color-struck," Madeline Grady said to me finally, after many nights at home beside her and her children.

"You've never heard of love of copper?" she said. "They'll love us black ones if we make a lot of noise, but when we keep to ourselves, like you do, they don't know what to do. But don't worry. They're young. You're a pretty enough girl. One of the boys up there will peel away for you, like my Grady did for me, and leave those yellow girls behind. You just have to let him take his time."

And that was another kind of humiliation. That she thought my solitude was a symptom of wanting love.

So that was it. The perimeter of this world, the one I had tried to escape to, was color. I recalled, with bitterness, that Mrs. Grady did not know how to read, but she sure knew how to count. In this world, the lighter girls were unsure what to make of me—by birth, I should have been their peer. But I was not, somehow, and I was studying to become something closer to a man, not what they understood as ambition.

I spent a lot of time in the outbuilding that had been newly designated as a library, books piled all around me, not reading a word. Instead, I read the books' frontpieces. Many had been donated by churches from across the East. There was an entire lot from one congregation in Philadelphia; another from a congregation in Albany, a stack that had the x's and handprints of a flock in Virginia. I would trace all the names of all these people who believed that I could be part of a bright shining future, but I couldn't bear to turn the page and begin to read.

It had been very easy to denounce Mama to her face and call her a traitor in my heart. I'd thought it was painful, but it was the easiest thing in the world compared with sitting here, feeling the weight of my mother's expectations and the world's indifference to my failure and my self. Mrs. Grady had taken to calling to me, as I left for class, "Go on, Black Gal, make me proud," and though I smiled at her each time she said it, knew she meant it with love, I could only hear a lie in her voice.

My rage at the world returned whenever I sat in that library. I knew what a stronger girl would do—sip her wrath like corn liquor, have it drench her ambition, sweat the rage out her pores as she worked harder and better, be smarter. But instead I suckled my anger like Lenore did the abandoned offspring of the barn cats, and it was about as effective as one of those little animals, doing nothing but mewling and flipping over in distress.

I knew I was not strong enough to touch a hundred white abdomens while feeling their contempt, while Mama stood beside me saying nothing. I did not think I was strong enough to pretend, even ten years on now, that the sons and husbands and fathers of the white women who sat behind our clinic's velvet curtain hadn't marked our houses with red chalk for destruction. And I knew, like the ache of a broken bone that hadn't been set right, that I was not strong enough to be faced with another Mr. Ben, and to fail him, and to have to live with that failure for the rest of my days.

I was not strong enough for this world, is what I meant, and it was a low-down, worming thing to discover about yourself when all around you, men and women who had been beaten, scorned, burnt, drowned, still found a way to come to this silence and sit within it and answer questions about what a lung was good for.

I began to think there must be something wrong with me: that I was slow or stupid, or merely ungrateful. Most of all, I felt a deep, burning shame in the center of my chest, that I could not work my rage better. When Mama was my same age, she had already finished her studies and was submitting herself to examination after examination, to try to enter medical school. She was working, in the evenings, with the local pharmacist, to learn how pills were made, and she was conducting her own experiments, and writing to friends to send the latest medical books to her to study.

But here I was, with an entire library open to me at midday, and I couldn't read a word.

I was only dull, hidden Libertie.

Dear Libertie,

You must make sure to ask that the latest anatomy books be found for you. The following is a comprehensive list of authors to trust:

Dear Mama,
The college's library is tolerable. The books have been donated by many kind churches. I've read the frontpieces of each and seen books from

Drs. Henshaw, Borley, Crawley and Madison and Fredricks (the older)

Ohio, Delaware, Virginia (of course), Connecticut, and even Maine.

For your review, I present you the following case: A girl came with Adipsia.

I must say that I miss you, and even Lenore (tell her she's a busybody), and if I

She had neither appetite nor thirst, and the thought of food was disgusting.

could but see you & stand beside you two & hear your voices,

So, in your professional opinion (ha), my good girl, what would you give

I would perhaps not be so lonely here, with you, but that's a silly thing

as remedy?

to wish, I know.

This impotent anger was another kind of grave. I thought I would be buried in it on campus, until one day when Madeline Grady chased me out of her house and told me to stay at the college for the evening "with the youth your own age." So one evening, when the dark came sooner, I did not hurry home to the Gradys' but wandered around campus until a few girls told me to follow them. And that is when I heard it. It was the queerest thing to hear the sound of a piano at night, outside, but I could hear it—the deep tones of the notes and then after it, the whisper of the hammer hitting the strings, because it was an older piano and someone was tuning it.

Music at night, music after dark, music finding its way to you across sweetgrass, can feel almost like magic.

A bunch of students, men and women, had gathered in one of the music classrooms, where a slanting upright piano had been pushed against a wall. Standing at it were two women, pushing the keys. It was a student-run affair—the room was decorated with holly and ivy, and there was hot cider, donated by one of the farms, and roasted apples and sugared biscuits. It was so hot that the windows were open to the cold night air, and from where I stood, pressed against one of them, my back stung with cold and the full front of me steamed with discomfort.

The first to perform was a sleek and chubby boy who had memorized his own dreary poetry—rhyming couplets intended to celebrate the beauty of the seasons but that thumped along forever. Then there was a girl who read a monologue, in the voice of Theda—a scandalous thing. And finally, for wholesomeness' sake, the Graces.

And then the two women who had been at the piano stood. Louisa Habit and Experience Northmoor. Louisa sang alto and Experience sang soprano. The two of them singing together, that first night I went out, made a kind of joyful noise—sweeter than what it sounded like when the LIS sang together at home or when the choir sang on Sunday. I watched them as they sang—I could see, under the cloth of their bodices, where their lungs expanded for more air, where they were holding in their stomachs to force out the lighter sound. To watch Experience and Louisa sing was the same as seeing a fast, small boy run or a man swing an ax and break up a tree. It was the same singularity of form and muscle, the same pushing of a body toward a single point on the horizon. I wanted, right then and there, to be as close to them as I possibly could.

Experience was tall and thin, with sharp elbows, and skin like a bruised peach. When she stood up to sing, she slumped her shoulders, as if she was afraid of her own height. Louisa, in contrast, was short, and as dark as me, and fat, with a flare of a burn scar down her forehead, which draped dramatically over her left eye. Whoever had tended to it when she'd gotten it had done well—It was nearly perfectly healed, only a dark flush color and, of course, raised above the rest of her smooth skin. She made up for it with pretty, round cheeks that flushed with red undertones whenever she took in breath to sing more loudly, and when she opened her mouth, I could see she had perfect pearls for teeth.

Mama had taught me long ago—the first tell of good health is the mouth. *Louisa has probably never had a toothache*, I thought, longingly. Experience, on the other hand, most definitely had. When she wasn't singing, she kept her fist curled at the bottom of her chin, at the ready to cover her mouth whenever she was called upon to speak, because her bottom teeth were rotten.

I imagined a whole life for them there, while I watched. I thought they would never be what Madeline Grady said everyone at the college was: colorstruck. They moved together as they sang, and I thought they had found an escape from this world. I thought if I got as close as possible, I could maybe escape, too.

When the evening was over, I stood beside them.

"You are wonderful," I said to Experience. Her eyes widened, and her shoulders shot back. I had startled her. I regretted it immediately.

"Well, thank you," she said.

"You and Louisa, you are both really marvelous."

"Mm-hmm," she said uneasily. She was looking through the crowd, for her companion.

"Are you first-years here? I haven't seen you yet."

"This is our second year here. We are close to graduation. We are the only two women in the music department," Experience said. "We wish, I wish, to be music teachers." She had spotted Louisa, and made to move toward her. I followed, determined to keep speaking.

"If you wish to practice teaching," I said, "then I would make an excellent practice pupil."

"Who's this?" Experience had reached Louisa, with me trailing behind, and now they both were looking at me, Louisa expectant, Experience as if she wanted to flee.

"Libertie Sampson," I said. I held out my hand for a strong hand-shake—a gesture my mother had taught, which the proctors here, at least, discouraged.

Louisa took it, and I started to speak again.

"I was saying to Miss Experience—"

Louisa snorted at that.

"Experience," I corrected myself, uncertain, "that if you needed to practice teaching a pupil, I am happy to do that with you."

"Do you sing, then?"

"A little. In church, of course."

"Well, come to where we practice. Near the market plots, by the river. It's easier there," Louisa said. And then she carefully pulled her hand out of mine and linked arms with Experience.

It was easy enough to convince them to let me listen to them practice. It was harder to learn their histories. Louisa was the more personable of the two. She was witty and liked to flirt with the boys, and even the lightest ones flirted back with her, because of the mark and her height and her chins. It was clear, everyone knew, that this was only in fun. She could imitate any animal sound with a whistle or a fold of her tongue—the call of a loon, the cluck of a turkey, the growl of a cat in the bush. She would use this menagerie to give a running commentary on the affairs of everyone at college. The handsomest boy, she referred to with the lurch of a katydid, and the prettiest, stubbornest girl, with a billy goat's whinny. Everybody liked Louisa.

Experience was harder to know—she seemed to walk about in a kind of mist, the only thing dispelling it the sound of an instrument or Louisa's voice. She was terribly serious about music. She could play any instrument you put in front of her. Her most prized possession was a small, battered metal pitch pipe. When I and the other students would gather to sing with her, she liked to mournfully blow it to call us to attention.

She would sit in the bare square of the future green, her skirts spread out before her, working on her scores, making notations, following the scrip of music.

I learned that Louisa and Experience were not from the same place.

Louisa was from Virginia, and Experience was from South Carolina. That's all they would tell me when I accosted them, giddy with the sound of their breath, after the first practice. The way they said it, quietly, with no more elaboration, I understood that they had been born enslaved, and that they were not prepared to tell me who or what they'd fought with to end up here, singing beauty in a cabin in the fields.

> *Willkommen,*
>> *lieber*
>>> *schöner Mai,*
>>> *Dir tönt der Vögel*
>>> *Lobgesang*

was what they sang in a round that first afternoon by the river.

And then, when they combined their voices, it was another thing altogether. I believed that to attempt to sing with them in harmony would be like pouring bacon grease into a vat of water.

But Louisa said, "I cannot trust you if you do not sing. Why are you around the two of us? Just to listen?"

"I'm not very good," I said.

Experience shrugged impatiently. "That's not possible."

"Not as good as you," I said.

Louisa sighed. "False modesty wins you no friends, you know."

So I took a breath in. And I did it.

When I sang with Experience and Louisa, it was as if my very self merged with them. I was, I learned, a mezzo-soprano, and they each took pains to teach me how to make my voice stronger.

"You draw in air here," Louisa said, pointing.

When I sang with them, my whole history fell away. There was no past, no promised future, only the present of one sustained note.

When we sang together, we three stood in a round so that we could see one another's faces—and it was almost unbearable, to sing a song and watch Louisa's face change slightly and Experience's voice respond, and then my own, struggling for just a minute to reach theirs.

When I sang with them, I entered something greater than my sorry, bitter self.

I thought that anyone with a voice as powerful as that could teach me how to bend my anger to my will. I sat on that riverbank, and I thought that I had finally found my ambition. It was not to set bones right or to become my mother's double. It was to befriend the both of them, to make them love me and sing to me for the rest of my life. I knew this was a silly wish, but in my discombobulation at Cunningham College, I did not stop to question it. I knew enough to keep it quiet, to not speak it outright—not to Experience or Louisa, whom I did not wish to scare away, and not to Mrs. Grady, and certainly not to Mama. I spent the rest of the semester doing the bare minimum of work so I would not fail out of class and so I could keep meeting the two girls and have them sing to me.

Mama had told me freedom would come by following her, and I had known it was not true for a long time. Now I had someone else to follow, I was sure, and the thrill of having a new direction filled me up, blushed my cheeks, almost made me like the place. I put away my sticky journal to my imagined woman in the water and delighted in these real women, in front of me, made flesh.

"I wish my mama could hear you," I said one afternoon. "I wish she could hear how fine you are."

"I bet you wish your mama could do it," Experience said, and though she was smiling slightly when she said it, I felt the sting in her words and I saw the bitterness in her eyes. I turned away, ashamed. I had said something wrong again.

Louisa took my arm in hers and walked with me a little farther down the riverbank. "You sure do talk about your mama a lot," she said.

"Do I?"

"Yes."

I looked down at my shoes. "I'm sorry," I said.

"It's not something you should mind," Louisa said. "It is hard for Experience because she lost hers. She doesn't know where she is."

"Oh."

My rage burnt for an affront that was far less than hers. And here were the two of them not even hot, not even warm, just righteously cool in their voices. I had hoped that there would be a place where I found other burning bushes like me, willing to make the world anew with riotous anger. The fact that they had none unnerved me.

"But you do talk about your mother a lot, you do know?" Louisa gently chided. "It is always what your mama would think or what she would say or what she would like to say. Sometimes, I think your mama's here with us on this riverbank."

I walked on, in silence, ashamed again, until we heard a loud, rude croak from a frog ahead of us, more like a belch.

"See," Louisa said. "There she go," and I swatted her arm in laughter.

Dear Mama,
I have met the two most extraordinary girls, whose voices

　　Dear Libertie,
　　Today we had an interesting case: a young Hebrew serving girl

I believe can lead us to a kind of promised land. I know that sounds like a

with inflammation of the uvula and palate and an inclination to swallow

  *fancy and like a dream, but that's what their singing is like to
  me. Together,*

during the night.

they could be the greatest singers our world has yet heard.

What would you prescribe, Libertie?

Dear Mama,

  *Do you remember, Mama, when there was the bad fever a few
years ago? And the churches took to pealing bells to count the dead?
Two tolls for a man, three tolls for a woman, one for a child. And
how at night you would hear each ring of the bell, and wait, wait,
wait for the next ring—whose life were you hearing called out?
Whose life was coming to you through the dark? The Graces' singing
is like that. Except you're waiting to hear about life beginning, not
ending. And it is marvelous.*

  PS. I would prescribe, I think, Cimicifuga.

Dear Libertie,

  *I remember that, of course, Libertie, but I'm not sure what you
mean by the rest. I am glad you are finding amusement there, but
please do not forget your purpose.*

  *Yesterday, a woman came to me with a toothache, caused by the
damp night air. What would you prescribe?*

Mama—

Nux m., cepa, rhus. Wind: aeon., puis., rhus, sil. Draught: bell.,
calc, chin., sulph.

Libertie

I would go to the barrels of water Madeline Grady kept in her yard and take off the cover and try to catch my reflection in the black-silver surface there. She once found me like this, and I said, by way of explanation, "I am not a good daughter."

"Well, that's just pure nonsense if I ever heard it."

"I don't think I can be what she wishes me to be," I said. "I feel too much, and she's never felt like this at all."

Madeline Grady fixed me with a hard stare. "I've never met a girl as hard-pressed on making life difficult for herself as you, Libertie," she said. "Usually, it's men get caught in that current. I always thought women had more sense. But I suppose you live long enough, you see everything." And she sucked her teeth and looked for her wooden ladle, and I hated her, a little bit, for seeing me so well.

I'd rather have had my mother and her obliviousness. There is a greater comfort in being unseen than being understood and dismissed.

Sometimes, I thought Madeline Grady was wiser than any of us, but Experience and Louisa were not admirers of her. When they found out where I lived, they exchanged a look that I eagerly asked them to explain.

"What? What is it?"

"Well," Louisa said, "Mr. Grady is a sad man."

"Why? What's the matter with him?" I said, alarmed.

"He is very brilliant," Experience said hesitantly.

"Yes, very learned," Louisa said.

"And why should that cause you to feel sorry for him?" I said.

They looked at each other, and then they gave me the same pitying look.

"Well, you have seen his wife?"

"Yes, you have seen his wife?"

"Yes," I said slowly. I did not want to hear all the unkind things I'd thought of Madeline Grady said aloud by these two girls.

But they were subtler than me. "It's a study of what can happen when you do not let pure romantic love lead you," Experience said.

"When lust takes over," Louisa said theatrically.

Then they both laughed. I smiled, as well. I wished, perhaps, they were joking.

"Madeline Grady was a laundress when they met," Experience said.

"Well, that's respectable."

"Yes, but she was not just a laundress. She sold beer and spirits from her home."

"That's how her first husband died," Louisa said. "The father of her two boys. He mistook a barrel of lime for beer one night and drank a whole draught before he realized, and then he died in agony."

"I didn't know," I said.

"And then, she went to see Grady, to help her claim her husband's pension, and in a matter of course, the two have their little girl, and are married right before she was delivered."

"And Grady, the best colored legal mind of his generation is interrupted before he even gets a chance to leave here."

"She has thrift and grift to support him," Louisa said. "She's got the constitution for it."

"Yes," Experience said. "Those shoulders." And they both glanced at my own, as if judging how broad they were, to see if they were as broad as Madeline Grady's.

"But it really is a study in what can go wrong when a brilliant colored man makes the wrong choice for a wife," Louisa said.

In the women's dining room at Cunningham College, there was a big panel of fabric, with green velvet leaves bordering a list stitched out in red thread, three meters high.

MAN IS STRONG—WOMAN, BEAUTIFUL

MAN IS DARING AND CONFIDENT—WOMAN, DEFERENT AND UNASSUMING

MAN IS GREAT IN ACTION—WOMAN, IN SUFFERING

MAN SHINES ABROAD—WOMAN, AT HOME

MAN TALKS TO CONVINCE—WOMAN, TO PERSUADE AND PLEASE

MAN HAS A RUGGED HEART—WOMAN, A SOFT AND TENDER ONE

MAN PREVENTS MISERY—WOMAN, RELIEVES IT

MAN HAS SCIENCE—WOMAN, TASTE

MAN HAS JUDGMENT—WOMAN, SENSIBILITY

MAN IS A BEING OF JUSTICE—WOMAN, AN ANGEL OF MERCY

The first time I read it, I thought, *Then what is a man?* I thought of my mother, of course, and myself. I tried to parcel out where she lay on the fabric, but she was somewhere in between. Men then, for me, were still too terrifying to contemplate directly. They were an abstract. The only man I had seen up close was Mr. Ben, and he was not described by any of the words on that quilt. The left side of the quilt may as well have been stitched in gold thread; that was how fanciful a man's character was to me. And I had never known anyone who would claim Mama had taste and not science, who would call her deferent and unassuming.

I regarded that quilt as a kind of private joke, something no one who had eyes could believe. I saw its falseness again when I came home to find Mrs. Grady sitting, skirt spread out in front of her, on the kitchen floor.

"It's the last of it," she said, turning out the flour sack. "The school is behind on paying for the laundry, and we'll be short by next week."

I flushed. "Mama sent you my share, didn't she?"

Mrs. Grady nodded. "It's already spent, girl."

"But why don't you tell Mr. Grady? I'm sure he will give you more for the household accounts."

And at this, Mrs. Grady laughed for a long time, rolling the sack into a tighter and tighter ball as she did so.

"It's me give him his money. Do you think we'd be eating our dinner under other women's drawers if Grady had anything for a 'household account'?" And then she laughed again.

But that night, at dinner, she said nothing, and when Grady looked up from his plate and asked if there was any more tea for that evening, Mrs. Grady just smiled and said she had forgotten it. And then a cloud passed over his face, a recognition, and Grady stood up and went to his study.

The Gradys may have followed the rules of that quilt, but only by a kind of willed fiction between the two of them.

Mama and Madeline Grady and Lenore insisted that men were to be babied and entertained, but not obeyed. The Graces seemed to revere obedience, at least in the abstract. Louisa and Experience, these girls I loved, who I thought held providence on their tongues, were so sure of themselves. I began to doubt myself. Perhaps the rules Mama and Lenore and Madeline Grady lived by were wrong. Or not wrong, but they seemed only to apply in the velvet waiting room and white-washed examination room of Mama's practice or in the humid air of Mrs. Grady's laundry. And how good was a rule, how strong, how sensible was it to obey, if it lost all meaning as soon as you left your front door?

I wondered who Experience and Louisa would pick if they could pick their mate, since it was so important. Both were ignored by the men of Cunningham College, though they did not seem bothered by this.

"The other ones here, they call us the Graces because they think they're clever," Louisa told me. "Look at Experience. She's bright, but gawky."

I tried very hard not to look at Experience. "No, she is not," I said.

Louisa laughed. "Yes, she is. Not naming it isn't gonna change it."

"I'm gawky," Experience said, and that set Louisa to laughing.

"And I'm like you, Libertie," Louisa said. "Pretty but dark. And fat. And this scar. Altogether helpless. They called us the Graces, and maybe it's meant to be an insult or a tease or a joke, but I think it's a love note."

"It makes it easier to sing for them," Experience said, "when you think of it that way."

"My mama made it a point to never comment on another woman's beauty, or lack thereof," I said, and this made them both laugh, though I wasn't sure why.

It was the same way when they sang. They looked each other in the eye, and it seemed like they always kept their gaze like that. Nothing broke it. It was deeper than whatever was stitched across that musty quilt in the dining room. It was the same connection that exists between a flower and a bee, between a river and its bank, between a muscle and a bone.

And it was because of that I thought perhaps they were right and Mama and Mrs. Grady were wrong, and something turned over again inside me, some resolve that pushed me away from Mama a little bit more.

I DID NOT go home for winter term, so my grades were given to me directly to mail to my mother, which I did not do. I was close to failing—not quite, but close, and I took the letter with this message and pressed it into my old anatomy book and put it at the bottom of my trunk, resolved to think about it when I could get the sound of the Graces out of my head.

Over the Christmas break, the snow was so high we did not have mail for many weeks, so that when my mother's letters came, there were five of them to read in a row, and each one, every single one, was filled with the addition of a new name: Emmanuel.

He is a student of homeopathy, recently graduated from a medical school in Philadelphia. He is eager to study under anyone, including, he says, myself, "though you are a woman" (ha).

It was only one pair of parentheses, but Mama may as well have written me in dried berry juice. What did this "ha" mean, from a woman who I knew would bristle at a dismissal like that? A woman who had never been fond of parentheses.

Madame Elizabeth has sent him to me—he is lately of the city of Jacmel, Haiti, before he came to America to study medicine. He

was not able to find a doctor who suited his interests in that city.
So Madame Elizabeth and the church who sponsored him have
sent him here, and he has been a welcome addition to the practice.

He sleeps in your bedroom—he has found it most comfortable.
He has also suggested a new way to organize the garden—we will
try it come this spring.

He recently saw one of our most persistent cases, Mrs. Cookstone,
the judge's wife, who lives on Pineapple Street. She was resistant
that a colored man should treat her, but Emmanuel is able to get
by. He is a high yellow homme de couleur (as Emmanuel is known
back home in Haiti, he tells us). She relented once she saw him.
She agreed that he should consult with her from behind a sheet.
Lenore conducted the actual physical exam, and Emmanuel asked
questions.

As you remember, Mrs. Cookstone is a bit of a nervous case, but
she has written already to tell me that under Emmanuel's care, she
already is quite recovered from the pain in her chest and is even able
to walk in her garden now, for a few hundred paces without needing
to sit down and rest.

And here, the letter continued, enumerating all the ways this
Emmanuel was a wonder.

Emmanuel has brought with him an album . . . He is collecting all
of the plants and wildlife of Haiti, and we spend evenings compar-
ing the plant life of his homeland to that of Kings County.

Emmanuel has created a tea that sweetens the breath, which
we are now able to offer our wealthier patients. Sales have boosted
clinic revenues by 2 percent alone this month.

Emmanuel is an especial favorite of our child patients and has a light touch with even the most fearful ones.

I counted each time she wrote that name. I knew enough that it was ridiculous to be jealous of a name on paper, but I could not help it, though I dared not mention it to Madeline Grady—or Experience and Louisa.

Mrs. Cookstone is now complaining of a pain in her calf muscle, which she says she also feels in her left shoulder. Emmanuel has already prescribed something that has done wonders, but I'm wondering if you can guess what it was.

This was even worse, to be set against a rival I could not even see, in a race I was no longer particularly interested in but, because of pride, I could not abandon. She wrote of Emmanuel with the voice of a proud mother. She praised him in a way she had never praised me—except for that one time, so long ago, when Mr. Ben first came to us and she had stroked my cheek and said, "Libertie is beautiful."

But she had never called me clever, or smart, or good with patients, or even particularly hardworking.

Now when she sent me problems to solve, she would write, *Emmanuel has already found the answer, but I wonder if you can.*

She did not send me cutouts from journals anymore, because *Emmanuel has asked to study them and add to his own collection.* She would send them to me when he was done.

Can you feel brotherly jealousy for a man you have never met? A figment of your imagination, a ghost of your mother's convictions? I did. I could not even store her letters in my chest, beside my list of grades—I felt that somehow the letters would whisper to one another, and my mother would instinctively know, back home in Brooklyn, how close I was to failing.

I SPENT THAT spring more in the music room than the library again, until, as the days began to lengthen, Louisa and Experience fell into a bitter disagreement.

A dean had suggested to the two of them that perhaps they should sing spirituals, that they should add these songs to their repertoire and then make a show of performing them.

Louisa and Experience had already brought in a little money for the fundraising efforts of the school with their singing. The songs they sang were German and Italian pieces—they prided themselves on this. They did not sing hymns, and they did not sing the songs we knew from church, or those our parents and grandparents and lost ones sang to keep from crying. The songs we'd all once sung in the fields. The songs that our parents sang at night or with one another, that we still sang now, even in freedom. No, in public, Louisa and Experience only sang in a foreign tongue, about springtime and love and offering apples to your beloved. But the college suggested they could raise more money if they sang the slave songs.

"There's that college out in Tennessee that's done it," Louisa said, worrying the cloth of her skirt. "And they've sung to the Queen of England."

Indeed, we'd heard of those singers and even tried to see them when it was reported that they were playing in Cincinnati. We'd even started out to make the long journey to hear them, but we'd turned around after half a day when the stationmaster told us it was not the real Jubilee Singers but a fraudulent group—four men and a girl who couldn't harmonize and made a mockery of not knowing the words.

"The group from Tennessee sang pain for the Queen," Experience said, in that strange hollow way she had, and this stopped both me and Louisa from speaking further as we tried to understand what she meant.

"They say the Queen gave them an ovation," Louisa countered. "She invited them to her palace, and they dined with lords and ladies." Even when she was impassioned, Louisa made everything she was saying sound like a joke, so I laughed at this.

But Experience shook her head. "I won't sing my sorrow for anyone," she said.

And then she blew her pitch pipe, to bring Louisa back to the music.

"She's stubborn, is all," Louisa explained to me, later. "She's thinking of herself and not of what can be done with what we have."

She took my arm in hers. We were crossing the square of dirt. The college president spoke to us all the time of the grass to go there— bright and healthy and cut short and orderly. Every Sunday sermon ended with his invocation of this future time, when the college and the men and women there would be so prosperous, so abundant, they would have a whole mess of earth that grew grass solely for strolling in, which no animal would eat from.

In the meantime, a few of the women students had sprinkled sunflower seeds around the grounds the previous summer, and now, in the spring, we could see the battered stalks poking up still here and there through the muddy snow.

"She's not thinking of all that singing could do for us," Louisa said, kicking at the flower roots.

"That's what you would do if the Queen said she'd give you a stack of coins to sing your pain?"

I was teasing, but Louisa stopped and looked at me gravely—one of the few times I ever saw her stop joking.

"Before I came here, I slept in the corncrib and I saw my mother and brothers sold. I sang for each one when they left me, but that's my own song, and I wouldn't sing it for a queen of anything. But this is the only home I have had or will ever have on this Earth. You can't just throw away a home. You do whatever you can to keep it." And then she took my arm again and walked me the rest of the road to the Gradys'.

There was a coldness between Louisa and Experience after that, and I saw them once, from afar, Experience loping a few feet in front of Louisa across the field, Louisa trotting to keep up. They sang together, but had stopped speaking, and it was awful to feel the silence returning, the silence coming back in, and I tried to think of something to make it stop.

I was not sure how to convince Experience. I knew my own mother didn't sing those songs. Her father did not pass them on to her. I only learned them from the women at the LIS, who sang them before, during, and after each meeting, who sang them to keep time as we did some tedious task, like piecing together the stitching in a quilt or rolling bandages. Sometimes, I sang the songs to myself with the words changed, to help me remember all the parts of a body—the names of bones and muscles and organs. I took a certain satisfaction in fitting those phrases into the loop of songs, the songs of work, the songs that made an art out of burden. But to say that to either Louisa or Experience, I knew, was a kind of insult.

It was a few weeks later when the women's dean, Alma Curtis, asked to meet with me. She tapped on my shoulder as I sat and ate in the whispered companionability of the dining hall.

"Stay behind, Miss Sampson, if you will."

Alma Curtis was a broad-shouldered woman of forty-five or fifty—back then, I thought of her as old. She was the only married woman who taught at the college. Just the year before, before I had come, she had married the college president, Thomas Curtis. After they had said their vows in the campus chapel and pressed their hands in front of the minister, Alma Curtis had dropped to one knee and bent her head, and requested, in front of the entire college, her husband's permission to continue her career. And President Curtis had raised her up, cupped his hands underneath her elbows, standing her steady, and said, "Of course."

Louisa and Experience had repeated this story often—it was always whispered when Alma Curtis walked by.

I had asked, "But how long did he wait to say yes?"

Louisa had blinked. "What do you mean?"

"Did he agree right away? Or did he make her wait?" I thought of a long silence in the hall, Alma Curtis holding her breath while her husband decided her fate, the flowers on the wedding bower shivering around them. And then I laughed. "It sure was clever of her, to ask for permission in front of a crowd like that."

I had meant it in an admiring way. I had thought, *What a slick woman!* in the same way that, back home, Lenore applauded the barn cats when one of them swiped the biggest fish head.

But Louisa had looked at me coolly. "What a cynic you are," she had said. "I happen to find it romantic."

So I had learned another rule I had gotten wrong, and every time I looked at Alma Curtis, I tried to imagine her as an agent of romance— invisible cherubs and steadfast ivy curling around her everywhere she went. Which was difficult to think of, because Alma Curtis's broad, jaundiced, straightforward face seemed to discourage anything like that.

I thought of this as I sat at the table, watching the other girls work together to clear the plates and food. When the room was nearly empty, when it had gone from quiet to silent, Alma Curtis sat on the bench across from me.

"We must discuss your performance, Libertie," she said with unbearable kindness. "The other deans, they were hesitant to take on a young lady in the men's course. They were not sure if she would be able to keep up. But your mother assured us, we were all assured, that you were capable. I personally intervened with President Curtis and asked that you be placed in the men's course. And your work, when you turn it in, is passable. So, then, what is distracting you?"

I could not exactly answer. I could only swallow and say, "I am unsure. If you would give me more time. Perhaps it is being so far from home."

She said, "You spend an awful lot of time in the music room."

We let this sit between us for a moment.

"Yes. Yes. You see . . ." I licked my lips, readying for the lie. "You see, I've come to a sort of conclusion."

Alma Curtis looked at me skeptically.

"The Graces—that is, Louisa and Experience—they mentioned that President Curtis wished for them to found a chorale. In the mode of the Jubilee Singers in Tennessee."

"Yes," she said. "I am aware."

"And Miss Experience," I said. I figured the formal address would help my cause. "Miss Experience was uncertain about performing the slave songs for a different audience. For our white friends."

Alma Curtis looked unconvinced.

"She says she would feel distressed," I said, "to sing the slave songs in front of them."

Alma Curtis sighed again and under her breath said, "These young people."

"So . . ." I wet my lip. "So I have been formulating an idea. A compromise of sorts. That they could perform in Brooklyn, for the colored people there. I know that the women's groups are planning many celebrations for the summer. We could raise some good money. I could organize it. My mother has friends in Philadelphia and Boston who would gladly support. It would be a kind of jubilee."

Alma Curtis blew out a breath.

"If anything," I said, "it would help convince them that performing is possible. And then, perhaps, they would not be so shy of mixed company."

The dean sat back for a moment. "This is what's been distracting you?"

"I very much love this college," I said, "and wish to aid in any way that I can."

Alma Curtis shook her head. "You may love it," she said, "but I have come to tell you that you cannot return next year. We do not have a place for you."

I searched her face to see if she might regret it, if she might leave me an opening to argue. But there was nothing, not even pity, not even sympathy. Just resolve.

She patted my hand, and then she stood up, shook out her skirts, and walked away.

"FOR COLORED PEOPLE," I said to Louisa and Experience later that day. "The women's club my mother founded will organize a benefit, and you two will be the stars. Louisa, we can raise the money for your home. And, Experience, you will not have to sing your pain for anyone else but people who already know it."

"If these colored ladies are so rich," Experience said, "why can they not just give the money to the college? Why do we have to sing for them?"

Louisa snorted. "Can't get nothing without giving nothing. Anyone knows that."

"They'll raise more if it's a celebration," I said. "A talented duet all the way from Ohio? If it is new people in town, we can get our friends from Jersey and from outside the city to come. It will be a whole celebration. You'll see."

I talked so much and promised so much that I found, by the end of the night, that I had made myself out to be some sort of impresario and not a failure. I spoke and felt my mouth form these lies, my tongue wet with them. I could hear the desperation in my voice. I was certain they would doubt me.

But Louisa was smiling again, and Experience had allowed Louisa to hold her hand, and so it seemed they believed me, after all.

There was no time to feel shame. There was only the beat of blood in my ears as I spoke faster and faster.

At the Gradys' that night, when Madeline Grady had pulled herself and her children and her husband into their bed a few feet from me, I lay on the stones that had been my resting place for nearly a year and pulled a stranger's cotton stocking up to my mouth and screamed the song I had been trying to sing, falsely, all these months. The song of my anger and my sadness, the song that I knew I could never sing in front of the Graces—I did not want them to disown me. I sang it for myself only: a thin, high thing, ugly and satisfying. I sang till my throat was raw and dry, and white flashed before my eyes, till I was panting. And then I lay back on my stones and told myself I felt lighter.

Dear Libertie,

You have only written me of music and nothing of your studies. Miss Annie tells me that you are planning, with the ladies of the old LIS, a concert in the summer—I would wish to know about it. I hope you will tell me of it when you come to stay.

Emmanuel is eager to hear of it, as well. I fear he grows bored here, out in the country, as it is. But he does not wish to go downtown and he rarely travels to Manhattan.

I am most excited for you two to meet. I think you will find him an excellent brother in study. He is so levelheaded, so calm, so persevering, that it is impossible not to wish to work as he does.

It is strange to have someone in the house who is not you, who is not my daughter.

I am eager to welcome you here, to your home, to where you belong, before you leave me again for your studies.

I hope this is not a sign that my Libertie is leaving me behind.

Your

Mother

Di m' sa ou renmen, epi m'ava di ou ki moun ou ye

Tell me what you love and I will tell you who you are

I had not counted on the Graces' fear of death. By the time we reached Philadelphia on our journey back east, we had slept in the barns and sheds and church pews of smaller towns, and I'd thought they would be happy for real beds in the city, which Madame Elizabeth had promised we would find in her home.

Louisa saw the coffins first, and she reached for Experience's hand. I think Experience would have spit at me if she could have.

Madame Elizabeth stood in the center of her shop and watched them. "I did not take you girls for being superstitious. I know you are good Christians and you know the only haint is the Holy Spirit."

She had three coffins stacked alongside the shop's dusty brick wall—a large one, for men, a slightly smaller one, for women, and then the smallest one, for children, stacked at the very top. The room was divided between coffins and dresses—on the left, the stacked coffins, on the right, a headless, armless torso in a long muslin skirt, horsehair blooming out of its stitched shoulders, and a table scattered with bolts of cloth.

Madame Elizabeth had us sit at the hearth that straddled both sides, to recover.

"Lord, but you must be busy," she said to me.

"Yes, I suppose," I said.

"A full year of studies done. I am sure you are tired." She smiled and held my gaze.

I shook my head and looked into the fire. "But is Mama well?" I said. And then, "She seems to have aid in her new pupil—"

"Emmanuel, yes." Madame Elizabeth nodded. "A fine boy, from a good family. He and Lucien were the best of friends, before they left for Haiti. He is very handsome, too." She directed this to Experience, the lightest of us. I had forgotten how color-conscious Madame Elizabeth was. Experience, realizing she was the intended recipient of this information, blushed and cleared her throat.

"Yes, Emmanuel's all right," Lucien said. He had been sitting by the coffins, wiping one of them down with a rag, and had been watching the Graces with a smile that was not altogether kind. "I wish Emmanuel'd stayed down here with us. It would have made my life less dull."

Madame Elizabeth laughed. "More like you would have gotten into more trouble than you already do."

"So you see," I said, "Mama has no need of word from me."

"Oh, Libertie," Madame Elizabeth said, "you're a smart girl. You know you'd whip him in any contest. Especially after a full year at school. You do not ever have to worry of being crowded out of her affections. You are too old to be jealous of a person you've not even met."

I glanced over at Louisa, who was following the whole conversation with interest. Only Experience had the thoughtfulness to look away, embarrassed. She stared at the fire, working to suppress one more yawn, then stood up suddenly. "I fear, Madame Elizabeth, that we must retire," she said very carefully, in a low tone she used when she was speaking to older people.

They stood and embraced Madame Elizabeth, who stayed in her chair, and waved to Lucien. Then they were gone.

I turned in my chair and made a show of asking Lucien about himself.

He had remained as pleasant-looking as he had been ten years earlier, and I realized, with a start, that he was lightly flirting with me, though it seemed to be more for the amusement of his mother, I realized, then any sort of genuine interest. He made his jokes and verbal flips loud enough for her to hear and when one was finished, looked sideways for her approval. Madame Elizabeth would sally him on with a tap of her fan or a pull at her shawl.

In one of his moments of joking, he called me "Black Gal," and I shivered.

"Do you remember?" I said. "Do you remember Mr. Ben?"

"Oh, Daisy!" Lucien cried in a nasal falsetto, and then fluttered his hands. "But of course."

Madame Elizabeth narrowed her eyes. "That poor man."

"Do you ever wonder what happened to Daisy?"

"If there's any justice in the world," Madame Elizabeth said, "her soul's repented for all the pain she caused that man."

"But how is it Daisy's fault," I said, "if Ben Daisy was the one who chose to die for her?"

"Well, listen to you, Miss Libertie," Lucien said. His eyes shifted between me and his mother, sizing each of us up.

Madame Elizabeth tilted her head and held her finger to her chin, a practiced pose of concentration. Then she said, "Love is a mysterious thing, and a gift. A woman is a keeper of love, and when she does not take that duty as sacred, then things like that happen."

Lucien sighed. "You lose your mind and end up trying to make love to a river."

"You are terrible," I said.

"Glug, glug, glug," Lucien replied, and I saw, from the way his mother held in her laugh, that the joke was not a gamble.

I stood up. "I should go to bed, as well, Madame Elizabeth."

"Ah," Lucien said, "we've made you mad."

"Lucien, stop it." Madame Elizabeth held up her arms, and I stepped awkwardly toward her. "Good night. And say your prayers for your mama and me." Her breath was murky with the smell of tea and sugar.

Madame Elizabeth and her family lived above the shop. The stairway to get to their rooms was clammy, built into the brick of the house. At the top of the stairs was a short hallway, dim, with only one cramped window at the end, which faced out onto the street. I hadn't taken a light with me upstairs, and Madame Elizabeth had not offered one, so I moved along the hallway, my fingers running along the doors. I counted, one, two, three—Madame Elizabeth had said the third room was where we should sleep. I reached for the doorknob and turned it and pushed, but the door would not move.

I tried again, turning the knob back and forth, the iron becoming sweaty in the heat of my hand. I thought for sure Experience or Louisa would rise to let me in, but there was nothing. I scratched at the panel. "Louisa," I called. "Experience." Still no reply.

I held my ear to the door and heard the faintest shuffle, as if someone in bare feet was moving carefully. Then I bent down to the keyhole to look through. There was no candle, only the very faint moonlight from the window in the room. I could see nothing, really. But suddenly I heard someone on the other side of the door gasp, as if she had been holding her breath for a long time. I blinked once, twice. And then, again, nothing.

I stood up from the keyhole. And I think, then, that I knew. I looked at the doorknob in my hand, shook it idly, almost forlornly, one more time, and then felt my hand along the hallway wall until I was back at the cold staircase, and then down to Madame Elizabeth and Lucien at the fire. The two of them had resumed work on a cape, spread out before them at the table. Madame Elizabeth looked up, six pins between her lips, while Lucien stood beside her with a line to measure stretched between his hands.

"They were already asleep," I said, not sure how else to explain myself. "And I shouldn't wake them. It's been so long since they've slept in a bed. They need as much rest as possible before their performance."

Madame Elizabeth looked back at her work. "Well," she said, her voice muffled by the pins, "sit by the fire for a bit, and then you may sleep here if you wish."

And so that was where I fell asleep that night, listening to the hum of heavy scissors cutting through damask.

That sigh behind a closed door in the dark was a song I had never heard either of them sing before. It was the same song I heard, sometimes, while lying on the hearth of the Gradys' home, many hours after everyone in the house had gone to bed. When I'd heard it there, I had instinctively pulled my blanket tighter around my head, hummed what songs I could remember from rehearsal, and, sometimes, resorted to clearing my throat loudly, to make it stop.

But I had not wanted to make whatever was behind that door quit. I had only felt a pang of longing. I had never wanted to know something so badly in my life. Not even when I saw Mama make a dead man walk, not even when I stared at the river for a lost lady, had I ever wanted to know something as much as I wanted the knowledge of what, exactly, Louisa and Experience were doing—no, not what they were doing, but what they were feeling—behind that locked door. Longing to know what had caused that smallest, sweetest of sighs made me shut my eyes tight as Lucien and his mother lazily quarreled about the best way to attack the fabric before them.

When Louisa had said that home was in Experience's arms, and when she had defended Experience from every call questioning her coldness . . . they had been traveling to another country, I realized. They had lived there all along, while I stayed a citizen of this one, a land without sighs.

Mama, before I had left for college, had made oblique mention of what could happen to girls in school—"Girls, when they are left on their own, they become each other's sweethearts sometimes"—but she had told it to me as something her white-lady patients sometimes fretted about, and for me, she made it clear, it was only another possible distraction to avoid on my way toward greatness. She had not suggested it could be like this. A closed door with a mystery behind it that I could never know.

Up until then, I had told myself that my disgrace at Cunningham College was a blessing. I'd thought I could endeavor to make this trip with the Graces into a permanent state of being—I could become their manager, writing to the respectable colored ladies of the North and finding drawing rooms and church floors and forest clearings where the Graces could sing. The three of us would never have to return to the place of my shame—we could indefinitely live in the admiration of colored women who would otherwise have scorned me for the failure I had become.

I did not see how that was possible now. Because in my fantasy, Louisa and Experience would stay with me always, would never leave me—we would travel together; there would be no secrets between us. And eventually, with a long enough proximity, I would understand the covenant between them and enter into it on my own.

But there was no room for me there. Perhaps that was what I had been responding to in their voices all along—their desire. As wide as their desire was, it could not make room for me. I knew that. It was a bride song, a song for twin souls, for one mate to call to another. And I, a fool, had mistaken it for a song of federation.

And so I was alone again. On the wrong side of a locked door. An interloper in what I had been so certain would someday be my country.

WE WERE TO take the train to New York for the last part of our journey—Lucien and Madame Elizabeth accompanying us. We left early the next morning—Experience's cheeks flushing red at the sight of me, cramped in the same chair, by the fire, but Louisa looked up at me through her lashes and said, "You should have knocked louder, for us to hear you."

She was so bold that, for a moment, I thought that I was mistaken, but I noticed that as she said this, her fingers trembled, and so I only nodded and looked away.

The train used to have mixed seating, but at the station we discovered it had a newly implemented car solely for colored passengers. Lucien wanted to contest it—"I'll speak to the porter," he said, but Madame Elizabeth waved her fan.

"I am tired," she said, and Lucien fell back beside her, willing himself to swallow all of it.

Experience and Louisa tried to smooth over the ride by telling Madame Elizabeth how comfortable a train was, compared to a stagecoach—even Experience made an effort to say something merry, though all four of us were watching as something slowly ate Lucien up from the inside. He would not look at any of us, only at the country that rushed by the open window.

He seemed to recover by the time we reached New York. I had not written to my mother directly, had arranged for the LIS to welcome Experience and Louisa at the church. But when we arrived, there was my mother, standing among the group of women, looking almost hopeful.

A year and a half away, I had not forgotten her face, but I was shocked by the changes to it. Her hair was not as bright—it was fainter— not yet given over to gray but closer to it than when I had left. And when I stepped close to her, I saw that her face was threaded with a thousand little lines of worry. As I embraced her, I heard Madeline Grady's instruction: *You've got to press the memory out.*

Even her embrace felt different—my mother's arms were not a place I knew well, but in my recollections of them, her arms had always been heavy and strong. They felt lighter now, and her skin, where it touched mine, felt soft.

Is Mama ill? I remember thinking for one terrible moment, but then realized, with a shock, the truth was more awful. I had not noticed her age when we were together. But seeing her, after we were apart, all her years on this Earth came down between us.

I pulled away.

"We have missed you," she said. And then she looked over my shoulder expectantly. "Is this your great cause, then?"

"Miss Louisa and Miss Experience," I said. I saw Louisa quickly reach for Experience's hand and then drop it as they moved forward to greet my mother.

"Libertie speaks so much about you," Louisa said.

"And this," my mother said, "is Monsieur Emmanuel Chase."

He was only a little bit taller than Mama. This is the first thing I remember noticing about him. He had been there this whole time while I embraced her, just back behind her elbow, but I had not noticed him in the excitement of reunion.

He held out his hand, the other tucked behind his back, the model of a gentleman.

I took it.

He was most nearly white—Mama had been modest when she said he could get by. He was even lighter than she was. His hair was fine, but balding at the temples, narrowing back into a widow's peak, the rest of it slicked back with oil, though curling at the bottoms. His eyes were deep and wide-set and black, and his mouth was thin. This was because he sucked his lips in whenever his mouth was relaxed, a habit his mother had switched into him. When his mouth was allowed to fully rest, as it did in sleep, his lips were as full as any of ours, fuller even than my own. His mother beat him because his lips were, in her imagination, the only sign that he was a Negro. Holding them in or letting them loose was a choice between life and death, she believed. But I would only learn this from him later, when I lay close enough to trace his mouth's outline for myself, with my little finger.

"It's a pleasure to meet you," he said, and then he turned and said the same to Experience and Louisa. He had a trace of an accent, I assumed it was French, and this made him sound even more distinguished. I felt a pang of acknowledgment, that this was the person my mother had chosen to relish instead of me. And, of course, shame with myself, that I had proven my mother's doubts correct, that she was right to bring him in when she thought I might not see my schooling through. And underneath it, running as high and bright as a mountain stream, a longing that Emmanuel Chase should think well of me, which I hated myself for even wishing.

Lucien rushed forward to embrace him and slap him on the back. It was the masculine version of the hundred little flatteries he had directed my way to make his mother laugh, though now he seemed to have forgotten her entirely, focused only on Emmanuel Chase.

"Long time, old boy. Too long, old boy. What a sight, old boy," Lucien said, his voice curving up into an approximation of a gentleman— different from the voice he'd used on me and Experience and Louisa.

To which Emmanuel Chase only said, "Yes."

And for that, I felt another pang, that Emmanuel Chase was very politely making a fool out of Lucien in public, a pastime I had liked to do myself as a child. But my jibes had never landed, because Lucien had never cared what I thought of him.

At the house, Lenore played much cooler than my mother had. She said, "Oh, look, a ghost," when she saw me, forcing me to accost her with apologies and swears of devotion until she grudgingly accepted my embrace.

The house was full then, for once, in the evening, with Mama, Lenore, myself, the Graces, Madame Elizabeth, Lucien, and Emmanuel Chase, who, I noticed as we all sat down to dinner together, had taken the head of the table. Mama sat to his right.

"There won't be much time to rest," Mama said, "before you must begin preparations for the performance."

"The Graces can rest here during the day," I said. "I've already volunteered for the LIS." I waved my hands, a flourish, in front of me. "Behold, a mule."

This made Mama laugh, at least. Lucien, too, though Emmanuel Chase only smiled and kept his face close to his plate.

"And you must tell us," Mama said, "how your studies are faring and what the college is like and, oh, how are Mr. Grady and his wife doing?"

I had expected this, and I had a dodge—what I had learned from so many years as a doctor's daughter. That nobody wished to speak of any greater subject than themselves. So I turned to Emmanuel Chase and said, trying to keep the envy and the fear of him from my voice, "My studies are boring, but a doctor all the way from Haiti, that is much more fascinating. Mama has spoken of your talents, but she has not mentioned much of your history."

Emmanuel Chase laid down his knife and fork, as if he was about to make a speech. I thought, *At least I have guessed right about you. You are vainglorious.*

"My father was born free here, in Maryland, and my mother was a slave. She escaped twice, to join him—the first time, she and my three brothers were recaptured; the second time, she made it away, but with only one of them. In Maryland, she and my father had five more children—I am the youngest. My father joined the Church of England. They do not have much of a presence in Maryland, but their faith is strong.

"Even before war broke out, he wished to leave this country, but my mother would not hear of it—she wished to stay, in case my two brothers ever found a way to return to her. But my father could not see how colored people could make anything of ourselves here. He petitioned the church to send him to Haiti—the president there had promised land to any American Negro who could come. And my father was determined.

"Right before the diocese agreed to send him, we got word that my two other brothers had died—one of a whipping, from an overseer in Mississippi, and the other drowned while trying to cross the Delaware River. So we left, certain we would miss nothing back here. We left the same day war broke out at Fort Sumter, though we did not learn of it until we arrived in Haiti."

Emmanuel Chase spoke as if he had practiced this speech many times in his head and had warmed to telling it. He paused for breath, for gasps, for admiring sighs, and Madame Elizabeth and the Graces humored him. I noticed, though, that he seemed to take their noises as genuine—he was not so savvy as to realize that these were the sounds women learn to make to keep men talking. I thought, again, *I know you*. And I widened my eyes as he spoke, made my smile slightly bigger. Then an extraordinary thing: as he finished his first speech, as he said "arrived in Haiti," he raised his eyes to look in mine, as if to say *I know you, too*.

He paused to take a sip from his cup of water, and I lowered my eyes and kept them down as he continued.

"So it seemed my father had gambled well, and he was very proud. But, as you can imagine, it was quite a shock for a young boy such as myself to be spirited away from Baltimore to Haiti. The first year there was very hard—my brothers died, as did two of my sisters. Before the year was over, my mother died, too. That left only myself and my sister Ella. And my father, of course."

"I'm sorry," I said, but he just blinked and continued.

"The second year, my father was able to begin to raise funds for his ministry, and our farm there, and so life became a bit easier. My father remains there. I plan to return, as I hope all freeborn men do one day. Perhaps even Lucien will come, if we can tempt him."

Lucien looked up, momentarily shocked at this, but he recovered. "Leave Philadelphia for Haiti and the rule of Negroes?" he said, and rolled his eyes.

Madame Elizabeth laughed and slapped his arm, and I saw Emmanuel Chase's gaze harden, his lips grow even thinner.

"It's where our people's ambition lies," he said.

But Lucien shook his head. "My father's Haitian, it's true," he said, "but I am an American by birth, and I'll stay here in her land, if I please."

"You'd stay here even as they kill us for trying to vote? You'd stay here even as they cut us down in Colfax and in Hamburg?"

"We'll fight them back," Lucien said. "We'll win in the end. The white men will learn that colored people mean business."

"You have too much faith in white folks," Emmanuel Chase said.

Lucien said, "You have not enough faith in colored people."

"Do you know a story my father used to tell me?" Emmanuel said. "He used to work with a white family just past Baltimore. He would send people their way, when they were escaping. But he had to stop when one of them told them what the white people were doing—inviting slave owners over for dinner and then asking everyone to debate the slave question, together, at the table. Black men, scared and tired and just trying to run, forced to sit and prove how worthy they were to the very men who should have been apologizing to them—"

"Emmanuel," Mama said. If it had been me getting angry, Mama would have stopped the whole conversation. She would have tried to drown my rage. But here was only a very quiet "Emmanuel," which he ignored.

"You can't ever be free in a place like that," he said. "In a house that runs by those rules. I can tell you, no one in Haiti has ever asked for such an indignity. It is our own republic. It's for colored men such as us."

"But they are not Christians," Experience said. "They are papists."

"And cannibals," Lucien said.

Emmanuel looked pained, as if Lucien had reached across the table and slapped him. "Your father would let you speak of his country like that?"

"He is who told me this of his country!" Lucien said. "Colored people are a cursed lot, but at least in our good fortune, we are cursed in the good Christian nation of America, where good government and understanding of God prevail—"

"You say that as they riot any time we try to sit in a railway car," Emmanuel said.

"Those are only potholes on the road to progress. We will prevail. We have the tradition of good Anglo-Saxon law and fairness to guide us. Haiti has none of that. We could go there, I suppose, to raise them up—now, I agree with you on that. As good Christian Negroes, we should act as a mother to our race, to bring it up to manhood."

"But there's still so much to be done here," Mama said.

Emmanuel had that pained look again, the one that had creased his face when Lucien called his countrymen cannibals. It momentarily flashed across his face, and then it was gone, suppressed. He looked at Mama with polite interest, though I was beginning to think that underneath, he was burning the same way I did.

He turned back to Lucien. "None of us will ever triumph," he said, "until we are completely free." Emmanuel may have sat at the head of the table, but he would not have dared to say this directly to Mama.

"But what does freedom mean?" I said. I could not help myself. I had heard something in his voice then that I thought—that I believed, that I flattered myself, that I hoped—was only for me.

The table stopped to look at me. My mother, I saw, looked the hardest. It was as if she was seeing me for the first time. But all I could think was, *I have embarrassed her again. She wishes I was not her daughter, that clever Emmanuel was her son.*

I closed my eyes, wishing I had not spoken.

"It means," Emmanuel said, his voice shaking, either from excitement or dread, I could not tell yet, "that we are wholly in charge of our own destiny."

"And we seize it, apparently, with violence and blood," Lucien said, "if we are to follow the Haitian model. That does not sound like freedom to me. Freedom goes hand in hand with peace and harmony and prosperity. But did you ever notice"—he leaned over to Louisa—"how the lightest ones burn brightest for revolution? Why is that?"

"They're closest to freedom and can taste it, so they'll do anything for it," Louisa said, laughing. She had begun to relax and regain her playfulness.

Emmanuel Chase laughed along, but he wouldn't look at her. He only said to Lucien, "Revolution already happened there."

"Here, too. Twice," Lucien replied. "It's hard work, but we'll prevail. Colored men will be free. And in the meantime, I don't have to speak French."

"It would give your father great pleasure if you did," Madame Elizabeth said.

Lucien slapped his hand on the table. "Mwen se yon American."

"I did not know you were such a patriot," Louisa said.

"Oh, but I am." Lucien leaned back in his chair and began to sing the first few verses of "Yankee Doodle Dandy" in the nasal tones of a northerner. "Please join me," he said.

Louisa scoffed. "I have a voice to preserve," she said, which made the whole table laugh, except for Emmanuel, who sat back, quiet.

It was hard to get a look at him, because every time I glanced at his face he stared back at me.

My mother declared that the Graces should sleep in my room, with me, and Madame Elizabeth should sleep in her room, with her, leaving Lucien to sleep with Emmanuel in Mama's old examination room, which Emmanuel would take, now that I was home. As the sleeping arrangements were announced, I watched Louisa and Experience's faces, closely, but neither one gave anything away. I imagined that they held hands underneath the table, and I felt a rush of sadness. I cupped my own hand, under the lace tablecloth, around empty air, and imagined what it would feel like for another hand to rest there.

I did not want to be in the room alone with them while we all undressed and pretended that none of us knew what had happened. I didn't think I could bear to hear any of the excuses they would give for why they had not opened the door at Madame Elizabeth's. It felt, perhaps, even more lonely-making to know they had not trusted me with the truth. So I made a show of announcing I would sit on the porch for a bit before bed.

"I missed the garden," I told my mother.

Lenore tilted her head. "Leaving home really does change a person," she said.

But Mama gave an approving smile and kissed my head before taking her candle and leading Madame Elizabeth off, so that they could gossip in peace in her room.

I sat on the porch for a bit, listening to the saw of flies all around the house in the night. It felt like the world was still drowsy from the winter, nothing alive out there in the dark was at its full pitch yet. I counted one Mississippi after another, trying to leave enough time for Experience and Louisa. I grew uncertain, though, if I had waited long enough, and so I stood up from the porch and walked out into the yard, trying to see if the candle was still burning in my room upstairs.

I tilted my head back. I could see the flare of light, where the flame sat on the windowsill of my room. I sighed, waiting for when the two of them would feign sleep and I could return to lie in my own bed, a stranger among friends.

"You hold yourself like that and you could swallow the moon."

I jerked my head back, and there was Emmanuel Chase, coming down the porch steps to stand with me.

I think I'd known that it would be this way. I think, if I was being honest, I'd hoped that it would.

He smiled, pleased with himself for the bit of poetry. "My nurse used to say that to me, when I was little."

"A nurse?"

But he was not flustered. He nodded and drew a very short, fat cigar out of his jacket pocket. He sucked on the end but did not move to light it. Not yet.

"It is like that in Haiti," he said. "The better families have servants."

"Other Negroes?"

"The people who live in the country, yes. They're used to work like that."

I blinked.

"I sound hinkty," he said.

"You haven't forgotten that word, at least, with all the French you speak."

"No," he said. "I haven't forgotten. Wherever there's niggers in this world, you need to have a word for uppity."

I laughed at that, and he smiled wide again. It was a kind of agreement between us.

I stepped back to look up at the window again, to hide my excitement. The candle still burnt.

Emmanuel came to stand beside me and tilted his head back, as well. Then he said, his voice lower, so that no one in the house could hear him,

"My nurse, we learned to call her Ti Me. It means Little Mother. She would tell me stories about the gods. Haiti has different gods than here. They came from Africa, on the ships with the Negro slaves, and stayed—they did not forsake the Negroes there, like they did the Negroes here. They are always around us there."

"You weren't scared?"

"No," he said, still looking up at the window. "My sister was scared and thought it was all heathen nonsense. But I loved them. Ti Me told me a story about the god who has the moon. The goddess. 'Yon lwa' is what Ti Me would say. She is called La Sirèn—"

"Haiti has sirens then? Mermaids, like here?"

"She lives under the water, yes. She rules the oceans—she is as changeable as a wave."

I shivered. "I knew someone once, who used to speak nonsense like that."

He sucked on the end of the cigar again, a sound almost like a kiss, which made my stomach lurch.

"Really?" he said. "So you've already heard of La Sirèn, who is so beautiful she takes men underwater with her, who possesses her subjects and makes them walk as though they had fins for legs. And they gasp—oh, they gasp—because they cannot breathe air anymore, and the only way to get them to stop is to douse them with water. I have seen it myself, as a boy, in the temples Ti Me took me to.

"Sometimes, La Sirèn gets jealous and she'll drown a man and take him down under and teach him her magic. When he comes back to the surface, his skin is light, as bright as mine, and his hair is straight, and he knows all about the world."

"Is that why you look like that, then?"

He laughed. "But you told me you already knew all about her. That another man has already told you this tale. And who was he?"

I felt the grass, insistent, on the bottom of my shoes. I felt the calm cold of the night air. "There was a man my mother tried to help. Madame Elizabeth tried to help him, too. He was a funny sort of man—he stole away here before the war. But he couldn't abide freedom. It was almost as if he couldn't understand it. That sounds wrong, but that's how he acted. He said his sweetheart, who had long died, was here with him, that she wore pink and white and loved sweet cakes and that he only wanted to be with her. He became upset when he caught her with three wedding rings on her finger, so he claimed, and he drowned himself in the river. All because he was sick with love and freedom."

Even as I said it, I felt a roll in my stomach. I had never given Ben Daisy's history like that to anyone so plain. To do so felt like a betrayal of Mama, and I half expected her to throw open the house's front door and stare me down. But the door stayed shut.

"Ah," Emmanuel said. "That was not La Sirèn. That was Erzulie Freda. She is the goddess of love, and she is married to the god of the sky, the god of the ocean, and the god of iron. She loves hard and loves beautifully, but she is never satisfied. She ends every day crying for what she has not done, what she cannot have. Your poor man had no chance against her."

He hadn't heard me, I thought. Or he thought my story was part of our dance. Or maybe what I had said about Mr. Ben was too monstrous. Imagine telling a revolutionary like him that freedom made a man sick. I felt a burn of shame at my perversity. I wanted to be better for him. So I did not say, "You misunderstood." Instead, I said, "I suppose you are correct."

The window was still illuminated. As I remembered Ben Daisy, the song I had made up for him came back to me, as loud as the flies drowsing in Mama's garden.

When I looked back at Emmanuel, I saw he was watching me, in the light of the moon, with those wide-set, watery eyes. He was still sucking on the end of the cigar.

"Why haven't you lit it yet?"

"You have to taste it first, before you can light it. I brought ten of them from home, and have been trying to ration them." Then, still looking at me with interest, he said, "I save them for special occasions."

I thought, with a flash, of how he had watched my face as he gave his speech at dinner, that silly remark about the moon.

"There is nothing special about tonight," I said, despite knowing what he meant.

"But there is," he said. "It is very rare that I can meet a devotee of Erzulie herself, this far north, near the waters of a river as cold and muddy as one in Kings County."

"So I am a goddess of love, then."

"If you insist," he said.

It was a game I was no longer sure how to play. To be earnest seemed wrong. I thought of Mrs. Grady's hectoring. I was not quite up to that, either. Louisa and Experience, they were true with each other. *Quick, Libertie, quick*, I told myself. *Something clever.* But all I could say was, "Why are you interested, then?"

"My father thinks the Haitian gods are demons. He thinks it is his life mission to get every Haitian to Christ and to forget the blasphemies. But I think those gods are our genius. The genius of the Negro people. Our best invention. And Erzulie, the goddess of love, she's called with honey and flowers and sweet things, and she speaks to the longing, the desire for perfection in this world, and our sorrow that we will never achieve it. And I try to stay close to people who know her."

"But none of it is real," I said. "It was a thing Ben Daisy made up when he couldn't stand to be here. And I was just a child. That's why I believed him."

Emmanuel Chase finally struck a match and lit his cigar, and the heavy smoke rolled over both of us. "It was real enough to drown the man. I think it is remarkable."

It was my turn to speak, my turn to say something fascinating to him, but I could think of nothing. My bedroom window was dark now.

I only pointed up above, at the moon, just a sliver of white behind a black ribbon of clouds. He followed my gaze. He breathed heavily, and another gust of too-sweet smoke came over us.

"Good night," I said.

"Good night, then, Libertie."

Upstairs, at the entrance to my own room, I stood at the door for a minute, my hand on the knob, afraid it wouldn't turn. But it did, easily enough, and in the dark I could just make out the two rounded forms of the Graces, on opposite sides of the bed, a clear space between them.

I crawled into the space. Louisa turned and breathed in, then coughed.

"You smell like a bad man," she murmured.

Experience sneezed.

"It was Dr. Chase's cigar," I said, even though I knew she spoke in her sleep. "He smokes in the garden at night. Cigars he has to work up to taste."

"Hmm," Louisa said. Then she turned on her back, away from me. Experience turned in the other direction.

For a long time, I lay between my two friends' love, my eyes open in the dark, breathing in the smell of the night curdled with the stink of cigar through the open window, where Emmanuel Chase, I guessed, still stood below, smoking at the moon.

IN THOSE DAYS, in Brooklyn, Tom Thumb weddings were all the rage.

The prettiest boy and the most docile girl of any Sunday school class would be chosen as the groom and bride. Churchwomen would spend weeks sewing a morning suit for the boy—silk and velvet cut down for a child's shoulder span. For the girl, a veil and train made comically long, so that she would look even smaller and slighter when she walked to the altar. To act as the reverend, they would ask the child who loved to play the most—one who could ignore his classmates' tears and keep the gag going with his comical sermon. People paid good money to see them, and to laugh at the children weeping at the altar, unsure if they'd just been yoked to their schoolyard nemesis for life.

This passion for children's marriages came on us quick after the war. It was a celebration and an act of defiance and a joke—we could marry legally now, even though we knew our marriages were always real, whether the Constitution said it or not. So real a child could know it, too.

Louisa had insisted we add one to our benefit.

"It makes the children cry every time," I said.

"We'll sing 'Ave Maria' to drown out their tears," Louisa said.

I looked to Experience, who shrugged. "They get to keep their costumes when it's over, don't they? Tears are a small price to pay for a new dress."

I'd laughed. "You are both hard women."

But I was not laughing while Louisa and Experience stayed at my mother's house, preparing their voices for the performance, and I stood in the church, six little girls lined up in front of me, four of them already weeping.

I grabbed the hot hand of the girl closest to me. "That's Caroline," Miss Annie called as I pulled the girl out of the church, past the graveyard, to the copse of trees where Ben Daisy used to wait for his love.

Now the little girl Caroline stood before me in tears. "Stay here," I ordered. I tried to be stern, but this only made her cry harder.

I knelt down and touched her shoulder. "You must know it's just for play? You won't really marry anyone. You just have to wear a pretty dress and walk down the aisle." Then, "Look, look here." I squeezed her hand once, then dropped it quickly and stepped ten paces away from her, until I was out of the trees, nearly to the graveyard's gate.

"Watch me, Caroline," I called. "This is all you have to do."

And then I counted to myself—one, two, three—and took the

exaggerated steps of a march to where Caroline, skeptical, stood in the shade. I held my head up and twisted my face into a grin, which, I realized, probably frightened her more.

"You walk and smile," I said through clenched teeth. "Walk and smile, and then you get to the front and bow your head and wait, and when everyone claps, it's over, and we give you sweets and flowers."

"That is precisely how marriage works," I heard from the set of trees, and there was Emmanuel Chase.

"Yes," I said. "Exactly that. Flowers and sweets. So what is the point of carrying on?"

"I don't want to marry Daniel," Caroline said. She had stopped crying and was watching us both with interest.

"It's the same as when you play with your sister or your friends," I said. "It's not real."

"That's not very kind to Daniel," Emmanuel said. "His heart will be broken."

Caroline looked at me uncertainly, her eyes threatening more tears.

"You confuse her for the sake of a joke," I said.

It had been all well and good to try to flirt with Emmanuel at night, while looking up at my window, my mother a few feet away. But it was less appealing here, in the woods, with only a six-year-old as witness.

Emmanuel Chase knelt down and said with great ceremony, for my benefit, "Listen closely to Miss Libertie." Then he stood up and smiled at me.

It was strange, to see the way Caroline looked at Emmanuel Chase— it was pure adoration, mixed with a little bit of fear. "Go on," he said to her, and Caroline closed her eyes and began to march, her knees raised to her chest, her arms stretched out in front of her, lurching toward me where I stood at the edge of the circle of trees.

When she reached me, she opened her eyes, her arms still held out as if she was balancing a great weight, and whispered, in a voice loud enough for him to hear, though she didn't wish it, "Is the white man still watching us?"

I lightly slapped her arms down. "Dr. Chase is a Negro, just like you," I said.

She looked at him over her shoulder again, to make sure, which he laughed at.

"Now walk back," I said, "slower. You do not have to lift your knees as high. March on my clap. And go slow."

When she reached Emmanuel Chase, he looked at her awkwardly, then reached out, turned her around by the shoulders, and sent her back to me.

So we did this a few times, sending Caroline back and forth between us, sometimes watching each other, until she grew tired. "I know it," she insisted. "I know it now. Let me be."

She did her slow, lurching march all the way back to the church, and then Emmanuel and I were alone together. By then, the shadows of the trees had grown long enough to reach me where I stood. I allowed myself to feel the cold for a moment, then stepped back into the sun. He followed.

We stood there, both looking at the church. Today, there were no props for him to play with. He looked almost nervous. It pleased me to imagine that I made him nervous. He raised one hand to his temple and then dropped it just as suddenly.

"I have thought a lot about what you told me," I said, to break the silence. He looked relieved.

"It really is remarkable," he said.

"This is where I used to play with Ben Daisy when I was a girl. But still, I don't know anything about the gods you talked about."

"Well," he said, "not many of us here do. But in Haiti, everyone knows them."

"Even the Christians?"

"Everyone's a good Christian in Haiti."

"I don't believe you."

"It's possible to be many things at once, Libertie."

I walked a little farther into the warmer part of the grass.

"You like riddles," I said.

"It's not a riddle. It's like the marriage you'll officiate."

"Another riddle," I said. "You aren't doing much to convince me."

"But it is," he said. It had caught his imagination now, and he turned toward me, eager to talk. "When a man and woman marry, they become one, correct? One being bound together, but two very separate people. They remain separate, but act and work as one, for the better of all."

"You are very modern," I said, laughing. "A woman remains separate from a man? She's not swallowed in him, whole, to replace that missing rib?"

I had found my rhythm with him now, I thought. I understood now why Madeline Grady teased so much. It made it easier to talk to a man if you pretended everything they said to you was false.

But Emmanuel Chase was hard to understand, because sometimes he became very earnest. As now. He reached out to catch at the tallest cattail and broke it off, then tossed it away, impatient. "I believe in companionate marriage," he said, rather proudly.

"So you are very modern."

"It is only logical that a man and wife should share friendship and charity and understanding. They should be friends for life."

This embarrassed me, and so I looked away. "That's where my father is buried," I said, pointing at the grave. FREEDOM stood out on it, as stark as ever, but his name had worn down, no longer deep in the stone but risen faint to the surface. "I do not know if it was that way between my mother and father, though it makes me sad to think she lost not only her husband but her closest friend."

"It is a pity. A house needs a man and a woman to function."

"I don't know about that," I said. "We did just fine."

He smiled, as if he disagreed but was too polite to say, and I felt a rush of sympathy for my mother, a wish to defend her.

"Was it like that with your parents?" I asked. "Were they companions?"

He didn't turn from my father's grave. "No," he said. "They were nothing of the sort."

And then he was silent, and we listened to the wind move over the grass and, behind us, an exasperated Miss Annie telling the children to quiet.

I was too embarrassed to ask him more. And he did not seem to want to relieve the silence; he stood in it as if it was the most comfortable place to be. Finally, I could not stop myself.

"Is it strange," I said, "being here in America, after so long away?"

"Everything is grayer. I had forgotten that. The trees, the clothing, the people's faces. Even the sun is grayer here than it is there."

"Is it so beautiful there?"

"It's a better world there," he said. "Or it will be. Very soon."

"You're not a patriot anymore."

"I am not as optimistic as Lucien or your mother," he said.

I looked up finally. He was staring at me again. "I never thought of my mother as an optimist."

"She is only that," he said. "What other word would you use to describe a colored woman who has so thoroughly decided to work with whites, who trusts the white women who come into her office telling tales about hurt spleens, but won't trust me to touch those same women with my bare hands?"

"They used to ask me to turn to the wall," I said, "when she was examining them. Mama said it was because they were jealous, that I was young and they were not any longer."

"I could understand that," he said.

He said, "When you blush, your skin glows darker somehow. It's remarkable."

"It should not be."

"You don't find this place changed, since you've been away?"

"I don't know," I said. "I missed it, I thought. It was mostly just— different. But now I am not sure I can call it home."

"Is that why you are now an impresario?"

"You can make fun if you'd like. I've never found anything truer in this world than Louisa and Experience singing. And the one thing my mother taught me, above all, is to fight for truth when you find it."

"That's very pretty."

"You are making fun again."

"No, it is very pretty. But also not true."

It was a thrill to hear someone outwardly doubt my mother. I had never heard it before, and a part of me leapt to him as he said it.

"She's taught you so many good things, though," he continued. "You probably got a better medical education as a child than I have now."

"I am not a very good student," I ventured. I almost told him right then, that I was disgraced. But then he said, "Oh, I find that very hard to believe," and I thought perhaps we were back in the language of flirtation, with no place for truth.

I wished I could be whatever it was that he saw when I stood before

him. It was clearly not the same person that the Graces saw, or Alma
Curtis or Madeline Grady, or even who Mama saw, when she looked at
me. He looked at me as if I was a wondrous being, as if my voice was a
song, as if I was magic. And I did not want to disappoint him.

By then, the sun had shifted, and we were on the cold side of the
field again. He held out his arm to me, and I took it, and he walked me
back toward the road, toward my mother's house.

"You are not at the hospital," I said. "Why?"

"It's too nice a day to be indoors." And then glanced at me. "Good,
you don't believe me. I told your mother I wished to work on some
notes back at the house, and when I was on the way there, I was lucky
enough to see you and the little girl in the field. A happy coincidence."

"My mother lets you come and go."

"I'm not a servant here," he said, sounding offended, which seemed
strange to me.

"She never did with me," I said. "I could only leave the clinic for
errands. She said if I got too used to wandering off on my own, it would
break my concentration. She knew it took me so long to work it up."

"So you were a servant then. The little scullery maid, forced to
become a doctor."

"It was not so bad," I said. "If you were a girl given to that work."

We walked on a bit longer in silence. Then I took a breath. "Has
my mother told you how she taught herself anatomy? When she was a
girl my age, there was a cholera outbreak downtown. She followed the
gravediggers for a day, until she found a baby's body, asked for it, and
took it to her father's barn to dissect. She did it because they wouldn't
let her work with the cadavers."

I am not sure why I told him this, this secret my mother kept. It
was a story she did not even trust to Lenore, and only told me when my

dedication waned, when she suspected I would not work hard enough, to shock me into diligence. It had worked, but I had told no one since.

Now I looked over at Emmanuel Chase. I had told him, too, to shock him, to see if it could shake that look off his face. But he was saying nothing, only looking back at me, as if what I had said was perfectly normal, as if he'd expected no less from me or from her. So I took an even deeper breath, and told him my greatest secret.

"I am not so passionate as my mother," I said. "I could not do something like that."

He nodded, and then he let his hand brush against mine and took it in his. We kept going like that, hand in hand, not speaking, only looking at the road laid out before us until we could see the turn for my mother's house. Then he squeezed my hand once and tossed it away from him. I thought, in this new language we were building together, that maybe it meant he believed I was passionate after all.

"Good afternoon, then, Libertie," he said. And he turned to go back the way we'd come.

I was at the front door again, but I could not bring myself to go in.

I had admired my mother, in her ability to use the people around her for greater good: the baby in the bush; Mr. Ben and his delusions; the matrons who funded her hospital. I had thought myself a coward that I could not do the same. I had burnt in anger at a physics of the world that my mother took as given. And even in that anger, I had failed to do anything, had been disgraced as a student. I was no one's promise.

But Dr. Emmanuel Chase still thought me good. Or, at least, thought of me as someone to admire. Mama had made it clear my anger was useless, unbecoming, superfluous in this world. But anger looked marvelous on Dr. Chase. It gave him a conviction, a heaviness, that he would not have had if he was sweet, if he was asked to be as polite as I was. He would be my avatar.

Through him, I could taste righteousness.

And he understood me. I thought.

To choose him would be to hurt my mother in a way I was not even sure of yet. I knew it would make a wound. I did not know then how deep, or how lasting.

I HAD BEEN a success in something after all, and there were too many people to fit into the church alone. The children would marry in the copse of trees, which we hung with garlands of flowers. Colored people came from Manhattan, from Jersey, from Long Island. Some even came up from Philadelphia, on the word of Lucien and Madame Elizabeth. The whole thing had turned into a kind of homecoming for the older people, some of whom had not seen one another since the war ended, who cried as they embraced, who walked together arm in arm, who stopped to whisper to one another or sometimes draw back to laugh at some change in fortune.

Sometimes, when I looked up from wiping a child's nose, I saw my mother in the crowd. She was on the arm of Madame Elizabeth, and the two of them were always in the midst of at least five other ladies. None of the former members of the LIS—that was not to be. But a few women stood gravely beside her as she spoke, and only allowed themselves to smile when Madame Elizabeth broke in and interrupted her.

Suddenly, Mama looked up and caught my eye, and I looked away. I crushed the purse at my side, just to hear the crinkle of a piece of paper there. It was a note, slipped under my door that morning in the small span of time between the Graces leaving the bed and when I turned over in sleep. The note was addressed to Erzulie, and it had been written in a hand I had not seen before but had known immediately who it belonged to.

"You need to say 'dearly beloved,'" I told Chester, the boy we had picked to play minister.

He looked up at me and twisted his face into a scowl.

"You need to at least try raising your hand at them," Emmanuel Chase called.

I raised my hand half-heartedly, but the boy had already jerked his arm free, and now he ran.

"You showed him your bluff," Emmanuel Chase said as he came closer. "You're too kind."

"You would not call me kind if you knew me."

"But I do know you, or at least the most important part of you," he said. "You are my Erzulie. You're the lover, never the fighter."

"You are very presumptuous."

"I know you," he repeated, still smiling. I wished he would repeat it forever.

I looked away from him, back out to the crowd. My mother still stood with her group of ladies, but she was turned toward us, watching.

"You cannot send notes like you wrote to me this morning," I said. I knew she couldn't hear us from where she stood—no one could have—but I dropped my voice anyways.

"I only write the truth."

"You should understand, I am not as sophisticated as you. I've only been from my mother's garden to her waiting room and back again. The only other place I know is the inside of an anatomy hall. I do not know the world like you do. You won't find a very satisfying game with me."

"You think I'm false."

"I think you are not hearing what I am saying."

"You've mistaken me if you think I only tease you. I wrote it to you, but I'd say it out loud to anyone here who'd ask. I'd say it even without their asking. You wish me to ask your mother now?" he said, and he turned as if to walk toward her.

I knew enough, at least, that in the next beat of the game I was supposed to grab his arm and stop him and laugh. But I stood with my arms at my sides and did nothing.

He turned on his heel and smiled wider. "You called my bluff."

"I do not understand you," I said. "You write declarations of love and marriage on the back of a scrap of paper I may not even see, and slip it under my door like an assassin, and then tell me your intentions are pure."

"So you read it," he said, "and it's true. I love and adore you, and wish you would be my wife. And you want to know if my intentions are good. I think that tells me all that I was hoping."

"I do not like games like this," I said.

Then I raised my voice to its normal tone. "We are about to begin. Excuse me."

It is a strange thing, to see something you have imagined over and over again finally acted out in front of you. It is almost like a kind of death, a loss of something, that the thing is not as you had thought it would be. I myself had laid out a path of pine needles, brown and dry in the July heat, from the end of the copse of trees to the stump of the altar. I watched Caroline shuffle down it, almost tripping over the hem of her too-long dress, to the little boy we'd chosen for her groom, who was looking not at Caroline or at the spectators who laughed and called out encouragement, but above him, at a cardinal in a branch of a tree.

When the child minister called out, "You may kiss the bride," the crowd began to laugh and jeer, but Caroline stepped forward, grasped her boy groom's head in her hands, and brought his face to hers in a cruel smack, which everyone cheered.

The Graces were to sing in the church, we had decided. But after the wedding was done, Louisa came to me. "We'll sing here, under the trees, where God and everyone else can hear us."

So Louisa and Experience stood side by side in front of a crowd of three hundred colored people. They did not look at each other, but before they began, Experience grabbed Louisa's hand and held it, and did not let go until the songs were over.

The sound they made, with just their two voices marrying in the air, filled the whole clearing.

> *My Lord,*
> > *what a morning*
> *My Lord,*
> > *what a morning*
> *Oh, my Lord,*
> > *what a morning*
> *When*
> > *the*
> > > *stars*
> > *be gin*
> > > *to*
> > > > *fall*
> *You'll hear the trumpet sound*
> > *To wake the nations underground*
> *Looking to my God's right hand*
> > *When the stars*
> > *be gin*
> > > *to*
> > > *fall*
> *You'll hear the sinner moan*
> > *To wake the nations underground*

Looking to my God's right hand
When the stars
be gin
to
fall
You'll hear the Christian shout
To wake the nations underground
Looking to my God's right hand
When the stars
be gin
to
fall

You read in the Bible about the voice of God shaking leaves and commanding bushes to burst into flame, about trumpets making walls fall, about the songs that can sweep waves across the planet's face, but it is quite a different thing to stand in the heat of July, the smell of damp lace and pine sap and other people's bodies all around you, and know those words to be true.

By the time they got to "What Ya Gonna Do When Ya Lamp Burn Down," the crowd joined in—men, women, and children, singing and slapping hands and the bark of the trees—Experience and Louisa in the middle, still hand in hand, their voices rising above it all. I think it is the closest I have ever come in my life to seeing true love, and for a moment my sadness and anger were gone. I only felt the warmth of something fulfilled, and I closed my eyes to make it stop, because it felt too much.

The rest of the afternoon was the bazaar and the feast—long tables brought out and set with cake. Plates of oysters, too, which Experience and Louisa had never seen before.

"You tip them back, like this." I showed them, and when I held one up to Louisa's lips, she began to giggle. "That smell!" she cried. Experience pinched her elbow and then blushed hard, and they would not tell me anymore what it was about, so I drifted away from them, alone again.

Emmanuel Chase kept his distance from me, walking among the crowd, talking to the prettiest women and girls, laughing with the men. I thought, *Had we really stood under those trees and talked of marriage?* I could not believe, would not have believed it, to look at him.

"You are in-fat-u-a-ted." It was Lucien who sang this. There was a slight weave in his step as he moved toward me, slapping the rhythm on his thigh. When he reached me, he smelled the same as Madeline Grady's barrels of beer.

"You know this place is temperate," I said.

"Not over there it's not." He pointed behind the trees, where a man was making his way gingerly out of the underbrush, passing another who was stepping in. "They have one barrel there, not too much, just enough to keep us all toasty."

"You disrespect our mothers."

"You keep acting so sour, Dr. Chase will never look your way," he said, and then began to laugh.

"You should leave, Lucien, before your mother discovers you."

"You never leave their skirts."

"You do not seem too interested in that either."

"You shouldn't run after the first man who makes your blood roll like a river, Libertie."

"I will see you this evening, when you've sobered up a bit," I said.

I did not like to admit it, but Lucien had troubled me. I walked through the rest of the bazaar, stopping to look at the tables with things for sale. Some of the younger girls had knitted a set of fingerless gloves, and I spent time pulling them on and off my hands, becoming angrier and angrier at Lucien's presumption. My feelings toward Emmanuel could not be so obvious as he wished to imply. I was not anything that a person like that could easily know—a man who looked to make his mother laugh first, a man who couldn't hold his own after one mug of beer drunk under the trees.

I opened my purse and took the piece of paper out of it again. There was my own hand, writing out the events of this day. And on the back, the other script, the one I'd seen that morning.

To My Libertie
    This is a note to declare my undying affection for you. I wish, above all, for you to become my wife. I think, if you are being honest with yourself, you would wish it, too.
    Yours,
    Emmanuel Chase

Not even a bit of poetry, I thought. I admired him for that. For speaking plainly. For avoiding some terrible simile about my eyes, as someone as low as Lucien would have done.

"You are back," I heard, and then I turned and saw it was Miss Hannah, standing with Miss Annie, both of them looking at me with a friendly weariness.

"Yes," was all I could say.

In the years since her brother left us for the water, Miss Hannah had grown smaller, so that now she stood at Miss Annie's shoulder, Her back was still straight, but her eyes were nearly colorless. I had thought her old when I was a girl, but more or less the same age as my mother. Now, I saw she was much older.

"Studies suit you well," Miss Hannah said, and I reached out to grab her hand.

"I have thought of you and Mr. Ben often," I said.

It was the wrong thing. Miss Hannah's face broke, and she lowered her eyes, and Miss Annie looked at me, exasperated. But Miss Hannah held my hand in hers so tight that my fingers tingled, and she would not let go.

"Have you seen?" she said. "He's here, with us."

She would not let go. I put my other hand on top of hers, and she clasped her other hand over that, so that we were bound together. She led me away from the table before I could snatch up again my slip of paper from where I'd stuffed it, underneath the pile of empty gloves.

"Here," she said.

It was a wooden marker. It was painted with the name BENJAMIN SMITH—the name Miss Hannah had chosen for him and herself. Someone had painted wings on either side, but they were so clumsy they looked like crescent moons.

The church, at least, had given him a prized space, in the middle of the yard between two larger stones. Miss Hannah gazed at the plot as if her brother's body was really underneath it, as if he could rise up through the grass to be with us.

"I am saving up for stone," she said. "I had this put up last year."

She still held my hands in hers. "You are a good sister," was all I could manage to say, but she did not seem to wish for more. She only wanted me to stand in her fifteen years of grief, beside the play grave of her brother.

It was colder and almost dusk by the time Miss Hannah let my hand go and I could leave the graveyard. By then, the celebration had quieted. Some men and women lingered, eating the last of strawberries that had been set out. A few children, waiting for their parents, slept in a pile underneath one of the tables.

There was no sign of Emmanuel Chase. When I went back to the table to try and find his letter, it was gone. I told myself, even though I knew it wasn't true, that maybe someone had swept it away with the dirty rushes or packed it with their extra pairs of gloves. I tried to find Louisa or Experience to help, but I was told they had already headed back to my mother's house. So I started the walk from the church alone, my hands still pressed from Miss Hannah's grip.

The lightning bugs were out already. They darted all around me, sometimes deep into the fields, sometimes just a few steps ahead. The light was almost purple, and it made me wish that Emmanuel was beside me—if only to be able to remark on how strange and beautiful it was, if only to have a testimony. I slowed, as if I was walking arm in arm with a companion. It did not seem fair that this whole night was stretched before me and I was its lone witness.

I was thinking about this, about the ghost of Emmanuel beside me, when I came to my mother's house and I saw her, standing in the open doorway, the light from inside blazing behind her.

"Hello," I said, startled.

And she said, "You're lying to me, Libertie."

"IT'S NOT ENOUGH," she said, "that my only daughter has not spoken a word to me since she has come home. That she has hidden behind friends and acquaintances. That she has not even given me a report of her year—"

"I wasn't—"

"It is not enough that she has not come to visit our clinic, has ignored my letters for months. But above all of that, I find she has kept her worst secret from her own mother."

How could she know? I thought. *Who could have told her that I had failed, that I was cast out of Cunningham College?* Briefly, I flashed in anger upon Experience and Louisa. But I had not shared my disgrace even with them. Who could have told my mother?

"You've lied to me. How long have you been lying to me?"

"I don't know what you mean, Mama."

"Stop! It makes me sick to hear it."

She had not moved from the door. She would not let me pass, I realized with terror. I stood out in that night air that had seemed so beautiful, so magical, just a minute ago. If only she would let me into the house.

I started up the stairs, but she moved from the door to meet me at the top step.

"How long? That's all I ask. I put the blame on you. How long?"

"Please, Mama, let me inside."

"I cannot trust you in this house anymore. How can I trust you even to sleep under this roof?"

I began to cry. "I am sorry, Mama. Please forgive me."

"I can't even trust those," she said, her voice thick. I realized, with a start, she was crying herself. "Your tears are lies, too."

"Please, Mama, just let me inside, and I will explain. I will explain everything."

"You cannot sleep here," she said.

"Please!"

"I cannot trust you underneath this roof."

I do not know how I managed to be on the ground, but I was. I had sunk all the way down into the earth, and could only double over and cry. I knelt like that until I heard the swing of her skirts as she came down off the porch, as she stood over me. I could smell her perfume, the smell of the lemon juice she used to bathe her lily petals and keep her skin soft and bright, the hot cotton of her waistcoat—my mother's good graces in the air around me.

And then she thrust something small and crumpled up underneath my nose.

In that queer purple light of the evening, I could just make out *my wife . . . you would wish it, too . . . Emmanuel Chase.*

"What is this?" I said.

"I am not a fool, Libertie. So do not treat me as one."

I took the paper from her hand and turned it over in my own.

"This is what's upset you?"

"You've compromised your honor with a man who lives in my house. Of course this has upset me! Have you lost your mind?"

She did not know. She did not know that I had failed. I heard myself give a short, hoarse laugh. And then she slapped me.

My mother had never hit me before. Even as a small child, she had not swatted me—only Lenore, on rare occasions, had done something like that. I cannot say it even hurt very much—her blow landed soft, like a brush of silk, as if she had changed her mind between raising her arm and swinging it down.

When it was done, we both could only look at each other in surprise.

She recovered first. "I cannot believe you could be so foolish."

"I haven't done anything."

"You have ruined your future. You have spoiled our plans."

I laughed again at that, in the same hoarse voice, which sounded foreign, even to me. "They're already spoiled."

She raised her hand again. "Don't! Don't tell me if you've sunk that low! Don't say it!"

I should have said, *I am a failure, but not in the way you think.* I should have said, *I cannot pass a simple anatomy class, and even if I raise all the money in the world from Tom Thumb weddings and girls singing, Cunningham College will probably not want me back.*

Instead, I said, to the dirt beneath me, "I will never be a doctor."

She sank down beside me. She was there on the road beside me, in front of our house, and her face now was merely her own, the moonlight masking the changes that had shocked me when I first saw her that day. My mother.

"You've given up your dream."

"It wasn't mine," I said. "You dreamt it for me."

"It was ours."

"I cannot join you," I said. "I am sick of the smell of other women's blood, Mama. Please."

"So you'll leave me," she said. "So you chose your body over your mind. So you were weak."

"I am weak. But I did not fail you like that. Dr. Chase has been nothing but a gentleman. I have conducted myself with honor with him—"

"I have no reason to believe you," she said. "You've already proven yourself a liar."

She sat back in the dirt. Then she lay all the way down in the dust until she was looking at the night sky. We sat like that: Mama seeing stars, and me not daring to raise my eyes from the dirt, until she sighed heavily and settled even deeper into her skirts.

"I gave you too much freedom," she said. "So much freedom and you gave it up for the first bright man who smiled at you."

"I don't want him, Mama."

She took my hand in hers, still staring into the sky. Her voice was smaller now. "I know these tricks, Libertie. I hear them every day from the girls and women who come into my clinic, all big with child from a man who's left them. They tell me, even then, 'I don't want him,' but it's only to save their dignity. You think he will do this to you, too? I should know that, at least."

"He hasn't done a single thing to me," I said. "And I assure you, I don't want him to."

"You think it's love," she said. "Maybe it is love. But it is quite a thing, to be a wife. It is not the same as a lover. It is not the same as a doctor—"

"I know that, at least, Mama."

"It is definitely not the same as being a free woman." She turned to me, her eyes shining. "This is your ambition? You could be so much more, Libertie."

"No," I said, my voice thick with tears. "I can't."

She gave a ragged cry, the most terrible sound I have ever heard in the world, and if you would have told me as a little girl that I would have been the one to cause my mother to make that sound, I would have called you a liar. But here I was, beside her, as she sobbed.

"Come, Mama." I pushed myself up, to stand above her. She looked so small in her circle of skirts, her head bent. I leaned down and pulled her up by her elbows. "Come, Mama. I am not lost to you yet. I will not marry him, if it makes you cry," I said. I would have said anything to get her to stop making that sound. I got her to her feet. I put my arm through hers. I walked with her slowly, through the yard, up the steps, through the still-open door.

It took a moment to realize we were not alone in the room. There was Lenore, and our houseguests—the Graces, Madame Elizabeth, Lucien, and Emmanuel Chase himself, who stood at the mantel, a look of nervous expectation on his face.

He stepped forward. "You told her?" he said. I realized he was speaking to me.

"She discovered on her own," I said.

Mama stepped forward and held out her hand. "Congratulations," she said.

As Emmanuel reached to take it, she doubled over, a stream of sick splattering the hem of her skirts.

And that was how we announced we were to be married.

EMMANUEL SAID WE could always elope. "We do not need to stand up before your mother and family. We could be married by a judge and leave for Haiti as soon as possible." But I knew if the mere mention of marriage had made my mother sick, it would possibly kill her if we brought more humiliation through an elopement.

So we planned for our wedding. Quickly, because in my harried scheming, I'd figured it would be another two months before Cunningham College's letter informing my mother that I was not welcome back would reach the house. If I was safely married by then, and on a ship to Haiti, I could spare myself the exquisite pain of seeing her further disappointment. I was a coward in that way.

It seemed to me marriage was as good a plan as any other. I would not be a doctor, but I could perhaps be a wife. This optimism sprang from the fact that I was still not sure what a wife would be, but I knew what a doctor was and that I couldn't be one.

We were to be wed quickly. Madame Elizabeth announced she would make my wedding dress and wrote to Monsieur Pierre to tell him she would not be home for another month. She installed herself in Mama's front parlor, with a ream of white cotton and one long panel of lace that we had managed to buy, which she assured me she would drape across my shoulders.

All of the preparations I had made for the play wedding just a few weeks before suddenly became real. We were to be married in the same circle of trees, as close to my father's grave as possible. I had insisted on that for Mama's sake, but my mother had looked at me blankly when I'd told her, then nodded. She was not speaking to me. She nodded or shook her head, but she did not share any words with me. She continued to speak to Emmanuel—with him, she kept everything the same—issuing him orders for the clinic, conferring with him on patients, showing him the books. It was only I who was enveloped in silence.

Madame Elizabeth tried to talk with her. Emmanuel himself asked her to please stop. But she would only say, "I'll speak to my daughter again on her wedding day."

The Graces had left by then. They were committed to two more dates in the North—one in Hartford, Connecticut, and one in Florence, Massachusetts. We'd watched them leave for Manhattan, and as the boat pulled away to cross the East River, I tried to remember that I had never fully belonged to them at all. I had always been left out. Emmanuel took my hand as he stood beside me. I told myself, *Soon, you will belong to him*, and the thought was both thrilling and made me sad. If you would have asked me then what my heart's desire was, it would have been to be with the Graces on a ferry or in a coach, maybe thinking pleasantly about Emmanuel Chase but not anywhere close to him in reality.

When we could no longer see the ship, we walked back downtown to Mama's hospital, to where Emmanuel now slept, in the red velvet waiting room of the clinic. He had agreed to leave my mother's house the night our engagement was announced. "Believe me," he had said to her as he held his bags before him, "I meant no disrespect to your household, Madame Doctor. You have been nothing but—"

And Mama had cut him off. "I believe you," she'd said, and he had been so relieved he did not hear what I had heard, the words unsaid, which were that she believed him—but not me, her own daughter.

Emmanuel and I allowed ourselves a half hour visit each day in the waiting room, when it had closed for the afternoon, while Mama and Lenore, on the floors above us, set the clinic right for the night. We would sit in that parlor, and Emmanuel would tell me what would come to pass in Haiti.

"In Haiti, you will meet my sister and Ti Me."

"In Haiti, Papa will be the first to greet you."

"You'll learn how to say that word, once we are in Haiti."

And I could almost believe him, I desperately wished to believe him, that the future was a promise. But then I would leave him and go back home.

Madame Elizabeth did not, of course, have her dressmaker's dummy in Kings County, and so instead she laid out the pieces of my dress on the parlor floor. Every night, there was a bit more to my bridal costume, and I would come back from my talk with Emmanuel and see it where it lay, deflated, on the floorboards, a kind of skinny ghost of my life to come. It made me sick to see it all flat like that. A bad omen.

"Put it on me," I told Miss Elizabeth, and she laughed. "I've never seen a girl so eager to be a bride."

The night before the wedding, Emmanuel Chase came for dinner, and it was almost as it had been when we had first met. Mama stood at the top of the table and raised her cup and toasted both of us. "A happy marriage to my Libertie," she said, and I felt the tears run down my face in gratitude that she had seemed to forgive me.

But when I went to embrace her later that evening and held her close, she whispered in my ear, "Don't do it," and I realized that she would never bring herself to forgive me, and I went up to bed cold.

Emmanuel Chase stayed the night, since he did not wish to travel back to the clinic so late. I lay in my room, feeling the heat creep back up my bones, imagining that I heard him crawling up the stairs to scratch at my door and beg for . . . what, I was not sure. I knew what happened in the marriage bed. I had known since a young age—Mama had not been shy about that. I thought of what would happen the next night and kicked the sheets off—they suddenly felt too heavy.

In the last week, our time together in the parlor had become something else. It was no longer a telling of what would happen once we got to that country I still could not quite imagine. Our time had become a kind of war between ourselves—or rather, a war of both of us against desire. I did not think a man could make the sounds that Emmanuel Chase made, as he reached first to grab my shoulders, then my arms, then my forearms, then my hands, where they rested in my lap—too daring, that. Then back to my shoulders and then my neck, which he pulled close to his, forcing me to bend my head toward his, as he desperately moved his mouth. I would watch him do all this and realize, with amazement, that I was doing the same to him, holding with the same urgency to his neck, mirroring the movement of his lips with my own.

And then we would hear a step above us, or Lenore or Mama drop a scalpel, or the sound of a canister rolling across the floor, and we would separate—those last few days, I'd heard him gasp as we did so—and pull apart, and sit in the velvet again, to quiet our breathing.

So I lay awake and waited to hear his fingernails draw across my door. But all night long, there was nothing.

At dawn, I rose. I could not stand lying there anymore. I crept down to the parlor and knelt on the floor, running my thumb up and down the seams of the wedding gown. Madame Elizabeth had stitched them with such care I wasn't even sure where they were. I discovered one stray tuft of a thread, and I almost pulled it loose.

That's how Madame Elizabeth found me when she came down an hour later. "You waste time in fancies," she said. "You only have so many hours in your wedding day." And she had helped me stand, directed me to the bowl of water she'd set out for my bath.

When I put on the final dress, the armpits and the neck immediately darkened, sweat leaking into tight cotton.

I was standing in the parlor, my arms above my head, as Madame Elizabeth dabbed underneath them with bicarbonate of soda, oohing and aahing about her progress, when Lenore rushed in.

"It is Miss Hannah," she said. "She's breathing heavy and almost gone."

So Mama and Emmanuel both left the house—Mama in her nicest shawl, and Emmanuel half-shaved. "I can come, too," I said, but neither stopped to tell me no; they were both already on their way.

Madame Elizabeth looked at me, full of pity. "It's probably best for you to stay here."

The house was suddenly quiet again, without them. It was almost like the old days. I lifted the hem of my skirt and headed toward the garden. "You'll spoil it!" Madame Elizabeth called.

I turned my head to look at her. "I won't."

Lenore had taken good care of the garden while I was away. I saw my mother's hand on the little pieces of wood she'd stuck by each row, and below it, sometimes, in Lenore's, a drawing of the leaves in question. I squatted, just enough, over the grass. I closed my eyes. I breathed in.

Mama still grew pansies. I picked the pinkest one, pulled it from its stem, and rolled the petals between my fingers till they tore apart. They left a stinging stickiness, made the palms of my hands dry and thirsty.

I held my palm to my nose, smelling my skin and the petals. I lifted my open palm to my mouth and licked it clean, each finger carefully, the bitter taste of flowers on my tongue. I reached out, with both fists, for the heads of more flowers and crammed them into my mouth. Did not the Bible say, *My beloved is mine, and I am his: he feedeth among the lilies?* I rolled petals over my lips and between my teeth until my mouth was sour with them. I'd read so many poems comparing beauty and love to flowers, but no one talked of how much they actually stung your tongue.

My haunches ached, from squatting. Finally, I stood up, placed my hand on the small of my back, and stretched backward to keep the hem of my gown out of the dirt. Then I left the garden and went back up the stairs, to wait for my groom and my mother.

Our wedding, I do not remember well. I only remember the sadness and shock from the loss of Miss Hannah. Madame Elizabeth and I cut the hem of one of Mama's old cloaks and tore it up into black arm-bands. Mama wore hers on her right arm, and I wore mine on my left, as she walked me down the aisle.

"A wife truly is a helpmate and a pillar," Reverend Harland said as Emmanuel and I knelt before him. "She is obedient to her Lord, her husband. We cannot raise up a great nation of man without a loyal and obedient wife and mother—as she stands, as she decides, so stands and decides the fate of the Negro people. The redemption and the triumph of the Negro race will come from the hearth, will come from the home, and will spread from there to the ballot box, to the pulpit, to the world. A wife holds the world in her lap and hands it to her husband."

While he spoke, Emmanuel and I looked straight ahead. I could see, from the corner of my eye, Emmanuel bend his head at the word "lord" and not raise it again till Reverend Harland pronounced us married. Then I turned to him. He kissed my cheek, and there was a smattering of subdued applause. He helped me to my feet, and we walked down the aisle, arm in arm, the whole church watching us.

The heat did not break. We stood out in the sun while the men shook Emmanuel's hand and the women looked from him to me and back again and then at the waist of my dress, trying to determine if it was thicker than it had been a month before, trying to find a reason we had married so hastily or even, I saw in the petty flash of a few eyes, why he had married me at all.

Our wedding night, we slept the same we had the day before—myself in my own bedroom, my husband down below. There was a moment when Lucien had leered and Madame Elizabeth had nudged Mama—"Perhaps we should leave the house to the newlyweds"—but Mama had looked so stern the joke had died, and so no one had tried to test her.

I lay as I had only a few hours ago, restless in bed, even the thinnest of sheets oppressive. Except now, there was the scratch at the door I had waited for. I opened it, and Emmanuel stood before me. In the dark of the hallway, his skin gleamed, so pale.

"We will wait," he said. "It is enough to wait." And then he leaned over and kissed me, this time full on the mouth. "You taste of flowers," he said.

"Flowers taste awful, you know."

He smiled at me, until I returned his smile, and then he left my door.

We were to leave in three days for Haiti, accommodations Emmanuel had worked so hard to secure as soon as I'd accepted him.

Vrè lanmou pa konn danje

Real love knows no danger

B ecause our ship was headed to Haiti, there was no embarrassment about our berth. On Haitian ships—at least this one—colored people were allowed cabins. Already, this world was better. The ship's captain knew Emmanuel's father, and so we had a private cabin, given over to us with much winking and nodding, so much that I could not look anyone on board in the eye.

Mama did not come to see me off—she took her leave at her own front door. Lenore was the one who stood on the pier below us and waved the white handkerchief for us, the last little bit of home I would see for a long time, maybe until I died. That thought brought a sharp taste to my tongue, a tightness to my throat. Not tears, because I had promised myself I would not cry about saying goodbye to that world, Mama's world; I had promised myself I would celebrate. I saw Lenore's handkerchief flash once more, and I turned my head to spit into the ocean, to get rid of that acid within me.

I spent the rest of the afternoon in the cabin. I was seasick. I did not know this about myself, as I had never traveled for so long on a boat before. It made me hate water and curse waves as we were rolled around over and over again. My head had a dull ache. Sometimes, Emmanuel would bring me cups of musty water, flat beer, sour cider. I could not eat the biscuits and dried fish that everyone else did. Even the sight of the curled tails, studded in salt, made me turn and be sick. I was miserable.

The only relief came at night. That first one, Emmanuel lay beside me, stinking of petrified fish, and told me to lie down on my stomach. "Take off your nightgown," he said.

I should have felt scared or shy. If I was a good woman, I would have felt trepidation at the first person besides Mama to see me whole. But all I felt was the roll of the waves, and relief that I could get the muslin off my sweaty skin.

I shut my eyes tight while he traced a botany lesson on my skin with a single finger

"Dorstenia," he said. "It looks like a tiny tree, crowned with a shooting star. You do not have trees like this, in America. It is a cousin of the fig. Its flower isn't soft and inviting . . ." Here, his finger traced all the way down to my hips, where they met my thighs, lingered there, then made its way back up. "Its flower is hard and standoffish. It is called a 'shield flower.' Its face looks like a wall of stone. But when you look more closely, you see the flower is made up of a hundred little blossoms, all closed off tight." He had reached my shoulders again, spread out his hands, felt the strength of my back.

"Why do you tell me these things now?" I asked. "You do not speak like a lover." I at least felt calm enough to tease.

"Because as my wife," he said, "there will be a whole new knowledge to learn, to aid me, and we may as well begin now."

His voice was light, so I opened my eyes and saw the shape of him roll above me, before I closed them again, still cowed by the waves.

"But what if I am too sick to remember?"

"I'm not speaking to you. The lessons are not for you. They're for
your body. She will remember." And then I felt his hand again, in the
middle of my back, drawing, I suppose, the flowers that made up the
shield of a Dorstenia.

He touched me until his fingers trembled. I shut my eyes even
tighter, pressed myself into the hay mattress of the berth. His fingers
lifted, and then I felt him turn over, onto his own back. He breathed
hard and heavy, as if he was at a gallop, and the sheet that covered us
began to shake.

I opened my eyes, sat up on my elbows, and watched him.

A man touching himself is a peculiar thing. My mother had told me
about women's bodies but not men's. I'd seen male members on barn-
yard cats before, and sometimes rude and red on a stray dog. I remembered, once, glimpsing one, folded over on itself in a nest of gray hair,
between the legs of an old man whom Mama helped to dying. I'd been
six or seven then, and Mama had had to ask me three times to hand her
her bag, before she'd looked up and followed my gaze. She'd pursed her
lips, pulled the man's cloak over him, and said, "You shouldn't make
patients uncomfortable with staring, Libertie."

At Cunningham, in anatomy class, they had asked me to leave the
room during the lessons on glands. I'd leaned against the side of the
building, staring out into the unfinished green, listening to the muffled voice of the professor calling out the body parts. When the class
was done, the men had left and I returned to the room, alone, to the
lesson written on the chalkboard, to name the parts to myself. Since
no one was in the room with me, I'd practiced saying them in different
voices—high-pitched, like a superior lady's, or low and growly, like a
cat's.

I watched my husband's hand move faster. In the dark of the cabin,
his skin was so dim—like a gray stone glimpsed at the bottom of a

well. His breath shuddered. The whole cabin, so close, became nearly unbearably hot. And then he groaned—like a body taking its last breath—and shuddered one more time and was quiet.

I looked at him. He was staring glassily at the beams of the ship. "I'm sorry, my love," he said. When he reached to touch my cheek, his hand was damp.

I did not leave my bed the next day. I tried to stand in the cabin, but the roll of the ship nearly forced me to my knees, so I crawled back into the berth and shut my eyes.

Emmanuel left me to walk on the deck. Above the groan of the ship as it moved through the water, I heard his high shout or some of his laughter.

The ship was a trading one that sold only a few berths to travelers. In the morning, he pulled me out of our bed to walk the deck with him. He said, "You cannot lie down forever. It will make everything worse." My legs did not feel like my own. I was scared, and I took just a few steps before going back down. I did not know if there were any other women on board, or if there were, if those women were colored. And in my sickness, I did not have the will to ask him.

That night, he did not even have to ask me to lie down. I did so gladly, eager to feel something besides the waves.

"Plumeria," he said, "are beautiful flowers. Long and thin and white. They look almost like stars, or maybe the legs of jellyfish. They could be as at home beneath the water as on land. They smell strongest at night." Here, he leaned over and smelled my lap.

"The smell is beautiful," he said. "So beautiful that three hundred years ago an Italian count stole it from the isles and made it into a perfume. The flowers make it to lure in sphinx moths, to do their polli-nating for them. The moths are driven mad by the scent, looking every-where for nectar, but the flowers are a flirt. Like my Libertie sometimes is. They have no nectar, but they've convinced the moths to do their propagating for them."

And here, his fingers stopped trailing on my spine and swept down, and his whole hand grabbed my behind.

He was already touching himself. I turned over, and he knew I would watch him, so he looked into my eyes, his face looking first furious, then frightened, and then so melancholy I worried he would weep. He finally closed his eyes. His shoulders shuddered, he groaned again, like the ship in the ocean, and then he was still.

I was determined to walk the whole ship the next morning. I did so on my husband's arm—he took me to the front and the other end. He made a show of calling me his "dear wife." He said, "We are to live in Haiti." I realized that the white men on board were mostly Northerners. It probably had not occurred to them, until that moment, that Emmanuel was colored. A few of them looked at him as if he had played some sort of trick. They, perhaps, had taken me for some sort of concubine. The crew was mostly Negroes—some American, but most from Haiti. They said, "Trè bèl" when they saw me, and tipped their hat if they had one.

There was one other woman on board, a white one, the captain's daughter. She looked to be my age, maybe a few years younger. She looked straight through me when we passed, made a show of looking straight ahead.

"How much longer is the trip?" I asked Emmanuel.

"We have been on this journey for five days," he said. "We have eight or nine more."

Before us, the sea stretched in all directions, the water a deep green. "Do you see there?" he said, leaning in to point, his cheek on mine. "Look over there. Dolphins jumping in the waves."

It only looked like flashes of light, and I told him so.

"No," he said. "They're dolphins."

"Or maybe they are sirens," I said "come to lure all these men to their deaths."

"La Sirèn has a song," he said solemnly. "They say her home is at the back of the mirror. In the other world."

He did not move his mouth from my ear. Instead, he chanted into it,

> *La Sirèn, la balèn,*
> *Chapo m' tonbe nan lanmè.*
> *M' t'ap fè yon ti karès ak La Sirèn,*
> *Chapo m' tonbe nan lanmè.*
> *M' kouche ak La Sirèn,*
> *Chapo m' tonbe nan lanmè.*

"What does it mean?"

"You have to guess."

"I do not know your language well enough yet."

"And you'll never learn it with that attitude."

"Tell me what it means."

He leaned in close again. He had been waiting for this. I had played the game he wished, without even knowing it. "You'll learn tonight."

That night, he told me to lie on my back this time. As he pushed my nightgown down past my shoulders, I covered my face with my hands. He said:

"*The mermaid, the whale,*

"*My hat falls into the sea.*

"*I caress the mermaid,*

"*My hat falls into the sea.*

"*I lie down with the mermaid,*

"*My hat falls into the sea.*"

I saw Ben Daisy's hat, covered in pansies, held to my mother's chest. I pressed my fingertips into my eyelids until the image was washed over in an explosion of stars.

"Take your hands from your face, Libertie."

I did what Emmanuel asked. We stared at each other for a minute, listening to the water move beneath us.

"Take off your shirt," I said to him finally. He did not break my gaze as he obeyed me.

His skin looked so smooth in the dark. I reached for it, to run my hands along it, and he drew his breath in, sharp, as if I had burnt him. And then he caught my hand in his and firmly placed it back at my side.

"What we do together, the word for it in Kreyòl is 'kouche.' It means to make love, but it also means to be born and to die, and to lie down, too."

"All those things at once?"

"All those things happen when we lie together. You must have felt that."

I looked at him. I twitched my hips, impatient. "So begin, then."

"Dogs' bloodberries." He reached for my breasts and began to softly touch them.

"What are those?" My voice was faint.

"They are little red berries—peppers, really—that grow at home. Women take them for their wombs—with the plant you have, vervain. It waters them. They become fertile."

"You are very poetic," I said. "For a doctor."

I disobeyed him. I touched the skin on his chest as he knelt above me, until he doubled over himself and shuddered, the wet of him falling across my thighs.

It was strange, to stand with him in the mornings, in daylight, in the middle of the ocean, and act as though what had happened between us at night had not happened. I could see, in the glances of the crew members, in the eyes of the white men on board, that they had guessed what we did at night, had imagined something even more. But here was Emmanuel, walking me carefully up and down the deck, as if he hadn't wiped his seed on my skin at dawn.

We were four days from landfall when it happened. He had drawn every one of the plants in his knowledge, some of them twice, and the sheets in our cabin were stiff and scratchy with his work.

"There is only one more," he said, "that I have not told you."

"What is it?" I said.

By now, when he shuddered, I held him. Sometimes, he pressed his face into my neck. When he touched himself, I allowed myself to look everywhere—his face, his chest, his arm moving ridiculously quickly. Even his member I knew now, like some other specimen to understand. It was still strange, but it had become expected.

"Persimmon," he said. "They are yellow, and you wait until they are so ripe they are swollen, almost bursting, and when you finally taste them, they taste like the gods."

And then he did what he had not done before. He pushed my legs apart and bent his head there, and moved his tongue until I was moving my legs apart farther for him, without shame, only urgency. Then he was in me and above me, moving with the same rapidity as he did his own hand, so that it was over quickly enough—the groan again, and then the collapse, though this time I could feel him as he grew softer, soft enough to slip from between my legs.

I had thought, from Mama, that all love was fair. That's the way Mama practiced it. Love was doling out the right amount of care to each patient and spending the right amount of time at each bedside. No more, no less. Mama's love was democratic. But Emmanuel was a despot in his love. He grasped at me—at my legs and my arms and my belly and back—as if, if he held on tight enough, he could claim it all.

Our final nights before we reached Haiti, I told him to be quiet. I looked at his body and saw a psalm. Mama had told me a daughter is like a poem, and so a mate's body, as made for me as mine was made for him, was like a psalm from God, I thought.

I am black but comely, I sang to him to make him laugh. He did, though he blushed, and it was another point of wonder, that about this my husband could be pious.

"You sing to me the poetry of nature, and I sing to you the poetry of God," I said to him. Again, he looked shocked, and that was a pleasure, too, maybe the deepest one, after all these nights.

> *Behold, thou art fair, my love;*
> > *behold, thou art fair;*
> > > *thou hast doves' eyes.*
> *Behold, thou art fair, my beloved, yea, pleasant:*   *also our bed is green . . .*
> > *A bundle of myrrh is my well-beloved unto me;*
> *he shall lie all night betwixt my breasts . . .*
> > *As the apple tree among the trees of the wood,*
> > *so is my beloved among the sons.*
> > > *I sat down under his shadow with great delight,*
> > > *and his fruit was sweet to my taste.*

This is what I sang to him, the word of God all jumbled up, as I held the back of him in my hands, as I tasted his skin and flesh and muscle and bone.

My beloved put in his hand by the hole of the door, and my very self, my inside, opened up to him. *I rose up to open to my beloved,* is what I sang when I saw Emmanuel's brow at my thigh, his head between my legs, his eyes closed, the only movement the ship and him.

He told me about all the plants discovered by man, and I sang back to him the fruits from God. I panted in his ear, "We are one, we are together, as you promised," and I did not think of who I belonged to (my mother) before I belonged to him.

I spoke to him God's poetry while he lay in me, the holy words which seemed to have spoken of us before all creation, all nature, all wrath.

BEFORE I HAD left, Mama had given me a satchel with five bags of powders she had ground herself. "You do not have to be a slave to him in that way, at least," she'd said. I had seen enough of her books, copied her columns of writings, to know that she gave this remedy to most of the women who passed through her clinic. The richer ones, she asked for payment; the poorer ones, she did not. And sometimes, a woman had had the course but came to Mama anyways, a few months later, her monthlies stopped and her middle thickening, and then Mama would shut the office door and I would hear the woman sob that Mama was fallible in this.

That would never be me, I thought giddily. My freedom with Emmanuel would come from children. We would build a nation out of each other. That was what we were traveling toward. And our new country needed citizens—babies, so many babies, so many beautiful brown babies, all fat and ready to fill a house.

So I took the medicine she gave me and, one day before we spotted land at Jacmel, I scattered it all over the rail. I told Emmanuel what I was doing, too, and he was delighted.

We were sure that where we were headed, we wouldn't need it. We were free to be abundant.

EMMANUEL HAD TOLD me, "Jacmel is the most beautiful city in the world."

It is a difficult thing, to be told something is beautiful by someone who already loves it best. As we approached, he watched my face avidly for my approval, and I tried to look expectant, to look amazed by what I saw. But it looked, at first, like any other town. I smiled and gasped, for his sake, and I did not think it bad, this first falsehood that stood between me, Emmanuel, and this land. I thought it was another sign of love.

The town hugged the base of the mountains—you could see them rolling up, as the ship approached. They were a deep, inviting green, and the buildings that came up to the shore were variations of white and pink and yellow.

We had come only with two trunks—one packed with our clothes, intermingled, the other full of Emmanuel's supplies: his doctor's bag, the plant specimens he had managed to collect in New York, and the homeopathic literature he was eager to bring back to Haiti. The rest of what we would need for our life together, he said, would be in his father's house. Since we did not have many possessions, we hired a man and a mule to take us to Emmanuel's home, which we reached by steadily climbing the road from the wharves, up through town. We passed the Rue de Commerce, where the traders and businessmen had their shops and then, farther, up the steep city streets, until we got to the quarter where Emmanuel lived, where the wealthiest lived and looked down at the harbor below. All around me, people spoke and called and laughed in a language I did not understand, and it struck me, finally, what I had done. The sun was high above us, my skin was warm and sweating, I was in a heat I did not recognize, climbing a hill a thousand miles away from my mother's face, and I had not heard her voice for longer than a moment in nearly a year. I could not help it: I began to cry.

"What is the matter?" he asked.

All I could say to him was, "I am a foolish girl."

The road got steeper. The dust rose to my eyes, making them even wetter. By the time we reached the house, Emmanuel had begun to walk many feet ahead of me, overwhelmed by the tears on my face.

When Emmanuel had whispered to me in my mother's waiting room about his father's house, I admit I had not paid much attention to his actual words. It was from his tone, the urgency of how he described it, that I had imagined it as something much grander than what was before me. He had spoken lovingly of the large shuttered windows that faced the street. Of the front veranda his father had built, with the iron railings. Of the oak front door that was always kept shut and, cut into it, the smaller door that the family used to pass in and out of the house. "We only open the doors proper," Emmanuel had told me, "when someone in our family dies."

The actual house that was before me was shorter than what I had pictured, but still impressive. The wood was painted a pale pink, and the black iron railings were winking in the sun. Emmanuel's father had been given the land when he came to Haiti ten years before—the promise to American Negro settlers fulfilled. He had traveled up and down the island, writing to the mother church back home, until they gave him the money to build a house worthy of the bishop that he was. At the very top of the house's flat roof was a weather vane with the imprint of an iron rooster. It was strange to have on a house in a place that felt as if wind had not been born yet, I thought, as I looked above and felt the sweat trickle down my neck.

At the front door, the mule driver untied our two trunks from the back of the animal and said something to Emmanuel. A joke—because Emmanuel threw back his head and laughed, and tipped him an extra coin.

"What was it?" I asked, wiping the sleeve of my dress across my face, trying to rub it clean of dirt and tears.

"He only noticed you crying," Emmanuel said. "And teased me about it."

"What did he say?"

"You have to learn the language sometime, Libertie," he said.

I thought at first he had arranged for the household to greet us; inside the hall, three people stood in a straight line. His father broke form first—a man a few inches shorter than Emmanuel, so just about level with my height. He was the same complexion as Emmanuel. He reached out to shake his son's hand. But he did not extend one to me, only blinked.

Beside him was Ti Me. She, too, was not quite how Emmanuel had described her. In Kings County, he had told me that Ti Me had been young once but had dedicated her youth to raising him, after his mother and siblings had died. I had pictured a woman old and bent, with gray hair. But the woman who stepped forward to greet me was probably at most thirty. Her skin was smooth. And she had bright, intelligent eyes, which darted over Emmanuel's face, then my own. She embraced him, as his father had, and pulled at his cheeks—scolding him, I guessed, for not eating enough. She was the only person in the house as dark as me.

Beside her was a woman Emmanuel's height. Ti Me was dressed in white, in this heat. But this woman was dressed in a rusty-red skirt and a black jacket. Her skin was as pale as Emmanuel's and his father's, but it had a bright-pink undertone, as if she was about to burn. Her hair hung in great stiff sections around her cheeks. Each section had been ironed once and then again, to get rid of the kink, and then violently curled. Her face was Emmanuel's, but leaner. His twin, Ella, I realized, with a start.

"And who is this?" she said as I stood beside Emmanuel.

"My wife," he said.

"You're married?" She raised one pale hand to her mouth.

I turned to Emmanuel. "You did not tell them?"

His father looked as if he was going to shout, and his sister was holding her stiff hair back from her face, her lips beginning to part—in a smile or a scream, I could not tell.

"You did not get my letters?" Emmanuel stepped back.

"You've married without my permission?" his father said. "And to whom?" He looked at me again, the whole length of me. I was, I could tell, in some way, lacking.

"Libertie Sampson. She is Dr. Sampson's very own daughter. A physician in her own right. A graduate of Cunningham College."

I pulled on Emmanuel's arm to stop him, but he would not. "A true scholar," he said.

"You married without my blessing," his father said.

"I wrote to you to tell you. I sent three letters to you to tell you of it."

"Who married you?" This was from his sister.

"The reverend of my church in Kings County," I said. "Reverend Harland, whom I believe you know, Bishop Chase."

Emmanuel's father looked from me to his son. "You are always too rash," he said.

I could feel myself begin to cry again. But I could see, from the corner of my eye, Emmanuel's sister watching me. So I stepped forward and unknotted the bonnet from under my chin. Once I had gotten it off, I moved toward Ella and took her in my arms. I held her there, though I could feel her body stiffen. I felt her tortured curls scratch against my cheeks, made harsh by whatever hot comb she'd lain on them. She smelled of dried perspiration and burnt hair.

"I am sorry," I said. "But I hope we can be sisters now."

I let her go and hurried over to her father, avoiding whatever look was on her face. "I am sorry, sir," I said, holding him in the same way. "I hope you can forgive your daughter."

I held him longer than I had Ella. He, too, was resistant, but I sensed that I should not let him go as soon, or this whole scene would be made even more ridiculous. As I held him, I could hear Emmanuel speaking in Kreyòl to Ti Me, who then shrieked—he must have told her I was his wife—and gave a short laugh.

"It is not funny," I heard Ella scold.

"Sorry, mum," Ti Me said.

I held on for a few moments more, for good measure, and then I let the bishop go. I stepped back to stand beside Emmanuel and watched his face, warily.

"It is not how I wished it would happen," Bishop Chase said finally.

"But we are here with you now, Father."

"Ti Me," the bishop said, "show them to Emmanuel's room," and then he left the foyer.

Ella had composed herself by then.

"Will you show Libertie the house?" Emmanuel asked her.

"We will have four for dinner, not three," she called to Ti Me.

Ella kissed her brother on the cheek. "We are happy you are here," she said. And then she left us.

Emmanuel and I still stood in the foyer of the house, which was so dim all I could see of that murky room with high ceilings was a flash of silver from a mirror hung on the farthest wall. All the shutters were closed against the afternoon sun.

To the right of the foyer, I could see a small room—with a table and chair, and a few books stacked on the end of the table—what must have been Bishop Chase's library. It, too, was dimly lit—its large window opening out onto the street also shuttered. There was a flutter in that room, and I realized that was where Emmanuel's father must have retreated.

To my left was a staircase, leading to the bedrooms. Directly in front of us was a dining room, its heavy oak table set for a formal dinner with six places, a single silver candelabra in the middle. The windows were unshuttered in the dining room, so that you could look out onto the back courtyard. It was full of a few flowering bushes and some clay pots growing herbs. The ground had been overlaid with stone. At the back of the courtyard was a small shed—the cookhouse, I realized—and farther away from everything, the latrine. Through the window, I saw Ella reappear, stalking toward the cookhouse.

"Come," Emmanuel said, taking my hand. He led me up the stairs, Ti Me behind us, carrying one of the trunks on her back.

"Oh," I said when I saw her struggle, and Emmanuel looked over his shoulder, then to me.

"She will carry it," he said carefully.

Upstairs were five rooms—more than I had expected. But then I remembered the mother and brothers and babies long dead. This house had been built for a much-larger family.

The doors for each room were shut. Our room was the first by the staircase. Its windows, at least, faced the backyard, so the shutters were open and the light was not as dim. There was a single double bed, the mattress dipped in the middle, a mirror, this one smaller than the one downstairs in the foyer, a chest of drawers, with a metal owl and a pitcher standing on it, and a wooden cross, above the bed.

Ti Me letting the trunk fall to the floor with a bang. She looked at me, pointedly, and said, "Ti fi sa a twò cho." Then she left us.

"What did she say?"

"You have to learn, Libertie."

"You won't even tell me this once?"

"She said you are a pretty mistress," he said.

I sat on the mattress and felt it dip further beneath me. "You and Ella do look a lot alike," I said.

"She was born three minutes ahead of me, my father tells me, but I've been playing catch-up ever since."

He sat down beside me and put his arms around me. I would have been happy to begin, but as we moved together, I leaned my head back and saw that the walls of the room did not reach the ceiling. The top of the room was open, and if I listened, I could hear Bishop Chase and his daughter and Ti Me talking downstairs, almost as if they were in the room beside us.

"Stop," I said. I pointed.

Emmanuel looked up. "Ah, all the rooms are like that in this house," he said. "If the gap was closed, no air could circulate. It keeps the room cool. So that we may do things like this." And then he pressed himself closer.

To live in a house where we all heard one another—I had not expected this. I thought, again, of my mother, and I wanted to cry. But I did not.

Instead, I pushed him away.

"They are waiting," I said.

THE CHASE HOUSEHOLD seemed to exist in some other country. It was situated not quite in Haiti, not quite in America. Outside the house, the business of the world pulled Emmanuel and his father to different parts of town. Bishop Chase rose early in the morning and refused to take a midday break, even when the rest of Jacmel fell quiet at the hottest part of the day. During that time, he would come back to the house to sit in his office and go over his papers—letters to his diocese back in the United States, to other bishops on other islands, to the deacons and priests in churches he had yet to even see. His progress in building his own church had been quick at first but had slowed in the last few years. The wave of American Negroes he had expected to come and bolster his original outpost, after the war was over, had not arrived. I suspected that they were of the same mind as Lucien, not willing to give up their bets on life in America just yet. But it was the bishop's belief that they would still come, in time.

I was to learn that Bishop Chase's favorite subject was how foolish American Negroes were. It was clear he considered himself as not quite one, which was strange, because he most definitely did not consider himself Haitian. He was a citizen of the imaginary country where his household was based, one of hardworking and disciplined colored people—though he was convinced that these were very rare. Haitians were lazy and kept too many scores. American Negroes were too short-sighted and did not understand history.

"If he hates both, who does he expect to join him in the new world?" I'd asked Emmanuel once, and he had looked at me, wounded.

"No one loves the colored race as much as my father," he'd said.

Well, he has a funny way of showing it, I wished to say. But I did not. I still thought it was love to say nothing.

At dinner that first night, I sat beside Emmanuel, my plate with two fewer potatoes than everyone else's. Bishop Chase leaned over his own plate, heavy with potatoes and topped with the leg of a chicken, and explained himself to his son.

"I have backed the wrong horse," he said.

Since they had arrived in the country, Bishop Chase and his fellow

émigrés had rallied around the politician Geffrard, who had managed
to become president for a time. Geffrard had given over lands at his
own palace to the American émigrés when they'd first arrived, and
when their initial crops had failed after the first growing season, he
had given them food from his own provisions. He had also taken land
from Haitians to give to the Americans. And the Americans were there
because the poorer Haitians had refused to return to the sugar planta-
tions that made Haiti such a jewel and a prize. Geffrard had looked for
the Americans to take the land and force the smaller Haitian farmers
into the type of destitution that would lead them to agree to the awful
work of making sugar for no pay. But Bishop Chase did not mention
this part of the deal they had entered into with Geffrard and his government. He only spoke of past and future glories.

Bishop Chase sighed. "No truer friend to the American Negro than
Geffrard."

"He has not been in power for nearly ten years," Emmanuel said.

"Do not insult Father." This was Ella.

"How is the truth an insult?"

"It is disrespectful," she said.

"A listing of history is disrespectful?"

"You would know. You understand disobedience better than I do,"
she said.

And then she turned to me. "Do you enjoy the food?"

I had never been looked at with such open hostility, but her mouth
was fixed into a very sweet smile.

"I like it very much," I said.

"You do not have to lie for politeness' sake. Haitian food is not like
what we have in America."

"This meal is very good."

"In America, you know, our meals are so much better for digestion," she said. "Here, it is always the plantain, the potato, and sometimes the goat. What I would not give for a gooseberry."

"Ah, but they are so sour," I said. "You were lucky to have a good one. There have not been good crops the last few seasons. When were you last in America?"

I had thought this would flatter her, but she narrowed her eyes and turned back to her plate, and the table was quiet for a moment.

"Ella has not lived in America since she was nine years old," Emmanuel said, laughing. I had pleased him with my unintended insult, I realized with dismay.

"If this is supposed to be proof of filial piety," Ella said, "it is not a very good one."

"Again, you are angered by facts."

"Ella has missed your arguments," Bishop Chase said, "though she won't ever admit it."

Perhaps, I thought, this was how siblings behaved. It was strange to see Emmanuel reduced to participating in someone else's game.

"You worry about Boisrond-Canal?" Emmanuel asked his father.

"He is a good man, I think. And he is friendly to the Americans. But he does not understand what we could build here, for the black man. For all black men. He is thinking of his nation, to be sure, but he does not understand cultivating allies with American Negroes. And then the Negroes I introduce to him, their heads are turned by white Americans, by the crumbs they are finding here and there . . ."

"Not crumbs," I said quietly, to my lap. Bishop Chase, at the pulpit in his mind now, did not hear me.

"They do not understand the future," he said. "And Boisrond-Canal . . . he does not understand our mission like Geffrard did."

"Father, Geffrard is not even in the country anymore."

"Good times will come again," the bishop said. "It is just hard to know when."

I ate in silence until I remembered. *At least I may have discovered something to charm them*, I thought.

"Emmanuel," I said, "have you shown your father your gift?"

"Not yet."

"I will go and get it now. I think he would enjoy it."

I stood up from the table before he could stop me, went to the foyer where Ti Me had left the second trunk by the stairs. In the dim light, I fumbled with the latches. The gift had been packed under Emmanuel's instruments and the dried cuttings wrapped in paper.

"Be careful, Libertie," he called.

But I would not be deterred. I called back, "I know how to unpack a trunk."

I gingerly laid each piece, each glass vial and book, on the ground until I found it, folded at the bottom of the trunk. I pulled it out, set it beside me, and repacked the pieces. When I came back to the dining room, the three of them were eating in silence. Ella did not even look up but kept her head bowed over her plate.

It was strange to have a bit of power over the two of them. To know something they did not. It had been so long since I felt this feeling that I relished it for a minute, holding the package behind my back.

"Well," Emmanuel said, smiling, "show it to him."

I shook the paper until it unfolded. It was a full print of all our colored heroes—there was Hiram Revels and Fredrick Douglass and John Mercer Langston, and even Martin Delany, my mother's old friend.

"*The Mystery*, out of Pittsburgh, made prints for Independence Day," I said. "Emmanuel bought it special for you, so that you could add it to your collection."

"Ah." Bishop Chase sighed. He looked at it from over his glasses but did not move to take it from my hands. "Yes. A thoughtful gift." Then he turned his attention back to his plate.

I was left to stand there, all that power in my hands on that print, while Ella smiled in satisfaction at her plate and Emmanuel looked at his father, exasperated. He seemed about to open his mouth, to complain again, but I did not think I could bear it.

"I'll leave it in the hall," I said, "to hang."

Back in the darkness of the foyer, I carefully folded the print and leaned it against the banister. I heard a rustling behind me and turned to see Ti Me. At her hip was a wicker basket, loaded down with linens. She stared steadily at me, holding my gaze. I smiled back at her. She did not move, did not blink, only looked into my eyes with a kind of curiosity.

I did not know what to do. But the way she stared at me, I began to think I understood. I bowed my head to her and made a short curtsy. When I raised my head, she looked at me a moment longer, then turned on her heel and was gone.

"You should touch it," he whispered.

"I can't," I whispered back.

"You did on the ship, without asking."

His voice whistled in my ear.

"We were alone then."

"We were not alone. All around us were tens of men who watched my pretty wife walk up and down the deck—"

"Emmanuel!"

"And still I had her all for my own. But in my own house, she won't touch it."

"I would," I hissed, "but they can hear every word."

He rolled his head back on the pillow, looked at the gap in the ceiling above us.

"They are asleep."

"I can hear them breathing."

"I did not take you for a nervous one, Libertie."

"I am not nervous."

"Nerves will not do well in our life here."

"I am not nervous."

"I thought you had a strong temperament."

"I do."

"Then prove it on me. Kouche."

He took my hand in his, guided it between his legs, where he wished it to go. I did not think I would ever get used to that. The wonder of it—rigid in my hand, not like any other organ. It was a curiosity. I had seen between the legs of more women than I could count, but this, this was strange. It was almost as if it did not belong on a body. As if it was some kind of a prank. I pulled my hand away from his, pressed hard on the end of it to see what he would do. He groaned. Why Mama hadn't told me of this, in all her anatomy lessons, the little bit of power here, I did not know. I wished that I could discuss it with her, or with someone. I could not even write it in a letter to the Graces, I thought. They would not understand.

Beneath my hand, Emmanuel was very slowly thrashing his legs under the sheet, as if the fit itself was luxurious. He was whispering something, too, low and deep: "Bon lanmou, bon lanmou, bon jan love."

"Emmanuel!" It was another hiss, higher than Emmanuel's voice, that seemed to fill the whole room.

His legs immediately stilled, but he could not calm his breathing.

"Emmanuel!" That hiss again, so shrill.

He put his mouth close to my ear.

"Go to the door," he gasped. "If you do not, she will try the lock. She won't leave till you answer."

"Who?"

"Just go! Hurry!"

When I opened the door, Ella was before me. In the light of the candle she held, her face was haggard and overly pale, as if the muscle beneath her skin was inlaid with lime. She did not tie her hair up for bed, like any other Negro woman would. Instead, she had set on top of the mass of it a yellowed nightcap, which threatened to slide off of it all.

She jumped back slightly when it was I who opened the door. Then she recovered.

"Is Emmanuel all right?"

"Of course, he is," I said. "Why would you think he was not?"

"I heard strange noises. As if he was in distress."

"He is not."

She sighed, exasperated, then strained her neck, as if to see around me.

"Emmanuel, did the food not agree with you? You have been so long away—"

"I am fine, Ella," he called back.

"Are you sure?"

"He is fine," I said, and made to close the door.

"You do not know him as I do. He has a sensitive stomach. Anyone making noises like that cannot be well."

"You could not know what those noises meant. You are not married," I said without thinking.

She breathed in heavily at that, so much so that her candle flame shook. I looked at her, aghast at what I had said.

"Ella, I apologize . . ."

But she turned and made her way back down the hall. I watched the back of her, the nightshirt and the wobble of the flame as she walked. I did not want to face Emmanuel.

When I turned back around, he was still in bed but sitting up on his elbows. He was grinning.

"I knew you were the right one," he said. "I knew you were not nervous."

"Your sister now hates me."

"It does her good."

"It doesn't do me any good to have her hate me."

"Ignore her. She doesn't matter."

"What does that mean?"

"Nothing. Only we are twins, but we have not shared the same life for a very long time. Not since we were children."

"What does that mean?"

"Come back," he said, "and I will whisper it to you."

I returned to bed. I pulled my knees up to my chin and turned away from him. He pressed at me for a few minutes, pleading. "It is not so bad, Libertie. She will understand in the morning."

But I stayed tucked into myself, even after I heard him turn over onto his own side, his hands moving fast, before he thrust one arm over to grab at my shoulder and then fell asleep.

I DREAMT THAT night that a million tiny white feathers broke through the skin of the palms of my hands, and when I waved, I felt the breeze flow through them. When I awoke, Emmanuel was gone and his side of the bed was already cold. From the looks of the sun, it was still early in the morning. I had not been so derelict as to sleep in. I dressed as quickly as I could and opened the door, and tiptoed down the hallway and to the stairs. There was no sound of Ella or Bishop Chase. Or even Emmanuel.

The foyer was empty. Bishop Chase's office was empty. I went to stand in the dining room, to look through the windows at the back courtyard. A group of children played there—a few in burlap shirts, another few completely naked, none in pants or shoes. They were slapping their hands together and shouting. I could just hear a bit of their song.

> *Li se yon esklav ki damou*
> *Li se yon esklav ki damou*
> *Li se yon esklav ki damou*
> *Libète moun Nwa!*

They sang it a few more times before I recognized, with a start, my own name. I turned away from the window, my cheeks burning, and moved through the rest of the house.

In the sitting room, Ella was already composed on the lone divan—a battered wooden structure with the horsehair falling from the bottom. Emmanuel sat at the table, writing. Ella was bent over some sewing in her lap.

"There she is!" Emmanuel called, and put down his pen to come and press my hands into his. Ella would not look up.

"Good morning," I said, to both of them.

"My love, I must go see Monsieur Colon, my mentor here in Jacmel. I have not seen him in so many years, and he would be offended if I did not see him first."

"I will come with you."

"It is not necessary," he said.

I looked from his face to Ella's bent head and back again. I narrowed my eyes.

"You will go with Ella and Ti Me to market. When I return, we can begin to unpack the things for my office," Emmanuel said. "Monsieur Colon is a very intelligent man. But he is suspicious of women, especially a woman as beautiful as my wife. I will have to be gentle with the news of our marriage."

"He, at least, warrants that consideration," Ella said to the sewing in her lap.

"You will be happier here, Libertie, than coming with me."

I said nothing, only glared at him.

"You will have time enough to meet the rest of the neighborhood. Half of them know you are here already. Did you not hear the song the children have already made up in your honor?"

I shook my head.

Emmanuel smiled and began to snap his fingers, slightly out of time. "Li se yon esklav ki damou, li se yon esklav ki damou, li se yon esklav ki damou, Libète moun Nwa! Which means, of course, that I am a slave of love to my black Libertie."

My eyes shot through with pain as I felt tears form, but I forced myself not to cry. He looked at me expectantly.

"Very clever," I murmured.

"Ha! You will learn. Anything here that happens at midnight is known by dawn. And by morning, the neighborhood has turned it into a song."

He bent his head to kiss my fingers. I bent my own to meet his.

"Please don't leave me with her," I whispered.

"I thought you were brave," he murmured back.

And then he was gone.

I turned to Ella, who had not moved from the divan. I sat down, primly, on Emmanuel's chair.

"What are you sewing?" I said.

She unbent her head and looked at me. She held up a lady's jacket—black fabric with red thread she was embroidering. The embroidery was so thick and close together in some places that the jacket looked crimson. In others, it was nearly black, with only a bit of red curled over.

"Very nice," I said.

"You cannot possibly understand it."

"It is a jacket."

"Yes, but you can't know it."

I frowned. "I do not understand," I said.

"Exactly," she said. She set aside the jacket, as if in a rush. "We must get to market."

"Ti Me!" she called suddenly. "Ti Me!"

Ella and I sat there in the quiet. She glared at me, her nostrils flaring slightly. Today, her hair was pinned up, but two tendrils framed her face. One still held the paper curler she must have put in last night, after she left our bedroom. The other was valiantly trying to hold on to a curl but was losing in the humidity of Haiti.

Ti Me was slow to come, but she finally appeared in the doorway.

"Mademoiselle," she said.

"We must get to market, Ti Me. Honestly. Fwi a ap gate. We will be left with nothing. Papa must not be made sick paske nou parese."

"Wi, mademoiselle." Ti Me looked from me to Ella. "Just let me get my basket first," she said.

THE MARKET WAS a kingdom of women. All around me, old women were bent with produce loaded onto their backs, baskets topped with the green fringe of sweetgrass. Some of the old women had gray skirts; others, blue and yellow ones. There were younger women, too, who walked faster, hips rolling, legs spread wide, hurrying past. And children. There were children everywhere—some clothed, some naked, all barefoot. I had thought, back home, with my mother and Madame Elizabeth and Lenore all around, that I was dark. But here, shining in the sun, I saw women with skin the color of the night sky.

The sound of the market so loud it was nearly unbearable, but it was sweeter than the silence in the Chase household. It was the hum of a hundred women talking and laughing and trading and gossiping, to make the day run. Every woman, it seemed, was calling out to the others, "Maren, maren!" It was the one word I knew, the one I had learned from weeks on the boat. *Sailor, sailor,* the women were shouting. But when I asked Ti Me and Ella about it, Ti Me opened her mouth to answer and Ella cut her off.

"You'll notice, the Haitian women are not very chaste," she said. "And it all stems from that. All of this does. All of this chaos around us."

Ti Me closed her mouth and drew ahead of us, the basket balanced on her head. She had left this conversation.

Ella followed my gaze. "Oh, Ti Me would agree with me," she said. "It is part of Papa's work, to bring a civilizing force to this great country. Look." Ella pointed one pale finger. Behind us, the mountains rose, impressive and lush and green. "This country could be rich. But a country is only as wealthy as its wives and mothers. You will see."

I was not sure how the same home could produce an Ella, so full of spite her fingers shook at the mountains around us, and an Emmanuel, for whom the very same mountains brought tears to his eyes. I could not make sense of it, and I knew asking Ella directly would not get any response I could understand. It was a question for the night, for the space of time held between two bodies in bed—the one place in this country, I was learning, where I could speak the truth. Emmanuel, too.

I smiled at Ella in response.

To see her out in the market was strange. She walked like a very proud duck—both ankles turned nearly out, toes pointed slantwise. Every few feet, she swept the hem of her skirt up. I think it was to protect it, but it seemed to swirl up more dust and muck from the road. Ahead of us, Ti Me walked steadily, her own skirts tucked up into her apron to keep them from dragging in the mud. This practicality, perhaps, was what Ella thought of as so unchaste. It was what a man would think, not a woman, who knew how heavy skirts could get with dirt.

Watching Ella, I tried to see where Emmanuel was reflected in her movements. It relieved me that I could not. How could I love a man so much and detest the person closest to him? I thought again of what he had said. That they had not shared a life in a long time. I looked around me at the streets, the women bent over, Ti Me now stopping at a market stall, talking with another woman, a fruit I did not recognize in the palm of each of her hands. She was weighing them. Then she leaned over, spat on the ground. The two women began to argue furiously.

Ella stood watching, her arms crossed over her chest. The little boy at the stall watched, too, occasionally looking up at Ella, trying to read her expression. I caught his eye, and he grinned at me—a genuine smile. I smiled back.

Suddenly the argument stopped. Ti Me shouted, "Madame Sara!" and the other woman began to laugh. She held up her hands, as if in surrender.

Ti Me looked back at me slyly over her shoulder. "Madame Sara," she said, and then she looked pointedly at Ella to translate. She did not want me to miss the joke.

"It is a type of bird," Ella said. "It's very small and yellowish and black and green, and it's always chirping. You see it around Marchand Dessalines. She called the market woman that because she, too, is small and always chirping, and she goes from one town to another to sell, always talking, talking. The Madame Sara can build its nest anywhere, and this woman can sell anywhere, too."

"It is a kind of compliment, then?"

"Ti Me is too soft," Ella said.

"She seems to do well."

"Yes, but you must understand. No one here respects you if you're soft. You must be hard and righteous to gain respect. Look, there." She pointed to the other end of the market, where a drawing of the Virgin Mary, sketched on a piece of spare wood in charcoal and mud, hung on a pole over a communal pump. "Popish nonsense like this, everywhere. A whole country that glorifies suffering and not sacrifice. It is a big job, to be here. I hope Emmanuel has made that clear to you."

"He loves Haiti. He says it is where the future of the Negro race lies."

"He is not wrong. If we can ensure the right kind of Negro is here, he is not wrong."

"No one born here is the right kind?"

"Not without education and hard work. We must make them, too. That's what you're here for, I suppose. Why he brought you. Though why he thinks you are good for that, I do not know."

"I beg your pardon," I said. But Ella was not so brave as to meet my eye.

Ti Me stopped her bargaining to toss her head over her shoulder and call to us, "Bon manman, bon pitit." She turned back, picking up the rhythm skillfully, as if there was no interruption.

"What does that mean?" I said.

"It is an old Haitian saying. 'If the mother is good, the child will be good.'"

I looked away from Ella, back to Ti Me, who was grinning at me now. She winked.

"Mèsi," I said to her.

"The people here are very fond of proverbs," Ella said, staring straight ahead. "None of them make sense to me, though. The best proverbs, of course, are in the Bible."

"But these ones sound very agreeable," I said.

Ella said nothing, only kept watching the haggle.

When the deal was finally struck, Ti Me looked from Ella to me expectantly. I smiled back, uncertain.

"What is it?" I said.

Ella wouldn't meet either of our eyes. She looked down at her skirts, and then she stuck one hand to her side and fumbled for her purse there. She unhooked it from her belt and handed it to me.

It was soft and heavy in my hands, the coins inside it spreading over my palms. It was like holding an animal and feeling about on its belly for its organs.

"I suppose," Ella said, still without looking at me, "that you should hold this now. Since you are now the first lady of the house. The purse and keys are yours."

Her voice was halting, and strangely high-pitched, as if someone else was forcing the words out of her with a pair of bellows.

"It is not necessary," I began, thinking that if I could spare her this humiliation, perhaps I could win her favor.

But her eyes flashed at me, and I understood it at once. *Don't you dare pity me. The likes of you could never pity me.*

What had Ella herself said? *You must be strong, in a place like this?*

I took the purse and stepped in front of her and counted out the coins, one by one, to Ti Me's hand, and when we reached the house, it was I who drew the big iron key from my waist and turned it in the door and let the other women inside.

I THOUGHT THE keys at my waist would change things. Emmanuel led me to believe it was so. When he saw them there at dinner, his eyes became bright, and later, alone in our room, he held each one in his hand, one by one, only the length of the key between us as he worked them off their ring.

"The keys used to fascinate me as a boy," he told me. "Ti Me wore them until Ella was old enough, and the sound of them, when Ti Me walked, the sound of their clanking, meant that we were safe. I was scared of this country then. I had not learned to love it yet. I wanted to lock it out all day and all night, and hearing the keys hit Ti Me's hip made me feel safe.

"I learned," he said as he let one key fall against my thigh and picked up another, to work off the ring. "I learned, as I learned to love this place, that the keys were an illusion. Why would you live in a place as beautiful as this and lock out the night sky? I promised myself that if they were ever given to me, I would exorcise their power. When we were sixteen and I found out that Ella got the keys because she was now the woman of the house, I was heartbroken. And she would never let me touch them, because she knew I meant to strip them of their power."

He picked up the last key, began to work it off the ring. "But I have something even sweeter. I have this day, where I see the keys at the waist of my wife," he said, "and you are mine, and I am yours, and it makes the fact of that even more real to my family."

He led me to our bed, where he gently pushed my shoulders till I lay on my back, and lifted my skirt. He placed each key, warm from his shaking hand, across my bare stomach, while I whispered that he should stop moaning—his father and sister could clearly hear him.

But his ecstasy over those keys did not keep him close to me. The next morning, Emmanuel left at dawn, as he had taken to doing. He spent his days on an endless round of visits. To his mentor, the one other doctor in town. To his father's friends and associates—the men who made up the American Negro colony in Jacmel. Sometimes, he came back to the house very late at night, even after his father had eaten and retired to bed.

I was left to spend my days with Ella and Ti Me and the bishop. I say "days," but it may as well have been the same day, over and over again, so little did it change. Ella was always awake before I was, even if, in the dark, Emmanuel and the rooster crowing outside woke me. She spent her mornings working at her embroidery in the parlor—her incomprehensible jacket. Around ten, she would stow it away in a basket she kept underneath the battered divan, and we would all go to the market.

Ti Me went to the same stalls each day and made the same bargains. I realized on the fourth day, from the rhythm of their voices, that this was not so much an argument but a friendly conversation. Sometimes, Ti Me said something quick and low that made the woman laugh and made Ella blush and sniff about morals. I wished then, more than anything, that I could understand. Always, at the end of it, both women turned to me—Ella sullenly, Ti Me with clear amusement at the awkwardness it was causing her—for the coins in the purse at my side.

We returned to the house for the hottest part of the day. Ella took to her room. She said she could not withstand the heat of the tropics, despite having lived there from childhood. Sometimes, I went upstairs, too, but I grew restless lying beneath the sheet, the shutters closed against the heat, listening to the world outside slow down.

When the world began moving again in the late afternoon, it brought the American women of the colony over to the house. There were about ten of them in total—wives of the men who had followed Bishop Chase, the helpmeets of traders and farmers—all of them with the same pale skin as Ella, not a black one among them. The darkest was a very thin woman with yellow skin and no husband, who taught the Haitian women in a kind of domestic academy.

They would all arrange themselves around Ella, who would lead the conversation, usually begun by relating an imagined indignity suffered in the market. The untrustworthiness and the untapped potential of Haitian women was the main topic of conversation. How great the country could be, it was agreed, if only those women understood their place in a chaste home. Instead, they wandered to market and upset the order of the world.

Like Ella, none of these women had been to America for a very long time. The America they described was a kind of dream, where Negro people lived in perfect harmony, with kind and just laws, and every Negro woman stayed home to stitch counterpanes while her husband entered the world. I could not tell if they had been so long gone that they really believed this fantasy to be true, or if it was a collective fiction they engaged in together to pass the time, but to hear it made me wish to scream.

I attempted, once, very early on, to set them right. I told them of the red marks the whites had left on our doors. I said, "There are men following the law right now whom white men string up on trees for exercising their rights."

There was a pause in the room. One woman covered her mouth. Another murmured, "Mercy."

Ella did not even look up from the sewing work in her lap. Her hands moved the needle in and out of the fabric, humming like a cicada. "But there is justice in America," she said. "It will be set right. Here, Negroes cut down other Negroes for politics, too. It is our own against our own. In America, we are not so uncivilized as that."

I very nearly rushed across the room and ripped the embroidery from her hands. Instead, I stood and left, and I made it a habit to do so every afternoon, when I had sat long enough to be deemed polite. The only thing that saved me was the knowledge that the world my husband was building, that I was sure I would soon join him in building, was bigger than what Ella or those women could possibly imagine. I held this knowledge close to me and it cooled me in the middle of these endless, turgid afternoons, as if I had pressed a wet cloth to the back of my neck.

At some point during each discussion, a woman would excuse herself to go to Bishop Chase's door, by prearrangement. "I forgot," she would say, "the bishop asked to see me," and she would get up, and none of the other women in the room would meet her eye, and Ella, especially, would double down in her viciousness as soon as the woman took her leave.

It was always the darker women, or, I should say, the less pale ones who went, and I thought that was what made Ella rage. She had the worst case of colorstruck I'd ever seen, and I figured it was so bad she was even begrudging these women the chance to talk a little salvation with her father in his library. I pitied her for it, and it made me even more wary of her.

The bishop himself avoided both Ella and me, and Ti Me, though he was home when we were, more often than not. He still did not say a word to me directly. Sometimes, he let his eye rest on the fold of my skirt or my apron and he frowned in disapproval, but he never spoke. It was strange to live in a man's house and serve his son and not speak to him, but I thought of Mr. Grady—how shy he had been, how he had avoided speaking to me then—and I thought it must be the same with the bishop. But I did not respect the bishop or yearn to know him half as much as I had Mr. Grady. I thought of him more as an example of the worst parts of Emmanuel, and it was a relief that he did not try to talk to me. Seeing him made me scared of the kind of man my husband could possibly become. And I did not want that for him. For no one was loved in that neighborhood more than he, and it was through this love that everyone else—that is, our Haitian neighbors, not the sour-faced American women who followed Ella's whims—said my new name with respect and pride.

"Madam Chase, se madanm mesye Emmanuel!"

I had always thought titles were silly. Or rather, the only one to be respected was "Doctor." But I took an inordinate, stubborn pride in my new name, in the name I was now called in the streets when I walked to market with Ti Me and Ella. *Madame Chase, Madame Chase, Madame Chase.*

"Call me that, please," I said, teasing Emmanuel at night, and this delighted him almost as much as the iron keys on my naked body.

"You know, Madame Chase," he said, "it is a kind of work, to call things by their true names. To change their names."

"A kind of work?"

"That is what we call the practice of Vodoun when it is done. A work. It is an industry for the spirit. It is a task of repair. And it can be as simple as giving something its rightful name. As I have and as the streets have done for you. And, look, you embrace it. And so we will be right."

I wanted, so badly, to believe him.

Dear Libertie,

I feel it is time to speak plainly. There is no reason not to anymore. I have tried, as your mother, to only speak to you the truth, to remain impartial, to have you grow up with a love as pure as justice. But what good has that done? You've still chosen the flesh, anyways. So let me be fleshy, here, with you, since it makes no difference.

I miss you more than I thought possible. It was different when you were gone to school, and I was sure you would be returned to me. But you have passed over into a divide where I do not believe you can ever come back fully. And I mourn your passing.

When your father died, I spent three weeks in bed. Nearly in bed. I was alone in the house—my own father had passed a year before. Reverend Harland came to see me only once. But when he came, I was sitting up in bed, my mouth open wide in a scream with no sound coming out. I scared him in my grief. The Reverend has never been a brave man. The only other person to come see me was Lenore, who came every few days to hold her hand over my open mouth, to make sure I was still breathing, and to bring biscuits, hard as stone, from some of the women at church.

I spoke to no one except you. I placed both hands on my stomach, and in the quiet of the house I cried to you about your father. How much I missed him. You'd quickened before he passed. I'd held his hand myself over you, where you tossed inside me and rippled the skin on my stomach like a wave.

So after he was gone, I lay in bed and watched you move inside me, even though I wished the whole world had stopped. In that house made still by death, I knew you would continue, at least. At least I would have Libertie.

Elizabeth would write to me of her great political awakening. I liked those letters because they burnt with the same passion your father had, for the world to be set right. Elizabeth was learning so much then—about how slaves really lived, about what our own lives would be like if we had not been born free. I am ashamed to say I had not thought of it before. Even with your father whispering revolution in my ear, I only thought of colored people as the most cursed race in the world. I thought we were merely unlucky. I thought it was a matter of luck. I had read the stories of daring escapes, heard the old ones speak, seen the haunted eyes of our newcomers, and was only glad it wasn't me.

Your father did not talk of his life before he was free. He would not tell me even what town he ran from, only that he had lived for a spell in Maryland, and for some time in Virginia. Who his people were—his mother, his father, his sisters and brothers—he would not tell me, and in the flush of love I did not press him. I saw how asking made his eyes sad. Besides, I told myself, our life together shared a different fate. He had found me, with my bright skin and farm and money and profession, and he would be safe always, because I loved him. That's how young I was then. I really believed that.

After your father died, Elizabeth's letters told me of the women who came to her, the front of their dresses wet with milk, their daughters snatched from their hands, and I feared that would be me. It would be me. You would be taken from me, and it did not matter that I was freeborn, and it did not matter that I could see the blue veins at my wrist. None of that would keep you safe. That's what drove me to give aid. And I decided when you were born that I would hide my heart from you, because I worried I would love you into nervous oblivion.

When you were born, when Lenore raised you up from where she'd placed you on my thigh, the first thing I did was check behind your ears for your true color. And I rejoiced for what I saw there.

Because a part of him would live on in the world. That beautiful color. His skin glowed in the sun, like yours did as a girl, as it does now. I could not look at you in your wedding dress—that black black skin against that field of white—because of the glow of it. I had to turn away, you were so overpoweringly beautiful.

When I saw the color behind your ears, I could no longer deny all the ways you could be taken from me.

Even I was not secure, and my papa was not secure, in our color, because we were known to be colored and we could have been taken at any time. And if you were taken from me, no white person would believe you were mine—they did not think it was possible that I would prefer your black skin to my faint yellow, that I could give birth to something as wondrous as you.

The whole world told me you weren't mine, whenever I held you in my arms outside of our home. And so I grew frightened for you. And I knew what I owed you was very great. I must raise you up to be strong enough for this world. I must teach you how to heal the people in it. Maybe that could save you, I thought. Again, I was still very young then.

You would not believe me now, but you were a happy baby. Your joy brought something back for me. You will see, when you have your own children—it is as if they are your new eyes and your new heart, and you feel sometimes you can live for a hundred years more, even after all the trouble you've seen. You actually want to live for a hundred years more, even knowing how cruel the world is.

Before you came, I stayed in this world out of a sense of duty only. It was my trust to fix it. I would get weary sometimes. I would think of what your father wanted—Liberia. I would think of what would happen if I had followed his desire to be there. Only a heavy sense of duty screwed my ankles down into Kings Country dirt.

But through you, I learned to love our land. I saw you learn to walk, first on the floors my own father had cut and sanded, then on the land that he owned. I saw you learn to talk by calling back to the birds in our trees. I saw when you cried, and I held you close. You would look over my shoulder at the hills around us to soothe yourself. I saw the land, my land, through your eyes, and I learned to love it again. And it was not a burden. None of it was a burden. You told me once, in anger, that you must be such a burden to me, and I tell you, Libertie, caring for you has been the greatest honor of my life.

But I think even now I have failed you, and I am full of sorrow.

Love

Your

Mama

Ti Me had handed me the letter without any expression. I was sitting with Ella in the parlor, and I'd made the mistake of reading it in front of her. I felt her eyes on me, avidly watching, and I felt my skin become hot.

"Good news?" she said when I was done.

"My mother is well," I said.

And then I crushed the letter into a ball and held my hand in a fist until I could go to my room, my husband's and mine, and stuff it in the desk drawer there.

As if that could save me from it.

I will write her back tomorrow, I told myself.

But then I thought of what I would tell her.

The children here have made up a mocking song about me. Emmanuel's father did not even know we were married. His sister hates the sight of me. I spend my days surrounded by people, alone. This is what I have chosen,

*instead of speaking honestly, "fleshly," as you say, to you, Mama, and fight-
ing to stay by your side.*

"Emmanuel," I whispered in his ear that night. "Take me away from
here tomorrow."

He was in my hand, his eyes were closed, he nodded his head back
into the pillow, I thought that we still had this, at least, despite everything else, and I felt a little stab of pride.

But how do you list that triumph in a letter to your mother?

WE RODE ON his father's horse, across a wide, flat expanse of
no-man's-land that was full of puddles of water as large as very shallow
lakes, that women and children and men walked and ran across and
trod across on donkeys, going back and forth from their homes in the
mountains to town.

I could feel the horse breathe beneath me. Every step up the mountain, he took in larger gulps of air. I could feel the ends of his lungs
swell. The horse wheezed louder the higher we went. I felt my ears pop
as we ascended.

A wife is like a horse. Laboring uphill with the weight of two people's love on her back. My skirts were beginning to get damp with
sweat. I thought of Madeline Grady, who had looked at me and said
with confidence, "Grady reads for both of us." Where did that surety
come from? *I should have watched her better,* I thought.

It was one thing to fail as a student. I had told myself I simply did
not have the aptitude to be a doctor. That I did not possess that piece of
flint that existed in my mother's soul, which was struck and made light
when she had a patient before her. My anatomy was different. I was not
built to alleviate the suffering of others.

But I was surely built to be a wife. Wasn't every woman? Even

Louisa and Experience were built for love. And I felt it for Emmanuel, sometimes so strongly it made me dizzy. I did not realize, though, that I could at the same time be so lonely.

I pressed my forehead into my husband's back. "I wish the Graces were here."

"Why? So they could make you laugh?"

"They would at least sing us love songs to cheer us, yes."

"They do not sing love songs," he said.

"But they do," I said. "Every song the Graces sang was a love song."

"No," he said.

"They are. Love is freedom."

His ribs shuddered beneath my arms. He was laughing. "You don't know anything," he said.

We got off the horse for the last bit. "Wouldn't it be kinder to tie him to a tree and come back for him?" I said.

Emmanuel looked ahead, farther up the mountain, then back at me. "If you wish."

We left the horse by a bush. I could hear him, even as we walked, behind me, eating leaves.

Every few twists in the road, we passed a house of one of the families that lived on the mountain. They were set back from the road and made of wood and stone. We could usually hear the family's rooster as we approached, sometimes a goat in the yard. At each house, a person, usually a woman, would come to the door to watch us pass. If she saw me first, she would frown. If she saw Emmanuel first, she would smile and bow her head.

Emmanuel called to each, "Bonjou, madam." Sometimes, a woman would call back, "Monsieur Emmanuel." But every single one recognized me and called me by my new name, though I had never seen any of them before: *Madame Chase, yon fanm ameriken.*

"They know us here," I said.

"I come here nearly every day. I have bragged about you so often they know you by my words." He laughed. "Before I left for America, I used to come here to study."

"You would bring your books here?"

"Sometimes I was studying books. But mostly, I was studying the plants."

"You will get used to this walk," Emmanuel said, taking my hand in his. "You will make it every day with me, once my office is set up again. We will learn this mountain together."

"You have a lot of faith in me."

"It is not faith," he said. "I know you."

We then walked in silence, and I could pretend for a moment that I was the person he imagined. To get to the water, you had to climb uphill till the backs of your legs began to burn and your knees felt as if they would shake, and your skirts, as they moved around your ankles, felt like a burden. I tucked the ends into the waist of my dress, running them through my legs, which delighted Emmanuel. But I felt annoyance at the walk and the heat that he had not prepared me for. We had left in the afternoon, because he had wished to talk with his father first and we had wanted to miss the highest heat of the day. But the heat had lingered, and even the woods all around us felt oppressive.

I did not trust his admiration for me. The only person who had ever watched my movements as closely as he did was my mother. And she had watched not with pride, but with a kind of patient assessing. She was waiting for me to make a mistake, and he did not believe a mistake was possible. Yet.

My mother's scrutiny was a burden. But this other way of looking, this besottedness, was just as damning. My mother expected great things and constant improvement. He seemed to believe in a perfection that existed apart from my actual self.

I watched my husband's slim back as he moved up the mountain. His skin did not brown in the sun, only turned yellow and pink. For this trip, he wore a straw hat with a large brim and a veil of gauze. Ti Me had brought it to him, and they had both laughed about it, a shared joke. *His back is muscled, but he is a little man,* I thought as he walked ahead of me. It was easy to forget this as we wrestled in bed, as I watched him leave me so many mornings. I thought, *I still do not know him, but I think about him at all times, so I suppose it makes no difference if I do or not. It is the same.*

"This is where the women come to wash," he said. Before us was a small pool, the water shallow. "This is where I learned to swim as a boy."

"You swim?"

"You will, too."

He stopped before the bank of the pool and began to take off the ridiculous hat, his shirt.

"Emmanuel—"

"The washing day is done. It will be dusk soon. No one will come."

He rolled his trousers up and waded into the water. Then he turned to me and held out his hands.

"There are two other pools above us. The water for this one comes from a waterfall at the top of the mountain. The pool just above us is about seventy-five feet deep. We will move to that one when you are ready. The best pool is at the top, near the fall. It is maybe a hundred feet deep, but the water is so blue you can almost see to the bottom. We will move to that one together. You'll see."

"You are very confident."

"Of course."

"If I refuse?"

He smiled. "I will demand it."

Following his commands seemed an easier way forward to whatever version of myself he imagined. So I put one foot into the water, then another. I stepped very carefully over to him. I could hear the water as it moved around my feet. If I was quiet, I could hear the clap of the waterfall above us. A deeper sound than the one I had listened for in the puddles and barrels of water back home, when I was a girl and believed in Ben Daisy's lady. Emmanuel held out his hands for me. I put both of mine in his.

And then he threw me down.

The water was not deep enough for me to lose my ground. I went under, onto my knees, but when I raised my head, I broke the surface again.

He was laughing, truly laughing. I thought, *I have misjudged him.* I thought, *I have made a mistake.*

"This is how my father taught me," he kept saying.

I tucked my legs underneath me, sat back in the water. I could feel my skirts filling with the damp, beginning to weigh me down. Emmanuel danced around me, whooping and laughing and splashing. When he got close enough, I held out my hand and pulled his arm, until he was in the water with me.

He rolled happily in the mud of the pool. But if I could have gotten ahold of him, if I had not been scared of the water myself, I would have held him under. If only for a moment, for him to feel what I felt. How could you be bound to someone, for life, to the grave, and fundamentally not feel the same things?

I pushed myself up out of the water, but I felt it still dragging at my skirts, nearly pulling me down again. Emmanuel was still sitting in the water, laughing. I slogged to the shore, one heavy step after another. When I got there, I tried to sit first on the ground, then lean against a tree. I could feel my skirts becoming clammy against my legs. I looked up at the sky. The sun was beginning to set somewhere. You could not see the horizon from this pool, just a pink streak across the sky above us. I was a thousand miles away from my mother because I was too much of a coward to tell her the truth.

In front of me, Emmanuel leaned until he floated on his back. He held his palms out. "This is the first step," he called. "You must make friends with the water."

Around us, it was getting darker. In the dimming light, the dirt road we'd taken to the pool glowed against the shadows of the trees, as if it was lit up from below. I could hear the sounds of birds from far away.

"Libertie, are you listening to me?"

"No," I said. "I am listening to the jungle."

"You are angry?"

"Shh," I said. "I want to hear the trees."

I heard a splash as he sat up. "You don't understand," he said. "That's the way you learn. That's how my father taught me."

"Your father is always right?"

"In this he is."

"You will ignore your father when he tells you how to be a doctor, but if it is about drowning your wife, he is correct."

"You're being dramatic."

"Half drowning your wife."

"You've never wanted me to feel something in the same way you do?" he said quietly, to the water. "That's all I wish for here."

I thought then that maybe we could try to understand each other again. I stood up. I unbuttoned the blouse that stuck to me, stepped out of the skirts that clung to my legs. When I was bare, I walked back into the pool and sat down beside him.

"Like this?" I set my arms on the surface of the water.

"Now lean back."

If you follow his commands, I told myself, *you can become the woman he believes you are.*

I felt the water creep up my spine, around my shoulders, and lick into my ears. Everything within me wanted to hold tight against it. My head dipped further below the surface, and all sound was gone now—except the sound of my own breath. My mouth and nose were still above the surface, and I took in one more bit of air, which felt warm now, when the rest of me was in cold water. And then I let go and trusted the water, and I was free. I opened my eyes a little bit. I could see the moon above us, and its light reflected, white and shimmering, on the water that surrounded me.

"Do you think," I said to Emmanuel, "it's the same moon over Mama right now? Do you think she is looking at it as I look at it, as I lie on top of water? Do you think she can know me right now?"

But he was tired of games by then. Or games that did not involve him. He sat up and crashed out of the water.

HE TOOK ME to the water every Sunday afternoon. But first, we had to endure the mornings. Those we spent in sweaty prayer with his father's congregation: the bishop sitting behind the pulpit in his heavy robes, the priest standing up to lead the service, Ella's sewing circle sitting in the front pews with some of the Haitians who had joined the church early on, and the newest converts always standing in the back of the church.

No one seemed to question this arrangement, not even Emmanuel, when I asked him about it. "It has always been that way," he told me. But Ella was more blunt. "They are our brothers in Christ, but they aren't of our sort," she said. "The Haitians of our station are lovely, but they remain papists. The ambitious workers here join our church because they know we have schools and aid and help, and they want that for their families. We love them very much and they love us, and we worship together, but we like to be with our sort. Don't pretend you don't understand."

In our pew sat myself, at the farthest end, closest to the church window; Emmanuel, seated beside me; his sister, beside him; and Ti Me, at the aisle. Once, when we were all supposed to have bowed in prayer, I glanced up to see her neck straight, the only head unbent in all the church.

The church was Emmanuel's father's greatest pride. A stone building with rough windows dug out of the walls and a high ceiling. There was only one cross in the whole place, he liked to point out. No idolatry here.

We sang hymns in English first, then the Kreyòl translations. Bishop Chase strongly discouraged any hand clapping. "Americans can take it," he said, "but it excites the Haitians too much." So the songs swelled, but there was always some large piece missing.

It was nothing like when the Graces sang. It was nothing like when we sang at home in Kings County. It did not look like any fellowship I had known, but the bishop was proud of it, and much of the time spent in church was giving thanks for his intelligence, his humanity, and his hard work here.

Ella did not approve of our swimming lessons. She said it was an affront to the Lord's day. But Bishop Chase said it was up to a man to decide how he and his wife would spend the rest of the Sabbath, and so Ella only complained once. When we left for the mountains, though, she'd make it a point to get on her knees in the parlor and continue her prayers.

The bishop continued to say nothing. But after the third swimming lesson, the priest began to preach from Ecclesiastes, about the wife cleaving to her husband's family, about the obedience of marriage. Bishop Chase sat behind him the whole time, in his heavy robes in the heat, not even succumbing to it by fanning himself, as the others did. He was silent, looking straight ahead at some life that none of us could see.

I would reach for Emmanuel's hand while the priest spoke, if only to show some little sign of defiance, and he would take mine, but just for a moment. Then he would set it back down on the pew between us. Even that small rebellion was too much in his father's church, though when I would ask him about it, in our bed at night, he would say, "It was hot, Libertie. Too hot to hold hands."

Libertie,

I have received the notice from Cunningham College. And I understand, now, why you married that silly boy in haste.

I am so angry with you. And you are not even here to rage at! What a clever trick you played on me, my girl. What a lesson you learned at mine and Elizabeth's knee . . . the lesson of escape! You turned something so good and righteous against me. You've used it to your own earthly ends. I cannot think of a more wicked girl than you, and you know I've known my share. You are a deceiver. You are an escape artist. You are a liar.

You chose that man over doing the hard and right thing.

You chose indolence and lust over hard work and humility.

I have no doubt that Emmanuel Chase believes that he loves you. I think you have convinced yourself that you love him. But you know and I know that what you have done is wrong and you have ruined our dreams, your dreams, for what you think is love.

It is not love, Libertie.

Love would not make you think you had to flee your only mother.

You will probably never answer me now. You will probably continue to ignore my letters to you. So be it! So be it! So be it! Know that I hold this against you, though, Libertie. Know how you've made your mother rage.

You sat in my waiting room and looked down your nose at me and told me I was not trying hard enough. That I did not understand how to change the world.

You sneered at the white women I courted to keep you in nice dresses and pay for your classes. You stopped only short of calling me a traitor, and it is you who have betrayed me! Who has broken me. Who has deceived me. Who stood before me in a wedding gown and said, "I love you, Mama." Who gave up your virtue to a silly man so that you would not have to face the truth with me. I see it now.

So all is lost. So you have chosen that life, irrevocably. Do you know a part of me still held out hope you would find your way back to this path? That if I let you go, you would return? But you were already gone, long gone, and did not even bother to tell your mother of it.

You are a fool, and so am I.

Your

Mama

This letter came on a Sunday, after church, and when I read it, it went with the others in the back of the drawer, and I almost cried, I did, that she knew the worst part of me.

But Emmanuel called me down to dinner, and he put his hands on my shoulder and he said, "What is wrong?"

And I was still good to him, in his eyes, so I said, "Nothing," and I resolved I would not answer my mother again. Not for a long time.

WHEN YOU LEARN to swim, your body is no longer your own. It becomes enthralled to another dimension, that of the water. Your limbs are weightless, but you can feel your hair and clothes becoming heavy.

"Do you open your eyes underwater?" I asked.

"Of course," he said.

So while I practiced floating, I imagined him just under the surface, eyes open and staring up at me. I was not sure, in that moment, which one of us possessed the other.

This will always be our life together, I told myself as I followed him back down the mountain. I truly believed, then, that this was the start of the world he had promised me. I thought of our time in the pool as his gift to me. During the week, he still would not permit me to join him in his medical work. He said he was not ready yet. Monday mornings in the empty house became easier, though. Ella and I sat side by side or walked to the market together, but my spirit was still on the water.

"You are not so different from me," Ella said after a few weeks of this. She sat in the parlor, with her embroidery still on her lap.

"I do not think I am so different," I lied.

"You do. You think you are better than me," Ella said. "Pride is not attractive on a woman."

"I assure you, I am humbled."

"Fanm pale nan tou de bò bouch yo."

"What does that mean?" I said.

"Three months, and you still have less of a grasp on the language than a baby." Ella still had her head bent over her sewing.

I closed my eyes. Willed myself to remember floating on the water.

"What is it that you've worked on for so many weeks?" I said finally. "Surely you are done?"

She lifted her head. She slit her eyes at me. Then she held up what was in her lap. A jacket, which she held by the shoulders and gave a good shake so that it uncrumpled.

I got up from my seat and went to sit beside her. "May I?" I said.

She nodded.

I took the garment in my hands and turned it over. Close embroidery in that bright red thread. I held it nearer to my eyes. It was words. An incantation. Maybe even a history. I could only make out a few of the words, but I realized she had embroidered a whole story on this jacket in Kreyòl.

"What does it mean?" I said.

"You are like a child, always asking that."

I stuck my thumb into my mouth and hummed, like a baby would. I had the satisfaction of startling her into a laugh.

"Your estimations are always correct, Ella."

"Stop."

"I am an infant and, as such, would be delighted if you schooled me in this."

She looked at me. I raised my thumb back to my mouth. "All right," she said. "He hasn't told you, has he, yet, of the bad year we had here?"

"When your mother and brothers passed. Yes."

"He has not told you, though, what else happened?"

"No," I said.

"We were thirteen," she said. "We had been here three years. We knew the language so well by then. There was a great crime, in Port-au-Prince. We lived there then—we had not yet come here to build the church in Jacmel. A man had sold his niece to the Vodoun priests, and they had slit her throat and drained her blood and drank it and ate her flesh. The government investigated and brought the bad people to justice. We watched them burn in the capital square. Ti Me, my brother, and I. We saw God's law that day. It was extraordinary. Emmanuel fainted, and Ti Me kept saying, "It is not right." She stayed at the square till the last of the embers died down. I think she was waiting for something. I do not know what. My brother was very upset. He said it was a tragedy. That they should never have burnt those terrible people. He still says it was a tragedy. He wrote to me about it, even when he was with you, in New York. So I began to make this for him. To remind him of the true history. I wrote it—see, I stitched it in thread. So he will always remember."

As she spoke, she'd taken the jacket from me and fanned it over her lap. She ran her fingers over the stitches, again and again, as if she was mesmerizing herself. The thread was red and ragged, from her touching it over and over, and the jacket itself, which had started out white, I think, was a dun gray. It was like a child's rag doll, pulled apart by the child's own desire. But Ella treated it like a prize.

I was not sure what to do, until Ti Me came to the door to say "Market." And then Ella tucked the jacket up and put it underneath the divan, as if it was the most natural thing in the world.

Oh, I thought. *Oh.* I saw now her stiff, irregular hair, her rigid dress. That she should know something of Emmanuel that I did not, even now. That he should hold this in him and only share it with her, and not with me, his wife. That he would not tell me this. I felt furious.

WHEN EMMANUEL AND I made it back to the water, I was ready.

"I did not think there was anything to tell," he said. By now, in our lessons, I had learned to wear a pair of old bloomers and one of Emmanuel's undershirts. He swam in the nude. I had become afraid that someone—a woman coming to wash her laundry in the dusk, a child looking for frogs in the mud—would find us, but Emmanuel seemed to almost relish the thought.

"You would not tell me about seeing those people burn?"

"You can't . . . She doesn't . . . You cannot always trust what Ella says."

"She told me she longs to burn heretics at the stake."

"She took our family lessons in differently."

"What does that mean?"

"She is different than me. She has been for a long time. I did not want to tell you at first. It is painful, and then I worried you would treat her poorly."

I was standing in the pool, just at the depth where the water reached my calves. Emmanuel, kneeling in the water, lay back. He said, to the darkening sky above us, "She was not always this way. Papa says she is mad, but I don't believe it is so."

I sank down into the water beside him. "I don't understand why you did not tell me there was something wrong with your sister."

"We made a pact, when she began to . . . began to . . ." I had never seen Emmanuel halt for words, except when we were together in the dark, but he did so now. "When Ella began to . . . talk like that. Father and I agreed. There is no one here to treat her. They do not have madhouses in Haiti. And I would not put her in one anyways—because she is not mad, I do not think. And if we were to bring her back to America, where would she live? She is best here. She is best at home. I convinced Papa of that. And if I can find something to ease her burden, then I will have done my duty by her."

"So you expect me to live beside her?"

"She is harmless."

"She spends all day dreaming of seeing men burn at the stake."

"She is. She seems to have taken a disliking to you, but she would never outright hurt you."

"You choose her over me," I said. "Every time."

Emmanuel had not stopped looking at the sky. He said now, "I cannot believe you would believe that. When I've shown and said so many times to you that you are my life."

I heard him turn in the water. "Do you want to know what she really is to me? Ti Me says she is like this because our family did not serve us well. The very first words Ti Me said to Ella and me when she saw us were 'Marasa yo rayisab.' Twins don't get along. Especially if they are a boy and a girl. The boy will always prosper, while the girl will suffer. Ti Me is a fatalist, like everybody here. But she believed she could help us a little. She wanted to take us to a houngan, to meet lwa yo, to set it right. Ella refused to do any of it. Even at thirteen, she called it 'popish magic.' Ti Me says that that is when we lost her, and that Ella will not return to us as long as she is so stubborn."

"Do you believe that?"

"Ella has always been like that," Emmanuel said carefully. "When we were children, she was given to fits of weeping. But then, I was, too. And we had so much to cry over—leaving America and coming here, and being hungry the first year while Father set up his ministry. We thought we hated Father then. And then Ma was gone. And then everyone else.

"Ti Me, when she came to us, she would make sure the colors of our clothes were identical, that our plates always had the same number of yams. Sometimes, if I was in the kitchen with her, I would see her switch our plates around, so that I was given Ella's portion and Ella was given mine. I did not understand it. I said, 'Why do you do this?' And Ti Me said that was how you handled twins. She said because we were twins, we were very powerful and prone to resentment. That we must be satisfied and watched for jealousy. That our mother had not known to do so, and look what misfortune had befallen the family. Our poor mother had refused to learn the laws that govern the spirit here. She did not do her duty, and that is why she and our brothers died when they set foot on this land. And Ti Me said she would try to make it right.

"When Ella heard all that, it only made her cry harder. We used to cry together, Ella and I, spend whole afternoons crying over the books Father made us study. But I was young enough that I thought maybe Ti Me could be right. Our first Christmas here was spent with Father and the other mission families, on our knees in the sun, praying to God. That afternoon, Ti Me told us she knew what would make us feel better, and that if we wished to feel happy again, we would come with her when she called us. And she did, later that night—Father was asleep, and Ti Me came to our room and called for both of us. I went right away. Ella only followed because I went first. I remember her in her nightshirt, her eyes wide in the dark, staring straight ahead in fear.

"Ti Me took us out of the city—we walked in the dark for what felt like hours. Ti Me was like our mother, but she was only a few years older than the two of us. So we were all children and able to walk far. I remember the moon was so bright and high above us—it looked like a rib bone, curved into the sky. I would look up at it when my feet were tired. We walked on the road out of Port-au-Prince, and then Ti Me turned down a path into the forest, away from the shoreline. We walked again there, in the dark, with the leaves pressing up on my skin. Ti Me is like my mother, I've told you so many times, but she is not a very affectionate girl, and when I began to cry at the brush of leaves, she only sighed and told me to walk faster. Ella kept whispering to me, 'We will be sacrificed, and it will be your fault.'

"We walked and walked until we made it to a small house, made out of woven grass, and a clearing. There was a pole in the middle, and tens of people sitting and standing, laughing, talking, greeting one another. There were maybe five or six children younger than me, awake that late, on their mothers' laps or riding their older sisters' hips. There were old people and young. A few women and men in white shirts, and white scarfs tied to their heads. Torches all around to illuminate their faces. It did not look like any kind of solemn ceremony. It looked more like what a picnic did back in America, except it was happening in the middle of the night in a clearing, with someone's dog running happily back and forth and in among the people. Someone was even passing around slices of fruit. When we got there, Ti Me had us squat down on the ground alongside some other children our age. It was only as I looked at them more closely in the light from the torches that I saw how many pairs of twins were there. Boy twins. Girl twins. A few that were boys and girls, I guessed, like me and Ella. We sat and waited.

"We had left the house probably at midnight. By the moon in the sky, I would guess we sat and waited for another hour or so. I began to yawn, and Ti Me reached out her arm, so I could lie against her shoulder.

"Then the music began—you haven't heard it yet. It's like the drums of heaven."

"There are no drums in heaven," I said.

"You're wrong, Libertie." Emmanuel still was not looking at me. He still was speaking to the sky.

"I saw the men and women in white walk in a circle around the pole, swaying in time, the women each holding a lighted candle. Sometimes, in their march, they would stop to twirl. Sometimes, a man would come up to them and press his forehead to theirs, and then both, man and woman, would twist around each other, only their brows touching.

"I watched it all," he said, "but Ella hid her face."

"They had a brown-skinned kid goat and a speckled hen. They slit the throats of both and then cooked them, and then put them in a jug with three mouths and offered it to the Marasa. These are the spirits of twins.

"When the spirits had eaten, a woman came and gathered up the meal and put it in a wooden basin. She balanced the basin on the top of her head and walked around the pole three times. Then she took the basin off her head and showed it to each of us, to all the children sitting around. She kept asking us, 'Èske li bon?' When she got to me and Ella, I nodded.

"When she'd showed the food to all the twins present, she took the basin off her head, cast it down, and commanded us to eat. Ti Me told us to eat as much as we liked, until we were satisfied, but just to be sure we did not break any bird or goat bones with our teeth.

"It was a mass of all us children, pulling the food up with our hands, pushing it into our mouths. Ella, though, refused to eat. She was too scared to defy the adults outright, but she spit the food into her hands when they weren't looking. In the frenzy, I ate double her portion, to help her out.

"'Èske ou te manje ase?' they kept asking. *Have you eaten enough?* There were many children, but the kid goat had been fat, the hen, too, and the juice ran down my chin. Every other twin's face shone with grease in the moonlight.

"All during this, they sang a song. It is the song of the twins," Emmanuel said. "Should I sing it for you now?"

The only sound was the two of us, shifting slightly in the water.

"Yes," I said.

He took a deep breath and began.

> *Mwen kite manman m' nan peyi*
>
> > > > > > > *Gelefre*
>
> *Marasa elou*
> > > *Mwen kite fanmi m' nan peyi Gelefre*
> *M' pa gen fanmi ki pou pale pou mwen*
>
> > > > > > *Marasa elou*
> *Mwen pa gen paran ki pou pale pou mwen*
>
> > > > > > *Marasa elou*

I walked through the water where Emmanuel still lay, churning up swells with each step. When I reached him, I sank down onto my knees in the cold.

"Do you understand it?" he said.

"I think so." I closed my eyes and began, haltingly.

> "I have left my mother in Africa.
> > > > > "I have left my family in Africa.
> "I have no family to speak for me.
> > > > > "I have no relations to speak for me."

"Marasa elou," he said.

I lay back in the water beside him. I began to shiver.

"That's when I started to believe," Emmanuel said. "That's when I understood what this land had for me. Ella is unstable. She has never adjusted to life here. But I have, and I've thrived because of what I have taken in. Because of what Ti Me did for us, for me, on that night. That was my introduction to the work, and it is my most cherished act here. Do you understand? Ti Me saved me. The work saved me."

"You believe it all then? About twins and home and songs," I said. "And you call your sister mad?"

"Of course I believe it. The new ways here, it's where the people are free. We cannot be a nation if we don't have gods in our own image. They made these gods—do you understand? Just as your mother made her place and you made your own. They go further, where we need to. We will never be free until we do as they do."

"You would believe in magic?"

"I would have us serve the spirits." He dipped back in the water then, almost gone under, but then I saw he was pulling himself out, to look at me.

"I had thought you would understand," he said. "I wish my father would understand. I think Ella, in her own way, does understand. It's why she is so frightened of it all. She knows there's power there, but she isn't sure what kind. I believe we will not become a people until we have gods that understand us."

"You speak in riddles."

"I have told you from the beginning. This is my ambition. I can bring what I have learned in America and help the people here, with what they already have. I am building a new world. In the new world"—he curled his hand around my wrist, under the water—"we will be equals, you and I. We will be who we wish to be. There will be no limits on what we can dream or what we can do. You believed it when we married, and nothing has changed. Do not let this business with Ella make you think it is not possible.

"I was not forthcoming about Ella, this is true. I worried she would mean you wouldn't marry me, that you wouldn't marry into a family with people who were unwell. But everything else I've told you about myself should let you know I love you enough to chart new gods for you."

When we left the rock pool, I was still shivering. Emmanuel walked ahead of me, his back strong and straight, his shirt soaked through. I could just make him out as the night reached up to hold us.

Manman Poul grate, grate jouk li jwenn zo grann li

Mother Hen scratched and scratched till she reached her grandmother's bones

Libertie,

I was too angry to write again for a long time. I wrote you many letters and burnt each one, because Lenore said they were too harsh.

I am still angry, to think what I have lost and what has been ruined.

This is the life I had imagined for you. That we would have that coach with the gold lettering. That you would carry on my good deeds. That you would be my great act of love in the world and my redemption. My apology to your father for not understanding where he came from. My atonement to our people for failing them over and over and over again, when I couldn't set them right.

You would be brilliant and set them right. But you are not even right within yourself, I think. And you cannot even understand what I had given you, all I had given you, to prepare you to fight.

They say the Negroes now are a different breed than in my day. The colored people are different. Bolder. And maybe that's what you are. Not my daughter but a daughter of a different age. Maybe your

boldness serves better for these times than my fidelity. Maybe my
Libertie is really the clever one, and it is Mama who is the betrayer.

Write to me, Libertie dear, and set your mama straight. Give me
your words, please. I cannot take your silence.

Love

Your

Mama

I NEVER WROTE her back, because I discovered on Fet Gede that I'd fallen pregnant. That morning, I woke up to the sound of the drums. The drumming was something I had grown used to—it came from the temples that dotted the road to the water basins, and oftentimes, as Emmanuel and I rode back in the dark, we could hear it echo around us, off the trees.

After Emmanuel told me his life's work, I tried to do my best to make it my own. I had thought it was all poetry—though better poetry than what I'd written for Mama or the woman in the water, because it was inspired by love for me. But it wasn't just poetry; it was the logic by which he governed his actions and his mind, and I told myself I must learn it if I belonged to him now.

I thought that it explained the long silences between him and his father. I looked at Ella and tried to see her with the compassion that Emmanuel did. Her heat-stiffened hair, her sweaty, pale skin, the way she looked with fear and anger at the women in the market. *Love her. Love her. Love her for it,* I told myself. But mercy is hard to cultivate, when it's for a stranger who tells you you're only as good as what's between your legs and ignores you for hours on end.

Emmanuel must become your religion, I told myself. *Submit to him as you would to any preacher. It is the only way to survive here. He is your helpmeet and your ally.*

During the day, I did well enough. I sat near Ti Me in the cookhouse and tried hard to learn the language, enough so that one day I could ask her about the gods she and Emmanuel loved.

But every night, I betrayed him, when I dreamt of being with my mother.

Sometimes, I dreamt I was a girl, working quietly and companionably with her in her study, the heavy smell of camphor around us. Sometimes, I dreamt I was finally driving the black carriage with DR. SAMPSON AND DAUGHTER drawn in gold on the side. In every dream, Emmanuel, marriage, my desire for him, was forgotten, nowhere to be found. When I woke, I would long for her again, even as Emmanuel's arm sat heavy across my breast, even as I felt the long naked length of him against my back.

Sometimes, in the dreams, she held me in the softness of her lap, as if I was a child, and swept a gold fan over us.

The drumming that had started all around us that October, that startled me from morning sleep and afternoon rests, was a relief. It shook my head free of grief, and to its rhythm I could sing *Love Emmanuel,* and so forget my mother.

"The idolatrous Haitians worship the dead," Ella spat to me, the walls of the sitting room, the sewing in her lap, whenever she heard the drums. Emmanuel had told me that, yes, the dead here held a special place. But what do you call it when you worship a memory of a living person, of one who has never been completely known to you, and when your worship is unwilling, driven not by a desire to honor but because you have realized the world didn't make sense with her, and does not make sense now that you are without her?

"Fet Gede is their All Souls' Day, but as with everything outside of America, the sense of humor here is keener," Emmanuel had told me in bed the night before the holiday. This was his favorite position to tell me stories—while lying down.

"Ella tells me that the men tie skeleton hands to their belts and circle their hips in lewdness," I said.

"In that, she is not wrong. If there was ever a holy day designed to speak to Ella's delusions, this is it."

Already in the night, we could hear music and laughing, louder than usual.

"It is one big celebration for the spirits of those who passed," Emmanuel said.

"It sounds macabre."

"It is not."

"If I went with you, I could see for myself if it is not."

"But then who would keep the peace with Ella and father?"

In the morning, my bed was empty.

Emmanuel had told me that he would spend Fet Gede with the houngan he was apprenticed to, a leader of a Vodoun house of worship that Ti Me had introduced him to—the very same man who had presided over his own feast of Marasa in the woods, long ago. He no longer hid the purpose of his trips from me.

The other Chases were planning to spend the day in public prayer—a pointed protest of the merriment all around them. I had already missed a chance to see how our neighbors on our street would prepare, because Emmanuel had deemed it more prudent for me to help the women clean the church and wash down the pews in preparation.

"I do not see why I cannot come with you," I'd said.

"They are already skeptical of my work," Emmanuel replied. "Your being here at least lets them see that I can be something of a family man. That my project does not exile me from any sort of decent life, which they would very much like to believe. If I were to do this work as a bachelor, they would claim I'd let my brain go foggy through lack of domestic love. If you outwardly assisted, they would claim that I was a corrupting influence on you.

"This way, they cannot discredit my work. Not if my own wife is at the front row of the choir, singing hosanna with everyone else."

"You have thought of everything," I said.

"The work is too important not to." He'd taken it as a compliment.

I took coffee with Bishop Chase and Ella, then waited as Ella went through her three shawls, deciding which one she should wear to service.

"The yellow one, I think," I said, hoping to goad her.

It worked. She quickly chose her black shawl and gave me a sly look, as if she had been triumphant. *I was learning how to manage her, at least,* I thought.

I walked with her to service, Ti Me beside us. Ella made a show of covering her ears whenever the drums seemed too close. In church, she threw herself down on her knees before the service even began, and shut her eyes tight. I did not sit beside her. What Emmanuel could not see would not hurt him. Instead, I stood at the back of the church beside Ti Me. It was not even noon, and the room was already too warm.

By the afternoon, my knees wobbled from standing and the noise outside was overwhelming. Bishop Chase raised his voice until he was hoarse, but it did not matter. Outside was a great rush of laughter and footsteps and singing.

I glanced over at Ti Me, who had stopped listening to the bishop altogether. Her face was turned toward the street. The expression on it was one of such open longing I felt a rush of pity. It did not seem fair that Ti Me should also be punished by my husband's sense of propriety.

I tapped her on the shoulder, and she startled.

I smiled, though, and whispered, "Ou vle ale la?"

She looked at me for a moment, as if deciding something.

I pointed out the doors, where a woman, her face streaked with white powder, her skirts hiked to her hips, was running past, a little boy laughing, trying to keep up with her.

Ti Me nodded, once. I took her hand and walked the two of us out of the church.

As the doors swung shut behind us, I heard the men and women inside begin to rustle, the priest call for us to return, and the whoosh of Bishop Chase's robes as he stood up from his seat.

I had finally done something to provoke a reaction from him, and I could not stop smiling as Ti Me and I ran through the streets in the sun.

"Ki kote li ye?" I panted. *Where is it?*

"Simityè a," she said. *The cemetery.* And then she squeezed my hand.

The graveyard in Jacmel was a little bit above the city, in the hills, so that the dead had a view of the ocean and the living in the town below them. In those days, it was not as big as it would become, but it was still an impressive place. The graves there were aboveground stone mausoleums. Some had columns and porticos; others were nothing more than solemn boxes with tops to shift off when the dead were buried. It was not like our graveyard back home, with its little pebbles, that I cut the grass from. *Who is cleaning father's grave now that I'm gone?* I wondered as we ran.

I thought of my mother, now left to tend two graves alone for the rest of her days, and felt a flush of shame, again—at my hasty marriage, at my foolishness. But I did not have time to feel sorry for myself, because as we drew closer, we were swept up by the crush of people at the cemetery gate, jostling one another, pressing close, hoping to get in and join their friends.

A man stood at the gate, his face dusted in white chalk, a top hat on. On his nose was balanced three pairs of spectacles, all with the glass missing. He had stuffed white cloth into his ears and mouth, like we do whenever we prepare a body for burial. He removed his cloth only to speak in a nasally, high-pitched singsong that I could not understand. Beside him was another man, taller, who was inspecting everyone who came past. All around us, everyone was eager for his scrutiny.

I nudged Ti Me. "Kiyès li ye?"

She snorted. "You talk to me in English. It will be easier."

"Who is that?"

"Papa Gede," she said. "And Brave Gede. Papa Gede, he wears the top hat, he is the first man who ever died in this world. He knows what happens to us in the land of the living, and he knows what happens to those in the land of the dead. The man next to him, that is Brave Gede. He guards the graveyard and keeps the dead inside. He keeps the living out. He decides who enters today to play with the dead."

"Will he let us in?"

Ti Me snorted again. She walked faster, through the crowd. I had no choice but to follow her.

When we reached the gate, the man in the spectacles widened his eyes and the taller man threw back his head. Both of them laughed as we approached and began to yell even louder. But whatever they were shouting did not frighten Ti Me; she began to laugh, too. And both men waved their hands, as if to say *You shall pass,* and Ti Me stepped boldly into the cemetery.

I tried to follow, but as I did, one of the men yelled something again, in that sharp, nasally voice, so strange.

Ti Me laughed to herself but kept moving.

"Why does he talk like that?" I asked her as I hesitated just past the entrance. I could feel the heat of the crowd pressing against my back.

"He speaks in the voice of the dead," Ti Me said. "The dead all sound like that."

"What did he say?"

"I will tell you after, mamselle."

In the graveyard, people were crowding around two tombs, pressing forward, laughing, singing. Some were resting against the walls of the dead, others placing bowls of food and drink on the tops. "These are the tombs of the first woman who died, Manman Briggette, and her husband," Ti Me said. "And here is the tomb of the first to die by the hand of man, and there is the first murder. They are all here to call up the dead."

All around us was the sharp smell of rum. A woman danced past, a jug held high above her head, the liquid sloshing out, down her arm, on her face. Some of it sprayed on me. I coughed when it touched my lips.

"It burns you, eh?" Ti Me laughed again. "Piman needs to be hot," she said. "You take a whole string of peppers, ten strings even, and mix them with clairin. It has to be hot enough to warm up the dead."

The woman with the jug stopped a few feet ahead of us, the crowd making room for her as she began to twirl and laugh and roll her hips. She splashed the liquid on her chest, poured it over her hands, rubbed it into her face. Someone handed her a long red pepper, and she took that, too, stuffing it into her left nostril. Another went in her ear, where it promptly fell out and onto the ground.

"That woman is ridden by a gede. The spirits found her, and she is their horse. They will move through her body. The dead are cold, but we can warm them up. He needs piman to warm him up."

The woman began to hunch down lower, to sing and to dance faster. A few people in the crowd joined her, others laughed, and some began singing another song altogether. Above us, the sun hung low in the sky, and I could see, from the cemetery gate, the harbor with the light shining bright over it, the sea turned to waves of white light in the dusk.

I had thought when I came here, I would be able to become a new person. That I would become someone for whom it did not matter that I had failed my mother. And, I supposed, that had happened. I became a wife and a sister and a daughter to people who could not see me. But was that any better than what I had been at home, beside my mother? I thought now, *It is useless.* I had thought then, *It is lost.*

I looked at the crowd rejoicing in the graves. The man closest to me pulled a femur bone from on top of one of the tombs and waved it in the air in slow circles. A few people walked with goats on leads or held in their arms. The sound of laughter kept up all around me. It had gone from a shock to a comfort to something that warmed me on the inside, that made my blood beat, that at least told me I was alive.

Ti Me had given up her role as nurse to me and was now standing by herself, watching the men and women sing. Sometimes, she sang along loudly; other times, she kept beat with hand claps.

Perhaps, I thought, I was destined to always be a child; perhaps it was silly to try to be otherwise. I thought of the life that lay ahead of me, a life of doing what my husband whispered to me late at night, of standing beside a Christian madwoman every day in church and pretending that her pronouncements were sane, of sitting across from a smelly old bishop who looked at me as the Whore of Babylon and had not spoken more than twenty words to me since I arrived. I thought of dying here, in this land, never seeing my mother's face again. I felt it, suddenly, in my chest: *I need her.*

I began to laugh. It did not start as a giggle. It was horrible. My stomach ached with it, my lips hurt from peeling back, and my bones were shaking. I was laughing so hard I could not catch my breath. My smile widened and widened until my eyes were narrowed and I felt the tiny, hot burst of tears at the corners of my eyes. The strangest thing was that I could not hear myself. I could feel the laughter bang in my throat, but in my ears was only the roar of the people around me.

Ti Me turned to look at me—both shocked and amused. "It's too much for Mamselle," she said.

"No," I gasped when I was able. "We stay." Even in my hysteria, I could see the skepticism on her face. But I wanted to do at least one part of this right.

I sat down on the dirt, against one of the tombs. Ti Me, still looking anxious, stood beside me for a bit.

She knelt down. "Do you want to know what he said at the gate?"

"Who?"

"Papa Gede. He knows everything. He knows who will die and who will be born. He said you are now with child—two, he said. I laughed because I thought he was joking. He likes to make jokes. Rude ones, especially about pretty young women," she said. "But I think—"

I began to laugh harder. I pressed my back into the tomb and rolled my neck. I could not say then if I wanted release from the moment or to be held in it forever. I was never good at deciding a side.

"No, mamselle, don't do that!" Ti Me put her hands behind my head, trying to still me. She brushed the dust out of my hair.

"If I am . . . If I am . . . If I am," I gasped, "so be it."

"Mamselle, you will hurt yourself."

"I have failed as a daughter, and I do not like being a wife. Perhaps I can be a mother," I said, and then I began to laugh even harder, until

Ti Me raised me up by the elbows, dusted off my church dress, and walked me, very carefully, out of the graveyard and back to my husband's house.

By the time we arrived, I had quieted down some. I could feel myself hiccoughing, the flutter in my diaphragm. I did not think what Ti Me and that man, whoever he had been, what they said about me—I did not believe it could be true. But by then, Ti Me was convinced. She had me lie down in my bedroom, checked the shutters to make sure they were closed against the street, and set a tincture of ginger leaves and aloe at my bedside, so bitter it made me wince.

The house was empty except for the two of us. I could hear the whisper of the bottoms of Ti Me's feet as she walked from my room, down the hall, and out to the yard. She had told me she would go to find Emmanuel, but I was not sure that I wished to see him yet.

Even in the heat, Ti Me had draped a blanket over me, and in my exhaustion I had let her. But now I tossed it off and pressed at my stomach, naming each part I imagined I felt through my skin. *The liver, the kidneys.* I imagined feeling the womb. I had not thought of this part of it, of falling pregnant without my mother there to name everything. I thought of the last day of our journey to Haiti, when we'd thrown the satchel Mama had handed me overboard and toasted to babies to come. I had done it to amuse Emmanuel, to amuse myself, really, by imagining what my mother would think if she could see me then. I had not let it occur to me that any of it could be real.

The world is only consequences, Libertie. I could hear her voice now.

"You do not always have to be right," I said to the ceiling above me.

There was a flash of light there, the reflection from the bowl of water and herbs Ti Me had left by my side. I watched as the light from the water skipped over the ceiling—back and forth, back and forth. It meant nothing. It meant everything. I was not sure where this thing called a will came from. Mama had it. Emmanuel had it. Even mad Ella, in her obsessions, had a will. But I did not. Would it come when whatever was in me was born? Or did I have a little more time to develop one, before this something else was here?

I began to laugh again, a little weakly. The heat of the graveyard was beginning to leave me. I could feel the sweat cooling on my face. By the time Emmanuel returned, led by Ti Me, both of them panting from running there, I was sitting up in bed, sipping from the bowl of water, in the last little bit of sunlight from the shutters I had thrown open wide.

"You are feeling better, at least?" Emmanuel said, his voice hesitant.

I set down my cup. "There was never anything wrong with me."

"Ti Me says you took fright."

"I was only overheated. But I am well now."

He sat down on the bed, motioned for Ti Me to leave the room.

"She told me what you heard at the cemetery."

"Do you believe it?"

"It would not be surprising."

"You do not sound delighted."

"It is only that there is so much to do, still, for the two of us," he said. He bent his head. He would not look at me.

He made as if to fall into bed beside me, but I pushed him away.

"You do not wish for this either," I said.

"There is not much to be done. It was not part of the plan, but I cannot say I can't see how it could be. Father will be satisfied, at least."

"He was about to yell at me, last time I saw him."

"You shouldn't have fled from the church like that, this is true. You could have left more discreetly," Emmanuel said. "But he forgave you when I said you might be with child. He remembers what that is like. He said, 'Women lose their minds when they are carrying. It is their burden.' But he was pleased. He will be pleased."

"Is that all?"

"I can see how it could help with a lot of things."

"I'm to raise it, to have it, here with a grandfather that hates its mother and a madwoman for an auntie."

"Don't call Ella that," he said.

I did not meet his eye. Instead, I looked at the reflection of the two of us in the mirror across from the bed—the back of his neck, red with heat, and my own reflection, dark in the shadows of the afternoon.

"I am not feeling well again," I said. "I want to rest some more."

He looked only slightly disappointed. He got up to close the shutters.

"No. Leave them open. The noise helps make the room bearable."

He tried to smile. "For tonight only," he said. Then he left me.

When I heard him walk all the way down the hall, I went to the desk and opened the drawer, the one he had told me was mine alone. The letters were crammed in until they tore, the paper crumpled into a fan. I took them out and brought them back to the bed and held them in the cradle of my lap.

Mama's need was too great. Think of that, I told myself. But who would have thought of that? I'd needed her and needed her and needed her when it was unseemly, and now here was the proof that she'd needed me back.

I tried to read her letters, but the words would not focus. My eyes would not let me take them in. I felt a pressure at my temples and suddenly very, very tired. To recognize that I had become another person for possibly a reason as foolish and flimsy as misunderstanding my mother—it was too painful to bear.

Fragments of the letters swam into clarity.

You do not write
You do not write
You do not write to me
Why?

Libertie
　　I cannot think of a greater freedom than raising you from a babe in arms to a girl. You were mine, and I decided what you heard, who you listened to, what words formed on your lips. It was intoxicating to have that kind of open dominion over another, even more so because I knew you would grow to become your own person, and that person could be shaped by me.
　　You do not write to me

And then the letters went back to a blur.

I closed my eyes and rapped my fist on the desk—once, twice, three times.

And then I sat down and took a fresh sheet and dipped my pen in the ink.

I wrote on one sheet, simple and direct:

　　I am with child.

I called Ti Me and handed it to her to bring to the telegraph office on the Rue de Commerce. I spelled out the address carefully with my own hand. I made her repeat it back to me.

When she was gone, I looked at the pileup of my mother's love.

I'll burn it all this afternoon, I told myself in a flash of resolve. *If I burn her words, I will be free of whatever she wants of me.*

Instead, I stuffed the papers back in my drawer.

OF ALL THE things she told me about limbs and wombs and bodies, Mama did not tell me what it felt like to feel life within your own.

Within a month of the time in the graveyard, I felt it. The women in Mama's care had always described it as a flutter, but this felt more like a determined, persistent churning. As if a current was gathering inside me. The first time I felt it was in the parlor, while Ella lectured. She had been so enamored of her own words she did not see my expression, or note when I left the room. By the end of the month, the wave was steady and predictable. I imagined the child there, as faceless as the skin of the ocean, as formless as a wave.

Emmanuel was afraid I would lose it. He was convinced that what we had wished for, for so long, could be snatched from this world. It was as if all those deaths of his childhood—his mother, his brothers— were around him again and he saw winding sheets and sorrow every- where. He said it was now too dangerous for me to leave the house, even for church, even for the daily walk to the market.

"I can manage," I said. "I can help you in your work."

But he was not convinced. "It is too dangerous. You could lose it. I would not want to lose it."

"I will be as likely to lose it in this house as I am on the streets."

"This is the one thing I ask of you, Libertie," he said. "I have not asked that much."

And I thought, *This is a lie. But he truly does not know it.* And I thought, *He really has been a kind husband to you, Libertie. He could be crueler.* And I thought, again, that I was as gormless as the wave inside me if I could not make sense of any of this.

It was easier, in the end, to acquiesce. I did not think I could live in that house with everyone except for Ti Me angry with me.

"I will stay in, for now," I said.

And he smiled and kissed the top of my head. "It's lovely when you're stubborn," he said.

For the first week of my confinement, I kept my usual schedule. That is, I sat with Ella in the parlor room and the two of us pretended to work, while the other women—American and Haitian—moved in and out of the house, to Bishop Chase's study for instruction and approval.

"Emmanuel tells me you are with child?" Ella said the first morning.

"Yes."

"Well, then," Ella said. "Your work is done."

I thought we could reach a kind of peace. That, even in her madness, she would retreat in the face of this.

But Ella was cunning. She began to smother me with nostalgia. Now, alongside talk of the justice and blood she and Emmanuel had witnessed so long ago, she told me story after story of their childhood.

"When we were six, we had a pet goat who disliked me but loved Emmanuel."

"When we were fifteen, Emmanuel learned to swim and tried to teach me, but I was a lady enough to refuse," she said pointedly.

"When we were twenty, Emmanuel wished me to marry, but I asked him who was worthy, and he said, 'No one.' Just like that, my brother said, 'No one.' He has always understood me."

It seemed such a lonely way to be twins, I thought, Emmanuel always faced out to a future he was sure he could dream into existence, and Ella always turned back to a past that had meaning only for her.

For relief, I sometimes sat in the stoop of the inner courtyard, watching the hens walk across the dirt, watching them eat the dust out of boredom. But even that was not free of Ella. "Emmanuel and I had pet chickens. Two of them. They were black with red speckles, and Emmanuel loved his, but he hated mine, and he tried to pluck her feathers while she was still crowing, and . . ."

My escape was the cooking shed itself. Ella refused to enter it. "When we were ten, Ti Me told us to never enter it," she said.

"You are not ten anymore," I said.

But Ella was adamant. The shed, she was not allowed to enter.

It was quiet in there. The only sound was Ti Me's feet shuffling across the dirt and occasionally the clank of a spoon on a pot. It was hot, but when it got to be too much, I sat in the doorway and looked back at the main house. By the time I'd found the safety of the shed, my stomach and thighs had grown so much that my knees spread apart when I sat down. A rash of spots had appeared on my skin, and my underarms were always slick. I wore the same tan smock every day while Ella went about sewing me a new dress, with the waist dropped, for my final months. And still I had not heard a word from my mother.

"Have you ever been with child, Ti Me?" I said.

She sucked at her teeth, and I realized I had offended her. I felt a pang of embarrassment. I saw, in the corner of the kitchen hut, the straw pallet where Ti Me slept.

I tried again. "It feels as though my body is not my own. It feels like it belongs to whatever's growing in there."

Ti Me shifted a pot from one end of her worktable to the other. And then she began to tell me about the last time she had been ridden by lwa yo. It was a few weeks ago, she said, and she was so tired afterward she nearly did not make breakfast the next morning. Yon lwa who had mounted her turns her devotees into unruly children, begging everyone for sweets, curving their backs against the swats to come. Ti Me had stood in the circle and cried like a baby, crawled on her knees and stuffed her fingers into her mouth while the spirit acted through her.

"It isn't frightening when that happens?"

Ti Me cracked a nut on the worktable. "Why would I be scared?"

"Because you have no control over yourself. You lose yourself. You lost your freedom and died in the spirit of something else."

"Eh," Ti Me said. "Everything born dies, no?"

Emmanuel came back to me at night, but it was no longer only to me. It was a mirror of the lessons we had learned on the boat to Haiti, except that now, instead of talking to me of flowers, he manipulated the skin of my stomach, pressing hard.

"Do you remember," I said, "not so long ago, teaching me to swim?"

"Of course," he said. He was watching my stomach rise and fall with my breath.

"You could touch me like that, again, if you wished."

"The time for that is over for now," he said.

At dinner each night, as Bishop Chase and Ella listened, he questioned what I had done with my days indoors.

"What did you eat?"

"Which cistern did you drink from?"

"How many hours did you rest?"

"Did you walk the length of the hall three times, or ten?"

"I do not think," I said after the fourth night of this, "that your father and Ella want to hear every detail of my confinement."

"On that we agree," Ella said cheerfully. "I do not."

"Ella, stop." Emmanuel turned to me. "It is something we should be proud of. And it is their future, too."

"It is not," I said in a rush of anger. "It is mine."

There was a silence while Emmanuel looked down at his plate, chastened.

"You will explain to her?" Bishop Chase was speaking to Emmanuel. Never to me.

"There's nothing to explain," I said.

Bishop Chase kept chewing slowly, then swallowed and took a sip from his glass. "Ti Me, a bit more please."

"Libertie," Emmanuel said, "I will resolve it later."

I pushed myself back from the table as best I could and walked to the courtyard stoop, to stare at the night sky.

It was not clear if the face of the moon that looked down on me now was the same one that looked down on my mother. And in that loneliness, I felt a longing for her so violent that it made me rise up from the stoop and begin to pace.

"You know," I heard. "Emmanuel really does love you."

I looked up. It was Ella, standing in the light from the doorway.

"I suppose."

"You know," Ella said, "when we were sixteen—"

"I do not wish to hear childhood stories right now, Ella."

"When we were sixteen," she said, "I saw my father stick his finger in the coo coo of every serving girl up and down this street, including Ti Me. I told Emmanuel what I saw, and he said not to lie, never to lie. I told Papa what I saw, and he struck me and told me if I did not behave, I would have to stay in the house forever.

"Emmanuel said then to me what he said to you. That he would fix it with Papa. And then I knew he loved me. He told me to try very hard to forgive Papa, and he would fix it. And I did.

"Emmanuel told Papa I was sick. He told everyone I was sick. My friends have believed I was sick since we were sixteen. But he told me just to pretend. And it has been a little secret between us. I did not want you to know. You are so young, and I did not think you would understand. But you should. The world thinks you are mad . . . It's the greatest freedom I've ever known. Emmanuel gave that to me.

"I say whatever I wish to anyone. What colored woman in this world has that? Not a one, not a one anywhere on this Earth. You felt it when you first came, no? I can sew it into a million little words. I am free to speak my mind. Emmanuel did that for me, and he'll do it for you.

Ella held out her hand. "Because he really loves you."

FREEDOM WAS BEN Daisy choosing the bottom of the water over its surface, and the Graces singing, and Mama leaving me to put myself together in the loam, and the woman with the white chalked face, a pepper falling from her ear, dancing for the dead.

I knew what freedom was, and I knew I did not have it as I lay in bed beside Emmanuel, hissing in the dark, wary of what words would fall over the gaps in the ceiling above us.

"Your father is a monster. Your sister is lost."

"She is not completely lost. She told you herself."

"You would have me live that existence?"

"No. If you would be sensible. If you would trust me. If you would hold on. You would see, we only have to please him for a little while longer to be free."

"How much longer?"

"When the child is born, if it's a son, he will be more agreeable. My father and I are opposed—you know this. You cannot believe that I am the same as him."

"You've condemned your sister to . . . I am not even sure what kind of existence."

"She trusts me. As you should trust me."

"Why should I trust you if you don't even understand what is wrong?"

"You are being impossible, Libertie." He turned his back to me. The mattress creaked. "Papa . . . what he is doing is no different than what the slave masters used to do to our foremothers. Where do you think your mother's pretty color came from? Where do you think mine did?"

"But that does not make it right."

"No. But this is a new world here, with new rules. He is making his. I am making mine. You know what mine will be."

"Neither of your rules are new for me, or for your sister, or for Ti Me." I thought of the banner at Cunningham College, with its list of what made men and what made women. "We have always lived under them, whether there or here."

He turned back. I could feel his breath, hot on my face; he had brought himself as close to me as possible. "You are protected and cherished. I cherish you. And because of that, he will respect you," he said. "You have my love and devotion and my promise to always protect you. And you live in a country where I am considered man enough to make that happen. It would not be so back at your mama's house. You know that."

"You do not understand."

"What is there to understand?"

"You have freedom to define yourself, and I do not have any."

"You would not be asking for this if you loved and trusted me," he said. "It is the same with your mother. She did not trust me to wrap a bandage around a woman's arm without her oversight. But I thought you were different than her. That you had a better sense of what was possible."

I could feel his expectancy. But I did not want to give it to him. To give it to him would have been betrayal.

I sat up in bed, put my feet on the floor, and began the walk to the cooking shed.

IN THE SHED, I slept on the worktable. There was a hole in the roof, through which you could see the stars. I fell asleep looking up at them and was awakened only when Ti Me came in and gasped.

"You scared me, mamselle."

"I am sorry," I said. "But I think I will stay here with you for a while, if you wish."

"You have scared Monsieur Emmanuel. He and Ella searched the house for you and now he is walking the street, calling for you. You did not hear?"

"No." I rolled over, onto my side.

"They are trying to find you."

"Just let me rest here, please. You will not get in trouble. I will tell them I told you to let me sleep here."

"You would be more comfortable upstairs."

"Do you know, Ti Me, that when you are with child, your ribs float apart? Just like logs in a river. Float right apart."

"You are ill, mamselle."

"I only want to lie here for a little bit longer," I said. "When Monsieur Emmanuel returns, I will go back upstairs."

I could not see her expression in the dark, but I heard her turn to go back to the house. I felt the room grow cool around me. I could smell the peppers drying on strings on the wall. The grain of the worktable mixed with the blood of all the chickens cut and quartered. It was almost comforting. It reminded me of Mama.

"You will not get up?" It was Emmanuel standing over me, speaking in his softest tones.

"No."

"You would sleep better inside."

"It is good enough here for Ti Me."

"She is not with child."

You and your father see to that. "No, she is not."

"Come," he said. I felt him pull at the back of my smock.

I hunched down further, my knees bunched up against the squash of my lower belly. "I will not move. So do not try."

"You are being ridiculous."

"I am only asking to be left alone for a little while."

He said something low to Ti Me, who sucked in her teeth. Then he was gone, and it was me and her, lying there in the dark, with the chicken feathers floating around us.

I turned around again to look at her.

"Is it true, Ti Me?"

She was quiet for a long time. I could hear her breathing into the straw pallet. Then she sighed.

"Emmanuel feels like a son to me," she said. "Sometimes, he feels like a brother."

"Bishop Chase did that to you, what Ella said."

"It was not like that," she said. "Miss Ella is young and misunderstands."

"I do not think so."

Quiet again. Finally, she said, "Bishop does many things to many girls. You know what a man is like. It is no good to wish for something different. It's not possible."

I listened to Ti Me's breath slow for a long time. I listened to the night all around us. It was a queer thing that the night here in Haiti was not frightening. It was almost like a friend. I thought of lying in the Gradys' parlor, overwhelmed by loneliness. Of the night around my mother's house, always threatening to be broken by someone else's need—the knock on the door, the summons of "Doctor, come quick!"

That was not part of the night here. Sleeping in the cooking shed meant I could hear the sounds from the street more clearly. The bray of a baby goat lost for a moment from its mother. The rising and falling hum of insect wings fluttering. And far away, the roll of the ocean. I imagined I could hear the creak of a ship there, too. Would I take it, if I could? And if I did, where would it carry me? I had once believed escape was possible.

Emmanuel had always accused me of not loving the country. But as I listened to the night, I realized I loved it. I loved this land. If there was an answer to any of this, it was in the hills and the water around me. I loved it maybe even more than Emmanuel did. I loved it enough to wish more for it and my life there than what Emmanuel or his father could imagine.

HERE IS HOW you live in the cooking shed.

You make sure to wake up each morning before Ti Me, to wipe down the table you slept on. You roll off the table very carefully—your belly is heavy by then. Before you decided to live in the shed, your husband joked that perhaps you were carrying twins, and you think, each morning, more and more, that he was maybe right.

Two women cramp a shed.

You are aware you are asking a lot of your host. You wonder if you are doing the same thing you despise your husband's father for, just more politely. Sometimes, you wonder if she wishes it was she with the belly full of babies under the smock. She never looks at your body. She lets her eyes drift over it.

You find it awkward to sit in silence with her in the shed, so you try to draw her out. You talk to her in her own language, but she laughs at all the words you don't know. So sometimes you both speak in English, and sometimes you alone speak Kreyòl, and she answers that with a crack of her knuckles.

It is not a real answer.

A body cannot answer a question.

You take to making pronouncements to her. "I will never step back in that house," you tell her, "as long as the bishop lives there."

And, "I don't think he ever loved me."

And, "I think I am the silliest pickaninny who ever lived."

And, "How is it possible to become free when you do not even know who you are?"

These questions make you reckless and queasy. Saying them aloud is like sucking on the grayest gristle of fat on a stewing chicken bone. It is like smelling oxtails boiling. You feel how you used to feel when you wrote to the woman in the water, that telling the truth of what you feel is a dangerous thing, that it could invalidate your very self. Then you think of that woman in the water, and how she led this man to you. He called you one of her devotees. This man who fundamentally misunderstood you, and who you fundamentally misunderstood. You thought he was braver than he was. You thought he had a bigger imagination. His imagination was a cooking pot with the lid on, boiling.

All this takes your breath away, which is already short, because two expanding baby skulls are lovingly pressed on your lungs, making you lose your capacity for air. You are running out of air. You are not sure your husband understands this.

Gasping, you try to make yourself useful. Cooking is very much like making medicine, you think at first. There is a certain amount of drudgery in mixing and chopping and measuring, though Ti Me measures by handfuls and pinches, which makes more sense than how your mother measured, you thought bitterly. Your mother with her scales and her pipettes, and you, as a child, having to wash them each night for her. You try to do the same here, telling yourself you are useful. Ti Me looks skeptical.

You offer to gather eggs in the morning for Ti Me, and she says she supposes that you could. Sometimes, the eggs are malformed, the tops folded over onto themselves. You look at the nests, at the brooding hens, and you feel . . . nothing. You'd imagined that you would feel a great kinship with the world of mothers, now that you will shortly be one. But you do not. The pregnant nanny goat with its red swollen belly still disgusts you, and when you see another woman with child waddle past the back of the courtyard, you only feel embarrassed of how little you yourself have become a mother. Of how much you are still lacking.

Getting the eggs is tricky, because you are avoiding your husband and his family. You try to either get up before any of them or stay in the shed until your husband and his father, at least, are gone. But at night, when you lay on the worktable, you still lie as if Emmanuel was beside you. You curl to the edge and make space for this boy, as if the two of you were still in bed.

You lose count of your nights in the shed. Eventually, your husband leads his sister to the door, leads her by the hand like a child, and has her stand and call, "Libertie, Libertie, I have something to tell you."

You do not come out of the shed. You sit in the dark and call back, "You can say whatever you wish from there."

You hear them scuffle, as if someone is about to leave. Then Ella yelps. Had your husband pinched her? Ti Me, later, will confirm that he had. Just like when they were small. But after the yelp, you hear Ella, in her grudging singsong, say, "I did not mean to frighten you, sister dear. Please forgive us."

You do not shout anything back to that. You can feel the two of them out there, waiting. You will not respond. Eventually, one of them shuffles away.

A few minutes later, your husband comes into your shed and says, "Ti Me, may we have a moment."

When she is gone, you say to him, "You've forced Ti Me out of her home."

"You have," he says back, and it shocks you a bit, his willingness to do battle. You have always known him as a lover. You have always felt that power over him. You did not expect him to be willing to fight. If you do not know yourself as his lover, as the one who makes his eyes turn soft and makes his voice weak and makes him bow his head to please you:

What are you?

What power do you have here?

You are frightened then that you've lost him. That maybe he was lost to you already.

So you square your shoulders and decide, no matter. If he's lost, then maybe you are ready to be something else.

"You are a liar," you say.

"I have never lied to you," he says in a sob, and all your resolve nearly leaves you. And it is maddening that he is right. You want to go to him and hold him, to hold him as you did when you were both at sea. But in the dark shed, you think of the gleam in Ella's eye, and Ti Me's quiet voice saying:

You know what a man is like.

It is no use to wish for something different.

It is not possible.

"Do you remember," you say, "when you wooed me and told me that we were equals? That we would be companions?"

"Have we not been?"

"You did not tell me your family's history."

"I have always thought—" He stops, his voice strangled with tears. "I have always thought that I could be myself with you."

"But your self belongs to this rottenness. Your self defends it."

"I don't know what you mean."

"Which self have you been? The one who wants a million sons to build a free nation? The one who lets his father corrupt a country with his lewdness and greed? The one who calls his sister mad until maybe she's become it? The one who imagines doing all of this means he's working toward freedom?"

In the dusk, you see how slight he is, again. How pale his skin is, and how it glows. You think of how much pleasure you took in his looks, how much you took pleasure in the pleasure others took in looking at him. You were Mrs. Doctor, Mrs. Emmanuel Chase, Mrs. Chase. Your genuine desire for him was all mixed up in knowing how much he desired you, and how much anyone—Ella seething in the sitting room, his father peering at you over his glasses, your mother, shocked and scared, the high yellow American women of the colony with their faces fixed in disbelief—how all of them could see it. It was so plain they couldn't deny it.

How much it would hurt if all that certainty of who you were, at least to them, was gone.

"You are unfair, Libertie," he says. He unbends his head. And for a moment, it is as it was when the two of you were in the mountains, in the pool, his hands holding you up, through the water, to the sky.

"I do not know what to do," you say.

"There is nothing to do," he says. "You are only upset and broody."

"No," you say. "I don't know what to do."

"Come back in the house, Libertie."

"I think," you say carefully, "I will stay out here for a little while longer."

He sighs. Bends his head again.

And then he is gone.

THE BEST PART about living in the shed was being close to the fire. I no longer had to listen to the string of chicken move past Emmanuel's father's teeth, or his sister sip each teaspoon of her consommé. The only sound I missed was the fork up against my husband's tongue.

I did not eat what the family ate. I ate what Ti Me did. Sometimes, we roasted plantains in the embers of the fire. Sometimes, she cracked two raw eggs in a cup and drank it, and I drank it, too. I did not have the nausea so many women have with pregnancy. Instead, I craved the scraps of Ti Me's worktable. Sometimes, she had to slap the potato skins from my hands—she would catch me gathering them up and sucking each one as if it was honey.

"You best not start eating the dirt, mamselle," she warned me. "You do that, and I'll have Monsieur Emmanuel himself come and get you."

It was true I had been tempted, but I took Ti Me at her word, though I kept a small handful of dust in my smock pocket, to lick at when she was asleep.

"Ti Me, do you love the younger Chases?"

"Non, mamselle."

"No!" I laughed, surprised by how she'd said it without hesitation.

Her expression did not change. "They are kind. They were good to me when I came to them as a girl."

"But you don't love them?"

"What does any of that have to do with love?"

"You never loved Emmanuel and Ella, then?"

She snorted. "I never love Monsieur Emmanuel. Or Mamselle Ella. I care for them like they are my brother and sister. I care for them better than a mother. But I don't love them. When I first saw them, they were so thin. And so pale. They got spots in the sun. They were so scared—scared of everything. Emmanuel told me they see their mama pass, right in front of them. Their brothers, too. Their papa, he would always pray. The children cry, and he would tell them to pray. They would cry on me at night. I have my mother—she still living, so I did not know what to do. She told me just to hold them. So I did."

"You were not tired of them?"

"What do you mean?"

"When someone needs you that much, it doesn't make you tired?"

"You are speaking nonsense."

"I used to think that as a little girl. And I thought that was what was wonderful about Emmanuel. He wanted me without asking anything of me. I thought that at least. But now I think he asks too much."

"He asks nothing of you."

"He asks me to live with a bad man and a girl who pretends to be mad and does nothing all day."

"But the bishop and Ella can't help who they are."

"Do you think they will ever change?"

"The bishop. What would you change? He wishes for a place he cannot return to. He does what any other man would do if they were him. It is no use trying to change him."

"That's what you always say, Ti Me. Nothing is ever of any use."

"It would be cruel to try and change the bishop. You can only live beside him and turn away from him when you can. And Ella, she is still a child."

"I am to stay here and take whatever the bishop says or tries to do to me?" I said.

"You want to know why you are so restless, causing all this family trouble?"

"It is Monsieur Emmanuel who's caused the trouble."

"Bah," she said. "Men do what they do. They are like a plow, moving through dirt—they just make the way. It's women like you and your fretting that cause a mess, disturb a rut."

"What's wrong with me, then? Why am I so restless, if I should already know to do nothing like you?"

Ti Me had begun chopping up the cassava for dinner. She did not stop as she said to me, "You've been claimed by the spirit. By Erzulie. And you will be unsatisfied and miserable till you devote yourself to her."

"Have you told this to Monsieur Emmanuel?"

"I told him the first night I saw you. I said, 'Monsieur, a woman like that doesn't know herself. You should never marry a woman so lost she does not recognize herself. Can't even place her own reflection in a mirror. Can't even see her own face on top of still water.' He said you were a clever girl, you would make do. But . . . here you are." She looked up from her work to where I lay, belly-up to the soot-stained ceiling of the cookhouse.

"If you wanted to," Ti Me said while looking at the large bowl of rice, "you could change it."

"What do you mean?"

She shifted the rice—once, twice. The husking sound seemed to mock me.

"It is Monsieur Emmanuel who believes in all that," I said. "I don't."

"Wi, mamselle," Ti Me said.

"Well," I said after a moment. "What would I do? If I believed the things you did."

Ti Me finally looked me full in the face. "You would have to kouche."

I felt my cheeks grow hot, and I looked down, embarrassed. I could hear the word in Emmanuel's voice, when he'd whispered it to me in the dark, describing how we lay and died and were born together.

Ti Me laughed at my expression. "No, not like that. It means that, too, but also it means other things. You will kouche . . ." Here, she gestured to my stomach under the smock. "Give birth. But what I mean is that when you kouche, you would dedicate yourself to yon lwa. You would go to the initiation and you would kouche—it would be like you are dying. We would cry for you and grieve for you, because we would know you are passing over to another side. We would kiss you goodbye, Emmanuel and I."

I shivered.

"You would cover your eyes, and you would be made to dance in circles. Over and over. When that was done, you would be led to a small dark room, and that is where you kouche again. You would stay there. You would be reborn. You would be as a baby in a womb. You would be brought food and rubbed down, as a new baby is. You would be raised back up to become a woman again. But you would be new. When you leave the room, when you are finished, you would keep your head covered for forty days. Because you would still be like a newborn baby, and your head is soft, and the spirits within your head, even though they have finally been fed, would still be growing strong each day.

"But"—Ti Me sighed—"even though you should kouche and it would solve a lot of your restlessness, it does not matter. You will not stay here long enough to right it."

I began to sweat. "I don't understand."

"You sent me to the telegraph office. You make me send a message. You will not stay here."

"I did not ever ask to leave."

"You can leave a place in more ways than one."

THE MAIL BOAT came only on Tuesdays. The telegraph office was only open in the afternoon. Because of this, everyone knew everyone else's communications. There were the back-and-forths of the American Negro colony and the comings and goings of the white French and American merchants who stayed in the city. And then there was the continuous flow of gossip from the countryside to the market street, which wound over the mountains from Port-au-Prince. It was hard to escape this web of foreknowledge. It had already told the town that I was with child, that I had spurned my husband, that I slept among vegetable peelings.

An uppity woman, to turn a good man into a beggar in his own home.

A woman too sure of herself.

A woman that dark can't play like that.

Dr. Chase will be ruined.

Bishop Chase will, too.

I wished for any other sound to drown it out. Sometimes, I drummed my fingers on the shed's table, just to break the rhythms around me. *If only,* my index finger tapped. *If only.* It did not seem fair that my deficiencies in womanhood, in wifeliness, in Negro life, should follow me all the way to this new world, where I was supposed to be washed clean, left out of those old songs, harbinger of a different one altogether.

So it felt like a kind of dream when all this changed and began to din around the fact that we would soon all be visited by a troupe of

Negro performers. They were making a tour of the Caribbean, had come from Florida to Cuba and then to us, in Jacmel. This news was received with great excitement—even Bishop Chase seemed pleased.

The only time I saw Ti Me genuinely smile in that house was when she came to the shed and told me that Bishop Chase had given a special dispensation to everyone in the colony, allowing them to attend the performance, even though theatrics were generally considered sinful.

She shyly pulled, from under her own cot, her better shawl, all white, the one she only wore at holiday time and kept folded over, with care, in an old burlap rice sack. As I touched the gleaming white linen, I realized my dilemma. I wanted to hear something besides the sound of our alley, the sound of our animals, and Ti Me's occasional voice. I was bored in the shed by then. It was comfortable as I grew bigger and my hips grew soft, but it had lost its charm.

To leave it, though, would mean some sort of a concession. I was not sure exactly to whom. Was it to Emmanuel, or was it to myself? Lazy Libertie, without even the conviction to withstand the offer of a traveling show. Mama had stood firm for less. I felt embarrassed that I had ever criticized her as a girl. A song, it turned out, was where my resolve ended.

"They say they are bringing a man who plays a horn," Ti Me said, her voice swooping up in glee. "And another man who has trained the birds to talk to him, and can talk back to them. He can tell us their stories."

"Do you really believe that?"

"And there will be a carnival, and people will dance."

"Yes," I said. I reached for the bowl of rice Ti Me was now washing.

"And they are coming all the way from where you did."

Every evening, when Ti Me left our shed to serve dinner, I sat on the floor near the door and looked out across the yard, at the main house. Sometimes, when she returned from her duties, Emmanuel followed her. I would sit by the door, and he would tell me, again, how much I loved him, how he loved the children inside me, how I needed to only step out of the door and into the world he was building for us.

My resolve broke a bit more each time he came—because I was furious with him, with his father, but I still loved him. I still wished for him by my side, to run my hand over his pale back in the moonlight, to feel his hands underneath me, holding me up in the water. With Mama, I had held on to the anger and let the love burn away. But with Emmanuel, there was no satisfaction in this burnt space between us. It only made me lonelier, and the loneliness made me long for him more. I would be weak, I knew it, and return to him. But not yet, I hoped.

The night that word came about our visitors, I stayed for a bit longer while Emmanuel whispered all his love for me.

"I would like to see the players," I said finally.

"I do not think that is a good idea, in your condition."

"I am not so far along that I can't go."

"You are too far gone. There will surely be a crowd, and if anything were to happen to you, we would not be able to get you help in the crush of people."

"Maybe I could go but stand apart."

"You would probably," he said slyly, "be able to hear them from our bedroom window."

So that is how I found myself sitting again in my husband's room, a chair drawn up to the sill and the shutters open, straining to hear what I could past the crowd.

Ella and Bishop Chase had left to listen. Ti Me had gone, as well. It was only me and Emmanuel in the house. I sat to one side of the window; he stood to the other.

"I do not think I will be able to hear—"

"You will. They are performing on the Rue de Commerce. We can usually hear what happens there."

Outside the window, the sun was bending deeper into the sky, and we could see, just over the roofs of the trading offices, the water of the harbor moving back and forth.

I am here, far away from my mother and my father's bones, I thought, *and I am looking at a sight they will never see.*

"Do they move?" Emmanuel said.

"What?"

"Do they move, the babies? Do they move a lot? Is it painful?"

"They are sleeping at the moment," I said.

He smiled at that, his face so eager. I took a breath. Stopped. Took a breath again.

"They move the most when Ti Me speaks."

"Yes?"

"Yes. You know, she does not speak often, but when she begins to talk about something, it is almost as if they swim towards her."

"Then they know her as the rest of us know her."

I narrowed my eyes. "Do not say that."

He blushed. "I did not mean it that way."

"Your father took advantage of a girl who acted as mother to you. Who was only a few years older than you."

"Everything is not as simple as you think it is, Libertie."

"But it seems very simple. You say you want a different world than your father's. This is a chance to start making it."

He looked out the window.

"If everything you do is for the good of our people," I said, "for the country yet to come, I wonder if what he did to Ti Me, if that was part of making a nation, too."

"You are grotesque," he said.

"I am only asking questions. I want to know."

"You cannot know everything," he said. Then, "Aren't you tired of fighting, Libertie?"

I felt a heaviness in my bones that took my breath away. I felt the hang of my belly, pulling on my back, and the crook of my spine from sleeping on a wooden table. I felt the swell of my feet, the itch at the back of my knees that I could not reach. The waves, just over the horizon, moved over and over again, and even that sight exhausted me.

"You must be tired," he said again. "I know that I am. You ask me to do something that I have tried to do since I was a boy, and I tell you I will do it. When the time is right. But we have to plan, to build new things. And while we build, it would not be so bad to lie down here, in our marriage bed, which belongs half to you, after all."

He was at my elbow then, pulling it gently, and I settled into the cup of his hand. I was ready to follow him—I would have followed him, and we would have lain down, curved into each other like two rib bones in the same breathing chest. But then I heard it.

I had almost forgotten that their voices were real. I had not heard them in close to eleven months. Sometimes, in those first few nights on the ship, I had imagined that they sang to me. If I was being truthful, when I woke up in the mornings since, I was always a bit disappointed that I had not dreamt of them the night before.

Emmanuel still had his hand on my elbow, but it did not matter. I turned toward the window, and it was all I could do to keep myself from leaning out of it, from wanting to jump down to the ground below.

It was my Graces, come back to me.

I could not hear what words they were singing from so far away. But I could hear the clarity of their voices, the way they met and married in the air. I could hear how they wound their way to me. I could hear, too, how the crowd had quieted when they began.

"It's Experience and Louisa singing," I said.

Emmanuel looked exasperated. "It can't be."

But it was—I knew it was—and I listened as closely as I could until they were done, and then I heard my heart beat faster.

"You must find them. They must know I am here, but you must find them and bring them to the house."

"How will I even get close? How will I get down to them?"

"Please go!" I said.

"I will go, if it makes you happy."

And he was gone, and I thought of this man who would go out into the streets to find them for me. I thought of Ella, saying sourly, an accusation, *He really loves you.*

I sat in silence, in the darkening house, until I heard the great door downstairs open and close, and Bishop Chase and Ella purring their kindest regards, and Emmanuel laughing, and then the two voices I missed most in the world, after the voice of my mother.

LOUISA AND EXPERIENCE looked better than they had when we'd left them. Experience was a little stouter—her chin had swelled slightly, a little dimple of fat sat in the middle of it. Louisa was standing straighter. They were both in new dresses, finer fabric than I had ever seen them wear.

When they saw me, they began to shout—"Ho!" and "My!"—even Experience.

Finally, Louisa said.

"You have seen her?"

"She came to our final performance," Experience said, "before we began our engagement with the troupe."

"It was too hard," Louisa said, "to manage things on our own. We were nearly run out of town in Connecticut and robbed in Syracuse. We would have given up altogether and returned to school if we had not met Mr. Ashland and the Colored Troubadours. And then they announced their tour of the Caribbean, and that they would even come to Haiti, and we knew we had to join, if only for the chance to see you again."

"Thank God Mr. Ashland is honest," I said.

Louisa laughed. "Yes, he is a good man. We travel for six more months, and then we return to America and find another way, we suppose."

"But you must stay here," I said.

Emmanuel moved forward. "Yes, please stay."

Louisa looked quickly to Experience. "Let us send Mr. Ashland word of our plans. We were to stay two nights here and then travel on to Port-au-Prince. Mr. Ashland tells us there is an opera house there, finer than anything you can find in New Orleans, almost as fine as Paris."

"There was," Bishop Chase said. "But it burnt down."

"Mr. Ashland is not altogether honest," I said, and was rewarded with another of Louisa's laughs. I realized I had not made anyone laugh, besides Emmanuel, since I'd been here. Not kindly, anyways. Sitting at the dinner table for the first time in months, my back felt heavy against the chair.

Louisa and Experience told us all the things they had seen on their travels. It was strange to see them in front of the Chases. They did not understand the Graces' irreverence but knew enough that these women were good, because they sang the word of God. Still, the bishop mostly looked back and forth between Experience and Louisa, as if they were saying words in a language he did not understand but he knew to be indecent.

"In Florida, there is a city that is governed entirely by black men and Indians," Experience said, "and they have built an amphitheater so fine a whisper sounds like a shout."

"In Cuba, they had us sing in the market square while a man slaughtered a bull behind us," Louisa said. "We thought it would be a distraction, but no one clapped until we were done."

"They even ignored the bull's very pretty bow when he was brought down by the mace," Experience added.

"They say we will sing for the colored people in New Orleans," Louisa said, "though Mr. Ashland claims he had to take special care that we weren't engaged at a fancy house."

Ella put down her napkin at this and looked pleadingly at her father. But he shook his head slightly, as if to say *Let it pass, for our guests.*

"And," Experience said, "every penny we earn, except for incidentals, is sent back to the college, Libertie."

"We write to Alma Curtis every three weeks to assure her we are staying virtuous." Louisa winked at me, and I felt my cheeks grow hot.

"She'll be proud to know how you've turned out," Experience said.

"How I've turned out?"

"Yes, she would be proud."

"But I've done nothing I've been educated for," I said.

They both look pained.

Emmanuel looked at me sharply. "You have done very well for yourself, Libertie."

"Yes," I said. "But Alma Curtis used to say I was a girl who could have an ambition."

There was a brief, awkward silence. And then Louisa looked across the table to Ella, to compliment her on her cloak.

"It's a coat of righteousness," Ella said cheerfully. "As righteous as good brother Joseph's was."

Louisa looked at me quizzically. I shrugged.

Ella continued. "This coat is stitched with the word of the Lord."

"Is that so?" Experience said.

Emmanuel cut her off. "Ella is excellent at needlework. She really is."

"Very refined," Louisa said.

Ella narrowed her eyes at her brother.

Emmanuel smiled at the Graces. "We have not had many visitors from outside the island. Probably only once a year, and then mostly other missionaries. It is an honor to have artists in the house."

"I am an artist," Ella said.

"Enough, Ella." Bishop Chase put down his fork. "Ti Me," he called. "Ti Me!"

She appeared at the dining room door.

"Take Miss Ella to the parlor, please, to wait for us while we finish dinner."

"But I am not done!" Ella said. "I am not finished."

Bishop Chase would not look at her; he only continued to chew.

Ella rocked slightly back and forth in her chair. "You cannot make me leave," she said. But when she saw Ti Me in the doorway, Ella stood up.

"I believe I am to retire," she said. And she bowed her head—once, twice—in each Grace's direction. Then she was gone.

I felt Emmanuel's hand on mine. I had been running my fingernails down the tablecloth, in one long swipe, like the claw of an alley cat. He wrapped his hand around my wrist and squeezed it. I knew he meant it kindly, but I only wanted to pull away.

I had thought, up until that moment, with the Graces speaking warmly and Emmanuel joining them in their jokes and conversation, that maybe I could do what my husband was pleading with me to do. But then I thought of a thousand more nights in this beautiful country. Would he order me from the table, as his father did, if I said something he did not like? And would I leave with dignity, like Ella did, leave in a fiction, or would I kick and scream as I wished she would do, as I wanted to do now, and be called mad and unruly.

It was quiet for a moment. Emmanuel turned to Louisa and Experience apologetically. "Ella has not had the opportunities you have," he said. "She has never been to school. She is a bit unused to polished company, but I hope you will not hold that against her."

"I would never hold it against her," Louisa said, and Emmanuel smiled as Bishop Chase raised his head in the air. He'd heard the music in her voice, but he could not quite place it.

I had the satisfaction, at least, of seeing his expression when the world did not make sense for him. If only for a moment.

THE GRACES WERE to sleep in the parlor, on the broken-down divan that we pushed to the parlor chairs. I stood in the doorway and watched as Ti Me prepared their bed.

Experience cocked her head in Ti Me's direction as she knelt over the chairs. "This is life in Haiti, then?" she said to me. "All you do is sit up here and make sure Emmanuel is happy when he returns home?"

"You do not have to take in laundry or mending to stay afloat?" Louisa added.

"You are what those girls at school always wanted to be: a lady of leisure."

I laughed. "Leisure is stifling."

"Listen to the cheek of this girl," Louisa said, leaning over to Experience, "telling you and me, you and me, dear Louisa, that leisure is stifling."

"I would give anything to be stifled," Experience said dryly, and this set all three of us to laughing again, so loudly that Ti Me looked up, annoyed.

"Lordy," Louisa said, when we'd made a configuration of furniture that finally seemed as though it would fit the two of them. "I would never have guessed that you live such as this. Experience and I, each night, would say 'Where do you think she is now? Do you imagine she sleeps in a hammock beneath banana leaves?' And now to find you living in something like Cunningham's dining hall, but just with warmer weather . . ."

I frowned. "That is unkind, Louisa."

"Is it?" She looked up. "I did not mean it to be. I only mean, your life seems different from what you told us it would be."

"Isn't that true for all of us?" I said. "Could you have imagined traveling the world with Experience, sleeping in stagecoaches, arguing with impresarios as naturally as if you were debating the merits of philosophy back at Cunningham?"

"No," Experience said. "This is true. We could not have imagined that."

"So then life is different for all of us."

"Is that why you have not written back to your mother," Louisa said, "only sent her one telegram telling her you are with child and scaring the poor old girl half to death?"

I started. "How do you know anything of that?"

"Our last performance, before we left the North, in Manhattan, she had heard we would perform, and she came. She showed us the telegram herself. She said, 'Will you write to her? Will you find out what she means? Will you send her my word?' And I said, 'I will do you one better, madame. We will be traveling to Haiti ourselves and can deliver any message that you wish.' And so she gave us this."

And here, Louisa reached into her pocket and handed me a folded-over piece of paper, much wrinkled where it had been pressed up against her hip.

"It is from her?"

"She said to place it in your hands if you were alive, and onto your grave if you were dead."

"She thought I was dead?"

"She said you have not written her a word since your marriage. I think she is justified in thinking you had passed."

The paper was the same yellowish shade as the pages in her accounting book. I could not bring myself to open it.

"Libertie, it is very cruel of you to send a telegram like that to your mother and never write a letter," Louisa said.

"I did not know what to say." My voice came out low. "How would you explain this house to her, if you had to explain it?"

"I guess that is fair," Experience said.

"Are you safe here, Libertie?" This was Louisa. "Are you well?"

I did not know how to answer her questions. I took the letter and bowed my head and said, "Good night. I will see you in the morning."

I had promised Emmanuel, for the sake of our guests, I would not sleep in the shed that night. As I climbed the stairs to our bedroom, I felt the letter wrinkle in my hands. I did not want the ink to smear.

When I opened the door, he was there already, of course, in bed. He looked up, expectantly.

"Are they comfortable?"

"I think so."

"Will you be comfortable?"

"I do not know."

"At least lie down."

I set the letter carefully on his desk. I pulled my smock over my head and dropped it on the floor, so that I stood naked in front of Emmanuel.

He sat up in bed. "Come closer," he said. "I mean, if you please."

I kept my eyes on him as I approached. When I reached him, he held out one hand, placed it on my stomach, put the other around my waist, and let it rest at the small of my back. He rested his head on my stomach, and I felt the whisk of his eyelashes as he closed his eyes. I looked away from him, to the letter on the table. I both wanted to stand here, with his head on my stomach, with his arms holding the world, and I wanted to crouch on the floor and read every word my mother wrote me. I did not know which way to move and could not break away. So we stayed like that, for a long time, listening to the house settle around us.

Finally, he sighed. "I have missed you," he said.

"Let us sleep," I said.

A little past midnight, I heard his breath grow heavy and knew he was fully asleep. I pushed myself out of bed, carefully pulled the chair from his desk, and sat, naked, on the planks of wood, reading my mother's hand.

My Dearest Libertie,

You do not write, and that may be because you are no longer on this Earth or it may be because you are still angry at me, but either way I miss you and wish to know where you are, so I write this letter to you and send it by way of your friends, the Graces, hoping that it finds you at peace, whether you are on this Earth or below it.

The house feels truly dead now. I do not like staying here most nights. Most nights, I sleep in the waiting room of the hospital.

I write to you from the dark of the waiting room. It is about ten o'clock at night. I've just heard the church bell ring. I was to attend a lecture tonight, but I did not feel spirited enough. Besides, the topic is one I think I already know well: "The Future of the Colored Woman." It is an argument I am too old and tired to add anything to, I think.

The speaker is a very smart young woman, like your friends. She travels from city to city to talk to groups about the colored woman—a marvelous business, one that could not have existed even ten years ago. I told her this, and she seemed unimpressed by her own strangeness. She smiled and said, "Yes, mum." And I suppose that counts as progress, when a girl like her does things I could not imagine and does not stop once to think of them.

I had hoped I had made you brave like that, Libertie. Perhaps there is bravery in being a wife. Certainly, there is bravery in being a mother. I think you will learn that soon enough, if my calculations are correct.

I have delivered more babies in the last six months than I ever did when you were here with me during the war. I do not know if it is a sign of hope or a sign of desperation, that our people have gone baby mad. I think there are now more colored people in Kings County than ever before. Sometimes on the street, I do not recognize a single face, and I think how this is both a good thing and very lonely-making.

The last woman I attended, it was not here in the hospital. She was a very poor woman. Her husband came and begged me to come to her. He said she had been in labor for many days and he worried that she might not make it. I was tired. I had thought I would go back to the house, for once, that evening, and try to sleep there. But the man came just as I was about to leave, so I followed him to his home.

They lived in Vinegar Hill, in a small wooden building beside a grog shop. The sounds of her laboring almost drowned out the sounds of the sailors singing shanties next door. She was a very small woman, but loud. I said to her husband, "It is good that she makes so much noise. It means she has fight left in her."

She was doubled over, walking up and down the room, and so I walked beside her, holding her hand. She had been laboring so long her hand was wet with sweat and kept slipping from mine. I told her, over and over again, what a strong woman she was. What a wonder she was accomplishing. It was her first labor, and these were the things she needed to hear.

Towards the end of it, she screamed once more, very loudly. Then she lifted up her skirt, and what did I see, but the baby's knee sticking out, foot dangling down, almost doing a little jig.

And the sight of it made me laugh, Libertie, the first time I had laughed since you had gone. I know it was a dire sight. A breeched birth is dangerous, and the woman could have died. But I heard the sailors singing that their love lived in the ocean, and I saw that baby's knee jerk in time, and I saw the woman's face, her blink of surprise, and I could only laugh. At the absurdity of the world. The ridiculousness of your absence. The foolishness of whatever I did to cause you to leave me.

You will be glad to know, the woman delivered safely. I had her husband hold her elbows, and I squatted down between her knees, and together we turned the baby until he was straight, and he was delivered, just two hours ago today, by the grace of God our Creator.

I was still laughing when I handed the boy to his mother. She and her husband must have thought me a madwoman, and I am sure they will speak to Rev. Harland about how dotty Dr. Sampson has become in her old age. But even now, as I write you, even though I know the gravest danger we were in, I cannot help laughing. And isn't that a marvel, Libertie? Is that what you would maybe call grace?

I am not sure what your answer would be. I wish I could see your face just once more, to know what your answer would be. You sent me a message that you were with child, and then nothing. I thought of closing up the hospital and traveling to Haiti myself to find you. But I prayed upon it and felt, to the bottom of my soul, that you will come to me if you are meant to. That I will hear your voice again, whether here on Earth or in heaven.

To my love, my daughter, Libertie
I love you.
Your
Dear
Mama

THE GRACES LEFT as suddenly as they came, to travel over the mountain to Port-au-Prince, in search of that burnt theater. Louisa took with her, rolled up and tied to the string of her bonnet, my letter for my mother, for whenever she saw her again.

After they left, I did not have the strength to move back down to the shed. And so it was in Emmanuel's bed, after all, where I gave birth to our children.

My labor began at dawn. I was woken from a dream of the grass on my father's grave by a sudden pain in my hips, running, like scales on a piano, up my spine.

I could smell the salt of my body all around me.

The whole day, I walked the house, while Emmanuel trotted behind me to keep up and Ella called out nonsensical advice and Bishop Chase looked, for the first time since I'd known him, genuinely nervous. By evening, I began to feel tired from the pain, and I shouted at the three of them, "Only Ti Me has any sense."

Ella was easily enough gotten rid of. She did not like the sound of pain, and she went back to her room, loudly announcing she was of better use praying for me.

But Bishop Chase did not want to leave, and he watched me, with detached interest, as I winced and Emmanuel stroked my face.

"Please," I whispered to Emmanuel. Even in pain, I did not have the courage to yell at the bishop. "Please ask your father to leave."

And he did. He went to his father and said, "Papa, go to your study."

But Bishop Chase would not. He stood in the doorway and watched me labor, and it was only when I started to undo the ties of my smock—I was so overwhelmed with the heat, with the pain, and just wanted to be free—that he turned and left the room.

I walked in pain, and Emmanuel was there each step with me. And I knew there was no other face on Earth I wished to see, at that moment, except for his.

I thought, *I have forgiven you.*

I watched him as he watched me, as his soft mouth moved, as he held my arm, as we paced the hall together. I thought of his father, whom he still did not have the power to even make leave a room.

I could hear, in the bedroom next to ours, Ella and her father praying. A whisper—they would never pray loud like the Haitians did, like the Graces dared to do. And that made me even angrier—that even now, they would scrape and keep an etiquette of God. Their hushed prayers came over the gap in the ceiling, and it nearly drove me mad. Emmanuel felt the muscles in my arm stiffen and rubbed me gently there.

"It is all right." He smiled, and I felt my love for him come back.

I have forgiven you, I thought, *but I do not think that will be enough.*

"What's wrong?" he said. "Why do you make a face like that?"

"It only hurts," I said.

At midnight, I sat up in our bed. Emmanuel lay beside me, his breath light.

The pain that was in my body was warm now. It was a pain I had seen when I attended births with Mama. The births back home in Kings County, when I was a girl—every one was a kind of celebration. Because we knew each new child meant we had a claim to the land, to our space of freedom there.

The very first birth I had seen with Mama had frightened me. I had wanted to run from the room while the woman bellowed and hissed, and the air became thick with the smell of something deep and hidden, something that smelled almost lost.

But Mama had given me a look, and I had not dared to leave her side, and on our walk home she had told me, evenly, "You will not understand until you yourself do it, but in birth is the freest you can be. You do not have to take your leave of anyone or do anything for anyone. You are even free of deciding for your body how it will go—it is deciding for you. Your only expectation is to follow, and that is a kind of freedom, if you let it be."

Now in bed, I felt the next wave of pain and wished that she were here.

The sheet beneath me became wet. Emmanuel was woken up by the damp. He cried out in joy, in excitement. And then he was up, calling for Ti Me and for boiling water and for strips of cloth and for oil.

I wanted to leave the bed again. I wanted to feel the floorboards creak beneath my feet. A line of sweat trickled from under my chin to my chest between my breasts, to the top of my stomach.

I was breathing as hard as if I was racing up the walls of the room. With Mama, sometimes, a woman insisted on laboring with a knife in the bed beside them, to cut the pain. I had thought it silly then, as silly as Mama declaring those moments an emancipation. I had never thought, fully, what it would mean for me to join them there.

"I want Mama."

"Yes," Emmanuel said. "Yes."

By then, Ti Me was there, holding my other elbow. I could feel inside me a great, deep churning. A new world was trying to break out of my body.

It felt as if my hip bones would grind apart. I looked over both their heads to the ceiling and cried up to it. I felt Emmanuel wipe my sweat and tears. My knees began to shake. My spine bore down around itself—I could name every bone as I felt each one break.

I pushed my feet on Emmanuel's shoulders, a gross inversion of all the times I used to do the same, in pleasure, at night on the boat. And then I heard nothing. Not Emmanuel crying, not Ti Me whispering, not Ella and Bishop Chase's prayers winding over the ceiling walls.

I heard only the blood rushing in my ears, as pure and steady as a river, and in that one last searing burn of pain, I heard my mother's voice, wordless, only the tone and timbre that she'd make over our family's graves.

I felt the heat of my blood between my legs, and when I looked down again, I saw Emmanuel covered in my blood and crying, and

Ti Me covered in my blood and smiling, and lying on each of my thighs, my son and my daughter, our children, my children, born into this world I would make for them.

My Dearest Mama,

You have received this letter delivered to you by Louisa and Experience. Know that, as of this writing, I am alive. By the time Louisa and Experience hand this letter to you, I will have delivered your grandchildren.

I do not know what I am or what I will have become by then. I am not sure I ever knew myself. I used to think this was a failing. Something to hide from you. How could I be a righteous woman, to serve the world as you did, if I did not know myself?

But that seems like so little of a concern, now. I may not know myself, but I know the loneliness of love. I know what toll forgiveness takes. I know that the world is too big to be knowable.

I have learned to swim. Emmanuel taught me at first. But I learned how to float myself. The water carries you up, even when you think you are too heavy. When I float like that, I think of you and your ledgers, I think of where you go when you order the world in your mind, and I think I am ever closer to joining you there. I wish you could see your Libertie, floating in cool water so blue it seems God would drink it, staring up at the sky. When you are worried for me, when you are scared for me, when you wish to know me, think of me like that.

Mama, I am coming to you. I will be there maybe even before this letter arrives. When I deliver these children, I will rest for as long as I can and then I will come to you. The Graces have already agreed to help. They have left me their cut of the last leg of this tour, they have left it with a ship captain in Jacmel's port, and when I am ready, I am to find out when he next sails to New York, and he will harbor me and my children.

I will miss this country. I think it is here, more than anywhere else, that is my home. But I cannot stay. What a horrible thing in this world, to know your home and also know you can never live in it. I will tell you what Emmanuel has done, or rather, what he chooses to continue to have done, when I am home with you again. Emmanuel is a man who I do not think is all bad, but he does not have a big enough imagination to imagine me free beside him. I have already forgiven him for it, though.

I will carry to you my two children. I will wear their swaddling clothes as my own skirts. We will see you again before this world turns in another new direction. We will, at least, turn together.

I learned a new saying here today. Nou bout rive nan jaden an. We have almost reached the garden. My friend Ti Me says it to me as she measures my belly, how far it is dropped, when I am ready for birth. But I think of it as my song to you, my mother, when I see you again.

Love,

Libertie

THE BOY WAS at my breast first. He drank, and every time I tried to look in his eyes, he closed them tight. But when I looked away, I felt him watching me. The girl, she did not want my eyes. She watched my mouth. She watched my lips form shapes and my tongue vibrate as I sang to them. I watched her watch the invention of music. Right there, I invented it for her. Being a mother means being someone's god, if only briefly. This is known, I think. But they are my gods, too. They are my country now.

Emmanuel,

Know that I have left you because I love you. I cannot stay, though, in a house that is built on silences. I cannot pretend, as Ella does, if she is even pretending anymore.

I believe you are a strong enough man to follow. I believe you can hope for more.

I love you, I do. I love Haiti, I do. I love you enough both to leave you and hope for more.

Do you understand?

Can you follow?

Remember when I told you of Ben Daisy and how he drowned for love? And you said, in flirtation, that he and I belonged to Erzulie. Ti Me also told me, in her careful way, that I am Erzulie's, that I will always be unsatisfied, that the beauty of this world will never be enough for me and I will always long for the other side of the mirror, the more perfect world.

But I wish for a different story, I think.

So when you come to me, tell me this one. The one you told me about the water where I learned to swim. Remember the story you told me, about the pools? You said that water did not belong to us. Not to the colored people of Haiti, not to the Negroes, certainly not to the whites who caused the soil to run with blood. No, you said they belonged to Anacaona first. You said she was a Taino queen, who ruled the land here when Columbus came. She was beloved because she could sing. She could sing her people's past, she could sing her people's present, she could sing through all the way to her people's future. She led her people in revolt against the world that was descending, revolt against the world that said it was the only world possible.

The Spaniards tried to break her. They gave her the choice of death, or to be one of their wives, trapped in lust. She chose death. She went to her end with pride, even though they hanged her.

She revolted, and you said that we could still hear her cries in the water there.

That is what you told me.

When you come to find us, because I believe you will become a strong enough man to follow us, this is the first story I want to hear from your mouth, the only one I will want to hear in your voice for quite some time.

I think you can break free. I believe you can. But I cannot do it for you. You have to do it yourself. I don't know if I, myself, am free. I hope to be. Our children are already, and I leave you now to keep them that way. I leave you to keep their sovereignty intact. But do not think that you are now alone. I promise you—we are waiting for you, in the new world.

Your

Libertie

ACKNOWLEDGMENTS

There are so many people who helped me bring this book into the world. First and foremost, I would like to thank my agent, Carrie Howland, who believed that this book was possible and pushed me to write the proposal for it. I would like to thank my editor Kathy Pories, Betsy Gleick, Elisabeth Scharlatt, Michael McKenzie, and the many others at Algonquin who have so enthusiastically supported the creation of this work.

I would not have been able to complete this manuscript without the support of many generous and unexpected grants. The National Endowment for the Arts, the Whiting Foundation, the Radcliffe Institute for Advanced Study, and the Hodder Fellowship at Princeton University all provided me with the material support necessary to complete this novel. I am forever grateful and humbled to be the recipient of these fellowships. In particular, I must thank Meredith Moss Quinn at Radcliffe and Tracy K. Smith at Princeton for your support and belief in my work. Tracy also graciously connected me with a homeopath, Wanda Smith-Schick, who shared invaluable information with me.

While working on this book, I have had the good fortune of meeting so many artists and writers who inspired me, who had conversations with me, who shared with me how they saw the world and helped expand my understanding. I also had the good fortune of continuing my conversations with so many friends. This made writing less lonely and made me a better thinker. Thank you to Ja'Tovia Gary, Min Jin Lee, Lauren Groff, Mira Jacob, Bill Cheng, Tennessee Jones, Alexander Chee, Simone Leigh, Madeline Hunt-Ehrlich, Lana Wilson, Naomi Jackson, Nicholas Boggs, Tanaïs, Naima Coster, Kerry Carnahan, Evie Shockley, Andra Miller, André M. Carrington, Kinitra Brooks, Megan Mayhew Bergman, Cara Blue Adams, Mike Scalise, Margaret Garrett, Rebecca Sills, Ilana Zimmerman, Phillip Williams, Tanisha C. Ford, Molly Brown, Jessica Grose, Sheila Pundit, and Deb Reck.

I was very nervous to write about Haiti—a country I admired but that I am not from. I was scared of writing something untrue, and so I had to read and talk with as many people as I could to try not to do so. Thank you to the historians Brandon R Byrd, Kate Ramsey, Wynnie Lamour, Kendra Field and Malick Ghachem, who answered my questions and shared so many resources.

In particular, thank you to the historian Orly Clerge, who answered my questions about visiting Haiti and provided so many resources. Thank you to Edwidge Danticat and Sharifa Rhodes-Pitts, who did the same. Thank you to Patrick Sylvain, who provided expert Kreyol translations.

Thank you to Rob Field and the staff at Weeksville Heritage Center, who provided me with access to the oral history recording that inspired this novel. My time working at that historic site changed my life and I am forever grateful to those who work so hard to preserve that legacy.

Thank you to Nicole Davis.

Thank you to my family—Ariel Greenidge, Kirsten Greenidge, Kerri Greenidge, Ron Nigro, Katia Nigro and Hunter Nigro, David Dance, Suzanne Dance, Tyron Dance, Kwame Dance, Eric Davis, Candice Corbie-Davis, and Fidel and Che Corbie-Davis.

And thank you to my daughter.